ONE
OF US

TAWNI O'DELL

GALLERY BOOKS
New York   London   Toronto   Sydney   New Delhi

G

Gallery Books
A Division of Simon & Schuster, Inc.
1230 Avenue of the Americas
New York, NY 10020

First Gallery Books hardcover edition August 2014

GALLERY BOOKS and colophon are registered trademarks of Simon & Schuster, Inc.

For information about special discounts for bulk purchases, please contact Simon & Schuster Special Sales at 1-866-506-1949 or business@simonandschuster.com.

The Simon & Schuster Speakers Bureau can bring authors to your live event. For more information or to book an event contact the Simon & Schuster Speakers Bureau at 1-866-248-3049 or visit our website at www.simonspeakers.com.

Designed by Davina Mock-Maniscalco

Manufactured in the United States of America

10   9   8   7   6   5   4   3   2   1

Library of Congress Cataloging-in-Publication Data is available.

ISBN 978-1-4767-5587-8
ISBN 978-1-4767-5594-6 (ebook)

For my Mom

a memory

DANNY

"COME QUICK BEFORE HE starts looking for you!" my grandpa hissed in a frantic whisper from below my bedroom window, where he stood on an overturned wheelbarrow with outstretched arms while my father roared drunkenly downstairs.

All I could see were a pair of enormous hands with palms lined in black grime and speckled in blue scars reaching out of the darkness. I closed my eyes, scrambled over my windowsill, and lowered myself into their comforting grip.

"Shhh!" he said needlessly as we raced across the backyard out into the street and headed past the row of silent houses identical to my own, filled with occupants who had decided long ago to ignore this strange ritual of ours and the cause behind it.

Even in the dead of winter I'd never remember to put on my shoes, and by the time Tommy and I reached his house my stockinged feet would be wet and freezing. In summer my bare feet would be scraped and stinging. We'd arrive each time on his front porch, huffing and puffing, and would both take a moment to gaze down the hill at the distant rooftop of my father's house and the dark window to the right. Earlier a lamp had glowed there with my mom's favorite floral-printed scarf draped over the shade. This is how I signaled him for help on the nights when my father's usual inability to notice my existence turned into the keen liquor-fueled observation that I should have never been born.

We crept through Tommy's small front room past shelves and stacks of books, and the picture of my great-great-grandmother Fiona with her haunted eyes that followed me everywhere, and the mounted deer head whose antlers were hung with every kind of bric-a-brac until we arrived in the kitchen where we finally allowed ourselves to turn on a light and relax.

Tommy's kitchen wasn't any bigger or cleaner than the one in my father's house or supplied with better food. It contained a lot of smells, but none of them were the appetizing kind. The overwhelming odors were those of something burning and a powerful lye-based soap favored by coal miners and mechanics that made my eyes water and the back of my throat ache. But despite these shortcomings, it was my favorite place in the world.

Without saying a word yet he'd take the milk bottle out of the fridge and fill a battered saucepan sitting on the stove. He'd keep watch over it, humming to himself, until it reached the required temperature, then he'd slop it into two mugs. Mine he'd fill all the way and add a generous amount of Hershey's syrup. His own he'd fill only halfway and make up the difference with whiskey and a dollop of maple syrup.

On this night, after he placed my cup of cocoa in front of me, he told me a story I'd never forget. I'm sure this wasn't the first time I had heard the tale. In fact, I'm sure he had told it to me when I was still in the womb, when he held me as a baby, when he sat in a lawn chair nursing a beer, watching me play in the driveway with my Hot Wheels—but to-night was the first time I really listened. The first time I remembered it.

"Boys, they were. The lot of them. Not much older than you the day they were hung," he began.

I knew he was talking about the Nellie O'Neills. Men executed in the middle of our town was horrifying enough, but the thought of a bunch of first-graders swinging in the wind was too much to handle.

"They were six years old?" I squeaked.

He noticed my distress and gave my hand a reassuring pat.

"I'm sorry, Danny. At my age, a twenty-two-year-old seems like a child. They were young men. Very young men."

"Like Rafe?"

"Like Rafe."

He took a drink from his cup and continued.

"So there they were. Standing hunched and damp on the gallows in a drizzling rain, their wrists in manacles, gazing out at the shifting black sea of umbrellas shielding the spectators come to see their deaths. Decent folk, the newspapers called the onlookers, the kind who said their prayers and pinched their pennies and turned a blind eye to the sufferings of anyone not exactly like themselves.

"Nearly two hundred of these leading citizens dressed in their appropriately somber finery were packed inside the prison courtyard along with dozens of reporters and the families of the condemned, while outside the walls, a crowd of several thousand gathered in a shabby, sodden bovine mass of morbid curiosity and dumb bloodlust."

"What's bovine?" I interrupted him.

"They were like cows."

"What's sodden?"

"They were like wet cows."

He sighed.

"Listen, son, I'm not going to talk down to you and use baby words, but you can't keep breaking in on a man when he's telling a story."

I nodded and vowed not to ask any more questions. I'd make a mental list and look up the words tomorrow in the dictionary at school.

"This happened almost a hundred forty years ago. The government had abolished public executions, but private ones were still allowed. Bankers, merchants, lawyers, politicians, and businessmen of every stripe along with their wives and daughters were there by invitation only holding tickets that everyone had tried to get. They were a pretty pale blue in color and adorned with a small gold seal and the signature of Walker T. Dawes, the man himself."

Everyone knew Walker Dawes. He owned all the mines and lived on a mountain outside of town in a mansion covered in windows that glittered on sunny days like the earth had been slashed open revealing crystal underneath instead of more black coal.

I wasn't sure how he could've been alive back when the Nellies were around and still be alive today. I chalked it up to the superhuman longevity of fairy-tale villains and comic book evil geniuses.

"Hanging was the cruelest way to kill someone. Too many things could go wrong. It wasn't like a firing squad, where the victim could take comfort in the certainty that at least one of the bullets would prove instantly fatal, or even the guillotine, where his fate wouldn't rest on the competence of a rope knotted by the unsure hands of men but in the dependable precision of a blade.

"If the Nellies were lucky, they'd been told, their necks would break and they'd lose consciousness and wouldn't be present for their own deaths. If they were especially lucky, they'd die of shock the moment the trap door fell open and they wouldn't have to endure even that much. But if they weren't so lucky they would be slowly strangled while their hearts continued to beat and their heads continued to know, and luck was something they'd been short on lately."

He stopped suddenly. My heart was racing and I was hanging on his every word. No one told these kinds of stories to little kids except for bigger kids and the ones around here were too dumb to make up anything this good.

"You know why they were being hung?" Tommy asked me.

This was long before I'd read about the Nellie O'Neills in history books, before I'd visit their museum in Nora Daley's attic, before their alleged ghosts would star in paranormal reality TV shows, but it was impossible to live in Lost Creek and not know something about them even as a young child. The town was full of their descendants, and the gallows where they had perished were still standing next to the little brick jail where they had spent their final days. I'd never been inside the prison courtyard, but the crossbars could be seen rising ominously over the crumbling stone wall, their shape and meaning not exactly clear to me, yet they filled me with a sick dread nonetheless. Like the first time I saw my mother standing by the kitchen sink, her eyes as empty as those of a corpse, softly, methodically stabbing holes in a raw chuck roast with a screwdriver, I knew I should be afraid but I didn't know why.

"They murdered someone," I answered him.

"They murdered two someones," he corrected me. "Two of their bosses. And they cut off a man's ear and cut out the tongue of a priest and were also responsible for a lot of random head bashing."

"Why did they do all that?"

"Back then the conditions in the mines were horrible. Beyond imagining."

A clammy invisible hand began tickling the base of my spine then traveled to the back of my neck where it grabbed hold and slowly began to choke the air out of me. The mines frightened me much more than a gallows ever could. I was claustrophobic and afraid of the dark, and the thought of toiling in cramped tunnels deep inside the earth gave me violent nightmares. I had never told Tommy what my dreams were about because I was ashamed, but I used to share them with my mom. She tried to comfort me by telling me I wouldn't have to work in the mines because I was smart and smart people could go to college and get good jobs. I clung to this assurance, but at the same time it didn't make complete sense to me. Tommy was smart and he had worked in the mines his entire life.

"The Nellies were a group of miners who tried to get conditions in the mines changed, but they were pitted against one of the richest and most powerful men in the country who didn't want anything changed. They tried peaceful methods at first, but things turned violent on both sides. Some people say the Nellies were right to act the way they did. Others say they were wrong. Some say they were saints, the American labor movement's first martyrs. Others say they were thugs, unpatriotic union organizers who turned to murder to further their cause."

"Who's right? Were the Nellies good guys or bad guys?"

Tommy shrugged.

"One man's hero is another man's terrorist. You'll have to make that decision for yourself someday when you're older."

"But they killed somebody. They had to pay for their crimes," I pointed out.

His blue eyes flashed the way they always did when he had a secret, their youthful sparkle as happily unexpected in the crags of his face as finding something shiny on the side of an old dirt road.

"Yes, but not all of them were killers. Ten men were executed. Only two were guilty."

"How could that happen?"

"Walker Dawes controlled everything. The police, the courts, the press, some say even the governor. He could do whatever he wanted and no one could stop him. By killing all those men without even proving that they were guilty, he showed everyone how much power he had and made sure no one would ever stand up to him again.

"James 'Prosperity' McNab, Peter Tully, Kenny Kelly, and Henry 'Footloose' McAnulty were the first to go that day. Does the name McNab sound familiar to you?"

I didn't answer fast enough.

"It's my name," Tommy went on. "He was my grandfather. Do you know what that means? He was your great-great-grandfather. Do you know what that means?"

He glanced in the direction of the living room. I knew what this meant. Fiona was Prosperity McNab's wife.

This was too much for me to absorb all at once. Tommy seemed to sense this and plunged on with his story rather than give me time to start asking the dozens of questions that were forming in my head.

"They wore black suits, and they carried crucifixes. Peter Tully, who was the youngest, only nineteen, also carried a lace handkerchief his mother had made for him and given him the night before when she came to say good-bye.

"They knelt and Father Daley read the prayers for the dying over the sobbing of the mothers, while the fathers worried their hats in their dirty hands and let their bewildered stares wander anywhere but to the gallows. The priest placed his hand on their bowed heads, blessing and absolving them, and ordered them to rise. They kept praying while the ropes were placed around their necks and the hoods were pulled down over their faces, and they were still praying when the floor dropped open. People said their lips could be seen moving beneath the hoods.

"My grandfather was still alive when they cut him down. This fact on its own was nothing astounding. Of the ten they hung that day, four were fortunate enough to have their necks broken after the drop was sprung. The other six were left swinging, their chained wrists jerking up and down and their bound feet kicking, while the ropes slowly choked the life out of them.

"Prosperity's heart was still beating after twenty minutes, the longest of any of them. When they laid his body on the wet ground and the sheriff took off his hood, they say his eyes bulged and his tongue stuck out of his mouth much to the terror of the superstitious Irishmen crowded around him. Some said his swollen lips moved as if he were trying to speak. Some claimed he did speak. Some heard him say, "Fi," some heard "vengeance," a word in English he probably didn't know. Regardless of what he said or if he spoke at all, the legend of a not-entirely-dead Prosperity McNab was born.

"Fiona was there that day and she made their son, Jack, come along, too. Everyone told her not to bring him because he was so young, but she insisted he must know the truth in all its ugliness. He must see the murder of his father so he would never forget it."

"How old was he?" I asked.

"Now," Tommy answered, shaking a finger at me. "*He* was your age and already a breaker boy. Just a few months earlier Prosperity had taken him to the breaker room for the first time and sat him down among thirty other filthy lads silently separating coal from the slate that flowed past them in a black stream down a chute. How it must have broke his heart to do that to his little boy. He knew never a laugh or a smile or a single word would ever pass between them as they picked away their little lives, hunched over until their spines began to curve and their fingers began to look like the claws of a crow. They never had a chance to go to school or know anything of the world. They had no games. They never played. When their workday was over, they were too tired for that. Their bodies and minds were acquainted with nothing except the difference between slate and coal."

I glanced away from Tommy, trying to come to grips with this latest revelation. Jack and I were the same age and more than that we'd both lost parents. My mom was still alive, but it didn't matter much since she was locked up. Some days I'd tell myself I wouldn't know the difference if she was dead or not, but I knew this wasn't true, because if she was dead, I wouldn't have to worry about her all the time. My pain would be smooth and easy to hold, having been polished by the finality of irreparable loss, not surrounded by the jagged edges of possibilities.

"After they cut down Prosperity," Tommy went on, "Fiona turned and walked toward a group of men in top hats and velvet-trimmed black coats standing off to one side behind the gallows. She walked up to one man in particular who wore a small white rose in his buttonhole and a single ruby stud in his shirtfront and stared him directly in the face."

"Walker Dawes," I whispered.

"What she was doing would have been unthinkable to most of the people there, but it was a day already filled with the unthinkable and Fiona was a woman who thrived on such situations.

"She pushed little Jack forward. He was terrified and sick to his stomach but he went. He craned his neck back and took in the tall, dark figure that loomed above him and regarded him without pity, kindness, or even the instinctual affection adults usually feel for children. He would tell me many years later that on the day he watched his father hang, Walker Dawes looked at him with amusement."

"You talked to Jack?" I asked him, confused and a little excited by the idea.

He reached across the table and ruffled my hair.

"He didn't stay a little boy forever. He grew up. Jack McNab was my father."

"Did he try to get revenge?"

"No. Nothing like that. On the contrary, he worked for Lost Creek Coal for the rest of his life. It was Fiona who never stopped talking about revenge. According to her, Prosperity never killed anyone or committed any crime as crime was known to be in this country or any other. She saw it only one way from beginning to end: her husband had stood up to Walker Dawes and for that he was murdered. The mortal sin and legal iniquity aside, she was not the type of woman who allowed others to mess with her own.

"Most people eventually came to regard her threats as the ravings of a deranged old woman, but some bought into the story that she had turned to the Devil to get what she wanted and had become a powerful witch."

"Was she? Was she a witch?"

"Truth be told, the only black art she ever practiced was the burning of the pot roast every Sunday, yet I trusted her predictions. I was certain injustice would be avenged. But not because I believed in curses or kismet."

"What did you believe in?"

"For the longest time I wasn't sure. I couldn't put a name to it. It was just a feeling I had that our family would get back a little of our own someday. But now I know."

He stood up from the table and walked out the kitchen door onto his back stoop. It was a warm night in late September with just a tinge of autumn chill in the air. I joined him and followed his gaze past the roofs of the row homes to the worn-down mountains crouched on the horizon. Soon they'd be a riot of color when the leaves changed. Tonight, bathed in the glow of a full moon, they were the deep dark purple of a fresh bruise.

It was an amazing story, terrible and wonderful at the same time, like my mother's love, like these precious, poisoned hills that were the source of our survival and our ruin. I didn't want it to end.

"What, Tommy?" I asked again. "What do you believe in?"

He didn't look down at me but said to the sky, "I believe in you, Danny."

I WATCH THE CORRECTIONS OFFICER with his back to us standing outside the Plexiglas-encased interview room. The fingers on his right hand hanging next to his pepper spray occasionally flex the same way a dog's paws twitch while he dreams of chasing a rabbit. I wonder if he's asleep.

Over the years I've come in contact with a countless number of men in law enforcement, a phenomenon that began when my mother was first incarcerated. I've developed great respect for some, but most have proven to be variations on a theme, adult versions of the boys who tortured me when I was a child, with the same no-neck bulldog compression of head to torso, the same tightly wired yet somehow easy manner that would enable them to crack open a few skulls then go home and eat a bologna sandwich.

"You seem distracted," Carson Shupe says. "Thinking about your trip?"

I pull my attention away from the guard and focus on the convicted killer of four young boys sitting across the table from me.

"How are *you* feeling?" I ask him.

"I'm fine. I'm good."

He looks at me with his strangely jaundiced brown eyes, the color of watery beef broth, and as usual I don't find anything there except normalcy. Despite what he's done, this has always been a relief to me because it confirms my faith in the mentally ill. They are rarely violent. On the contrary, the desire to harm others is deeply rooted in the psyche of the sane. We're all capable of killing someone, although everyone isn't capable of killing just anyone.

Carson unclasps his fingers and tries to spread out his hands and raise them in a sign of acceptance, but his restraints shackled to a bolt in the metal tabletop keep him from doing this.

I glimpse his mutilated fingertips, shiny and pink with smooth scar tissue. Since he was a child, long before he began his career of unspeakable crimes, he's been obsessed with removing his fingerprints. He's tried rubbing them off with sandpaper, coating them with Krazy Glue and peeling them off, slicing them off with a razor. Even here in a maximum-security prison he's been able to get hold of matches and lighters and burn them off. The few times he's been in solitary, he's gnawed his fingers with his own teeth. His compulsion has nothing to do with a desire to conceal his identity, but originated from a wish to erase the one thing about him that made him unique from others. Carson has always desperately wanted to be like everyone else.

"Are you coming?" he asks me in a casual, pleasant tone, as if he is inviting me to dine with him instead of watch him die.

"Do you want me to?"

He shrugs.

"It would be nice to have a friend there."

My mind wanders back to my childhood again at the mention of the word "friend" and my complete lack of one. In all fairness to the boys who bullied me, they couldn't help themselves. My very existence practically begged for it. I was tall, spider-limbed skinny, skittish, bookish, pale, with a shock of almost black hair and equally dark eyes smudged with purple exhaustion that gave my face an otherworldly appearance.

Kids who called me anything called me the Ghost. I liked to think the nickname was meant as a compliment to my athletic prowess, referring to my ability to disappear on a cross-country course as much as my pallor, but I knew this wasn't the case. I was spooky. I had murder in my present and my past and someday in my future I'd choose to make the study of it my profession.

"I'll do my best," I tell him, "but I can't promise. I don't know how long I'll be gone."

"This sick grandfather you're going to take care of . . . Is he the one who watched his father hang?"

"It was *his* father who watched *his* father hang."

"I guess a lethal injection is better than hanging. Anything is better than drowning," he adds when I don't comment.

I know where this observation comes from. He found his mother passed out drunk in the bathtub when he was ten years old. This fact alone didn't traumatize him nearly as much as his own decision not to try and help her. He walked down the stairs of their apartment building, out into the moist Miami sunshine, and took a bus to the nearest public beach, where he sat in the searing sand and watched the hypnotic ebb and flow of a much larger body of water bringing dead fish to shore.

He pictured his mother as he had left her and was amazed by her resemblance to them: her mouth dangling open and her skimpy sequined cocktail dress clinging wetly to her skin, giving her the same opalescent sheen as their scales. He knew when he returned he might find her in the kitchen, raw and shaky, wrapped in a faded, tattered aqua bath towel making a Bloody Mary; or he might find her submerged in the bathwater glassy-eyed and bloated like the fish. Either way he had made the conscious decision to no longer interfere. Leaving her alone in the tub had been his participation in the act of natural selection. Since then he's become almost obsessed with the concept and convinced that it doesn't work.

His thoughts continue down their expected path.

"Have you had any luck contacting my mother?" he asks me.

"I'm afraid not."

"There has to be an address where her publisher sends all those royalty checks."

"Apparently the money is electronically transferred to a bank account in her name, but she's no longer at her last known physical address."

He presses his fingertips together and begins to flex the digits like a bellows.

"Do you want her to be there?" I ask.

"No. If she's there she'll embarrass me."

"Then why is it so important that I find her?"

"I want her to know. That's all. I want her to be reminded."

It's a difficult question for me to ask but one I feel I must for both of us.

"Do you blame her?"

His lips twitch slightly while he considers my question, pursing and relaxing as though he's contemplating blowing a smoke ring. He's a calm, quiet man, intelligent, personable, compact, fastidious about his appearance and almost prim in his outlook on life; the kind of man the neighbors will defend on the six o'clock news even after the facts begin to come to light.

A pained expression passes over his face and he leans toward me across the table. His eyes darken and he lowers his voice to a lewd whisper that makes the hairs stand up on the back of my neck.

"Everything bad that happens in this world is the fault of someone's mother," he says.

"Time's up, Doc," the guard announces, entering the room along with an almost identical version of himself. "He's gotta go."

I stand and so does Carson, who waits patiently while they unfasten his handcuffs from the table and his ankle chains from the floor. His lips begin their nervous puckering again. Perspiring scalp glimmers beneath the thinning hair on top of a head that looks too heavy for the thin neck straining forward from a pair of soft, hunched shoulders in a flesh-colored prison jumpsuit he somehow remarkably manages to keep spotless and wrinkle-free. Beneath the harsh glare of the fluorescent overhead light, he casts the pitiable shadow of a turtle outside his shell.

I stop in front of him. He bobs his head toward me. Before the guard intervenes and jerks him backward he's able to blow on my shoulder.

"Lint," he says.

"Thank you," I reply, brushing at the sleeve of my navy Ralph Lauren suit jacket, originally worn years ago during my first appearance on *Larry King Live* at the height of the Wishbone Killer trial. It's since been relegated to prison visits and weddings of people I barely know.

"You're the only one out there who doesn't think I'm crazy," he adds. "I appreciate that."

One of the guards glances in my direction with a smirk on his face.

I realize this is a seemingly bizarre comment considering my testimony at his trial and ongoing expert insistence that this man is in complete control of his mental faculties is leading directly to his death.

His lawyers mounted a vigorous insanity defense, but his heart was never in it. If they had been able to successfully convince a jury he was out of his mind, he would have been allowed to remain alive in a secured psychiatric facility, but it was obvious to me he'd rather die than have his sanity doubted.

I know why he feels this way. I have a crazy mother, too.

One of the officers escorts Carson back to his cell. The other walks me out.

I watch Carson go and I'm hit with a wave of loneliness. I admit I've come to depend on him. I find it easier to talk to him than to anyone else I know, and his suggestions for dealing with my problems have proven to be remarkably insightful. Still, I'm not sure I could ever be comfortable having a serial killer for a life coach.

"You coming for the big day?" the guard at my side asks me.

I glance at his name tag: Pulanski. I remember him. The last time I was here he wanted my opinion on the legitimacy of type 2 bipolar syndrome. His wife had suddenly become afflicted with it in the middle of their divorce and was using it as the reason she couldn't hold down a job and required substantial spousal support. He wanted to know if it was similar to type 2 diabetes and would go away if she lost weight.

"I don't know," I answer him.

"You ever seen one?"

"An execution? No."

"You ever been responsible for one before?"

"If you mean is this the first case I've worked on where someone has been sentenced to death and exhausted his appeals, the answer is yes," I reply. "But I'm not responsible."

"The guys say you're gonna write another book. That's why you've been spending so much time with Shupe."

"I have no plans to write a book about him. His mother already did that."

"Yeah, I know. Did you read it?"

"Yes."

"What was it she called you?"

His eyes dart in my direction. I can tell by the barely suppressed mirth in the look he gives me that he knows exactly what she called me; he just wants to hear me say it out loud.

"A pedantic buffoon and a spotlight-grabbing windbag."

His face splits into a broad grin before immediately returning to the humorless blank mask required by his profession.

"I've never met the woman," I tell him. "I've never spoken to her. And I'm sure she doesn't know what any of those words mean. Of course, she had a ghostwriter."

"Maybe the ghostwriter's an ex of yours?"

I smile but it's merely a nervous tic. He's making fun of me. My means of dealing with abuse has never evolved from childhood. Whether verbal or physical, my instinct has always been to run.

Carson assures me this is a perfectly healthy response and probably one of the reasons why I've survived so nicely, but it's not appropriate in every situation. I can't very well take off sprinting down the sterile prison corridor, my jacket flapping behind me, the hard soles of my shoes making rat-a-tat echoes, inmates pressed against bars whooping and cheering on my flight.

We pass through a security checkpoint. The moment I see my iPad, my BlackBerry, my neatly folded burgundy cashmere scarf, the shiny gold of my special credentials provided by the Philadelphia County District Attorney's Office, and a hardcover copy of my latest book with my name, Dr. Sheridan Doyle, finally larger than the print of the title sitting safely inside my briefcase, my panic diffuses.

I used to try to get people to use my full name instead of Danny, not out of any love for the former or dislike for the latter, but as a way to be taken more seriously and to distance myself from my past. But after years of listening to comments about me being named after a Sheraton Inn (i.e., "Ho-ho, is that where you were conceived?"), I finally abandoned the project.

Outside a January gust of swirling snow hits me in the face. My car is already packed with my laptop, clothing, toiletries, running gear, and a garment bag with several suits and jackets. There will be no call for the suits, but I always like to have a few with me no matter where I go.

When the doctor called to tell me that Tommy was being released after having been hospitalized with pneumonia, the conversation felt like a slap in the face. I never knew about his illness. I'd never considered the possibility that my grandfather could die. He may be in his nineties, but he's still as strong as an ox, and if his health ever began to finally fail him, I've always been confident his stubbornness would continue to keep him alive. His father and grandfather both died young under tragic circumstances, and I've often thought much of his longevity has been due to his unflagging belief that Death owes him.

I still need to swing by my office to pick up some case files and have a final meeting with my secretary, Max.

I've already locked up my apartment. It's a spacious two-bedroom with only a few pieces of carefully selected furniture and even fewer personal items. I like to think my style of decorating is a study in tasteful minimalism, but not everyone sees it this way. My cleaning woman calls my apartment the Tomb.

I've lived in Philadelphia for over twenty years, beginning when I came here to attend Penn, and with the exception of doing my graduate work at Yale, I've never resided anywhere else. I'm not sure why. I don't have any great loyalty or attachment to this particular city, but I do like my neighborhood. It's upscale and trendy but not too much of either. Gentrified brownstones are interspersed with gastropubs and tiny overpriced boutiques where no more than two customers can enter at a time to browse through one rack of clothing while being snubbed by a texting salesgirl. But there's also a seedy bodega on the corner that gets robbed weekly and a tattoo parlor across the street from me catering to pierced, shaggy-haired women I'd never approach but love to watch who come and go in a stream of tight leather, ripped jeans, and unapologetic cleavage.

As a forensic psychologist, I do most of my work on the road, conducting clinical interviews and psychological testing in prisons, mental hospitals, and the offices of prosecutors and defense attorneys. I also spend a fair amount of time in court and in TV studios, sitting on small uncomfortable sofas in faux living rooms with thickly made-up talking heads clutching huge mugs of coffee asking me to provide commentary on cases that they never bothered to research.

I could easily dispense with having my own physical office, but I like being able to say I have one. Years ago when I first hired Max I believed I didn't need a secretary either, but again, I wanted to be able to say I had one.

The first time I met him he was a woman named Stacy in her midthirties, doped up in a hospital bed, her face purple and swollen beyond recognition, arm fractured in two places, three broken ribs, having just been told by the detective who took her statement that there was a strong possibility charges would be filed against her for the death of her lesbian live-in girlfriend who she had just killed claiming self-defense by stabbing her in the neck with a pair of scissors.

When I told her I was a psychologist, she picked up a pen the cop had left behind and wrote "fuck you" on the back of her hand, which she held up to me in a fist.

After she regained the use of her jaw, I interviewed her once. If it was possible, she looked even worse than she did after being beaten. She was a frail, jittery mess of bony limbs, stringy striped blond and black hair, dull eyes sunk into deep pools of shadow, and cracked lips clamped on a succession of cigarettes she wasn't allowed to light. Her case didn't go to trial. She wasn't charged. I had forgotten all about her by the time she contacted me almost eight years later.

I agreed to meet her for coffee and was stunned by her transformation. A well-spoken, smartly dressed, egg-shaped man with the stare and calm implacability of an owl greeted me. His entire appearance reminded me of the bird: short spiky reddish-brown hair, large round-framed glasses, a fitted velveteen jacket swirled in shades of gray paisley. He wore a bracelet of glass beads and feathers.

He explained that back when he was a she after her near brush with death and even closer brush with love gone bad, she did what many women do in these situations who don't turn to God: she turned to carbohydrates.

He then produced a picture of an extremely large woman. He explained that this had been him. She had lost sixty pounds. He still had forty to go.

He then went on to tell me that what had finally made him turn his life around, to not only quit all addictive behaviors, but go back to school and get a degree and also change his sex, was a quote he had read in one of my books.

I was more than a little surprised. I don't write self-help books or anything remotely inspirational or motivational. I write about killers.

"'What lies in our power to do, lies in our power not to do,'" he recited to me over a skim milk latte. "That includes accepting our gender," he added.

I told him the quote was from Aristotle, not me.

He said he didn't care; I was the next best thing.

Today he looks like a different kind of bird. With his hair shellacked in the center of his head like a crest, his eyes outlined in black, and wearing a satiny azure pantsuit, he's the personification of a blue jay.

We make small talk then settle down to business. He perches on the corner of my desk and opens a red suede day planner with LIFE written across it in tiny crystals.

"We could've had this conversation over the phone," he tells me.

"I know."

"You wanted to say good-bye to your office."

I look around me. Unlike my home, my office reveals more of a personality, although it's not truly mine and it's not even entirely reflective of the personality I've adopted since leaving my hometown and making my way in the world.

The walls are pale blue, the color chosen because it made an ideal background for my two Velázquez drawings and the Seurat, and the two charcoal studies of avenging angels mimicking the style of Michelangelo, as well as my diplomas and framed photographs of me posing with Larry King; Nancy Grace; Matt Lauer; Governor Corbett; the Wishbone Killer; Liza Minnelli; Johnnie Cochran; the Scranton Bomber, Senator Casey; Kelly Ripa; a half dozen feathery, bedazzled showgirls (conference in Las Vegas); Siegfried and Roy (same conference); Jane Fonda; Dr. Phil; Dr. Drew; Dr. Ruth; Dr. Oz; Dr. Sussmann (my internist); and Earth, Wind & Fire.

The sofa and my chair are upholstered in warm rust. My desk is a reproduction of an eighteenth-century, severely male monstrosity but scaled down enough to get through the office door. A china figurine of a collie is displayed prominently next to my banker's lamp, a reminder of the dog I never had.

There's a quiet flamboyance in the decoration of the room that gives the people who come here something to think about if they find it necessary to think about me at all.

"What a strange thing to say."

He raises his eyebrows at me.

"You haven't heard yourself talking these last few days. You sound like you're going off to war."

"It is hostile territory."

He lets the subject go. We know just enough about each other's personal lives to realize we don't want to know anything else.

"Make sure you get in touch with your publicist," he begins. "She wants to go over some details of your upcoming book tour and begin lining up interviews. Also give your editor a call to tell her how much you like the cover."

"I'm not sure I do."

"It doesn't matter. Say you do. It's a good author photo of you at least."

"I look aloof."

"You are aloof. We finally have a shoot date for the episode of *Blood, Lies & Alibis*. You've also been asked to be a commentator on an episode of *Deadly Affairs*. A stripper who had her boyfriend kill her husband then had another boyfriend kill the first boyfriend. They want an expert to explain that she wasn't a sociopath, just someone who craved constant attention and wasn't able to solve her own problems."

"You've just described everyone on Facebook," I say.

"And you've been asked to do an episode of *Women Who Kill*." He pauses. "But I went ahead and passed on that one."

I nod. Another subject we don't need to get into.

"You have three active cases right now. The personal-history notes, test results, copies of the police statements, et cetera, are all here."

He pats a stack of folders sitting next to him on the desk.

"I've emailed you dockets, dates . . ."

He waves his hand in the air signifying more "et cetera."

"I've gone through your website email and there were a few requests from students I've forwarded on to you. As always I've taken care of the women and the crazies.

He snaps the planner shut and stands up, signifying it's time for me to go. He's right about me not needing to see him in person. We could've had this conversation over the phone.

"Are you going to be okay?" he asks me.

"Of course I'm going to be okay."

"You need a girlfriend."

"No one *needs* a girlfriend."

"You need a friend."

"I have friends."

"Friends you actually see."

"My friends aren't imaginary."

"That's not what I mean. How about a pet?"

"I have Sal."

"He's your tailor."

He helps me into my overcoat. The thought behind the gesture is feminine, but the forceful way he shoves the garment onto my shoulders is masculine. This is typical of Max's androgyny. Meeting him for the first time people are never sure if he's a woman with no waistline and the hands of a meat packer or a man with a girlish smile and too much love of texture.

"I'm fine," I tell him.

He takes a moment to scribble on the back of his hand with a washable marker like he did during our first meeting. It's a private joke between us and something he always does whenever I travel.

He holds up his fist.

For the first time since we've begun this tradition the words startle me. They're no longer a jest but advice from someone who has stumbled upon the fact that my deepest fear and deepest desire are the same.

COME BACK is written there.

I PROBABLY SHOULD HAVE rented an SUV. The roads can be treacherous this time of year, but I couldn't bear the thought of making the four-hour drive in anything less than the glove-leather comfort and sealed silence of my Jag.

I leave the wind and snow behind me. The interstate is clear of ice and for a little while, a heatless sun manages to shine through the clouds. As I approach the humped, shrugging shoulders of the rolling mountains from my boyhood, they prove to be strangely comforting, the lines of stripped trees sprouting from the pale earth reminding me of an old man's stubble.

It's not until I leave the main roads and take the unmarked turn off Route 56 between Hellersburg and Coulter that the uneasiness starts to get the better of me. I speed past the scattered roadside knots of rundown homes with porches draped in Steelers black and gold and enter country so suffocating in its silent grimness, I immediately long for any sign of mankind, even the shuttered King Kone.

The trees press too closely against the crumbling shoulders of old blacktop. The light seems to shrink. The hills crowd uncomfortably near. Even knowing the thought is nonsense, I wish they would take a few steps back.

A little farther along and the forest begins to thin, then drops away into hillside farms in varying degrees of decay. Some with all their buildings standing. Others with only a house and the skeleton of a red-blistered barn. Still others are nothing but a weed-filled cellar or a lone chimney with snarls of fallen barbed wire lying about.

After a sharp deadly bend marked with a cluster of small plastic crosses and artificial flowers, a collection of houses can be seen at the end of a coiled, shedding snake of a road. The usual words used to describe towns situated at the bottom of valleys—huddled, nestled, snuggled, cradled—don't seem to apply. This one looks like it's been spit there.

It used to be a well-tended place back when the mines were still operating. At one time it was home to two thousand people; now only a little over two hundred reside here, not even enough to fill a single cell block in the prison I just left.

The houses sag and need paint. Broken windows are stuffed with rags and driveways are blocked with disabled cars on cinder blocks. Yards are filled with every kind of junk imaginable, from discarded washing machines and bent bicycle frames to old mattresses and green Hefty garbage bags bursting with beer cans. Behind it all sit the watchful hills with a huge gaping wound of strip mining slashed across them. Some colossal earth-moving equipment is still parked there even though it's been silent for years, a constant reminder that even the biggest machines can be bested.

The history of the entire region summed up in a glance: Man ruins Nature; Nature ruins Man.

I begin my descent down the hill toward a town whose infamy makes the cheerful greeting of a welcome sign unnecessary and somehow cruel. The relief a visitor feels once he leaves is how he knows he's just been to Lost Creek.

two

TOMMY'S NOT HOME WHEN I arrive. I'm not surprised. When I told him I was coming he began ranting about how he was going to have his doctor's medical license revoked for violating his patient confidentiality, how he was stronger and healthier than I could ever hope to be, and how the crime-ridden, godforsaken city of Philadelphia with its pedophiles, pickpockets, and pathetic excuse for a football team needed me much more than he did, but I expected his bluster.

Twelve years have passed since I last set foot in my hometown. Once my mom began her revolving-door lifestyle with various mental health care facilities in the region before ending up at White Hospital, I stopped making my yearly Christmas visits. It wasn't a difficult sacrifice. Holidays had never been pleasant occasions for us. For most families they're a time to celebrate what they have; for us they've always been reminders of what we've lost.

I still saw Tommy from time to time when I'd visit Mom. Wherever she happened to be, he'd meet me there and we'd have a meal afterward that he called dinner and I called a late lunch. The get-togethers never went well, though, and now standing on his front porch I realize I made a mistake trying to separate him from this place.

I push open his door, never expecting for one moment that it could be locked.

The curtains are drawn. I turn on all the lights in the small front

room bursting with books. The bits of wall not taken up with shelves are covered with travel posters of Ireland and amateurish paintings of rural Irish life where every man is pink-faced and clad in some shade of green and every woman smiles beatifically at one of the multitude of children clinging to her skirts.

In the midst of all this serene Celtic lushness, the only representation of Irish life in America that Tommy has seen fit to display is a framed photo of one of the memorial services held for the Nellies each year on the date of their execution. A group of men wearing white pillowcases over their heads with heavy nooses tied around their necks stand silently in front of the gallows. Their bound hands hold flickering candles.

I purposely keep my back to Fiona, choosing instead to greet Tommy's prized flea-bitten mounted deer head first. His antlers are strewn with ball caps, random pieces of string and wire, the set of house keys Tommy never uses, a Terrible Towel, and a string of twinkle lights. I stroke his velvety nose the same way I used to as a child, only then I had to stand on the couch to reach him.

I can feel Fiona watching me, so I give up and turn around. If it's possible, she's grown even more fearsome.

She stares out at me from the heavy wood frame, where she sits stiffly and primly in a straight-backed chair with her hands folded in her lap. Her once long dark curls are pulled severely to the top of her head in a wiry gray knot and her lips are clamped together in a face that's covered in hairline cracks, as if it's made of a fine bone china and someone's tapped it all over with a spoon.

In my fifth-grade geography class we learned about Aborigines in Australia who wouldn't let outsiders take their photographs because they were convinced the camera would capture their souls. I was sure my great-great-grandmother Fi believed the opposite, that the camera was a way to preserve her soul and release it long after she was dead on members of an unsuspecting generation who were only trying to relax after school and watch reruns of *Gilligan's Island*.

I never came right out and told Tommy I was afraid of her photograph, but one day I did get up the nerve to ask him if pictures could be haunted. I should have known better.

Of course they can, he said.

I set down my bags and head to the kitchen. It's an extension of the front room; the only sign one has become the other is the difference in flooring and smell. The brownish-orangey carpet gives way to pinkish-gray linoleum and the scent of musty cushions and Bengay becomes the stench of cooking grease and burnt stuff.

The table is covered with one of the many cloths my mom used to embroider during her manic phases. This one she completed when she was hugely pregnant with Molly not long before she went to prison. I remember her sitting on the couch with the material draped over what used to be a lap I could sit on, but what had become a monstrous growth she insisted was a baby, while I was convinced it was the biggest kick ball from school that had recently gone mysteriously missing. Her fingers darted above and below the circle of fabric pulled taut in its frame, making small pings like sprinkles of birdseed bouncing off a drum.

Her skill was impressive, but to me it was also frightening. Like everything my mom did, I knew the calm of her competence was only a prelude to a crushing fall or an explosive launch, neither of which could be controlled by anyone, least of all her. Were the stitches going to eventually slow into a week she'd spend curled up in bed staring at a wall too depressed to even wipe the drool from her chin? Or were they going to quicken into a whirlwind of activity and jabbering explanations that I'd helplessly endure until the inevitable crash into full-blown hysteria and danger?

I run my fingers over the top of the faded blue fabric. It used to be a vivid turquoise edged with smiling suns, smirking stars, laughing clouds, winking moons, and dancing rainbows. I loved it but fought the love I felt. I had to find something wrong with it and I did. It wasn't the human qualities she gave to the celestial bodies that bothered me, but the fact that she mixed day and night.

The guilt comes rushing at me, and I don't try to get out of the way. I've become adept over the years at keeping it at bay for long stretches of time. It used to lap at me constantly like the tiny whitecaps that whispered around my ankles after a speedboat went by while I waded in the reservoir swimming area holding my mommy's hand. Now I save it up and let it knock me down all at once like a tsunami.

All the times I didn't visit her in prison. All the times I haven't visited her since. My inability to forgive her even though I know none of it was her fault. My inability to help her then and help her now.

As always my guilt can't be separated from my bitterness and it comes pouring over me as well.

What about the times I did visit her in prison? How many little kids could handle that? And the times I have visited her since despite the inconvenience to my personal life and my career and the toll it takes on me emotionally? What about my ability to forgive her enough to have a relationship with her at all? My ability to keep her in first-rate homes and hospitals while others in her situation are left to rot in appalling institutions or abandoned to the streets?

The battering ceases. The waves subside. My black thoughts slip from shore back into the depths of my psyche where they will wait gathering their strength again.

Once again, bitterness trumped guilt. I wearied a long time ago asking why her? But it seems I will never be able to let go of why me?

I look at the tabletop again and notice a bag of Wise potato chips and a bottle of Jameson whiskey sitting in the middle of it, Tommy's idea of lunch. He's never been what I'd call a healthy eater, but his diet used to be a little better when he also had to occasionally feed me. At this juncture in his life he subsists entirely on alcohol, salty snack food, and charred animal flesh. I suppose I have no right to criticize. He's lived to be ninety-six. I should probably urge him to start his own fitness empire. We could call it Swill and Grill Your Way to a Better You.

Nothing has changed since the last time I was here. Nothing has changed since I was a boy. This failure to evolve is one of the things that used to drive me crazy about Lost Creek and its inhabitants, a betrayed, conquered people enslaved by the notion the jobs may come back; a company town without a company.

I walk to the back door and look out at the identical rooftops spilling down the hill. I couldn't understand why people didn't move where the jobs were. What was the appeal of this crappy little town? Or if they were determined to stay, why not try and make it better? And one of the ways to do this would be to encourage people to be smart instead of beating them up for it.

My eyes begin to search out the roof of my father's house and I pull them away, dropping my gaze to the floor where I find a collection of Tommy's footwear sitting on a mat: mud-caked work boots, ratty old-man slippers, and a pair of rubber wellies. The contrast between them and the toes of my own glossy mahogany Louis Vuitton loafers temporarily immobilizes me.

My earliest memories of my father are of his feet. Not flesh over bones, or cracked yellowed toenails, calluses, corns, blisters, bunions, random sproutings of dark wiry hair, or whatever else might have been hidden beneath his work boots, but the leather, steel, and hard rubber soles that he wore every day to do his job.

I knew every scuff on them, every bit of unraveling stitching. I marveled at how long a pebble could stay stuck in the same piece of tread. They'd walk toward me and come to a stop inches away from my face where it was stuck to the floor with blood or vomit or sometimes just the gummy spills of a kitchen now that Mom was no longer around to clean it. I smelled mud and motor oil and, amazingly, beer. How could even his boots smell like beer?

"What'd you say to me?" he'd always ask after I hit the ground.

I took him literally. I'd try with all my might but could never recall what I'd said to upset him. Can I have another piece of bread? I got a star on my math test?

He'd slowly dig his metal-tipped toe deep into my shrunken belly while I looked up and concentrated on the red, white, and blue enamel of his American-flag belt buckle that I secretly coveted, knowing if he were to read my thoughts he'd kill me.

He didn't believe in sharing. I often thought this philosophy was behind his dislike of me. His son was one of his possessions, and I was the boy who lived inside him and was making him be someone my dad didn't want him to be.

Thinking about both my parents at the same time would overwhelm me no matter where I was, but doing it here amplifies the pain.

The little house suddenly feels claustrophobic. Tommy could be any-where driving around in his rust-freckled, mint-green Chevy truck, the two of them coughing and sputtering together, looking for someone to annoy or charm depending on how you feel about him. I have no way to find him. He doesn't have a cell phone. He could be gone for hours.

I change and go for a run.

I start off with the lofty intention of at least ten miles, but the day is cold and my muscles aren't willing after all those hours sitting in a car. A couple miles out of town, I decide to loop back, my purpose for running in the first place having already been served. I don't do it to stay in shape or clear my head or puff up my ego with my latest PR. I do it because roughly once a day I'm overcome by a fear of being caught.

When I reach the stone wall surrounding the old jail the same human instinct that makes us all slow down and gape at car wrecks makes me slow to a jog and glance inside the entrance at the cracked walls covered in graffiti, the muddy ice patches, the disintegrating brick jailhouse, and the black specter of the gallows standing in the middle of it all.

The structure looms, sinister in its simplicity and inexplicable per-manence. The platform sits on top of a twelve-foot-high scaffold now black with age. One of the trapdoors dangles open. Two are missing al-together. Most of the steps are rotted through. A perverse bird has built a nest on one of the crossbars and no one has dared to remove it.

With the advent of ghost town Internet sites and TV shows about the paranormal, the amount of tourists has increased sharply, but I think these particular visitors are often disappointed in what they find.

Searchers of terror are a type of thrill seeker who crave the excite-ment of the discovery, the scare, the escape, and Lost Creek offers none of this. The horror here is real but it's out in the open, in the light, and can't be left behind once confronted. The gallows are terrifying not be-cause they're haunted by the dead but because they were conceived by the living.

The prison and the courtyard are cared for by the long-suffering members of the Nellie O'Neill Society, aka the NONS, a rebel offshoot of the local historical society that has always vigorously asserted the executed miners' innocence. They conduct guided tours on weekends, maintain a museum in Nora Daley's attic, provide the hoods and nooses for the annual memorial service along with the baked goods, and have been trying to raise funds for a commemorative statue for as long as I can remember.

They also employ an unpaid groundskeeper named Parker Hopkins, who works for beer and the sheer joy of riding a tractor mower. This time of year he spends most of his time in Kelly's Kwik Shop across the road drinking instant hot chocolate laced with peppermint schnapps, lamenting the lack of money in the budget for a snowblower.

But no one is here in the middle of a cold January weekday.

I'm about to turn and leave when I notice something lying on the ground near the gallows. I think I know what it is but it can't be. I have to check it out.

I have my phone with me and instinctively think of calling Rafe. I have his number but lose my nerve. I don't know what I'd say after all this time. I dial 911 instead and tell the dispatcher I've found a body.

three

THE TWO YOUNG COPS introduce themselves. The first is Billy Smalls, and I have to say he's aptly named. I'm sure he took a lot of abuse about this fact when he was a child, which I assume wasn't all that long ago. Short and slight, ginger haired, with big ears and a smooth, wide-eyed baby face, he seems too young to do this job or any job other than sell lemonade.

The other is Troy Razzano. He's a dark-haired, dark-eyed, good-looking kid, but is already starting to get thick around the middle from the doughnuts, drive-thrus, and 2 a.m. Denny's Grand Slam breakfasts of a small-town law enforcement diet. If I had to pick one reason why he became a police officer, I'd say it's because he likes how he looks in the uniform. Even if he lives to be as old as Tommy, I'm sure he'll want to be buried in it. I picture Billy being buried in SpongeBob SquarePants pajamas. The kind with feet.

"Sheridan Doyle?" Billy repeats my name. "Your name sounds familiar."

"Yeah, I've heard of you, too," Troy muses.

"I grew up here. I'm visiting my grandfather. But you might know me from my books or TV appearances on the news, talk shows, crime documentaries . . ."

Recognition fails to register on their faces.

"I'm a forensic psychologist," I explain further. "I've been involved in some fairly well-known cases. The Wishbone Killer, the Scranton Bomber, the Dolly Decker kidnapping . . . I'm *Dr.* Sheridan Doyle—"

"Hey, that's it," Troy cuts me off. "Rafe knows you. He's got one of your books."

"Yeah," Billy chimes in. "Rafe knows you."

A thrill of childish pride rushes through me as if I've just been picked first for any type of team. I don't know why I think I'd have the slightest idea how that feels, but for a moment, I'm sure I do.

"So he's still working?"

They both smile and nod.

"Oh, yeah," they say in unison.

"He's a detective now," Troy provides. "The first one we've ever had. Everyone jokes the chief made up the position for him because he knew Rafe could never handle not wearing a uniform and having to pick out his own clothes so he'd be forced to retire, but it didn't work."

They fall silent. I wait for them to walk over to the body, but neither one seems eager to look at it. I imagine the Creekside Township police rarely deal with suspicious deaths, but even so, there's nothing gory about this one. I already took a look at him. I don't know why they're keeping their distance.

I start toward the man. They fall in beside me.

"You're an old-timer," Billy says to me. "You probably know a lot about the town's history. Is this the first guy to ever be killed here? I mean other than the original guys who were killed here."

"I'm forty-three," I state irately. "That hardly makes me an old-timer."

"Sorry."

"Why are you assuming he was killed?" I ask. "You haven't even seen him. It could be natural causes."

"How about that?" Billy says, crouching down near the body. "It's Simon Husk. I thought I saw his car over there."

"What do you think did it?" Troy asks me, tentatively.

"Don't you mean, *who* did it? Not *what*?" I reply.

He doesn't say anything.

"I don't think anyone did anything to him," I go on. "There's no blood. No sign of trauma on the body. Heart attack, maybe."

I glance at the boys. They look skeptical.

"He was an older man, overweight," I explain. "Smells like a smoker. Looks like a drinker. A diabetic."

"How do you know he was a diabetic?" Troy asks me.

"He's wearing a MedicAlert bracelet."

Billy barks a laugh.

"You're a regular Sherlock freakin' Holmes, Razzano."

Troy shifts around and hitches up his utility belt hung with twenty pounds of equipment featuring a huge flashlight, which is the most formidable object on it. In this well-armed community of hunters, veterans, and Second Amendment–loving patriots, his holstered Glock carries the intimidation factor of a squirt gun.

"Yeah, you're probably right about the heart attack," he concedes.

"Do you have an alternative theory?" I ask them.

"Isn't it true you can be scared to death?" Troy wonders. "I mean, can't something scare you so bad it gives you a heart attack?"

"What are you saying?"

"There's no such thing as ghosts," Billy jumps in.

"They could be zombies," Troy says to him in a private aside that leads me to believe this isn't the first time they've had this discussion.

"What are you two talking about?" I ask, even though I already know the answer.

"The Nellies . . ."

"We don't believe in them," Troy adds quickly. "But what if Simon here believed in them . . . ?"

He leaves the idea hanging in the air for all of us to consider.

Simon Husk certainly wouldn't be the first person to have ever allegedly seen a ghost at the gallows, or lingering in the jail, or roaming morosely through the field where the Nellies were buried without so much as a rock a child might use to mark a pet's grave to commemorate their final resting place.

The town has been the continual darling of ghost-hunting societies and research foundations for as long as I can remember. They show up periodically with their cameras, recorders, thermometers, and gadgets to gauge electromagnetic disturbances. Believers and skeptics alike have reported sightings of glowing orbs of light and faint bluish mists accompanied by sudden drafts of cold and suffocating feelings of dread. Every Halloween someone sees and hears Prosperity trudging along a road with his dinner pail swinging by his side whistling "Yankee Doodle."

"Husk just sold the gallows and the jail to Walker Dawes, and he's going to tear it all down and drill for gas," Billy informs me.

"The gallows are being torn down?"

I can't believe Tommy didn't tell me this.

The young cops nod in unison.

"Why now? Why after all this time?"

They both shrug.

"The Nellies could be mad at Simon for selling the gallows, so they killed him," Troy continues theorizing.

It's obvious from their expressions that they believe it's a possibility, but they laugh and shake their heads when they notice me staring at them.

"We're just messing with you," Billy says, squaring his slim shoulders.

We're interrupted by the sound of a car door slamming and one side of a heated conversation ringing out clearly in the cold white dawn silence.

A man in rumpled gray pants, a pair of Caterpillar boots with bright yellow laces, a strobing red-and-blue-striped tie, and an olive green corduroy blazer all topped off with a camouflage hunting jacket comes tromping toward us, taking a slight detour in order to kick a Pepsi can across the prison yard.

They were right about him not being able to pick out his own clothes.

"I don't care," Rafe shouts into his phone. "It's not my car anymore. I don't own it. I don't drive it. And I'm sure as hell not going to pay to replace its timing belt."

He pockets his phone but continues his tirade.

"When we were married she'd go for days, weeks, without talking to me. Now we're divorced, she wants to talk to me all the time. What are you looking at?" he snaps at Billy, who flinches at the edge in his voice.

Rafe stares him down with a surly blue squint, then flashes one of his disarming smiles that somehow manages to be both angelic and menacing at the same time, set in the fine-featured, booze-ravaged face.

He turns to me.

I wait breathlessly for some kind of sentimental greeting. Will he embrace me? Shake my hand and pat me on the back? It's been twelve years and I've accomplished a lot during this time; will he be too choked up to speak?

"What the hell are you wearing?" he asks me.

I glance down at my running attire: Sugoi RSR running tights, a North Face Apex ClimateBlock zip jacket, neon-orange reflective Saucony gloves, and a waterproof Asics beanie. I've come a long way from the wrestling team's hand-me-down shapeless gray sweats, tube socks for gloves, and Steelers knit cap topped with a big yellow pom-pom of my youth, but I doubt if he considers this an improvement.

Before I can come up with a response, he digs out a pink Jolly Rancher from his coat pocket and strips off the plastic wrap.

I remember he only likes the watermelon ones.

"Are you still trying to quit smoking?" I ask.

"Once a year."

He pops the candy into his mouth. I listen to the clicks and clacks of it hitting his teeth as he moves it around his mouth.

"How're you doing, Danno?"

His words whisk me back to the day we first met and he sat with me in the kitchen where I would one day get to know my father's feet while the other police officers took away my mother in handcuffs and the remains of my infant sister in a body bag no bigger than a backpack and he pushed a Tootsie Roll across the tabletop and asked me the same question.

I automatically started to say okay, my conditioned response, then I looked up and met his stare full of anger and concern but no pity or blame, and for the first time in my young life I felt I could be honest.

"Not very good," I told him that day.

"I'm great," I tell him today. "How are you?"

"Still kicking, which is more than I can say for old Simon here."

He kneels next to the body. We wait for his appraisal. Rafe's the only one here well acquainted with the sight of death. He only ever mentioned Vietnam once to me during all the time I've known him. I don't know any details about what he saw or did there, but I've always assumed it was bad for him. I've spent a few nights at the Red Rabbit with him years ago watching him drink with a mechanical purpose I know has to be motivated by something more torturous than life in a used-up coal town and four divorces.

"He's dead all right," he announces. "What was he doing here?"

"We don't know," Billy answers. "His car's parked on the street. Looks like he drove himself here."

"I thought he sold this land to Dawes."

"He did."

"I'm going to go talk to the wife," he tells the boys. "You two wait for the coroner."

"But . . ." Troy sputters.

"What's with them?" Rafe asks me.

"They're spooked," I tell him.

"I'm not spooked," Billy insists roughly.

Rafe grins. He opens his eyes wide and makes ghostly moans while fluttering his fingers at them.

"What do you think? Old Prosperity and Footloose are finally getting their revenge? Souvenir sales are going to skyrocket for the NONS," he whoops.

He abruptly turns and begins walking back to his car and I happily trail after him, instinctively falling into the puppy dog role of my youth.

He looks back at me over his shoulder.

"You gonna tell me why you're here?"

"I was out for a run."

"I can see that. You run all the way from Philly? I mean, why are you in town?"

"I came to take care of Tommy."

"Make sure he doesn't hear you say that," he snorts. "Tommy's the last guy who will let someone take care of him. He's out of the hospital. He's doing fine as far as I know."

He stops and watches me, clicking his candy against his teeth, waiting for me to explain why I'm really here. For once in my life, I can't put something into words, except to say I need to see my grandpa in the flesh.

"Why don't you come with me?" he suggests. "We can catch up."

"Come with you on an interrogation?"

"Interrogation, hell. I'm gonna go tell Bethany Husk her husband's dead. We can get a beer after."

"Aren't you on duty?"

"On duty," he snorts again.

He reaches into his pocket and holds out a piece of candy to me.

"I'll go off for an hour or two. No one will miss me."

four

AFTER MEETING FOR THE first time on the day of my mother's arrest, Rafe continued to keep an eye on me. He'd stop by occasionally with a candy bar or baseball cards. Eventually he started taking me on ride-alongs in his police car.

I was eager to go but soon discovered there was nothing exciting about his kind of police work. It consisted for the most part of driving around and sometimes sitting in the gravel lot behind the beer distributor's waiting for someone to break the speed limit on Jenner's Pike. Everyone did, and since it wouldn't have been fair for him to only ticket people he personally disliked, he devised a sort of game for us to play where I'd pick a number and we'd count the cars that went past until we reached it and then went after the unlucky one. He never rejected my choice of a number whether it was two or twenty-two. Once I picked 116. We spent several hours playing checkers on the board he set up between us in the front seat, but only thirty cars passed during that time so no one got a ticket that day.

When something out of the ordinary did happen, it never involved a car chase or a shoot-out or any kind of confrontation with a criminal or evildoer like police work did on TV. From what I could see, Rafe's job consisted of cleaning up the messes of ordinary people and then directing them—sometimes with the help of handcuffs—toward others who could help them find ways to cope with their mistakes and disappointments. Saving them from the bad guys turned out to be nothing more than saving them from themselves.

The giant Husk house sits alone on a hillside, a reproduction of an antebellum mansion constructed without any of the craftsmanship or natural building materials used in the Old South. It's a testament to how much square footage can be encased in vinyl siding and covered in stain-resistant carpeting.

Rafe pounds at the front door with the flat of his fist, ignoring the faux-brass knocker. A woman in her sixties wearing gold jewelry and a purple velour jogging suit answers.

"Mrs. Husk?" he asks.

"Yes?" she asks, crinkling her brow uncertainly.

He shows her his credentials.

"I'm—"

"Rafe," she suddenly gushes before he can finish introducing himself.

A sentimental smile lights up her face and I'm not surprised. Every woman in the county between the ages of thirty and seventy has had some sort of intimate dealings with Rafe, whether real or imaginary.

"We went to school together," Mrs. Husk explains to me while never taking her eyes off Rafe. "Do you remember—?"

Rafe nods and pops two Jolly Ranchers into his mouth in rapid-fire succession.

"Mrs. Husk," he cuts her off.

"Bethany," she offers.

"I'm here to talk to you about your husband."

Her smile and the misty softness in her eyes vanishes.

"Simon?"

"I'm afraid he's dead."

"Oh my God!"

She slaps a hand covered in chunky rings like small brightly colored ice cubes to her mouth.

"What happened?"

"It looks like he died of natural causes, but we won't know for sure until we get the coroner's report."

"I don't understand. Where? How?"

"We found him at the gallows."

Her eyes brimming with tears grow comically large.

"The gallows?" she repeats in a fearful whisper.

"That's what I'd like to talk to you about if you feel up to answering a few questions."

She gestures inside the house at an enormous green living room with cathedral ceilings, gold carpeting, and a huge coffee table inlaid with green and yellow pieces of the kind of rippled plastic seen in cheap church window reproductions.

Rafe follows her and takes a seat on the edge of a green-and-gold-striped couch and I'm immediately reminded of a farm machinery sales-man waiting for an airport shuttle in the lobby of a Midwest Comfort Inn. Bethany Husk practically disappears inside a barrel-shaped suede chair that looks like a big moldy marshmallow.

I decide to remain outside and stretch. Cavernous, color-coordinated houses make me nervous; along with traditional claustrophobia, I also suffer from a reverse type where I feel trapped by too much useless space.

The view from here would be beautiful on a sparkling October afternoon when the trees are a splash of enameled colors, but in January it's a vista of depressing shadows. Bundles of sooty bedsheet clouds sit heavily on the tops of the distant hills. Down in the valley through a black screen of bare tree branches is the gray stream from which the town took its name, meandering sluggishly among patches of snow like a vein on the underside of a wrist.

I can almost make out the town from here. There was a time when Lost Creek Coal & Oil owned every part of it: the rows of houses, the brass and marble bank where footsteps echoed like gunshots, the square, squat brown brick post office, the all-important company store, the jail, and eventually a school with a cafeteria that would also serve as a gymnasium and a place for town meetings and the laying out of bodies after a mine disaster. The only things Walker Dawes didn't own were the Red Rabbit and the two churches. For some reason he decided to let someone else profit from a miner's need to drink and his wife and mother's need to pray.

After the Nellies were executed, the gallows were never used again, but Walker made sure they weren't torn down. He claimed he left them up as a reminder of what happened to men who broke the law, but the miners knew the real message behind them was that he was the law.

Unlike his father, Walker Dawes II, or Deuce as he was better known, was a superstitious man. He never liked the fact that the gallows had remained standing, but even after his father passed away and the land was his, he was too frightened to destroy them. He wanted to sell the place but no one wanted to buy it until Warren Husk, a prosperous farmer with a morbid streak, showed up. Warren knew how badly Deuce wanted to get rid of the jail and the gallows, and he used it as leverage to put together a deal where he was able to buy up hundreds of acres of the surrounding land as well at a bargain price.

I never answered Billy Smalls, but to my knowledge no one's ever been seriously hurt there, aside from the men who were put to death, which is nothing short of amazing considering the amount of kids who have climbed up the gibbet over the years in response to dares or as part of macabre midnight games.

As children we were surrounded by irresistible life-threatening hazards: water-filled quarries, railroad tracks, abandoned mine shafts, mountainous bony piles that were the site of legendary dirt bike accidents, but none were as appealing as the gallows. We were too young to have a sense of mortality. We couldn't comprehend the horror of facing our own deaths or watching a friend jerk like a hooked fish from the end of a hangman's rope, but we were already well acquainted with the concepts of cruelty, treachery, and the dark art of survival. Whether pretending to be a miner or one of Walker Dawes' hired thugs, we understood what happened to the Nellies and we loved and feared their story the same way we did the one that belonged to our fathers.

"Simon's greed was greater than his fear," Rafe announces as he joins me again, stuffing a brownie into his mouth.

He hands me one. I shake my head. He eats that one, too.

"Everyone knows he was obsessed with the gallows. He's been

afraid of them ever since he was a little kid and thought he saw the ghost of Prosperity McNab."

"Seriously?"

"He saw a ghost outside his bedroom window and the next morning someone had written 'Fi' in blood on the bathroom mirror."

"In blood?" I repeat.

"Well, not exactly blood. It turned out to be his mom's lipstick."

"Prosperity's ghost was running around with a lipstick?"

He nods and grins with a mouthful of chocolate-coated teeth.

"It was obviously some stunt someone played on him, but Simon never stopped believing. He's always been too superstitious to get rid of the gallows. He thought if he tore them down the Nellies would come back and kill him. But apparently Walker Dawes offered him a sum of money he couldn't pass up."

He finishes his brownies and brushes the crumbs from his hands.

"It's been big news around here. There are some people who think the same way Simon did. They believe if the gallows fall, the Nellies will rise."

He makes the same googly eyes he made at Troy and Billy earlier.

"That's ludicrous."

"His wife said he's been going to the gallows a lot lately. That's the part that doesn't make sense."

"Why not?"

"Because he was scared of them."

"Maybe he finally wanted to confront his fears at the source before the gallows were no longer his," I offer.

"And one of the times he's over there, he drops dead. You have a problem with that?"

"None at all," I reply.

"Me neither. But just to be safe you think I should question Prosperity? You think he's gone back to his grave? Or he could be sitting over at the Union Hall with a beer and no one would even notice him. Just one more living corpse with a Miller Lite and a bad cough."

"Well, I'm glad everything makes sense and I'm glad you were able to escape. I was starting to get worried. The widow seemed awfully fond of you."

He doesn't respond. I know from experience he won't talk about his Lothario past, although I do remember him telling me once that he was amazed he got through high school without getting a girl pregnant. He was drafted right after graduation, then within six months of returning from Vietnam, and spending all of them drunk, stoned, and brawling, he did exactly that.

On the night he was packing his Firebird getting ready to skip town, his future first father-in-law, Trooper Stan Zilner, stopped by his trailer, sat him down in the kitchen, laid his service revolver on the table between them, and explained to Rafe that he knew a few extreme guys like him, guys who'd been in Nam, guys who teetered on the edge of good and evil. A push in one direction and they'd end up toppling into the dark abyss of criminality, a push in the other direction and they'd find themselves on the solid ground of law enforcement. Stan gave him the choice of becoming a cop, marrying his daughter, and raising his grandchild, or being pulled over by a state trooper who would discover a large amount of illegal narcotics in his possession and might possibly have to shoot him if he resisted arrest.

Rafe chose the first option. Ironically, out of the three elements comprising the scenario, the one he had the most misgivings about—being a police officer—turned out to be the only one he was good at.

He gets a call. He walks away from me to take it then returns frowning.

"I found Tommy for you," he says.

"Is he okay?"

"Oh, yeah, he's fine. But the manager at Carelli's Furniture isn't doing so good. She wants him out of there."

"Why is he in a furniture store?"

"You'd be amazed where he pops up. Let's go get him."

He bends down, scoops up a handful of snow, and swallows it: a country boy's method of cleansing his palate. He takes another piece of candy out of his pocket.

"Why don't you get a patch?" I wonder.

"That would be cheating."

"There are no rules for breaking an addiction."

He makes a slow turn, taking a final inventory, noticing things I'm sure I don't, reminding me of an old hunting dog grown white around the muzzle. I wouldn't be surprised if he raised his nose to sniff the air. Instead he bares his teeth and tells me, "There are rules for everything, Danno."

five

RAFE AND I ARRIVE at Carelli's Furniture on the outskirts of town, a flat tan warehouse with a glassed-in showroom at the front of the building filled with overstuffed recliners, sectional sofas, dining room sets, and a line of contemporary furnishings where Mrs. Husk probably found her church-window coffee table and marshmallow chair.

I spot Tommy's truck parked in the handicapped space in front of the doors. He's in his nineties and uses a cane and could easily get a handicapped license plate, but he refuses. Instead, he's written a sign he puts on his dashboard that reads: "I'm 96 and if you got the balls to tell me to my face I shouldn't park here, I'll move my truck for you. Otherwise, screw off."

He's been doing this since he turned ninety, making a new sign every year in order to adjust his age, and as far as I know no one has given him any trouble.

A woman in a pumpkin-colored skirt and jacket and brown sensible shoes greets us at the door. She has clipped streaky blond hair she keeps nervously tucking behind her right ear.

"I'm the new manager," she greets us.

Rafe shows her his badge. She studies it longer than necessary.

"Where's your uniform?"

"I'm a detective," he explains.

"They have detectives here?"

"Just the one, ma'am. Yours truly."

"What is there to investigate—"

"Excuse me, but where is he?" I interrupt before Rafe has a chance to answer her in a way he probably shouldn't.

She waves toward a couple dozen couches all crammed together in the center of the room, some facing in, some facing out, some facing each other.

Tommy's sitting on one with his cane propped nearby, eating from a container of party nuts, watching his wallet-size portable TV, the only advance in technology during the past thirty years that he ever praises, aside from Internet porn, which he's never seen but thinks is a good idea.

There's not a single customer in the store.

"What seems to be the problem?" Rafe asks.

"He won't leave."

"Has he caused any type of disturbance?"

"No. But he won't leave. He shouldn't be here."

She pushes her hair behind her ear again and blurts out, "Do you know who he is?"

"Maybe."

"He's Thomas McNab. He was telling me about his grandfather and the Nellie O'Neills cutting people's tongues out if they squealed on them. The Nellies were bloodthirsty killers, and he's related to them."

Rafe arches his eyebrows.

"Well, he's not looking particularly bloodthirsty today," he says.

"You think it's funny?"

"Ma'am, what exactly is the problem?"

"He can't be here," she states flatly.

We go inside and before we can even begin to make our way through the maze of sofas to get to Tommy, he recognizes Rafe.

"Called out the storm troopers on me, did you?" he shouts at the manager, who pretends to busy herself fluffing pillows.

He narrows his eyes suspiciously in our direction, then his face splits into a grin when he recognizes me.

"So you came after all. I told you not to. Are you so famous now you get a police escort?"

I'm flooded with relief. I wasn't sure what to expect, but he looks exactly the same as he did the last time I saw him and the time before that. I don't see any obvious signs of a prolonged illness. He has on the same red-and-black-checked Woolrich coat he's worn for as long as I can remember, and one of his Lost Creek Coal & Oil ball caps covers his unruly head of snow-white hair. The ladies of NONS are always telling him he should take off his hat so they can see his pretty hair. He growls and grimaces over the compliment, but I know he secretly loves it.

I lean down and give him a quick embrace. I don't expect him to stand up. He spent forty years crouching in a coal mine; the resulting arthritis in his knees makes rising from a sitting position no easy feat for him.

"And Rafferty Malloy. My favorite Malloy. The only Malloy with a good singing voice and an equally good throwing arm."

Rafe extends his hand for a shake.

"I haven't used either in a long time. How are you, Tommy?"

"Couldn't be better."

"Heard you were pretty sick there for a while."

"It was nothing. You think pneumonia can kill me? My lungs are Teflon coated."

"You do look good," I tell him.

"And you look ridiculous. Don't tell me you've been out running already."

He and Rafe exchange looks that say I'm clearly crazy. I'm used to this response here. In their opinion, the only time a man should run is toward a goalpost or away from a skunk.

"I'm sorry I wasn't at the house to greet you," he goes on. "I left you some lunch, though."

"Potato chips and whiskey?"

"I didn't have any tofu."

He lets his gaze return to the TV screen in his lap where he's watching the Home Shopping Network, one of his favorite pastimes. He regards it purely as a form of entertainment. To my knowledge, he's never bought a single item from them.

"Have you ever seen anything so disgustin'? Little doggy booties for sale? Gourmet doggy cookies? These animals live better than I ever did. Look at that. Steps. Little steps to put next to your bed so your old lame dog can get up there with you when he can't jump anymore.

"Get yourself a man," he leans forward and shouts at the woman in the advertisement who's lying in her bed urging a white feather duster of a dog up a set of miniature red-carpeted stairs.

"Well, look at her," he sneers. "What man would have her?"

"She probably has a man and he probably sleeps with the dog, too," Rafe tells him. "Ménage à dog."

Rafe's comment sends Tommy into a gale of laughter that ends in a coughing fit. He reaches for the empty coffee can he takes with him everywhere and spits out some of the black, tarry phlegm that fills his lungs. That it hasn't drowned him yet is a miracle. All of the miners he worked with are long dead, many for decades.

I catch a glimpse of the manager watching him with an expression close to horror frozen on her face.

"So what can I do for you boys?"

"We hear you've been telling some stories," Rafe says.

Tommy breaks into another paroxysm of laughter ending in another bout of hacking coughs and spitting.

"Lord, I told her some good ones. I told her after they killed the first foreman they cut out his heart, roasted it over an open fire, and served it up with some soda bread and a nice tart apple butter."

He breaks off into more laughter.

"And Fiona had a necklace made out of his fingertips—"

"You have to leave, Tommy," Rafe cuts him off.

"And where should I go? I can't stay in the house all day. Drives me crazy. I have to go somewhere."

It's true. Tommy's never been one to sit still, especially alone, but he's outlived all his friends. He's outlived his entire generation.

"You can't stay here."

"Fine," he says dejectedly.

"Why don't you go to the Union? Shoot some pool," Rafe suggests.

"Bunch of kids. Not a man there over eighty."

He ponders his situation.

"I guess I could go to the Bi-Lo. I need a few groceries. I tried to go last night but Owen was there and I had to leave. I can tell you everything he had in his basket. It's burned into my brain: a pack of hamburger patties, a bottle of Mountain Dew, two cans of corned beef hash, five boxes of single-serving mac and cheese, and a thirty-six double-roll pack of toilet paper he was lugging around under his arm. A man who lives alone and shits a lot."

Tommy's hands begin to tremble with rage.

"I told Arly he was a sonofabitch. I told her. She didn't have to get married, you know. I would've never thrown her out."

Rafe glances at me, knowing that I'm the reason she did get married whether she felt she had to or not. Having Owen Doyle's child and not marrying him would have probably been an equally perilous situation. She was doomed the moment the sperm met the egg.

A wave of sadness washes over Tommy and he flops back into the couch, his milky blue eyes becoming clear and then sparkling with tears.

For a moment, he does look old. He's become alarmingly thin, but he's not frail. If anything he looks tougher to me than he ever has, as if his body decided to consume any part of him that was soft and weak and leave only bone and gristle.

"I'm sorry, Danny," he says quietly.

He reaches out his gnarled hand to me covered in the familiar miner's blue scars like pieces of pencil lead trapped beneath the papery, age-spotted skin.

I take it and help him stand while Rafe puts the lid on his can of nuts and turns off his TV.

"No hard feelings?" the manager asks Tommy with a nervous tic at the corner of her mouth as we pass through the door.

"Of course not, young lady," he replies, flashing his most charming smile. "You have a lovely day now."

"She's terrified of me," he whispers proudly in my ear.

We arrive at his truck, but before he gets in he smiles back and forth between Rafe and me.

"Aren't you going to ask me about Simon Husk?" he says suddenly.

"How the hell do you know about that already?" Rafe asks.

"Nora was on the scene right away and she called me. You know how the NONS love me."

"She called you here?"

"She called Birdie and Birdie called Betty and Betty and I had run into each other earlier at the Kwik Shop and I told her I was headed out here. Told her I need a new couch. Aren't you going to ask me if I think the Nellies murdered him for selling the gallows back to Dawes?" he says ominously.

He has the vaguest touch of a brogue and speaks with the cadence of an Irishman, but this lilting quality to his speech doesn't come from Ireland. It comes from growing up in a closed-off American community of Irish immigrants.

Tommy's never set foot in Ireland, although he's always talked about going, and I've offered more than once to take him. I can't imagine anyone more Irish than him, but I know if he ever finally made it over there he'd be an obvious American.

It's the same problem his ancestors faced when they first came here. They weren't Irish anymore, but they weren't American yet. They were neither, and they were both. They were Irishmen living inside an American skin; they were Americans living inside an Irish head.

They were forced to carve out a new identity and a new culture for themselves here in the hills of Pennsylvania. Ireland had no place for them. America didn't want them. The mines became their country and the Nellies became their justice system.

"There was no murder," Rafe assures him. "And the Nellies had nothing to do with it."

"Right, right," Tommy says with a wink. "Move along, folks. There's nothing to see here."

I tell Rafe I'll take a rain check on the beer. We say our good-byes and I get into the truck with Tommy.

I know it's useless for me to ask him to let me drive, so I sit back and brace myself in the passenger side of his truck as he careens down the middle of steep, twisting roads, not seeming to care at all if another vehicle whips toward us from the opposite direction.

Most people become cautious as they grow older, but age has made Tommy even more reckless. Instead of viewing the remainder of his life as something he should protect and savor, he sees it as something left over that he needs to gulp down before someone else gets their hands on it.

"Do you mind if we go to the Bi-Lo? I don't have anything to make for dinner tonight."

"It's Bi-Lo, Tommy. Not *the* Bi-Lo. It's a grocery store, not a casino."

He beams happily at my correction, something I've always loved about him. He was the only person who ever made me feel like my thirst for knowledge was a good thing and that speaking up when a mistake was made was a positive response, not an act of arrogance.

Nothing excites Tommy more than learning something new, which is one of the reasons I can't understand why he's lived all these years in a town full of people who seem like they don't even want to know the little they can't avoid knowing. He loves books. He's the most voracious reader I've ever known, a trait he credits to Fiona, who was a self-taught reader and always made sure he was surrounded by the written word.

She raised Tommy. His own mother died in childbirth and his father, Jack, died ten years later in a roof fall in one of Walker Dawes' mines. This string of McNab men who grew up without fathers would end when Tommy had a daughter, my mother, Arlene. She gave birth to me, a son, but my father is a Doyle, not a McNab, something Tommy has forgiven but will never let me forget.

"Why didn't you tell me the gallows are coming down?"

"Must've slipped my mind."

"I don't believe that for one minute."

"Why should I care?" he asks. "They should've been torn down over a hundred years ago. They should've never been put up in the first place."

"But . . . ?"

"They're a reminder," he concedes.

I can't begin to understand what those morbid pieces of wood truly mean to Tommy. Even though I had an ancestor die there, they've never had much of an emotional impact on me. I was just one more kid who got a cheap horror-movie thrill from them, but for Tommy, they weren't the stuff of an overactive imagination or the symbol of some distant historical event. Fiona used to take him there every Sunday afternoon. She held his hand exactly the same way she had held the hand of Jack, and they would stand in silence as if before a church altar while he'd be forced to envision what had happened there to a man who had been taken from him and had left a hole in his life. I never would have known Prosperity McNab, but he would've been Tommy's grandfather.

"Of something horrible," I add.

"Maybe," he says. "But consider this. You see a person on the street with a scar on his face and you might feel pity or repulsion or admiration for surviving his ordeal, but regardless, you're always going to be intrigued. You know he has a story to tell."

I smile to myself but also feel a little frustration toward the man. It's just like Tommy to think having a story to tell is more important than removing a disfigurement that could lead to renewed self-esteem and overall better mental health.

I'm not sure I agree. I think I'd call in the plastic surgeon. A new face might be good for this town.

GROCERY SHOPPING HAS NEVER gone well for the two of us. We get our own baskets as soon as we enter the store and split up.

I pick up a few things and end in produce, a section of the store Tommy regards with dubiousness and scorn. My father would never be caught in the produce section either; this is one thing he and Tommy have in common.

Certain people find my father charming in small doses. Owen Doyle is the epitome of the tragic Irishman reeking of booze and splendid self-pity, capable of wit and good humor, but only as a precursor to throwing punches and recriminations. He wholeheartedly embraces the fatalism of our ancestors—a race of islanders damned with lousy weather and cliff faces instead of sultry sea breezes and soft sandy beaches—and used to have quite a few followers who listened to him preach from his favorite bar stool at the Red Rabbit every night about the futility of effort.

I was a disappointment to my father and his feet, who did their best to raise me right in his mind. A mother's love is unconditional, but a father's has to be constantly earned, and no matter how hard I tried, I could never please him. I eventually stopped trying when I began to realize the kind of man he wanted me to be was the kind of man I feared becoming.

I'm grateful when I see Tommy limping toward me after his foray throughout the rest of the store, his basket containing a bag of Blazin' Buffalo and Ranch Doritos, a bag of Fritos corn chips, eight pork chops, four Delmonico steaks, and two dozen chicken legs.

He glares at the bag of salad greens in my hand.

"Do I look like a rabbit to you?"

"It's for me. Don't worry," I say, tossing it into my own basket holding a quart of low-fat milk, three apples, two yogurts, and a half dozen minicupcakes from the bakery frosted in pastels and covered with rainbow sprinkles.

He notices the childish treats. He knows they must be for my mother.

"I'm going to go see her tomorrow," I say. "Do you want to come along?"

He shakes his head wearily.

"It's good for you to have time alone. I'll see her next week."

I nod my agreement and we let the topic of my mother and his daughter drop without any satisfaction or resolution as we've been doing all our lives.

He suddenly grabs my face roughly in his big hands.

"It's good to see you, Danny," he says.

My dejection lifts as I realize wanting to lay eyes on him again isn't the only reason I needed to come home.

"It's good to be seen," I say back to him.

six

THERE'S NOTHING TO SEE, nothing to hear, no one to run from or run to. I open my eyes and find utter black: an absence of light so impenetrable and inescapable, it has its own weight.

My breath comes in shallow gasps. The air is dense and filled with a metallic grit. I try to move but I can barely raise up on all fours. Sharp rocks dig into my back, my knees, and the palms of my hands, and a chilly dampness soaks through my clothes. I inch forward and hit a wall then turn and hit another. Each time I pick up one of my hands, I don't want to put it back down again for fear of what I might touch.

I don't know how much time I spend crouched, barely moving, suffocating and shivering before I spot something that looks like a glimmer of light. I reach for it, thinking it's next to me, only to discover it's far in the distance at the end of a tunnel. I creep toward it helplessly, not with any feeling of relief or hope, but with dread and revulsion. I realize I'm not seeing light at all but a kind of phosphorescence, the same sickly yellow glow I've seen on mushrooms in the woods late at night.

I keep moving toward it until I finally understand what I'm seeing and by then it's too late to turn around, and besides, I have nowhere to go except back into the black. The waxy clumps splattered against the rock walls are the remains of a person. I can make out part of a foot, an eye socket, an elbow, a pair of lips. Even though the man is in pieces, it's obvious he hasn't been dismembered. He looks as if he's been dissolved.

I begin to make out more and more pieces of more and more men. Suddenly I know what's happened to me: I'm in the bowels of a stone beast, and these men are being digested.

One of the puddled faces tries to speak to me, but his words are strangled in the thick, shiny ropes of tar that come spewing out of his cracked black lips. He tries again and this time I can make out his words. He tells me to get him a beer. The voice belongs to my dad.

I wake screaming, and I'm a child again waiting for Tommy to come rushing into the room where my mother used to sleep, scaring me almost as much as my dream, a haunted scarecrow of pale, skinny limbs in faded oversize boxer shorts, white hair sticking up like straw, and a grimace of toothless terror stretched across his face, brandishing whatever weapon was at hand: an empty whiskey bottle, a flyswatter, a bathroom plunger.

He'd stumble to the bed, clutching his chest, his eyes bulging, his cheeks caved in since he didn't have time to grab his dentures, and I'd be distracted from my own fear by having to calm his. We never talked about the content of my nightmares. We both knew I had good reason to have them, although in some strange twist of mental self-preservation, they were never about my mother and sister. I let him believe they were because I could never reveal to him what they were really about. They were shameful. I was afraid of the mines.

The moment passes and I sense the grown man's body I inhabit now. I know I'm not a child, but the rest of my disorientation continues. I don't know where I am. I can't see anything.

I flail around in a blind panic until I realize my head is buried beneath several throw pillows and Tommy's afghan. I sense Fiona staring at me from across the room. I close my eyes again while waiting for my heart to stop thudding and my hands to stop trembling. My chest is slick with sweat.

I used to have this dream all the time but my father has never been in it before.

Tommy limps into the room, the tap of his cane heralding his approach. He apparently didn't hear my screams because he says nothing. He's dressed to go outside in his coat, cap, and wellies.

"For someone who only eats rabbit food you look damned terrible."

"I fell asleep on the couch," I offer as an explanation. "Where are you off to?"

"A lot of talk flying around about Simon Husk. I thought I'd go contribute to it."

"What kind of talk? Don't tell me you're going to encourage the avenging zombie coal miner theory?"

He gives me one of his winks, which are as much a part of his mode of communication as his words.

"I'm keeping an open mind."

I close my eyes again and listen to his departure. I'm still shaken by my dream, but I can't allow myself to dwell on it. I'm about to go see my mother and I need to put all my energy into mustering the courage I need to face a completely different kind of nightmare, one I can't wake up from.

SINCE HER RELEASE FROM prison almost twenty years ago, my mom has lived off and on with Tommy, but he can't make her stay with him and I can't make her stay with me either and I wouldn't want to attempt it. The thought of my nomadic, delusional, kleptomaniac, bipolar mother being anywhere near a city is a terrifying prospect.

She's been in and out of civil psychiatric hospitals over the years, but the doctors can't force her to stay there either. Like many people who have been diagnosed with a mental illness, she believes she's perfectly sane, and those who think she's crazy are the crazy ones. Even more than that, they are her enemies.

She's sick but not sick enough in the eyes of the law and the medical community to allow her family to commit her. She would have to physically harm someone or herself in order for that to happen, and she has never hurt anyone in her life, except for killing my sister, for which she spent twenty years in prison.

Each time she's been admitted to a hospital—usually after disappearing for weeks at a time, showing up in a random town where she's been arrested for some petty theft or act of vandalism, and then being found incompetent to stand trial—she becomes a model patient and is released. She's cooperative and quiet and spends all her time reading and crocheting hats for orphans. The notes from various doctors in her records describe her as "smart," "friendly," and "pleasant." It's only when the subject of her illness comes up that she becomes "difficult," attacking not only the "ignorance" of their claims against her but the "stupidity" of their entire profession including her own son, who she never fails to mention is a psychologist, too, even though she wanted him to be an astronaut (something I never knew until I read it in her file).

Tommy went to court once to try and become her legal guardian with the authority to force her to take medication. At the hearing, Mom was demure and charming and told the judge she was not mentally ill, that all her life people have been calling her crazy just because she has a lot of energy. As proof of her sanity she showed him her social security card, named the first eight United States presidents, and explained the difference between skydiving and skywriting. She also complimented his eyes and told him he looked too young to be a man of the cloth.

He didn't grant the petition, claiming the court cannot deprive an individual of her legal rights just because she seems somewhat confused and has an unusual personality. He didn't see her on a bad day.

The J. M. White Hospital admits people who have been sent from jail or who pose a danger to themselves or others. Mom ended up here two years ago after stealing a bicycle in Hellersburg and riding into the middle of moving traffic causing a three-car fender bender where fortunately no one was seriously injured including herself. She told the police she purposely ran into one of the cars because the driver was a child molester.

The criminal charges were dropped but she was committed to White, a temporary relief for both Tommy and me. As psychiatric facilities go, it's not a bad place and it's only an hour's drive from Lost Creek.

I find Mom alone in her room. She's had three roommates since she came here. I've never met any of them. The first one she felt sorry for, the second one was a spy, and the current one is reputedly a close friend of Oprah's and puts on airs because of it.

The roommate's dresser top is covered with junk, but Mom's is clean except for the pile of her hand-crocheted hats. Each one is a different color that corresponds to a positive personality trait she has stitched across the front: blue is "compassion," green is "forgiveness," purple is "tolerance."

She doesn't believe in accumulating possessions. She says they weigh her down. But the few things she does have, she guards fanatically.

She's sitting in a chair with a book in her lap wearing the Christmas bathrobe Tommy picked out for her years ago. It's bright green and covered in prancing reindeer. She still wears her reddish-blond hair long and straight. It's streaked with silver like she's just finished combing sugar through it. She's small, almost waiflike, and has a child's round face, button nose, and freckled cheeks.

Each time I see her I'm struck again by how young she looks on the outside. I've seen many older people whose faces have been ravaged by time, but the eyes peering out from behind their masks of wrinkles are bright and youthful. Mom is the reverse. She's done her aging on the inside. Her face seems relatively untouched, but her once lively green eyes have faded into a dull gray the color of pond ice.

The only time there's any vitality in them is when she's having a manic episode, and then they blaze with a black intensity that I imagine must fill her head with the same kind of burning ache that comes when frozen fingers regain their feeling in a heated room. I know she is seeing something not of this world.

"Hi, Mom."

She doesn't respond. She doesn't look at me.

I walk over, give her limp body a hug, and hold out the cupcakes to her. My heart sinks as I remember how she used to take to her bed leaving my dad and me to fend for ourselves for days at a time. Her condition was so eerily complete and alien, she even spooked my dad into acceptance. The shouting I expected to hear never came. He'd come out of their bedroom, silent and uneasy. Sometimes he wouldn't check on her at all, content to take my word for it that she was "sad," and he'd sleep on the couch. I think he was afraid she might be contagious.

Please be okay, I silently beg her.

She smiles at the cupcakes and relief washes over me. She opens the package and takes a yellow one for herself.

"Dawnyelle's favorite color," she tells me.

Dawnyelle was an unwed teenage pregnant schizophrenic. Mom immediately knitted her a yellow hat called "hope" upon her arrival at White Hospital, then set to work on a blanket for her unborn baby, who Mom told me in a whisper was going to be a "half orphan."

This was well over a year ago. I have no idea what happened to either of them and I don't have the energy to navigate Mom's explanation if I were to ask.

"How are you?" I ask her instead.

"I'm fine. Why wouldn't I be fine?"

"No reason. We're supposed to get more snow," I say, beginning the careful small talk.

"I remember when you were little we had snow all the time for Thanksgiving," she says.

Against my will my mind drifts back to my childhood again, to Thanksgiving days spent at the prison. It was one of the few times out of the year when children were allowed to have physical visits with their moms. After our strip searches, we were led to a room with sets of plastic tables and chairs to spend fifteen uninterrupted minutes with our mothers before they were taken to the cafeteria to poke listlessly at white slices of turkey-flavored mystery meat topped with gelatinous globs of snot-colored gravy.

I'd crawl into her lap and she'd stroke my hair and hold me while I watched snowflakes fall softly in my mind and imagine what it would be like to build a snowman with her or have her pull me on a sled or have her waiting in the kitchen holding a cup of hot chocolate when I got home after playing with the friends I didn't have, but I also knew those times would be fraught with anxiety for me, possible precursors to disaster. I'd be forced to dig even deeper into my stores of fantasies about having a normal mom to come up with something truly comforting, but once I got there those times with her were warm and safe until I'd suddenly remember the truth, and as much as I feared my father's home, I wanted to go back there. Being snuggled up against my mother with her arms around me was somehow worse than my dad coming at me with his rage. With him I felt the fleeting panic of a cornered animal, but with her I felt the permanent agony of the obliteration of my nest.

"It's January, Mom. Thanksgiving was over a long time ago."

"I know that. I didn't say it was Thanksgiving now. I was remembering Thanksgiving. Everyone thinks I'm stupid."

"No one thinks you're stupid."

"I'm very smart."

"I know you are."

She finishes her cupcake and brushes the crumbs off her fingers.

"Can you get me my mirror?"

One of her few cherished possessions is a cheap silver hand mirror that appeared among her belongings after one of her arrests. Tommy assumes she stole it.

I open her top dresser drawer and can't help noticing a work sheet from one of the hospital support groups she attends called Lifestyle Choices. She's just begun to fill it out. Under short-term goals, she has listed: buy a car, purge evil, hem striped skirt, get out more. Her long-term goal is gardening.

I give her the mirror. She eagerly takes it from me and gazes intently at her reflection.

"I'm getting old."

"You look great."

"I guess I am old. I guess it's better to be old than dead."

She hands the mirror back to me, all the excitement she felt over it and her cupcakes draining away in front of me.

She stares at her pale hands lying lifeless in her lap like two broken albino bats. I prefer them to be busy. I look around for the latest hat she must be knitting or handkerchief she might be embroidering.

"Is something wrong?" I ask.

If ever there was a loaded question to ask my mother, this was it.

"Did you take your pills today?" I follow up casually.

She smiles at me.

"I saw Molly."

Her proclamation catches me completely off guard. I stare at her, dumbfounded, with no idea what I should say next.

"No, you didn't," I tell her.

"I saw her."

"Molly is dead."

"She was here last night. In my room. With Great-grandma Fi."

This information given in such a matter-of-fact manner sends a chill through me.

My mom used to hallucinate about my sister when she was in prison. She used to think she was still alive. She'd talk to me during our visits about Molly being in a crib back in her cell, and I remember one particularly horrifying time when she sat on the other side of the Plexiglas cradling an invisible infant and cooing to her. I couldn't get her to pay any attention to me, and when I finally cried out to her in frustration over the dirty phone receiver that always smelled like beer and french fries, she turned her burning black gaze on me and said, "What's the matter with you? Don't you love your sister?" Then she stood up and screamed at me, "Don't you love your sister? Don't you love your sister?" She was still screaming it when the guards dragged her away.

"You know that's not possible, Mom," I say calmly. "They're both dead. You probably had a bad dream."

"No. They were here in this room. Standing there."

She points to the foot of the bed.

"They were holding hands. Molly was all grown up, and Fi was young again. Not like in her picture. They were the same age. Young women. They couldn't talk. They stood there staring at me with their mouths open. Their skin was gray. They were angry."

My chill deepens to a shudder.

"I'm sure it was a dream," I tell her again.

"I don't want them to come back."

"Mom, it was a dream."

"I want a gun."

"A gun?" I cry. "What are you talking about? No, Mom, you can't have a gun."

"Why not?"

"Well, because—"

"I know. People think I'm crazy."

I don't comment.

"Then I want a dog. A dog would warn me if they come back. I don't like the idea of them walking around while I'm asleep. Do you think they'll hurt me?"

"No one's going to hurt you," I promise her. "It's all in your head."

"Don't say that to me," she says, irritation mounting in her voice. "Everyone's always telling me everything's in my head. I know what's real."

"I know you do."

"Stop saying what you think you should say! I'm not stupid!"

"I know."

"You wish I was dead."

Her words cut through me. There were times as a child when I wished she were dead. Not because I hated her, I told myself, but because I loved her. If she were dead maybe there'd be an end to her pain, I'd reason, but deep down I knew it was my own pain I wanted to ease. Maybe I wouldn't have to think about her every day if I knew she was safely in Heaven instead of locked up in jail. Maybe people might feel sorry for me and be nice to me because I was a boy without a mother, instead of giving me dirty looks and calling me names behind my back because I was the son of a baby killer.

"Please, Mom. Don't say that. I don't wish you were dead."

She gets up from the table and for a moment I think she's going to slap me, but she steps up next to me and peers intently into my eyes.

Who is she seeing? Who is any mother seeing when she looks at her grown son? The baby she nurtured, the little boy she knew so well, the stranger he became.

Is she disappointed? Does she see my failure? Does she hate me for not being able to help her?

She gives me a quick hug then drops to the floor where she retrieves something from under her bed.

"Here."

She extends a brown paper lunch bag toward me. My name is written on the outside in crayon.

"I made you a hat," she says. "Don't open it until you get home."

I take it from her and say my good-byes. Visits with Mom can drag on for hours or be over in a few minutes. She gets distracted easily and either wants me to leave or doesn't care if I leave or demands that I stay.

I'm on my way down the corridor to the elevators when her attending psychiatrist, Dr. Versey, calls out my name. I've only met him once but have spoken to him on the phone several times.

"How nice that you've been able to find some time to see your mother," he says to me, the implication being that I don't find the time often enough.

We shake hands and eye each other up and down. He's wearing a gray plaid, polyester-blend department store suit and some type of unidentifiable black shoe with white salt stains on the sides. I'm wearing dark wash Burberry jeans, a Ferragamo turtleneck, a Calvin Klein tweed jacket, and Dior Homme sneakers. I win.

"Doesn't it make you feel good? Aren't you glad you got to see your mom?"

"Yes," I answer him.

I'm not lying exactly. I'm always happy to see my mom, but it's a wretched kind of happiness, similar to what a wounded soldier must feel when he wakes up and finds out he's going to live but without his legs.

"How is your mother?" he asks like an old acquaintance who hasn't seen her in years.

"Shouldn't I be asking *you* that question?"

He laughs.

"I think she's doing wonderfully."

"She seems good."

"Did she discuss her plans with you?"

My mind jumps back to the work sheet. Which ones? Gardening or purging evil?

"Her plans?"

"I see."

He clears his throat.

"Patient privacy laws being what they are, I shouldn't even be telling you that she's about to be released."

"What?"

"We only have a hundred and twenty-eight beds."

"What does that have to do with anything?"

"Your mother is fine."

My scalp begins to prickle.

"'Fine' is a relative term."

"I realize that. What I mean is, considering her illness, she's doing very well right now and we simply can't justify keeping her here any longer, and once the legal restriction is removed, she's free to do what she wants, and she wants to leave. She's made that very clear. I can give you the names of some excellent private facilities."

"Believe me, I have all the names. I really have to get going."

Before he can say another word, I walk quickly away from him down the corridor and turn the first corner. I lean against the wall trying to look as nonchalant as possible and take deep breaths. It's been a while since I've had a panic attack, but if anything could trigger one, it would be this information.

I open the paper bag my mother gave me thinking I can use it if I start to hyperventilate and find an orange hat inside. Along the band is stitched A GOOD SENSE OF HUMOR.

seven

AFTER VISITING MY MOM I always try to dwell on a good memory and disregard the fact that now I know most of them were the beginnings of one of her manic episodes that were destined to end in disaster.

Driving back to Lost Creek today, I think about the time we painted the garage pink. I wasn't sure Dad would like the color, but Mom kept assuring me he would. She painted like a fiend and by the time we finished, I agreed with her that he would have to love it. Who wouldn't love a garage the same color as Bazooka bubble gum?

She was so pleased with the results she wanted to share our good fortune with others, so we went next door and started painting the neighbor's peeling front porch. It was a perfect sunny day and as I watched the old drab gray flecks beneath my feet disappear beneath a pretty, glossy coat of pink, I felt anything was possible. Even this bleak, run-down town could be given a new life. With Mom and me leading the way, this could become the most beautiful place in the world.

Then the neighbor came home and she and Mom got in a big fight that ended with Mom throwing the remaining paint on her and running away.

Mom still hadn't returned by the time Dad got home from his shift. He stood in the driveway for the longest time and just stared. His gaze was so intense and his stance so fixed, I started to think maybe he liked it after all.

Tommy's truck came rumbling up a few moments later. He parked and slowly got out, unable to take his eyes off the offending structure, too. He held out a hand to me, still grimy from a day of work, and said to my father, "I'll take the boy."

I spent two days at Tommy's house and when I returned the garage was painted mud brown and Mom was in her bed silently staring at the wall plucking loose threads from her sweater.

I can hear Tommy's voice in my head trying to comfort me as clearly as if he were in the car with me now.

"I know your mother has her share of problems, but at least you have a mother. Your great-great-grandfather Prosperity never knew his mother because she died *before* he was born."

This was the way Tommy always began this particular story. He doesn't have to be with me for his words to soothe me. I settle back behind the wheel of my car and listen.

"Prosperity's mother wasn't one of these women who died *during* childbirth. This, at least, was a phenomenon a fellow could try to begin to understand once he finally learned that women carried babies around inside themselves before finally expelling them into the world in a manner no one dared to seriously contemplate.

"To expire during the commitment of an act was common enough. Soldiers were often shot dead while in the middle of soldiering. Prosperity's friend Billy Kelly—the more reliable of the Kelly boys—loved to tell of his own uncle falling down dead in the middle of haying. Everyone had heard of the woman in Goleen who died while in the middle of pouring out tea for the parish priest.

"But to die *before* you began to do something, this was something entirely different, and Prosperity was greatly impressed by the idea. Throughout his young life, he would raise his fists to anyone who failed to give his mother the proper respect due to a woman who had shown such willpower and foresight. As far as he knew, very few people accomplished anything of worth after they were dead.

"He would never know the exact facts of his tragic beginnings, although Fiona would eventually unearth the details after they were married through a correspondence she struck up with the aunt who raised him.

"The truth of the matter was that his mother did die during child-birth—not before—but she was half-starved, frail and sickly, and lost consciousness after the first wave of pain and passed away shortly there-after. The doctor had to cut the infant from her body, a procedure so gruesome for the times that the two neighbor women attending him were struck dumb by the sight of it and could never bring themselves to gossip properly about it in the future.

"Whenever they tried, their minds would fill with the poor young girl's face, looking as pale and quiet in death as a sleeping child's, sitting atop the flayed, bloody carcass, and all they could manage to do was cross themselves and mutter ominously that she died before the child was born.

"Like his mother dying before he was born, Prosperity's father had left before he was born. He had gone to England to look for work, since there was none to be found in Ireland. He hadn't known the girl long or well, just long enough to marry her and well enough to get her preg-nant, although no one was ever quite sure of the sequential order of these events. People tried to contact him after the birth of his son and the death of his wife, but he was never heard from again."

I feel a little better after recalling Tommy's story, although I still dread having to tell him Mom is getting released again. He's too old to deal with her anymore and I can't have her live with me in the city. She needs to be watched constantly. I don't know what we're going to do. The enormous expense aside, facilities for the mentally unstable have become few and far between, and many of them are terrible places not much better than the prison where Carson sits waiting to die.

Tommy seems physically fine. We talked last night over dinner and decided there's really no reason for me to stay, but I can't leave him here alone with Mom. At least not at first.

I'm distracted and not paying much attention to the drive, but even so, I can't help noticing the commotion going on at the gallows.

One of the town's black-and-whites is parked there along with

Rafe's car. The surrounding streets are also full of cars and pickup trucks. A crowd has gathered inside the prison yard and formed a motionless chunk of rapt parka-clad humanity with a hundred arms, all of them holding phones aloft taking pictures and video of the gallows.

I don't see Tommy's truck anywhere and I decide to stop partly out of curiosity but mostly because I might be able to learn some town gossip before he does.

A woman in a winter coat and rubber boots is sitting on the gallows in a chair and a man is sitting on the edge of the scaffolding holding a rifle with his feet kicking casually at the air.

I recognize the woman as Birdie Connolly, the activities secretary for the NONS, a plump, pleasant grandmotherly sort with soft white hair like a cap of cotton balls. She's tied to the chair with what looks like clothesline, but she doesn't seem to be in any distress. Her lower arms poke out from the layers of rope and she's busily knitting.

The man is the NONS volunteer groundskeeper, Parker Hopkins. He's in tan winter coveralls and an orange ball cap with an expired hunting license pinned to the front. His gun rests in his lap and his head keeps drooping forward. Despite the cold and the fact that there's a bound woman behind him, he looks like he might fall asleep.

Looking around me at the expectant audience and back again to the two patient players on their empty stage, I almost feel like I'm attending a Lost Creek interpretation of *Waiting for Godot*.

Rafe's here along with Billy and Troy. They're in uniform and he's in his camouflage hunting jacket and if possible, pants that are even more wrinkled than the ones he had on yesterday. His blue tie is covered in leaping green and orange frogs. I pray it was a Father's Day gift from a grandchild.

A bulky woman made to seem even bulkier by the metallic sheen of her gray ski jacket is standing next to them. It's Moira Kelly, a member of one of the largest local tribes. The patriarch is a good friend of Tommy's, a descendant of Prosperity's best friend, Kenny Kelly, who swung in the noose next to him, and the owner of Kelly's Kwik Shop. Moira's one of ten offspring that were produced during the twenty-odd years of

Mrs. Kelly's childbearing capabilities. The oldest sister, Glynnis, was Rafe's second wife. Moira is somewhere in the middle and manages the store for her father. She and Rafe don't get along.

"What's going on?" I ask Rafe and the two young cops who aren't doing much of anything.

"Parker's taken a hostage," Rafe replies without emotion while rolling a piece of candy around inside his mouth.

"What?"

"He's trying to keep the gallows standing," Billy Smalls explains. "He says Simon Husk was just the beginning and more people are going to die if they get torn down."

"He's trying to keep the gallows standing because once they're gone and Dawes starts fracking, he'll have no place to mow," Rafe adds.

"I think it's kind of cool," Troy says.

"Cool?" I wonder.

"I mean, all the attention the town's getting. It's been a while, but we got a paranormal-reality TV crew coming here again. Someone from the show called the station about it."

"I hope it's *Ghost Sniffers*," Billy joins in. "We might get to meet Wade Van Landingham."

"Who's Wade Van Landingham?" I ask.

"He's this psychic who sniffs out spirits," Troy explains.

"Intuitive investigator," Billy corrects him.

"I don't think it's *Ghost Sniffers*, though," Troy goes on. "I think it might be *World's Creepiest Destinations*."

"How about that, Moira?" Rafe says. "There's a TV show about your lady parts."

She gives him the finger.

"Isn't anyone concerned about what's going on here?" I have to ask. "He has a gun."

They all stare at me almost with pity.

"You know Danny Doyle, Tommy's grandson?" Rafe asks Moira.

"Sure. He's been in the store. He's never friendly, though."

"That's not true," I practically gasp. "I always say hello."

"You never mean it."

"How can someone not mean hello?"

"Don't you live in the 'burgh'?" she says to me.

"I'm on the other side of the state. Philadelphia."

"Eck. Philly. I hate that place."

"Have you ever been there?"

"You don't have to go somewhere to know you don't like it."

"Yes. Yes, you do."

"I'll never understand why anyone wants to live in a city."

I just nod. I don't want to get involved in a discourse on the evils of urban life. I'm well acquainted with small-town moral superiority. I don't bother telling her the worst things I've experienced have all happened here.

"Parker!" Rafe suddenly shouts. "Give me your gun."

Parker's head jerks up.

"No."

"Come on. This has gone far enough."

"It's not even loaded," Parker shouts back, holding his rifle up in one hand.

"Then why the hell do you have it with you?"

"To make it look like I really kidnapped her. We want to get on the news."

Rafe looks around him at the multitude of cell phones hard at work posting photos to Facebook and sending video to YouTube.

"Here's what's going to happen, Parker. You're not only going to get on the news. You're going to attract the attention of the state police, who might already be on their way here, and once they get here I can't help you."

"What do you mean?"

"Right now this is a harmless misunderstanding, but if a trooper shows up this becomes kidnapping and assault with a deadly weapon."

"What if I say I'm here willingly?" Birdie chirps up, her knitting needles flying.

"Which carries a life sentence," Rafe finishes. "You think about that a minute."

Another woman detaches herself from the crowd and starts heading in our direction. She's half the size of Moira, wearing jeans, harness boots, a fleece-lined denim jacket, and red mittens.

Moira notices me watching her approach.

"Stop eyeballing my sister," she warns.

"I've never eyeballed anyone in my life," I tell her, trying to control my exasperation again. "I don't eyeball."

"You were eyeballing," Rafe says.

Moira leans toward me and lowers her voice.

"Here's the lowdown. Her name's Brenna. She's single. She's got two grown kids. Two ex-husbands, both assholes. One's a deadbeat, the other's a foreigner."

I glance at the sister again. Was she actually married to a foreigner, I wonder, or just someone from Altoona?

"You need to put an end to this, Rafe, before he really gets in trouble," Brenna says upon her arrival.

"I agree," I say.

She gives me a frank look with a pair of golden brown eyes that remind me of an amber amulet my mom stole from somewhere. She keeps it in a change purse along with her mother's wedding ring, her own wedding ring, a charm bracelet of multicolored stones I bought for her at Woolworth's when I was eight, a tiny bird carved from blue marble that she also must have stolen, and some petrified candy corn.

"What if I say I won't press charges?" we hear Birdie cry out.

"You know Danny Doyle?" Moira asks her sister.

"Not really, but I think I remember you," Brenna says. "You were about four or five years ahead of me in school. You were some big cross-country runner."

"Not many people remember cross-country," I respond eagerly.

"That's for sure," Moira comments.

"I wasn't too bad," I add. "My sophomore year I finished in the top thirty at states."

"Congratulations," Brenna says.

"Big deal," Moira scoffs.

I turn and glare at her.

"I finished sixth my senior year."

"Double big deal. Who cares if you won it? How many runners get to shake hands with the president, or get a sandwich named after them, or get to bang one of the Kardashians?"

"What is she talking about?" I ask anyone.

"That was ages ago," Brenna says to me, "but I've heard of you recently. Why would that be?"

I'm about to suggest one of my many television appearances or the publicity surrounding one of my books, when all the warmth drains out of her honeyed eyes.

"I read an interview where you said your hometown is full of ignorant yokels."

"I'd never say anything like that."

"Those were your exact words."

"I'm sure the quote was taken out of context."

"How do you take that out of context? You meant the good kind of ignorant yokels?"

I start to defend myself. I open my mouth, but the festering childish words stay inside me where I've learned it's best to keep them. *People were mean to me first!* I want to shout.

I don't get a chance to say anything. She and Moira walk away.

Living well is supposed to be the best revenge, but it hasn't proven true in my case. I should take some satisfaction in my success. I should own up to my comment because I said it and yes, I meant it and yes, it's true. And all of that aside, no one around here thinks twice about making fun of the way I dress, the way I talk, where I live, what I eat; why shouldn't I make fun of them?

When I left for college, I thought I was going to fit in just fine in the Ivy League, but once I arrived there I was instantly branded . . . an ignorant yokel.

It didn't matter how smart I was or how ambitious, how many books I had read or obstacles I had overcome. I could earn my way into those hallowed halls with my brains and my fleet feet, but I was woefully unsophisticated and painfully poor and could never be a true part of the world that had formed the majority of the student body. I did befriend some of the rich and spoiled, but it was implicitly understood I was invited to their parties and onto their yachts and into their opulent homes as an observer, a foreign exchange student of sorts from an inscrutable barbaric land of past-due utility bills, faded hand-me-downs, and Tater Tot dinners.

The truth is I've never belonged anywhere, and as much as I hate to admit it to myself, I wouldn't mind belonging somewhere.

I can feel Rafe looking at me by not looking at me. I don't know what he's thinking and it doesn't matter because he would never express it out loud.

During all the years I knew him while growing up there was only one time when I got into trouble and he was called upon to intervene. He gave me a talk that probably didn't last more than a minute, but when it was over it was understood by both of us that this was the only life lesson he was ever going to put into words for me and that I should find a way to make it applicable to every crisis of conscience I would ever have in the future.

In third grade, in a gallant effort to engage boys in art class, our teacher asked us to draw pictures of the deadliest monsters we could imagine. Then we had a contest where we were randomly paired up and the class voted on which monster would win a fight between the two until we came down to the ultimate victor.

The other kids drew hideous creatures with blood dripping from their dagger claws and gnashing teeth. Some were fire-breathing; others acid spewing. One had machine guns for arms. Another shot lasers from his eyes.

I drew a dome-shaped shell covered in armored plates and a poisonous slime. Inside, my monster could be seen curled up sleeping. He had no means of attack. He won by surviving.

It was the only time I ever flunked a school assignment.

The other kids teased me mercilessly and even my teacher sniggered. By the end of the school day I had moved past my usual response to this kind of treatment. I didn't want to take flight; I wanted to fight. I was mad. The hottest part of my anger didn't stem from the abuse, but came from the fact that I loved my picture. It was a great work of art, a hundred times better than the caveman drawings the other kids had done, and no one appreciated it.

I wasn't in any mood to negotiate the vagaries of school bus bullies. Lost Creek Elementary was a couple of miles from my house. Some of the route was along isolated country roads, but I had walked it before and I didn't care.

I started out and soon I came upon another boy. He was a first-grader. I didn't know his name. I assumed he lived in one of the nearby houses behind the school or he wouldn't be walking alone at his age.

His age. I thought about it for a moment. Six. I was six the first time I went to visit my mom in prison. My great-grandfather Jack McNab was six when he watched his father hang. It was a milestone age, an age when a boy should already be a man, but this kid was obviously still a baby and more than that, he was fat, the one physical attribute on the list of reasons why other kids could call you names and destroy your self-esteem that I didn't possess. Never mind the irony that I got made fun of for being too skinny.

It would be so easy. I wouldn't have to strain my brain at all. And it would make me feel good. It must make them feel good or they wouldn't do it all the time.

I jogged up beside him. He turned his big round face toward me in fear but then a brief flicker of hope shone in his eyes as he recognized the too-tall, too-skinny, too-quiet, nerdy, pale, weirdo, smart kid with the mom in jail and thought he was safe.

"Hey, Fatso," I said and waited for the rush of joy that was supposed to accompany hurting someone.

It didn't come. Watching his demoralized gaze drop to the ground, his shoulders bunch up, and his lower lip begin to quiver actually made me feel worse.

"Hippo," I tried again and gave him a shove.

"Don't," he said to his feet.

"What'd you say to me?" I responded automatically, not realizing I was quoting my father.

"Don't, please," he sniffed.

I shoved him harder.

"What's the matter with you? Aren't you going to fight back? Are you chicken?"

My next push knocked him on all fours. He scraped his hands on the roadside gravel and banged his knees and burst into tears.

I still wasn't feeling good. I was feeling worse. Before he could get up, I pushed him again and he fell over onto his side. I let loose and began flailing at him. It wasn't punching or even slapping. I didn't know how to do either.

"I hate you!" I yelled at him, but I was lying. I didn't hate him. I didn't even know him.

I hated that my mom was in jail. I hated that my sister was dead. I hated that my dad didn't like me. I hated that no one liked me. I had a lot of hate in me but it wasn't directed at individual people; it was directed at circumstances. How do you beat up a situation?

He covered his face with his pudgy hands and I instantly recognized him as the monster in my picture hiding in his armored shell.

By this point, I was crying as much as he was. I ran off into the trees.

I didn't venture back onto the road until it was starting to get dark. A few people slowed their cars and asked me if I wanted a ride, but I gave them my name and told them where I lived and promised I could get there on my own and they went on their way.

Finally, I heard the sound of a slowing engine behind me and one solitary whoop from a police car's siren. I turned and saw red and blue lights sparkling in the gloom of the fading day.

It was Rafe. The same man standing beside me now, only then it was Young Rafe with his sulky good looks in his uniform with a gun strapped to his side. A law enforcer. A protector and server. The only person who ever took the time to explain to me what was happening to my mother. A man I admired but didn't envy. A man I wanted to mimic but didn't want to be.

I trudged over to his open window.

"Did you beat up that little kid?" he asked me.

"I didn't beat him up," I replied.

If only he'd have been there, he'd know this was appallingly true.

He waited with his engine idling.

"Yes," I finally admitted.

"Why?"

I shrugged.

"I don't know," I said honestly.

"Get in, Danno."

I climbed into the car and I wanted to stay forever in the warmth and safety and the silent camaraderie. The only thing that could've made it better would've been a pizza.

My own house would be empty and without food. My dad had been on disability for over a year now and was rarely home, spending most of his time at the union hall or drinking at the Rabbit. This was okay by me for the most part, but sometimes it was okay to have him around. I got lonely and he and his feet weren't always mad at me.

Dad would probably never find out about the incident, but Tommy certainly would. He'd be disappointed in me. If I had beat up a true bully he'd be thrilled, but picking on a little kid was never okay.

Rafe looked at me then looked away.

"Before I was a policeman, I was a soldier fighting in a place called Vietnam. You ever heard of it?"

"I think so."

"I'm not going to dwell on the subject. All I'm going to say is it was the worst place in the world. I suppose the Vietnamese like it, but for people from Pennsylvania it was like being in hell. Hot as an oven. Red earth."

He stopped himself from going on. I could see the effort on his face.

"We had to fight in the jungle with forty pounds of weapons and equipment on our backs, but the heaviest thing I carried around was my hate."

I thought about this revelation the same way I'd contemplated the little fat kid's age. I could see Hate hunkered on top of Rafe's soldier backpack, a bristly black monkeylike beast with yellow eyes and long sharp twisted claws weighing him down.

"Who did you hate?" I asked.

"At the time, the enemy. The North Vietnamese."

"Why were they the enemy?"

"We didn't really know, but it didn't matter. We were soldiers. It was our job to defend the country, not our job to decide when it needed defending."

"Why'd you want a job like that?"

"I didn't. It was given to me, and even though I didn't want to do it, I couldn't say no."

"Like when my dad makes me scrub the toilets?"

"Exactly like that."

He put the car in gear and began driving.

"I was a soldier and we were in a war so I had to shoot people sometimes. They were always far away or hidden in the jungle. I never had to see anyone up close. Then one time I did. I had to fight an enemy soldier with my hands. The way you did with that boy today."

The comparison was ridiculous, but I knew he wasn't making fun of me and that made it even worse.

"We had both lost our rifles, but I was finally able to get my handgun free and I pointed it at him. I should've shot right away. That's what I was supposed to do but I didn't. I looked at him and he looked at me. He was just like me. Probably the same age. Had a mom and dad somewhere who loved him. A family. A house where he grew up. Maybe a girl he liked.

"I understood in that moment that I'd been lied to my whole life. There's no us and there's no them. There's just everyone. And as soon as I realized that, all my hate went away.

"He was just like me," he repeated.

"What did you do?"

"I killed him."

In the silence that followed I struggled to find the lesson I was supposed to take away.

Tommy was a talker; Rafe wasn't, but they both only opened their mouths when they had something meaningful to say. Most people did the opposite.

"You got rid of the hate, but wouldn't it have been easier to kill someone you hate?" I eventually asked.

I knew I had asked the right question because the answer explained everything.

"Yes," he said.

"Let's go, boys," I hear Rafe say beside me.

He and Billy and Troy start walking toward the gallows.

Rafe's sixty-one now. The years have put their stamp on him but somehow haven't aged him. Maybe that's because he was never young to begin with. He's always just been.

Parker's eyes dart in all directions, searching for his best avenue of escape, but he thinks better of it and falls backward onto the time-blackened wood in surrender, where he lies motionless, trapped by his snowsuit as surely as any toppled baby.

eight

SCARLET

THE FIRST TIME I saw a dead person I was nine years old. Actually, I didn't see an entire person; I saw parts.

Twenty-eight men were killed in an explosion in one of my dad's mines. I was playing in his study when he got the call. He stood beside his desk, a slim figure in silhouette against the daylight outside the window. I couldn't see his face, but I knew he wouldn't look sad or even upset. Nothing ever bothered my dad unless he wanted it to.

"Twenty-eight," he said into the phone.

His fingers began to tap on the lovingly polished surface of the mahogany desk that once belonged to his great-grandfather, the original Walker Dawes.

He noticed a mark on it, frowned briefly, and rubbed it away with his fingertip.

"Well, double digits are never good, but it could've been worse. Let me change and I'll be there in fifteen minutes."

He turned around, intending to head out the door, but spotted me on the floor with my collection of Strawberry Shortcake dolls spread out before me. He bent down and gave me one of his best boardroom smiles.

"Hey, there, Button."

"Is something wrong, Daddy? Where are you going?"

"There's been an accident," he replied, tousling my hair. "It's nothing that concerns you."

My mom agreed with him. Not only did the mine explosion not concern me, it *really* didn't concern her. She departed the next day to go stay with her parents in New York and avoid the "unpleasantness," as she called it. My little brother and I were left in the care of Anna, our nanny, which wasn't anything new.

Anna strongly disagreed with my parents. She thought the accident did concern me very much and to prove it, she packed me up in her pea-green Pontiac two days after Mom fled and the bodies had been recovered and drove me to Lost Creek. She left Wes at home with the kitchen staff.

The nearest hospital and morgue were dozens of miles away from the mine and there were too many bodies to fit in the funeral home, so they laid out the pieces of men in the elementary school gym.

When we arrived, the building was surrounded with vehicles: cars, pickup trucks, ambulances, fire trucks, police cars. People stood around in murmuring knots or stared numbly into white Styrofoam cups. Some cried quietly while others held them. Men were crying as much as the women. Big men. Tough men. Men who looked like they could break my dad's arm as easily as they snapped kindling across their knees.

I had expected hysteria. I had heard my dad tell my mom that "all hell was breaking loose" in Lost Creek. I expected women collapsing on the ground sobbing and tearing their hair out. I expected angry men shaking fists and brandishing shotguns while claiming someone was going to pay for this. I expected other men in uniform rushing around authoritatively calming everyone; instead it turned out the men in uniform cried just as much as everyone else.

I had believed in Hollywood's version of tragedy, but this was real life, and in real life hell wasn't something that broke loose; hell was something people kept quietly hidden in the shadows of their everyday lives, but every now and then they couldn't stop it from stepping out into the light.

Anna grabbed my hand and maneuvered me through the cars and trucks and people.

Everyone stared at us, but I didn't mind. I was used to people knowing who I was, but this was a different kind of acknowledgment. There was no awe or respect in their glances. No humility in their silence. They stared at me frightened and full of animal distrust, as if they were a pack of woodland creatures watching me walk through the smoldering ashes of a forest I had just burned down.

We walked into the gym. It also served as the cafeteria and auditorium. School had been canceled for three days, but the smell of pizza burgers still lingered. There was a stage at one end with old snagged blue curtains and a counter at the other end where the kids lined up to get their school lunches slopped onto their orange plastic trays. Both ends had scuffed backboards hanging from the ceiling with basketball hoops and torn nets mounted on them. There weren't nearly as many people in the gym as outside, and the ones who were there didn't notice us at all.

The bodies and pieces of bodies were covered in sheets and spread across the gym floor. The sheets must have been torn off beds and donated by townspeople because they weren't a uniform institutional color. I noticed a pink one and a lavender one. One was yellow with tiny orange flowers, one striped in shades of blue and green, and one decorated with cowboy hats and boots. It was smaller than the others and obviously belonged on a child's bed. The lump beneath it was smaller, too, and for a moment I wondered if a dog had died in the explosion.

A policeman stood beside a table near the other doors talking to a doctor with a clipboard under his arm. The table was covered with a white sheet and had a couple of small lumps. Two tear-stained women—one older than the other with her arm around her shoulders— stood together over one of the sheets while a priest talked quietly to them. A pastor in a polyester suit holding a Bible and wearing a white tie with a large gold cross pinned in the middle of it talked quietly to an elderly couple standing away from the sheets.

I looked up at Anna and thought she was about to say something to me when a young woman came through the doors behind us, walked past us, and headed toward the policeman, her high heels click-clacking over the polished wood floorboards.

She was attractive in a skittish sort of way and had the most amazing shade of hair I'd ever seen. It was almost the color of a yellow marshmallow Peep. But it wasn't her hair or youth or slavish use of blue eye shadow that made her stand out compared to the others. It was what she wore: a slinky black party dress and a pair of strappy red stiletto heels.

I didn't understand. I was enthralled. I couldn't take my eyes off her.

She talked to the policeman and the doctor and from out of nowhere, two other men appeared. I could tell they were miners by their steel-toed work boots, their dirty hands, and the exhaustion carved into their faces. They had been digging for bodies for two days and nights.

They greeted her and it was obvious they all knew each other. The four men talked earnestly to her. I couldn't tell if they were trying to talk her into something or out of something. Finally the two miners stepped away and she lifted her chin and squared her shoulders, and I suddenly understood everything about her.

She had dressed up for the occasion the same way people dressed up for church and funerals. Out of respect for the worst thing she would ever have to do in her life she had put on the prettiest thing she owned. Her husband had probably bought her those shoes and that dress with the money he earned at the job that had killed him. He probably loved to see her in them so she had put them on to come down to the school gym and identify what was left of him.

The doctor pulled back a section of the sheet on the table. The policeman looked away.

I stared at her shoes. I wanted those shoes.

She suddenly lunged for whatever was under that sheet. It turned out to be part of an arm, from the elbow down, charred black, with a hand attached to it.

The doctor tried to intervene but she pushed him away. She began fiddling with the dead fingers. She was trying to pull off a ring. She yanked and the finger came off instead.

A strange noise came gurgling out of her mouth. I thought she was finally going to cry, but it was laughter: high-pitched, screeching, hysterical laughter. She laughed and laughed and laughed.

Everyone in the gym watched, but no one made a move to stop her.

I suppose I should've been scared or grossed out or sad, but I wasn't any of those things. As I looked around at all the bewildered pain on all the helpless faces, I wondered if life and death was different for poor people. Maybe being alive was the bad part for them. Surely it was better to be ribbons of flesh seared into a coal seam than to be that crazy, ruined girl.

The doctor was able to get the finger away from her and put it back under the sheet. She kept laughing. The priest went over to talk to her, and she laughed harder.

"This is your father's fault," Anna whispered icily to me. "He's a murderer. All of the Dawes men are murderers."

"I'm going to tell my dad you said that."

"Go ahead. It wouldn't be the first time he heard it. Besides, he doesn't care what anyone thinks about him."

"He cares what I think."

She squeezed my hand tighter and shook it.

"Look closer," she urged me. "Doesn't it bother you? What do you see?"

What I saw bothered me but I didn't feel bad. It was their own faults, after all. Everyone knew coal mining was a dangerous job. I didn't feel regret. I didn't feel in any way responsible for what I was seeing or that my father was responsible either. I sensed something wasn't fair, but injustice without a defined villain is only bad luck. I sensed waste, but I wasn't sure what was being wasted unless it was the red shoes because they might not ever be worn again.

"Parts," I told her.

She glared down at me and I dug my fingernails into her palm. She stood it for as long as she could before whipping her hand away, hissing at me. It was a game we played: which one of us could inflict more pain.

She wasn't allowed to inflict physical pain on me, because I was a child, so she settled for the emotional and psychological kind that didn't leave marks on the outside. I, on the other hand, could do whatever I wanted, and even though I enjoy a good mind fuck just as much as the next gal, I preferred real, honest hurt.

I like red shoes to this day. I have at least a dozen pairs of them. I like red in general but not because of my name.

People always think I must be named after the color or the plucky heroine from *Gone With the Wind*, but I'm not. My father's great-grand-father died of scarlet fever, and my father idolized him to the point of obsession. The Dawes men never sire daughters and always name their firstborn sons after themselves, so when I was born, my parents were completely caught off guard and had no idea what to call me. My dad insisted that despite my gender deficiency, they still had to find a way to pay tribute to his revered ancestor. And that's what they did. They named me after the disease that killed him.

I haven't been back here for almost twenty years, and when I say here I mean the mansion the Original Walker built back in the 1800s. It sits on an expanse of private land about five times the size of Lost Creek. We have our own zip code.

My father loves attention but he also tires of it quickly and needs to retreat into isolation, while my mother must be constantly admired by people who mean nothing to her. They resolved the problem by buying four other homes in more exciting locales where my mother spends most of her time. Dad joins her now and then when he wants to be reminded why he spends most of his time alone.

He's a man of extremes in everything. He once told me that it's okay to be very poor or very rich because the lack or excess of money frees your mind to dwell on loftier subjects, while the people in between spend their lives obsessed with the pathetic mundane trappings of mediocrity. It's why we have a country infested with shopping malls, tractor mowers, aluminum siding, and sweatpants.

The people in between would all be better off dead, according to Dad. At least he practices what he preaches. He works tirelessly to keep himself very rich and his workers very poor. He'll have none of that middle-class blandness associated with his name.

I've never spent any time in the town except for my visit to the school with Anna. I've never even seen the infamous gallows, although I've heard enough about them and seen enough pictures, including the painting in my father's study. Last night while relaxing in my hotel room after my flight from Paris to Philadelphia, I watched a repeat of a reality TV show where a group of paranormal investigators skulked around the gallows and jail looking for the ghosts of Prosperity McNab and his fellow Nellies. They didn't find them, although they insisted they felt them. I wasn't convinced.

I'm on my way to Barclay, the only town around here large enough to have a motel. I have no idea how this meeting with Anna's cousin is going to unfold, but even if it turns out to be nothing, I want the option of not sleeping under the same roof as Walker and Gwen Dawes.

Maybe I'm a little crazy for doing this, but my curiosity has been piqued to the point where I can't think about anything else. Anna's been dead for a long time now, and I didn't even know she had a cousin in Lost Creek who described herself in her letter to me as Anna's best friend. I was immediately pissed off. I was Anna's best friend. She also said she was the only person Anna would trust to keep this kind of secret and I'm a huge sucker for secrets.

The rest of the letter was vague in content, a bizarre conflicting mix of angry half-formed threats against me and desperate pleas to let her help me while hinting that there was some horrible skeleton in the Dawes family closet Anna had told her about and only I could stop her from revealing it to the world.

I tried calling her but she wouldn't speak to me. When I told her my name, I heard a panicked gasp on the other end before she hung up.

I make a trip back to the States every couple of years. I usually don't venture farther than my apartment in New York City, but I decided this time to visit the old homestead and to pay a visit to dear cousin Marcella Greger to discuss this terrible secret and her misguided belief that she was Anna's best friend.

After checking into the Barclay Holiday Inn with a marquee advertising karaoke night and the upcoming nuptials of Tyler and Brytnee (I asked at the front desk and her name wasn't misspelled), I take a seat in the chlorine-saturated air at a table in the bar with a view of the atrium and the indoor pool.

I'm about to go back to the front desk and complain about a lack of service when a waitress finally appears. She rushes over to me, apologizing profusely, and explaining that they don't get many customers in the middle of a weekday and that she's all alone.

She's young and cute despite her awful brassy blond dye job and too much foundation and metallic shadow that completely overpowers her pretty blue eyes. It would be very cool if she was a descendant of the yellow-haired girl with the red stilettos.

"My name's Heather," she tells me. "What can I get you?"

"Jack Daniel's and Coke and please put more Jack in it than Coke."

"Okay," she says, biting her lower lip, "but I'll have to charge you for a double or I could lose my job."

I smile at her.

"And you wouldn't want to lose a great job like this one."

We both look around us at the Holiday Inn atrium, at the empty poolside tables with their drooping, lopsided umbrellas faded not by sun but by age, the fake palm trees, the stacks of chairs against a wall waiting to be set out again for the next retirement banquet or wedding reception.

In the distance, an ice machine clunks and growls. In the pool, three pudgy children shriek, splash, and smack each other.

"It's a good job for here," Heather asserts.

"There's a whole big world out there."

"I know, but I like it here."

"Why? Don't tell me it's because of a boyfriend."

"No."

She blushes. I love girls who blush.

"I don't have a boyfriend right now. I don't know why I stay here. I guess 'cause my family's here. I got lots of friends, too."

She gives me a quick once-over, appreciating what she's seeing even though I know she doesn't realize what she's seeing: the five-inch heels of my Louboutin boots, my Moroccan print Albert Elbaz tunic over black skinny jeans, my distressed leather Versace motorcycle jacket, my lips glistening with Guerlain Folie de Grenat, and the six-carat ruby on my right ring finger.

"Are you here on vacation?" she asks me. "You look like you're on vacation."

"Why would someone come here on a vacation?"

She laughs.

"I admit there's not much going on. It's sure not Disney World."

"It's not even Carpet World."

She laughs again.

"But it's a nice place," she insists.

"If you like rust and fat people."

"Oh my God, I can't believe you said that."

As if to prove my point, an obese woman in a cherry-red one-piece looking for all the world like a gigantic jacks ball, carrying a *People* maga-zine and a Big Gulp, comes walking toward the pool, her flip-flops slap-ping in time with the rhythmic rumble of the ice machine.

She stops at the edge of the pool and screams at the children to stop screaming.

Heather blushes again.

"Then are you from around here?"

"I used to be but I moved away a long time ago."

"Yeah, that's what people do. They either move away or stay. Where do you live now?"

"Paris."

"Oh my God, that's so exciting. Can you speak French?"

"Tu es une fleur sur un tas de fumier."

"What did you say?"

"You're a flower on a pile of shit."

Her blush deepens.

"Thanks."

She's sweet. I'd like to take her back to my room and strip off her polyester uniform, wipe the gunk off her face, and jab her all over with one of my mother's vintage hat pins for dying her hair that color. She'd thank me for it later.

"I better go get your drink."

She hurries off and returns quickly.

"Anything new happening around here, Heather?" I ask as I take the glass from her.

"Nothing's gone on here for a long time, but all of a sudden there's a lot going on."

"Really? Like what?"

"Well, do you know about the Nellie O'Neills?"

"Of course. I grew up here."

"Well, the gallows are coming down."

"You're kidding!"

"No, I'm not."

"Unbelievable. After all these years."

"And yesterday the man who owned them and sold them back to Walker Dawes so he could tear them down was found lying dead right next to them."

"No!"

"My grandpa says Mr. Husk died of natural causes and he should know. He's a cop here in town and he saw his body. But there are a lot of people who are saying the Nellies had something to do with it."

"What do you mean?"

"There's a curse on anyone who tries to get rid of the gallows."

"Do you think people really believe this?"

"You'd be surprised. It is kind of suspicious. Mr. Husk was scared of the gallows. He thought they were haunted. When he was a kid he saw the ghost of Prosperity McNab outside his bedroom window and then the next day he found the name of Prosperity's wife written on a bathroom mirror in lipstick."

"Lipstick?" I try not to laugh since she's obviously taking all of this very seriously.

"That's what people told him it was, but he was convinced it was blood."

"You know a lot about Mr. Husk."

"One of my aunts cleaned house for them for a long time. She used to hear Mrs. Husk blabbing on the phone all the time. Making fun of her husband was one of her favorite things to do."

The blush returns.

"How about you, Heather? Do you believe in ghosts and curses?"

"No, not really. But I've always thought it was really creepy to keep those gallows around all these years. How about you? Do you believe?"

"I believe people need to make up things to help them cope with the randomness of death."

She looks confused.

"Huh?" she says.

"I knew a girl at the private school I used to attend who had everything going for her. She was rich. She was beautiful. Everybody loved her. Then one day out of the blue she had some kind of bizarre seizure that killed her. She was only fifteen. We found her in her room. There was foam all around her mouth and her lips were blue and her body was covered with these disgusting blisters."

Heather's eyes fill with horror.

"There was no explanation for this terrible tragedy. Wouldn't it have been better for all of us if we could have believed she was the victim of a curse?"

"I'm—I'm not sure," Heather stutters.

I finally take a sip of the drink and frown at her.

"Can't you do better than this? No one's going to find out. Come on. Live dangerously. Life is short."

She rushes off and returns a few minutes later. She sets my drink back on the table and leans toward me. I feel her breath tickle the inside of my ear.

"I made it extra strong," she whispers.

nine

ON MY WAY TO Marcella's house I decide to drive through Lost Creek. I marvel at how bleak and depressing everything looks. The original shanties the miners lived in fell down a long time ago. The homes standing now were built at the turn of the last century and they're not much of an improvement: rows of flimsy boxes built into hillsides so steep they appear to be leaning. At first glance most of them look abandoned, but driving slowly past I see curtains in dark windows and muddy footprints on front porches and other signs of habitation.

The streets come together at the bottoms of their inclines to the only level part of town, where there are a few shops and businesses and several buildings that were obviously a source of pride in their day: a bank with a marble façade and padlocked revolving doors; a hotel still wearing some of its faded Victorian colors—mint green with peeling lilac gingerbread trim—turned into apartments with To Rent signs hanging in its shuttered windows; the one and only department store, its display windows crisscrossed with plywood and graffiti.

Across the street from the bank is a bar with a red door and a sign depicting a lop-eared, red-eyed rabbit holding a pint of foamy beer and a plain brick building next to it called Kelly's Kwik Shop. Its windows are filled with flyers and ads.

I park my rental Rover and walk into the store, pausing to glance at a piece of cardboard with "Nellie O'Neill Merchandise Inside" written on it and a brass historical-landmark plaque beside it. This is the site of the original Lost Creek Coal & Oil company store.

I feel a little thrill as I pass through the door, realizing every one of the Nellies would have spent some time in this very room. They would have walked over these same floorboards and stared at these same walls, but my excitement is short-lived when I discover that the interior has been completely gutted and modernized to resemble every other crappy convenience store that's sprung up over the past forty years: buzzing fluorescent lights, cracked linoleum, the smell of burnt coffee, aisles of candy and snacks with a few light bulbs and packs of batteries thrown in, a refrigerated section in back stocked with soda pop and ice cream, and a glass case of cigarettes behind the cash register. I don't see any so-called food that doesn't come in a wrapper or a can.

Two elderly town matrons dressed in the floral-patterned blouses and color-coordinated polyester pants apparently mandated to all rural females over the age of fifty are absorbed in conversation with a large woman behind the counter.

One of them is wearing a brick-red overcoat with a black velvet collar over her ensemble and a plastic kerchief even though it's not raining, and the other has on a knee-length nubby cardigan of the most disorienting mixture of pinks and purples I've ever seen.

A bleary-eyed, scruffy man in a snowsuit the color of a coffee stain and a bright orange ball cap is perched on a nearby stool drinking dejectedly from a mug topped with whipped cream. His face is chapped from the cold and he keeps wiping his nose on his sleeve.

"Hello," I greet all of them.

They smile and nod.

The old ladies have kind faces, but I can tell from the gnarled arthritic knuckles and the small humble gold crosses dangling from both their necks that these are hard old-country broads who are no strangers to disappointment and pain and would easily turn their backs on me if they thought I was here to cause any trouble for their tribe.

I start browsing through the strange, sad collection of Nellie O'Neill souvenirs: books on the subject, key chains, mugs, pens, T-shirts, CDs of Irish folk songs, rosaries, crucifixes, fake white roses with accompanying cards explaining how each Nellie was given a white rose in his cell the night before his execution, and two hand-carved wooden models of the gallows.

Sitting in the midst of it all is a framed needlepoint sampler that reads, "In memory of James McNab, Peter Tully, Henry McAnulty, Kenny Kelly, Denis Daley, William Fahey, James Shaw, John Kerrigan, Charles Sullivan, and Jack Donoghue."

"I don't believe in curses, but you gotta admit it's damned strange," the woman behind the counter says.

She's younger than the other two but not young. She has a mean moon face and I instantly don't like her.

"Oh, come now, Moira," the woman in the coat chides her. "There's nothing that strange about it. The man had a heart attack."

"At the gallows," her friend in the sweater pipes up. "And after selling them back to Walker Dawes."

Moira nods.

Heather was right. Everyone in town *is* talking about the death of Simon Husk.

"Stop it, Birdie," the woman in the coat says. "The two of you have caused enough hysteria for one day."

She glances at the man over the tops of her glasses.

He doesn't look up from his mug but seems to sense her displeasure with him. He shifts in his padded suit.

"Parker had his heart in the right place," Birdie says in his defense. "He was trying to protect us."

"Baloney! Protect us from what? You of all people, Birdie, should know how hard we've worked to be taken seriously. This kind of publicity degrades the Nellies and all that they stand for."

"Which is?" I butt in.

They all look my way. Even Parker.

"Can I help you with anything?" Moira asks me.

"No, thank you," I reply. "I'm just looking around."

"Are you here to see the gallows?"

"In a way."

"Where are you from?"

"Here."

"Here?"

"Yes." I tap one of my lacquered fingernails on the countertop. "Right here."

She makes a frankly skeptical appraisal of my outfit.

"Can someone answer my question? What exactly do the Nellies stand for? Which side are you on? Do you believe they were innocent? Completely innocent? As in they didn't club one of their pit bosses to death in front of his house while his wife and children watched from in-side, or slit the throat of another one while he was asleep in his bed, or cut off the ears of an informer, or cut out the tongue of a priest, or set fires and dynamite railroad cars, or that they did but they were justified because of the treatment they received in the mines?"

"You shouldn't be disrespectful," Moira tells me.

"A person who sells T-shirts that say 'I got hung up at the Lost Creek gallows' is accusing me of being disrespectful?" I wonder aloud. "I'll take one of these, by the way."

I push the shirt across the counter toward her.

"I'm not the one selling this stuff and I don't get any money from it. All the proceeds go to the Nellie O'Neill Historical Society. Right here's the president, Nora Daley."

I look at the old lady in the coat. She pulls a business card out of her pocketbook and explains she's also the curator of the Nellie museum in the attic of her house.

"And I'm Birdie, the activities secretary," the one in the sweater in-forms me. "I did the needlepoint."

"It's a pleasure, ladies. I didn't mean any disrespect. I was simply asking a question."

"That's fine by us," Nora says. "We're happy to answer. Our claim is some were innocent and others were provoked. They deserved some form of punishment but not death. There were killings on the other side, too."

"Sounds like a reasonable claim to me. Remind me again, what's the story behind their name?"

"Nellie O'Neill was a widow back in Ireland," Nora begins. "She and her six children were turned out of their home by an English land-lord's bailiff for not being able to meet the rent. When she resisted and threw herself in the mud at his feet begging for more time, he called her a name that so upset her youngest boy he threw a clod of dirt at the bai-liff, who turned around and horsewhipped him to death in front of his mother.

"Later that night, the bereaved Nellie, mad with grief, snuck into the bailiff's home and with the help of the housemaid, she stabbed him to death with the same knife he had used earlier that evening to carve the lamb he served to his own family.

"She was found, tried, and hung, and her remaining children were scattered to the wind."

"Right," I say. "I remember now. The Nellies were the ultimate ma-ma's boys."

"If you're from around here you should know all this," Moira snaps at me.

"I was sent away to school when I was very young and it was trau-matic. You wouldn't understand. I doubt you've ever lived anywhere but here. I'm sure you're too afraid to venture out into the world."

Her face reddens.

"Some people stay where they was born and raised because they want to, not because they're afraid to leave."

"I suppose. But it's rare. Most people who stay do it because they're afraid to leave, and most people who leave do it because they're afraid to stay. If you stop and think about it you'll find that fear is the motivating factor for most decisions people make in their lives."

"That's a terrible way to look at life," Birdie says.

"It's the truth. What are you afraid of?" I ask them. "And don't say spiders or the dark. What really freaks you out?"

"Spiders," Birdie replies right away, clutching her arms. "I hate spi-ders."

"Being lost in space," Parker volunteers from his stool.

Birdie chuckles.

"I don't think you have to worry much about that."

"Cancer," Nora answers seriously.

"People who throw things when they get mad," Birdie adds to her list, "and spoiled potato salad."

"None of you are afraid of ghosts?" I ask.

They laugh and shake their heads.

"Of course not," they assure me.

I pay for my T-shirt and also a box of Little Debbie Oatmeal Creme Pies. When in Rome.

AS LONG AS I'M here I decide to finally take a look at the gallows up close and personal.

The site is a disgrace. The brick wall surrounding the yard is crumbling in places and has its fair share of graffiti, none of it artistic or witty. The gallows themselves aren't impressive at all except for their size. Original Walker added two extra crossbars in order to be able to hang four men at once. Walker's Wonder they called it in the newspapers. No one had ever attempted to build anything like it before. Say what you like about Walker Dawes, when it came to business, he was one efficient bastard.

Standing before them, I try to feel something. I envision the families of the Nellies waiting to watch their men swing. Most of the executed were very young if I remember correctly, although back then a boy would have started working in the breaker room when he was five, gone into the pits in his early teens, and could already be married and have a couple of kids by the time he was twenty.

What were they thinking? Aside from the terror and obvious grief, they must have been angry. I mean, really, really angry; the kind of anger that had led to the Nellies committing the acts that landed them here in the first place. Every single man, woman, and child probably felt the same way, but only a few had acted on it.

I guess you couldn't blame them. They'd been duped. They were told there would be plenty of work for them here in America. They were promised fair wages and decent homes. Their children would be able to go to school. They'd have religious freedom, too, and best of all, they'd be thousands of miles away from English persecution. This was the propaganda spread by guys like O. W. (the Original Walker), American mine owners who were just beginning to feel the need for cheap unskilled labor to dig the coal, which was quickly becoming the nation's most desired fuel and would make them all filthy rich.

What the Irish found was very different from what they expected. They had left English landlords behind only to encounter something much worse: American businessmen.

Nothing hurts more than betrayal. I know. I've experienced my fair share of it. And I have to say—but never to my father—that I completely understand where the Nellies were coming from.

Anna was the source of most of my information about the Nellies, and that meant I received a decidedly biased account. Her great-grandmother was Peter Tully's aunt. I asked my dad once if he knew my nanny was related to one of the men his grandfather had been responsible for executing. He said he didn't care; throw a rock around here and you're going to hit someone who claims to be related to someone who died that day.

Anna had experienced betrayal, too. She told me about her boyfriend and how he got another girl pregnant and married her, but how she still loved him and he still loved her. I was a kid and didn't understand anything about romantic love, but even so, I thought the situation sounded messed up.

Anna was not attractive and I thought that might have something to do with why she clung to this loser, but I also sensed part of the reason she looked the way she did was because she didn't try. No makeup. Dowdy clothes. Unfortunate red curly hair, the frizzy kind. But looking back on her now, I think she had a pretty good bod and she had deeply dark eyes, unusual in a redhead with a fair complexion. When I did something she approved of, they shined with the same pretty gloss as my black patent leather party shoes after a good polish.

I make my way into the jail next. It's one more unremarkable structure. Four cells with nothing in them except a small wooden cot on either side.

Again, I try to imagine what went on here. I picture the men lying on the boards, looking up at the one small window, watching the ever-present flakes of black soot twirl through the openings between the bars, listening to the construction twenty feet away from them of the means of their demise.

The sound would've been deafening in the jail, but it didn't matter where you were in town. There would have been no escaping the grinding of the saws and the ringing of the hammers. The mothers, wives, and sisters would have had to listen to it as they went about their daily chores.

I pause to read the descriptive plaque. It goes on and on about the deplorable conditions in the mines: the frequencies of explosions and roof falls, the dying canaries, the pitiful wages, the debt passed down for generations, the lack of schools, the absence of any labor negotiating power.

I know what it would say if Walker had written it: Life isn't fair.

I take a final look at the gallows on my way back to my car. This time I try to imagine what Simon Husk felt as he stood here during his last moments on earth. What horror visited him that was powerful enough to stop his heart? Not a curse but his belief in a curse, or did the ghost of Prosperity McNab appear to him again after all these years? If he did he must not have had his trusty lipstick with him this time. The desire to draw a big red clown smile on Simon's face would have been irresistible.

ten

ANNA GREGER WAS NOT a happy woman. I don't think I ever saw her smile or heard her laugh or say a nice thing about anyone. I assumed part of her disposition had to do with how she'd been treated by her boyfriend and by the bad-hair fairy. Imagine my surprise then when her cousin turns out to be cheerful and chatty, almost annoyingly so, once she gets over the initial shock at seeing me on her doorstep.

"I'm Scarlet Dawes," I announce to the stunned face of Marcella Greger.

I don't need to ask who she is. The family resemblance isn't striking but it's there. She's obviously much older than Anna was when I knew her. She's much heavier, too, and has big, blunt features that make me think of a face carved into a totem pole. She has the same hair, though, only Anna let her curls grow long and wild; Marcella shears hers close to her head like a carroty sheep's wool. She has the same dark eyes, too, but these ones don't seem to have any intelligence behind them so they don't glimmer; they're the flat brown of mud.

She slowly opens her mouth and her chin disappears into the folds of her neck. I wait for her to speak but she just stares at me.

"I assume you're Marcella Greger, Anna's cousin."

"I-I-I," she begins to stammer.

"Oh, come on," I say, smiling at her. "You can't really be that surprised to see me after sending me that letter then refusing to talk to me on the phone. You had to know I'd be intrigued."

She continues to stare and say nothing.

"Anna had a terrible secret about our family that she didn't blab to the world while she was still alive?" I go on. "I'm sure that fact alone will turn out to be more unbelievable than the actual secret. Can I come in?"

"Yes," she's finally able to answer me.

I lead and she follows.

From outside, her house is nothing: a little white, vinyl-sided affair with a one-car attached garage sitting all alone on the side of a rarely traveled country road. Her nearest neighbor is on the other side of a hill and not visible from her yard. Across the road is a sagging barn, stripped of paint, its walls gaping with holes, and what looks like an abandoned farmhouse, but you can never tell around here. Someone could still be living there.

Inside, the house is something else. I have to pause for a moment to get my bearings before diving in. I'm a minimalist, and Marcella Greger is obviously an accumulator.

Every available space in the small front room, including the windowsills, is covered with knickknacks: figurines, candles, blown-glass animals, vases, perfume bottles, teacups, piggy banks, seashells, commemorative plates. The one common quality the items seem to share is that they are all ungodly bright colors. Even the shells are painted in neon greens, oranges, and blues.

The walls are peony pink and the carpet is lavender. A rainbow-striped afghan is thrown over the back of a sofa piled with stuffed animals and rag dolls. The table lamps have plastic shades depicting scenes from Disney cartoons. Suncatchers made of bits of colored glass hang in all the windows and freckle the room with yet more color. I feel woozy.

"I'm sorry. It was such a shock seeing you out there. I forgot my manners and everything."

Marcella hurries around in front of me and plants herself in my way. For the first time since meeting her, I notice what she's wearing: turquoise blue stretch pants, furry green frog slippers, and a yellow sweatshirt with Minnie Mouse cavorting across the front of it in her traditional red and white polka dots. Shrink her down to four inches in height and Marcella would make a very nice addition to her own collection of crap.

She smiles fondly at me and for one very uncomfortable second I think she's going to hug me.

"It's so nice to meet you. Anna loved you to pieces."

"I know. I was her best friend."

"Can I get you something?"

"Blinders."

She laughs.

"I know it's a little crazy in here. Some people think it's too much."

"No," I say, feigning disbelief.

"Yes, they do," she assures me with a nod of her head. "I guess it is very colorful. I can't help it. I love colors. The brighter the better. I think it comes from my childhood. My dad was a miner. Matter of fact, he worked in one of your dad's mines. I guess that's no surprise being from here. Anyways, I grew up in a world of soot and smoke. Everything was gray. Even flower petals got soot on them. Didn't seem like we had any color at all in our house. I think that's why I love it so much now."

She comes to the end of her childhood account and gives me a wistful look. Once again I think she's going to hug me. I let my attention be diverted by a large rainbow, at least two feet long, sitting alone on its own shelf in an obvious place of honor. At one end of it is a pot of gold and at the other is a lecherous-looking leprechaun.

She catches me staring at the piece.

"Isn't that something?" she says rapturously. "One of my nieces got it for me for my sixty-fifth birthday. It's a real sculpture. Made of bronze. Signed by the artist and everything. Try and pick it up. Go ahead. You won't believe how heavy it is."

I do what she asks and make a show of how I can barely pick it up. She laughs appreciatively. It has a nice heft to it. With a good swing, the weight of it could be lethal.

"Can I get you something to drink?" she asks me.

"A drink would be nice."

"You mean a drink drink? I don't keep alcohol in the house except for a few beers in the fridge. Well, and I also keep a bottle of Southern Comfort I use to make hot toddies in the winter when I catch a cold. It's something my family's always done. I got used to it. But I don't drink otherwise."

"Southern Comfort's a little sweet for me, but if you put it over ice and mix in a little water it should be fine."

I follow her to the kitchen but don't step inside it. Like the other room, it's overwhelmed with clutter and chaotic color. Her refrigerator door is completely hidden beneath clipped coupons, store flyers, overdue bills, and notes to herself all stuck to the appliance with an array of mismatched, random novelty magnets ranging from farm animals and flamenco dancers to prancing picnic food and the cast of *The Flintstones*.

"I have a terrible memory," Marcella explains to me, motioning at the refrigerator.

She catches me studying the individual notices and doesn't seem to like it.

She looks nervously back and forth between me and a large number 228 written in red marker and underlined five times on a piece of paper tacked to the middle of the door with a Pittsburgh Penguins magnet. She suddenly steps between me and the refrigerator.

"Why don't you go sit down in the living room and I'll bring your drink?"

"Fine."

I walk back to the couch, move aside some stuffed animals, and take a seat.

"It's interesting to find out about you after all these years. It never seemed to me that Anna had any kind of a personal life," I call to her while I wait.

"Well, you were a kid," she shouts back at me. "You probably don't remember. And it wasn't like she had much of a personal life."

She joins me again, carrying a watery bourbon for me and a mug of microwaved stale coffee for herself.

"So what is this secret she told you?" I ask.

"Well, she didn't exactly tell me. I found a letter she wrote. Well, it wasn't exactly a letter. It was more like a confession. Or no, not even that. A statement."

"A statement?"

"Yes. I suppose I should start at the beginning."

"I suppose," I sigh.

"When Anna died, all her belongings came to me since I was her closest relative. I gave her clothes and things like that to Goodwill, but I kept a box of papers and personal items I meant to sort through one day but I never got around to it. Her death was so horrible, I didn't want to think about it at the time, so I put the box up in my attic and forgot about it.

"Recently I've fallen on some bad financial times. I won't go into all that unless you want me to."

"No, that's not necessary," I tell her.

She looks disappointed.

"I might have to sell my house. My sister and her husband have a trailer on their property that their son and his wife and kids used to live in when they were just starting out. Well, actually, it was after they were starting out. See he got into some trouble with—"

"I get the picture," I interrupt her.

"Well, I've started to go through some things and I finally went through Anna's box and I found this letter. Or statement. Or whatever you want to call it."

"May I see it?"

"I don't have it with me. I put the original copy somewhere safe. Not in the house. But I did make a copy for myself."

"Then can I see the copy? I won't doubt the authenticity of the original one."

She hesitates.

"Why did you go to the trouble of contacting me in the first place if you didn't mean to show me the letter or at least tell me what it says?"

My words apparently make sense to her. She gets up slowly from the couch and thumps over to a desk in the corner of the room. I didn't notice it earlier because it, too, is hidden beneath dozens of gaudy knick-knacks.

She opens the middle drawer and takes out a piece of standard white paper with a small amount of print on it. She gives it to me and I read it in an instant. It's only four sentences long. I even recognize Anna's handwriting. She was left-handed and wrote in rigid, backward-slanting capital letters. She told me once she never learned to write properly because the nuns at her Catholic school wouldn't let her use her left hand because they believed it was a sign of the Devil. They even went so far as to lash the evil hand to her side with a piece of rope. She was never able to master her right hand and almost flunked out of school because her assignments were illegible.

"Why would she make something like this up?" Marcella asks me. "It's too weird. If she wanted to make up something bad, aren't there a lot easier things to make up? And why write it down?"

I don't respond.

"I didn't know what to do so I went to see your mother."

"My mother? You showed this to my mother?"

She nods.

"And what did she say?"

"She said it was nonsense. It was obviously the ravings of a lunatic. And she reminded me how she killed herself. But I knew Anna probably better than anyone. I never believed she killed herself. Especially in that way."

"You didn't know her better than I did," I correct her. "And if it wasn't suicide, how did it happen? She was murdered?"

"No, no, no, nothing like that. I don't know what happened. It just never made sense to me."

"Well, I was with her all the time. And I'd have to agree with my mother that she was a disturbed woman. This is crazy."

I set the piece of paper on the coffee table and take another sip of my drink.

"So let me see if I have this straight. You didn't get any reaction from my mother so you decided to try me next. Why not my father?"

"Oh, I could never talk to your father."

"Why not? My mother is much scarier and far more dangerous than my father. He's actually very open-minded. I'm sure he wouldn't have believed this either, but he would've been entertained by the idea of it."

"This is more about you than him."

"I disagree. I think he'd find this much more upsetting than I do."

"This doesn't upset you? I mean, if it was true?"

"It's not true."

"But if it was?"

Marcella's beginning to annoy me. I stand up and stroll across the small room, my heels leaving indentations in the pale purple plush of her carpeting.

I catch sight of my reflection in one of the windows. A woman dressed like me in a place like this is so wrong, it almost seems right. I envision a haute couture photo shoot for *Vogue:* "Paris Malaise Meets Flea Market Nausea."

I turn back to Marcella.

"Why did you go see my mother? What could you possibly gain?"

Her face reddens.

"Who said I wanted to gain anything?"

"You asked her for money, didn't you? And now you want money from me."

"I wouldn't want much, just enough to keep my house."

I'm surprised by her answer. She doesn't make any denials or beat around the bush. Even though she's trying to blackmail me, I know she doesn't think she's doing anything wrong. The Dawes family has plenty of money. She's only asking for a little of it in exchange for doing us a favor. This way she'll be able to save her kaleidoscopic little nest and we'll be able to save our lily white skins.

"The problem with blackmailers is that they can always come back for more," I tell her. "And even if you do pay them, there's no guarantee that they won't talk."

"I'm very trustworthy. Ask anyone," she replies, not seeming at all offended by what I've just called her.

"Somehow I don't see me wandering around Lost Creek asking people if you can be trusted."

I walk around behind the couch. She doesn't turn to watch me but keeps looking straight ahead, trying to maintain her composure.

"If I don't give you the money, what are you going to do?"

"I don't know," she says.

"I think you do."

"No, I don't. I don't want to make any trouble for anybody. Really. But if this is true there's some people that's been badly hurt and some people who should pay for their crime."

I swing the bronze rainbow, two-fisted like a baseball bat, at the back of her head where it connects with a dull, wet crunch. She's propelled forward onto the coffee table then topples onto the floor where she lands faceup with an enormous thud that shakes the house enough to make her dozens of little treasures shiver and tinkle against each other on their shelves.

I probably could have trusted her to keep her mouth shut. That's not the point. I didn't like the idea of her knowing. I don't want anyone else knowing until I find out for certain that it's true and then I'll decide what to do with the information. Until then, I don't want to be bothered by thoughts of Marcella Greger. I can't stand it when people bother me.

eleven

MY MOTHER CAME FROM South African diamond money and my father came from Pennsylvania coal money. It was a perfectly conceived carbon-based romance. Not exactly a match made in heaven; more a match made in the black bowels of the earth, but one that's managed to survive for more than forty years.

In her youth, Mom was a striking platinum blonde with killer cheekbones and a long slim body with a neck like a swan; beautiful but not desirable, an ice princess, the kind of woman people never tired of looking at because she was so perfectly pretty, but the kind no one could ever imagine doing something as savage and sticky as having sex.

My dad was striking, too, back then and almost as pretty as my mom. He had doelike dark eyes, long lashes, full lips, and a luxurious head of wheaten hair he wore shoulder length and combed straight back from his face like a lion's mane. He would have been called effeminate except for his square jaw and a nose that was anything but delicate.

The combination of the two of them should have produced an Adonis of a son, but two attractive people do not necessarily make attractive offspring, just as two homely people can occasionally startle the world with a beautiful child. It's the way the genes mix, not the genes themselves, that matters.

Wes is not bad looking; he's just not anything great. He's a coarser, bulkier, duller version of my dad. They resemble each other yet somehow manage to not look anything alike.

Wes was the kind of son most men long for. He never rebelled in his youth and would have done anything Dad told him to do, anything to win his approval and stay in his good graces, but Dad had no interest in having one more fawning toady hanging around him. He'd spent his whole life telling people what to do and being instantly obeyed. Among his own kind he wanted initiative, spirit, original thought, and even a bit of recklessness. I gave him all this and more and I think he enjoyed what he considered my "antics" (except for hanging Mom's cat in a tree), but nothing I ever did impressed him for the simple reason that I didn't have a penis.

The birth of Scarlet Dawes broke the string of male-only offspring in the Dawes family stretching back for as many generations as anyone could remember. The disappointment Walker felt when he heard the news must have been crushing.

I doubt he had much patience for the tales of his wife's heroic seventy-two-hour struggle to expel me before finally succumbing to the C-section that would scar her perfect pale middle for life. Her postpartum depression was easily blamed on the difficult labor, but I always assumed some of it came from her inability to make a boy. Now I know this failure may have affected her in ways that even someone as perceptive as me could never have imagined.

The first Walker was a pretentious peacock who appreciated aesthetics, but at his core was a grasping, driven man who wanted people not only to be in awe but to cower. The result of this philosophy when it came to building his home was a fifty-five-room, turreted, Gothic edifice, but one made of a rare ashen rose stone he had imported from New Mexico. On sunny days, the hundreds of diamond-shaped window panes sparkle fiercely, but I never found this to be a pretty sight. To me the entire house seemed to be on fire.

Clarence opens the front door on my second ring. He hasn't changed a bit. He always seemed old to me, even when I was a kid. I rarely noticed him. He went about his job with the stealth of a spy, occasionally appearing in some random room where he'd stand silent and still like a piece of human furniture, but I never doubted his control of the household. Even Anna seemed intimidated by him, but I think this was because he didn't come from around here so there was no way for her to gather up every piece of gossip about him and his family. She regarded him as a loose cannon because she didn't know anything about him and therefore didn't know what he was capable of doing.

His face registers a moment of surprise at the sight of me, but he's too good at his job to allow any sign of unpreparedness to show for long.

His eyes flicker away from me.

"Miss Dawes, what a pleasant surprise. Are your parents expecting you?" he says while fixing his gaze firmly over my shoulder like a new recruit addressing his drill sergeant.

After Anna's death, he was never able to make eye contact with me again. He looked around me but never at me, his eyes straining in all directions like a blind man who knew he wasn't alone in a room but wasn't able to find the other person he sensed was near him. Sometimes I wanted to grab his hand and place it on my shoulder just for fun and call out, "Here I am," but I was always afraid once he found me he'd start screaming and my feelings would get hurt.

"I don't think so," I answer him. "Are they here?"

"Your mother is. Your father is in New York on business but expected home later tonight."

I bob my head to try and put myself back in his line of vision but he glances beyond me at my car.

"Do you have any bags?" he asks.

"No, not now."

I walk past him into the house.

"I won't be staying tonight. Where is Mom?"

"I saw her in the kitchen a moment ago."

I hand him my coat and walk quickly through the house, not bothering to glance in any of the magnificent rooms. I know the contents by heart and I'll have plenty of time for reminiscing later.

Mom's in the kitchen, like Clarence said. She's just leaving it carrying a cut-crystal pitcher full of gin and tonic.

She looks good for an old lady. She's still thin, still fashionable in a pale gold lounging outfit of loose silky pants, a sleeveless turtle-neck shell, and matching cardigan. Her hair's white now but the shade isn't all that different from the shade of blond it used to be. She's kept it long and has it piled on her head in a silvery smooth chignon. She has wrinkles, but they don't take away from her excellent bone structure.

When she sees me, she lets out a small shriek and drops the pitcher on the floor. It shatters on the ceramic tiles into a million glass shards.

The liquid seeps toward me. I pick up my foot so my boot won't get wet.

"Hello, Mother," I say.

"Scarlet, you almost gave me a heart attack."

"Did you think you saw a ghost?"

"What on earth are you doing here?"

"Visiting my parents."

"Why didn't you let us know you were coming?"

"I wanted to surprise you."

"Well, you succeeded."

To my amazement, she drops to the floor, ruining the knees of her satin pajama pants with the spilled booze, and begins scraping the glass shards into the palm of her hand.

"Mom, you've got servants to do this."

"Clarence!" I call.

He's already in the room. He must have heard the glass break.

"Mrs. Dawes had a little accident," I explain. "Could you clean this up and bring her a fresh pitcher of drinks into the sunroom? And I'll have a Jameson on ice."

"Of course."

Clarence gets down on the floor beside Mom.

"Mrs. Dawes, are you okay?"

"Yes, yes, I'm fine."

"You cut yourself."

"It's nothing."

There's an awkward moment where Clarence can't figure out if he should get up first and assist my mom because he's a servant and his job is to be helpful, or if this will offend my mom because it will remind her that she's old.

My mom solves the problem by getting up first. She's not as spry as she used to be, but it doesn't take her too long.

"I'm a mess," she announces once she's back on her feet. "Excuse me. I'm going to change and I'll meet you in the sunroom."

Mom has changed the décor since the last time I was home. The sunroom used to be filled with tons of plants, bright pink wicker furniture with plump floral-patterned cushions, and soft chenille rugs. It was always warm like a jungle.

Now everything is modular and white. Armless chairs. Lacquer cubes for tables. Sectional leather sofas with chrome legs. Vanilla shag rugs. It's the kind of room that screams out for a muddy footprint or a blood trail.

Mom reappears. She's changed her entire outfit even though her pants were the only thing that got wet. Now she's wearing drapey wide-legged coral pants and an even drapier sheer blouse over a camisole.

She has a million of these kinds of outfits, but I guess it makes sense: loungewear is the uniform of the professional lounger.

She stands in the doorway and attempts a smile. I notice she's bandaged her hand.

I walk toward her with my arms open.

"How about a hug?"

She embraces me with all the maternal enthusiasm of a stop sign.

"You look good, Mom."

"So do you."

Her eyes run expertly over my midthigh length dove-gray sheath with a fine silver thread running through the tweed. I changed after visiting with Marcella.

"Nina Ricci?" she inquires.

I smile and nod.

"Did you end up getting that Galliano we looked at? The blue tattered silk?"

"Of course."

She takes a seat on one of the sofas and I sit on a cube. I openly stare at her, but she avoids looking at me. I think she may have some idea why I'm here.

"Those Dior peep-toe booties are adorable, too," she tells me. "You have the legs to wear them."

"So do you, Mom."

"I'm too old for that now. Women my age shouldn't wear miniskirts and stiletto heels."

"Some do. What about Beebee?"

Her wounded hand flutters in the air in a gesture of annoyance.

"Oh, don't get me started on Beebee. Did you see them, by the way, when they were passing through Paris last month?"

"I did everything possible to avoid them. They're pigs."

Now she finally looks at me. Her eyes are as blue as they've always been. Age hasn't faded their intensity. I used to wish I might see some fondness or kindness in them or even mild interest, but any stores of soft emotions she ever possessed were gone by the time I knew her. Whether she lost them during her own childhood or if her years with Dad did it, I'll never know.

To her credit, she's the only person I know who can make a heated, vulgar feeling like disgust look cleanly, coldly lovely.

"Why do you have to be so hateful?" she asks, tilting her head to one side like an elegant well-fed shorebird calmly contemplating a fish she has no need to eat.

"I'm not hateful," I tell her. "I don't hate anyone. In order to hate, you have to care first. You know I don't care what people do just as long as they don't bother me." I pause.

"Is Dad here?" I ask her.

"He's in New York."

"You didn't go with him?"

"He was only going overnight."

"How's Wes? The girls? I brought them gifts."

This piques her interest. I almost detect a twinge of panic on her face. Does she think I'll tell Wes what I know if it turns out I know what she thinks I might know?

She's always been closer to Wes than she is to me. He's more im-portant to her. Again, it's a penis thing.

"Are you planning to see them?" she asks.

"I don't know what my plans are."

Clarence finally shows up with the drinks and the tension level drops dramatically.

I sip at my whiskey while Mom practically gulps at her gin and tonic. It can't possibly be her first drink of the day. I chalk up her eager-ness to nerves.

"Do you remember that awful prison of a boarding school you sent me to when I was thirteen?"

I expect a frown or a pout of disappointment but she gives me a strained smile.

"Where did that come from? You always say things so abruptly."

"It's called honesty."

"No, I think it's called abruptness."

"Well?"

"You were out of control," she says, relaxing back into the soft white leather. "We had to send you somewhere. And even if you'd been a model child, you still would've been sent to a private school in your teens. You know that. Wes went to a private school, too."

"It was a nuthouse. We had to see a shrink twice a week."

"It most definitely was not a nuthouse. It was a private school with an agenda. No different than a Catholic school. If we had sent you to one of those, you would've had religion classes instead of psychoanaly-sis. It's the same thing."

"Religion is a form of therapy?"

"Whatever gets you through the night, dear, as the saying goes."

She holds her drink out to me and smiles again.

"Cheers."

We clink glasses.

"Any particular reason you brought this up?"

"I don't know. I guess I'm feeling nostalgic. The year I was sent away was really the end of my living here. After that school there was another one and then college and then real life."

"You've always been welcome to come back anytime."

"That's big of you, Mom. Actually, the main reason I came back was to talk to Anna's cousin, Marcella. Have you ever met her?"

"It's idiotic," she says, her fine features puckering prettily again in disgust. "I can't believe you'd be taken in by something like this."

I don't say anything. I just watch her and drink.

"It did occur to me that she might try to get money out of you after she couldn't get it out of me, but frankly I didn't think she'd have the nerve or the resourcefulness to be able to track you down."

"I think it's true," I tell her. "The accusation is too bizarre to be something Anna just made up. And why write it down? Why keep it all those years?"

"How am I supposed to explain the actions of a crazy person? The woman was seriously disturbed."

"Then you're saying it's not true."

"Of course not."

"Then you won't mind if I show the letter to your husband?"

She bows her head slightly. This time when she raises her glass to her lips, I notice a slight tremor in her hand.

"We both know he'll insist on knowing if it's true or not, and he won't take your word for it," I go on. "And there *is* a way to find out the irrefutable truth nowadays. A very easy way."

I continue staring at her, willing her to look up at me, but she won't do it. She slowly, distractedly swirls the ice in her glass and watches it closely.

"I always wondered why you kept her as a nanny. She never struck me as being well suited for the job. She didn't really have any qualifications. Now I know. It was to protect your secret. She knew what happened. Not only that, you forced her to help you."

"I didn't force her to do anything," she counters harshly, finally glancing up at me, then immediately dropping her stare back into her drink.

"I told you it's a lie."

"So I can show it to Walker?"

I get no reply.

"Personally I think he'll be more bothered by the deceit than the violence. What do you think?"

"What do you want from me?" she asks in a low voice.

"I want to know if it's true and if it is, there's one other person involved in all this who's just as guilty as you are and maybe even more repulsive. I want a name."

She raises her gaze and sits perfectly still, holding her glass in two hands now like a beggar might hold out a cup for some change. She fixes her eyes on a point in the past. I watch her and wonder if she thinks about it every day, or only occasionally, or maybe never, and which of these would make her a more terrible woman.

She has always been capable of exquisite acts of ruthlessness because she has no allegiance to anything but her family and her wealth, but now she knows I have even less than that.

"I want a name," I repeat.

"Go away, Scarlet."

"Sorry, Mom, but you've just guaranteed that I'm going to stick around. I'm going to stay until I find out what I want to know. What I deserve to know. What do you have to say to that?"

Her eyes open so wide they seem to fill her face and a pale blue pulse begins to flutter beneath the tissue thin skin of her fragile throat.

She's afraid, but the moment passes.

A private smile spreads slowly across her lips and she raises her glass to me in another salute.

"Welcome home, darling."

twelve

DANNY

LIKE MANY BOYS WHO never knew their own fathers, Carson Shupe was a collector of father figures: a math teacher who was the first person to tell him he was smart; a young loan officer who lived briefly in the apartment across the hall who was the only man he ever remembered *not* sleeping with his mother; a black mechanic who worked in a nearby garage who let him hang out and drink Cokes and watch him work on cars; a long-winded assistant manager at a White Castle who was his first boss; a potbellied pharmacist who also lived across the hall and who *did* sleep with his mother and also molested him for several years when he was a child.

In speaking about all of these men, Carson painted pictures of astounding individuals who possessed a rare mix of machismo and sensitivity. They were patient and caring, yet stern and demanding; encouraging and playful, but tough and dogmatic: all the qualities a boy wants in a dad and all the ones he needs. I highly doubt they were any of these things. I imagine the one quality they all had in common was time on their hands.

They're all here, though, sitting in the gallery at his execution. It's bigger than I expected and much more opulent. The seats are upholstered in red velvet. The walls are covered with colorful tapestries of hunting scenes. A chandelier of polished deer antlers and candles hangs from the ceiling. The flames sputter as if unseen lips are blowing on them, and the wax drips liberally onto the laps and the tops of the heads of the spectators, but no one seems to notice.

The district attorney is here and all the members of the prosecution team. I wave at Sam, the assistant DA I worked with the most. He sees me but doesn't wave back.

Carson's defense attorney is here, too, and the two psychiatrists who testified on his behalf. Behind them sit a quartet of silent, broken men, and I know without knowing that these are the fathers of the murdered boys.

I search but none of the mothers are here. I realize there are no women here at all.

Men continue to file in: prisons guards, inmates, the judge, reporters.

Along the very back of the theater where the light is dimmest I see a group of figures I can't identify. I strain my eyes and begin to make out their white hoods. They start to slowly shuffle down the aisle toward their seats. Their ankles and wrists are shackled.

It can't be the Nellies. The Nellies are dead and there's no such thing as ghosts. It must be Tommy and the others in their memorial service getups. But why are they here? They have nothing to do with Carson Shupe.

And why am I looking at the spectators? I should be sitting with them. We should all be facing the stage.

"Tommy!" I call out.

I expect my voice to echo around the cavernous room but it goes nowhere.

I hear the clack of Rafe's candy coming from under one of the hoods.

"Rafe!" I cry.

"Mommy!" I cry.

She materializes out of the blue along with Molly and Fiona. They're all the same age. They're all young women the way Mom described them in her hospital room. Their skin is gray. They stare with their mouths open. Fiona is dressed in an old-fashioned long dress from her era. Molly wears jeans and a Speed Racer T-shirt, the cartoon I was watching when Mom's screams ripped through the house when she found Molly missing.

Mom is in a straitjacket.

"You were supposed to protect her," she says.

"I was too little," I plead with her.

"You were her big brother. It was your job."

Carson strolls in wearing street clothes. He joins the women. He stands next to my mom and puts his arm around her shoulders. On one of his mangled fingers with the shiny pink tips is a big ruby ring.

I start to tell him to keep his hands off my mother, but before I can get the words out all of their faces begin to melt then become the shifting images of a hologram: his face is my face; my mother's face is his mother's face; Molly's face is the face of a strangled boy; Fiona's face is the face of the Devil.

I try to run but my ankles are wrapped in heavy chains. My wrists are, too.

"Hello, Danny," a soothing voice says behind me.

I turn and find a man in a red suit. His hands are clasped in front of him and he smiles sadly at me.

"Who are you?" I ask.

"Why I'm Walker Dawes."

He unfolds his hands like the spreading of a fleshy bird's wings and reveals to me the blood-slick head of an unborn infant.

Vomit rises in my throat.

He opens his mouth to speak to me again and my father's voice says, "Go get me a beer."

I jerk awake with such force that I shake the entire couch and hit the end table. A lamp goes crashing onto the floor.

I let out a shout. My ears are ringing with the sound of my heart banging. I fell asleep in my clothes again and my shirt is drenched in sweat.

I wait for either my mom or Tommy to appear. We brought Mom home yesterday and installed her back in her childhood bedroom. It's directly above me.

Nothing happens.

I take deep breaths until I feel like I can stand. It's still dark outside but dawn will break soon.

I get a dish towel and drape it over Fiona's face, then return to the kitchen to make some coffee.

While listening to the drip and gurgle of Tommy's pot I settle down on the couch and open the box containing the files for my most pressing case, hoping to distract my thoughts and calm me down. It's the death of Baby Trusty at the hands of his mother, Mindy Renee Trusty, a cute student from an upper-middle-class family who loves *Gossip Girl,* skinny jeans, and pineapple on her pizza, and is shaping up to be, in my opinion, one of the most cold-blooded killers I've ever met.

I put aside all the materials from the DA's office: medical records, witness statements, autopsy reports, psychiatric reports by no fewer than six defense experts; then my own voluminous notes from interviewing her family, friends, neighbors, teachers, classmates, former boyfriends, and Mindy herself. I stop when I get to the folder containing her MMPI, the Minnesota Multiphasic Personality Inventory, the most widely administered standardized psychological test.

She finished the 366 questions in record time, only looking up from her scratching pencil every now and then to complain about the fact that she was missing a yoga class and to glare at her cell phone, which I had confiscated, turned off, and left in plain view on the table in order to watch her reaction.

I scored her test that same night. There were no significant clinical elevations in the curve, no signs of mental illness, depression, or any type of thought disorder. Her profile showed her to be absolutely normal, yet she had given birth to a baby alone in a bathtub in a hotel room less than three months earlier, cut the umbilical cord with scissors she had brought with her, stuffed loose change down the baby's throat until he suffocated, cleaned up the mess, put the baby's body into a plastic bag provided by the hotel for overnight dry cleaning, and put him in the trunk of her car with the intention of driving to her grandparents' farm near Lancaster and burying him somewhere in the woods. She might have gotten away with all of it if she hadn't passed out from dehydration and exhaustion and wrecked her car. No one had known she was pregnant; she had gone to great lengths to conceal her condition.

Her defense team is putting forth the all-purpose standby excuse for crimes that seem otherwise unimaginable; she snapped.

The problem with this argument is that no matter what certain attorneys, the media, and pop culture like to insist, mental illness doesn't work this way. People don't just snap. Any criminal—whether sane or insane—is a long time in the making and exhibits many signs throughout his or her life of impending danger for anyone who chooses to notice.

Traditionally, infanticide cases are rarely even prosecuted, and when they do go to trial, they are the single most successful use of the insanity defense. It seems incomprehensible to a jury that any mother would willfully kill her own child.

Being mentally ill is an easy explanation to accept when someone does something this awful. People prefer it over the only other available explanation, which is what I'm going to present to them in this case: Mindy Renee is a monster.

My own mother is one of the few women in this country who has been convicted and sent to prison for killing her own child, and if ever there was a woman who was obviously mentally ill and should have been acquitted, it was her. But she was a victim of circumstance, time, place, economics, and a fact of the case no one was able to overlook for even a moment: there was no other conceivable suspect.

Random lunatics didn't break into people's homes in the country, kill an infant, and bury her in her own backyard, and my father had an unassailable alibi; he was in a coal mine when Molly went missing.

The circumstantial evidence against my mother was overwhelming, but even so, Tommy never believed she did it. At the time I did my best to be on his side and defend my mom, but my support was halfhearted. I wasn't convinced, even though a few things didn't make sense to me.

I was there when my mom first realized Molly was gone. I had just come home from school and Mom was lying on the couch taking her nap while Molly was taking her nap in her crib.

Mom greeted me and asked me about my day, then took my hand and we walked upstairs together.

I'll never forget her screams or the terror on her face as she flew wildly around the little room I shared with my newborn sister, throwing herself on the floor and looking under the crib, slamming open the closet door, my toy-box lid, the dresser drawers, running to the window and pressing her forehead against the glass with a sob.

If she had killed Molly and buried her in our backyard where Dad found her body later that night, why would her shock and anguish have been so real? If she was acting, who was she acting for? Me? I was five years old.

I knew Mom did strange things, sometimes dangerous things, yet I also knew her actions were never motivated by anger toward others. She would have never purposely harmed someone.

I knew how much she loved Molly. I saw how she smiled at her and heard her sing the same lullabies to her that she sang to me. She held my little hand in hers and helped me gently stroke Molly's tiny arms and legs and talked about all the fun things we were going to do together. If she had hurt Molly it would have been an accident, and her first response would have been to get help for her. It would have never occurred to her that she should try to cover it up. She didn't think that way.

My mother could tell the most fantastic stories involving her ongoing delusions that were completely untrue, yet at the same time she was incapable of telling a lie.

I told all of this to Rafe when he took my statement. I was sure he believed me, but like me he also believed my mom was crazy and by definition, crazy people did crazy things. They were completely unreliable. They were always doing stuff that was out of character.

I've since spent my entire adult life discovering just the opposite is true: the mentally ill are the most predictable people in the world.

Mom never stopped denying that she killed Molly, but to the jury, it was painfully obvious that she had killed her. This fact wasn't being questioned. Why had she done it? What had led to this horrible tragedy? These are the answers they wanted to hear.

Over the years, people may have whispered to each other behind closed doors that Arlene McNab was crazy, but no one ever knew this for sure, and even if we had known, nothing would have been different. Our family could have never afforded treatment for her and we wouldn't have wanted her to get any. In a coal town in the 1970s, psychiatry was only for the truly crazy, and crazy was nothing more than a catchall term for the weak who couldn't cope. In a culture where a boy blowing off his fingers with butane and blasting caps was considered to be a whiner if he asked to go to the hospital, a woman claiming she couldn't get out of bed to make dinner because she was depressed wasn't going to be met with much sympathy.

Yet at the trial she desperately needed a psychologist to say she suffered from manic depression, but Dad and Tommy still couldn't afford one. They also couldn't afford a competent attorney.

I didn't attend the trial. Tommy felt any sympathy the jury might feel for my mom would be outweighed by the damage the experience might do to me, plus he thought the ploy could backfire and the jury might want to protect me from my mom instead of return her to me. I guess my dad agreed with him.

The public defender assigned to Mom's case also pointed out that if he were to put me on the stand for the purpose of saying nice things about Mom, this would mean the prosecutor would also get a chance to talk to me, and he would ask questions that would make my mom appear to be exactly the kind of violent, unstable woman who might kill her baby.

It was the only smart move Mom's lawyer made, and any good that might have come of it was overshadowed by his crucial error of putting Mom on the stand, where she said over and over again that she didn't kill her baby.

This insistence sank her insanity defense. Everyone had already decided she had done it. All that was left was to decide if she deserved leniency because she was ill, and the jury made up of hardscrabble blue-collar cynics believed there was nothing saner than telling a bald-faced lie to save your own skin.

I leave Mindy's MMPI in the box. I can't work. I need to get out of this house. This place has always been my safe haven, but it's also filled with bad memories. As a child I rarely slept here without having a nightmare, and now it seems the same thing is happening again.

I pass on the coffee. I eat a banana and go out for a run.

I don't pay any attention to my route. I know all the roads and I'm not worried about getting lost, but today this works against me as I get too absorbed in my flight and trying to survive the cold. I come to an unpaved road I haven't taken before. I know I should turn back and head for home. My eyes sting from the cold; the icy air burns my lungs; my hands, face, and feet are numb.

This new route is no different from any other back road around here. The hard-packed surface of mud and gravel glimmers with patches of ice. It's heavily wooded on both sides. This time of day the bare tree branches are starkly black against the iron-gray sky and I'm struck by the macabre thought that the coal-rich land has been stabbed again and again, spurting its lifeblood into the frigid air where it hangs frozen.

As I'm cresting a hill I hear the rumble of trucks and see lights below blazing against the indigo wall of the predawn hills. The massive piles of slag, the ebony sparkle of coal tumbling off a loader into the back of a truck, the double-wide trailer that serves as an office, the dark yawning entrance to the four-foot-high tunnel sunk eight hundred feet into the side of a mountain: I didn't know there were any operating coal mines left near Lost Creek.

I hear a truck coming up behind me. I turn and make out a pickup behind the glaring headlights and prepare myself for some abuse.

The truck slows as I expected and the passenger-side window rolls down.

"You looking for a job? Sorry but we're not hiring."

The voice is female and taunting and vaguely familiar. I move closer and find Brenna Kelly behind the wheel.

"It's a joke," she explains.

I don't know what to say.

"Anyone ever call you a fanatic?" she asks.

"Are you referring to the running?"

"You've got to be crazy to be out on a day like this. Get in. I'll take you down to the office and get you some hot coffee then drive you home."

"That's not necessary."

"Get in," she repeats.

The tone of her voice is commanding but not domineering. There's a gentleness to it that makes me think she knows what's best for me. I'm tired. I do what she wants.

A group of men in coveralls and hard hats stand outside the trailer stomping their feet in steel-toed safety shoes and blowing into their cupped hands to keep warm. They greet Brenna with grunts and nods.

"You find yourself a hitchhiker, Lou?" one of the men asks her and the rest respond with smiles they try to hide by bowing their heads.

"Just a man in need of a cup of coffee," she replies.

"I don't know what you heard, mister, but Lou's coffee ain't that good. Sure as hell not worth coming all the way out here to get it."

They all laugh at this.

"Lou?" I ask her.

"It's a nickname."

"She's an army lieutenant," one of the other men provides.

"Not anymore."

"Six tours," he says.

"Now I'm an accountant," she tells me.

"An accountant who can shoot you between the eyes from three hundred feet away."

More laughter. She smiles back at them. I decide to smile, too.

"This is Danny Doyle," she introduces me. "Tommy McNab's grandson."

At the mention of Tommy's name, they all quiet down and stand a little straighter out of respect. I'm glad she didn't introduce me as Owen Doyle's son.

A tall, lanky man with a gray beard steps forward.

"How's Tommy doing?" he asks me.

"He's fine."

"He was sick, right?"

"Pneumonia. But he made a full recovery."

"There ain't nothing can kill Tommy. 'Cept time."

The rest of the miners nod their agreement.

"This is my brother, Carl," Brenna says gesturing to the man who just spoke, "and this is Ricky, another one of my brothers."

One of the other men steps forward. He's not quite as old or tall as Carl and he's a little meatier, but the family resemblance is obvious.

He shakes my hand. I'm relieved when I get it back.

"And this is J. C., Todd, Jamie, and Shawn. Is Tim around?"

"He won't be back till this afternoon. He's checking out that new generator."

"Right," she says.

She leads me into the trailer. The men silently watch us go. I assume they're going to make fun of me as soon as I'm out of earshot.

The office is deliciously warm. The circulation begins to return to my face and extremities and they burn. My muscles are starting to cramp up but there's nothing I can do. I'm not going to stretch and I refuse to sit down and then have Brenna watch me try to get to my feet later groaning and wincing like an old man.

"I wasn't aware that there were any mines still operating around here," I comment.

"There's just this one and another one out near Coulter. They're small. We only employ forty men. They're prized jobs, believe me."

"So you work for Walker Dawes?"

"Technically, yes, through a complicated financial and legal arrangement that's pretty common in the industry now. Tim Franklin operates it, but his company is a subsidiary of Lost Creek Coal. Tim bought the rights to the coal cheap in a tax sale from another company. Dawes is into a lot of fracking now. And clean coal."

"Clean coal," I interject. "Mention it to Tommy and he spends the rest of the day saying things like, 'How'd you like a plate of dry water?' or, 'Maybe you'd like me to hit you in the head with this nice soft rock?'"

She smiles while taking off her coat and gloves.

"I know a lot of guys who feel that way, but they'd never turn down the work. Jobs are jobs."

"How's this mine doing?" I ask.

"Like most mines this size. It's profitable only if everything goes absolutely right, which is hardly ever. The next two shifts have to fill forty trucks or we're out of business."

"Is that a lot?"

"One twenty-by-twenty-foot cut fills three trucks."

She sees that I have no idea what she's talking about, but I'm flattered that she thought I might.

"It's a lot because we lost a couple hours yesterday. A problem with the generator. No generator, no fan. No fan, no air. Every hour of downtime costs about two grand."

She brings me a cup of coffee and walks back to her desk. I wish she would have stayed a moment longer. She smells good: a clean floral soapy scent combined with cinnamon and ginger. I remember Moira said she likes to cook. Maybe she has nightmares. A lot of veterans do. Did she wake up screaming, too, and bake a pie before coming to work?

"Thank you," I say. "Six tours of duty. Were you in Iraq?"

"That's one of the places."

She cocks her head to one side and eyes me critically.

"You look like you're thinking about giving me your business card so I can call you if I ever shoot up a shopping mall and want to use PTSD as an excuse."

"That's the kind of thing I could help you with, but I'm not thinking that."

"So Tommy's feeling better. Is that why you're here? To see how he's doing?"

"It's been a while since I've been back and I thought it was time."

I drink my coffee while she goes about getting folders out of a filing cabinet.

"I've never seen Rafe and Moira together," I say, attempting to fill the silence, "but from what I've heard, there's more bad blood between them than between him and Glynnis."

"You know how that goes. Glynnis got over the divorce but Moira never will. Sometimes it's easier to get over someone wronging you than it is to get over someone wronging someone you love."

"Rafe didn't exactly wrong her."

"Rafe's a good man. He'll do anything for you except give even the tiniest bit of himself. Most women expect at least a little piece."

"Most women want all of it."

"Really?"

She fixes me with an intensely probing gaze, the meaning of which I can't quite determine. I'm reminded of the other day and how our first meeting had ended on a sour note. I don't want to get in an argument with her again.

Fortunately the trailer door bangs open and her brother with the viselike grip steps in.

"You got any tape?" he asks Brenna.

She goes to the desk and tosses a roll of reflective duct tape at him.

He catches it and begins ripping off pieces he wraps around the cuffs of his sleeves and his pant legs.

I silently congratulate myself on the fact that I've never had a job that requires taping my clothing so parts of my body won't be chewed off by machinery.

"How are you doing?" she asks him.

"I'm fine. What kind of question is that?"

"The kind of question a sister asks her brother when she'd like to know how he's doing."

"Everything's great."

He throws the tape back at her and stalks past me on his way toward the door.

"Nice to meet'cha," he mumbles.

"Is anything wrong?" I ask her once he's safely outside again. "You look upset."

"His wife lost her job," she explains. "They have four kids. This job has been a godsend for him but it might not be here tomorrow. I don't know what they're going to do."

She pauses.

"I look at their situation and all I can think is how lucky I am that my kids are grown and it looks like they're going to be okay."

"You're old enough to have grown kids?"

"I got pregnant with my first right out of high school. They're eighteen and twenty. My son's in the army and my daughter's a freshman at Pitt. She wants to be a doctor. We'll see what happens. Not bad for a couple of yokels."

I glance at her to see if she's smiling but she's not.

"I tried to explain that."

"I know what you were trying to say, but you didn't have to be mean about it."

"People here were mean to me first."

Her frown deepens.

"Listen to yourself. You sound like you're five years old."

I open my mouth to protest but she won't let me.

"What about you? Any kids?"

"No."

"Wife? Ex-wife?"

"No."

"There doesn't seem to be anything wrong with you. You make a good living. You're not bad looking."

"Why do you have to assume there's something wrong with me because I've never been married or have any children?"

"Most people do it, that's all. Whether they should or not. Sometimes whether they want to or not. It's what we're supposed to do, so we do it."

"Is that why you got married?"

"The first time? Pretty much. Plus I was pregnant."

"What about the second?"

"Rebound guy. French. Met him in an airport coming back from one of my tours. The accent really got to me."

"You married a guy because of his accent?"

"Pretty much."

"I once slept with a woman because she used the word 'lain' correctly in a sentence."

She giggles at me over the rim of her coffee mug, and despite the snow that's begun falling softly outside the trailer window, my mind drifts back to high school and that last week before summer break when

the girls were allowed to wear shorts. All those bare legs and round bottoms and flashes of soft bellies between bandanna belts and faded halter
tops. They'd glide by with glitter-painted toenails sticking out from
plastic sandals, laughing like Brenna and tossing their heads, filling the
halls with the tantalizing smell of their fruit-flavored Lip Smackers and
cheap roll-on perfumes, as unself-conscious as flowers, not understanding the meaning they brought to the world simply by being in it.

I was never allowed anywhere near that particular garden until
today.

thirteen

I LET BRENNA DRIVE ME back to Tommy's house, and I tell her I owe her a favor.

Mom's in her reindeer bathrobe busy at the stove. Tommy's sitting in his chair cleaning his rifle, wearing one of her hand-crocheted hats. It's a green one with the word FORGIVENESS stitched across the border. Mom is wearing a purple TOLERANCE hat.

My orange GOOD SENSE OF HUMOR hat has been given to the deer head.

"You know you can't shoot ghosts," I tell him. "They're already dead."

He glances up from his gun.

"Raccoon's been in my trash again."

"Do you want some breakfast?" Mom calls out.

I walk over to her and see what's on the menu.

"You need to eat, Danny, or you'll never fill out. Have some creamed dried beef," she instructs, dragging a wooden spoon around a frying pan full of bubbling red and white muck.

"Wonderful," I say. "Our yearly salt requirement satisfied in one meal."

"When you have food you should eat it," Mom explains. "We might not have any tomorrow. Or we might be dead or we might be held captive against our will."

She explains these scenarios without expression, apparently not the least bit upset by the possibility of any of them occurring. She obviously took her pills this morning. The medication helps control her illness but it also erases her personality. People's identities are shaped by their beliefs, even if they're wildly untrue; eliminate them and their lives become banal. My mother sees herself as the heroine in an epic tale of good versus evil, even though the extent of her good deeds might only be painting a garage or knitting hats, but when she's medicated, she believes she's weak and useless.

"Do we have any cereal?" I ask.

"Lucky Charms," Mom replies.

I sigh and look behind me at the boxes of cookies and snack cakes sitting on the table. On the way home from the hospital we made another stop at *the* Bi-Lo.

I can't stop my mind from drifting back in time to our own kitchen was filled with the dozens of cookies she used to bake. They were wondrous creations: peanut butter blossoms with Hershey kisses in the center; warm, gooey pecan tassies she called fairy pies; ginger snaps that smelled like autumn; thumbprints filled with dabs of glistening raspberry jam. But my favorites were the sugar cookies, the hearts and stars and bears and shamrocks frosted in every color imaginable and topped with sprinkles and gleaming silver candy balls.

I never knew when I'd wake up in the morning or come home from school to find them already made or when she'd have me help her. Afterward we'd drive around town giving them to people. The trips would start out full of fun and good intentions, but one time we ended up far from home lost and out of gas, and another time she got caught up in the excitement of our mission and started driving too fast and hit a phone pole. I broke my wrist. She bloodied her nose and broke a rib. The car suffered the most damage. Dad took away her car keys after that.

A vivid picture of her emerges, young and lovely, with shiny red hair like a new penny, pulled back in a ponytail. She's rubbing her big belly, talking about how the next batch of cookies we make will be for Molly. (She already had her name picked out. She was certain the baby was going to be a girl.) How she won't be able to eat them because she'll be too little. She won't have teeth. I laugh at this. I can't imagine how weird she'll look without teeth. Mom laughs, too. She ruffles my hair and tells me I will always be her special boy. Molly will be her special girl and she wants me to love Molly as much as she does. I promise her I will.

I dashed off to the school bus and left her behind, seeming painfully well and deceptively content, alone with the dozens of dazzling cookies she had made in the middle of the night stacked all along the counter-tops.

When I returned home from my few hours of kindergarten, every single one had been destroyed. The kitchen was covered in crumb carnage. Mom sat at the table, her eyes as empty as the ones in Tommy's deer head, her hands, her hair, her cheeks streaked with frosting and sprinkles. I burst into tears, not sure if I was more upset about the loss of the cookies or the loss of my mother yet again.

They were ugly, she told me in her chilling monotone. She was worthless. She couldn't do anything right.

Tommy has put on his coat and cap.

"Going to get the mail," he tells us.

On his way out, the phone rings and he snatches up the receiver without bothering to glance at caller ID. It's an irrelevant service for him since he would never *not* answer a call. He enjoys berating telemarketers even more than chatting with friends.

"Yes, this is Thomas McNab," I hear him say. "He is. Sure you are."

He turns to me with a skeptical grin and holds out the phone.

"Some joker wants to talk to you. Says he's Walker Dawes. Probably one of your psycho pals from prison."

"Hello?" I say hesitantly while watching Tommy out the window make his way across the porch and down the icy steps with the help of his cane.

"Yes, hello. Is this Sheridan Doyle?"

The voice on the other end is smooth and refined with a tinge of affectation to it.

"Yes?"

"This is Walker Dawes."

An irrational fear courses through me. For a moment, I'm convinced I'm speaking to the original Walker Dawes, who could only be calling from the grave, or in his case from the cold, airless, marble interior of his family's mausoleum. I can't think of anything to say.

"I hope you don't mind me calling you at your grandfather's home. I heard you were here taking care of him while he recovers from his recent illness."

"How did you know?"

"Oh, little birdies. Spies. Snooping is my hobby."

"I'm sorry, but I'm a little confused. You don't know me."

"No, but I know of you, and I'm sure you know of me."

"Yes . . ."

"It's because I know of you that I'm calling. I'd like to discuss something with you. It's a little delicate so I'd prefer to do it in person. Will you be free later today?"

"Possibly."

"Wonderful. Do you know where I live?"

I've met and worked with and even befriended the rich and famous. I'm certainly not impressed or intimidated by this man's wealth or his reputation, yet now that I'm being offered the chance to finally meet him I'm not sure I want to. I'm not flustered by who he is, but there's a part of me that's unnerved by what he's always represented to this town.

"If I head north, it's the first fifty-room mansion to the left," I reply.

"Very good," he laughs. "Actually, it's fifty-five, but who's counting?"

He hangs up and I'm left staring at the phone, not completely sure what just happened but certain of one thing: I can't wait to tell Tommy about this.

I look out the front window and see him standing on the side of the road in front of his mailbox with a collection of bills and catalogs in one hand and a single piece of paper in the other held close to his face.

His expression is almost fearful. He's so preoccupied with what he's reading, he doesn't even look up when I open the front door and call to him.

I run out and join him at the mailbox.

"Danny," he says simply and holds out the sheet of paper to me.

I look at the words typed in the center of it.

SHE'S INNOCENT. YOUR GRANDDAUGHTER'S STILL ALIVE.

"Who would do this? Who could be this mean?" he asks in a mystified pleading tone, too sad to be angry. "It must be a prank."

He hands me the envelope. It's typed, too. There's no return address and it has a Barclay postmark.

This isn't the first time someone has anonymously harassed us because of my mother's crime. Back when it happened, Tommy's house and truck were vandalized. Someone spray-painted "murderer" and "baby killer" on his front sidewalk. Someone threw a rock through one of his windows. Yet even at the height of my mom's notoriety, no one ever sent a note like this one. No one ever claimed she was innocent, and certainly no one suggested that my sister was alive.

"After all these years," Tommy says, shaking the note at me. "What do you think it means?"

"I don't know."

He puts a trembling hand on my arm and he's suddenly a confused, vulnerable old man who needs my help and I don't like it. I don't know what to do. I never realized until this moment how much I've always depended on him to be able to weather any indignity or assault, to be invincible and eternal like the hills.

Tommy holds the piece of paper out to me again.

"Could it be true?" he says.

I know how much he's always desperately wanted to believe in these words, but there's no denying the fact that Molly was killed. Her body was found buried in our backyard. Mom's the only one who could have done it.

I put my arm around his shoulders and we walk back into the house together. My cell phone is ringing when we get inside. It's Rafe.

"Have I got something to show you, Danno," he says.

fourteen

I NEVER USE THE WORD "wow," but it's the only word that comes to mind.

"Wow," I say.

"Is that your professional opinion?" Rafe asks.

"Level-four disposaphobe."

"Huh?"

"That's the psychiatric term for a hoarder. Level five is the most severe, but she had some boundaries. She kept the floor relatively clear and her compulsion was very specific. She was attracted to color, sparkle, and childish objects that represent happiness and fantasy."

"Reminds me of . . ." He pauses and scratches his head. "What's the name of those stuffed animals? My girls used to play with them. They were all different colors and had a cartoon about love and sharing. If you watched more than thirty seconds of it you wanted to go outside and kick a cat."

"Care Bears," I provide.

"Yeah, that's it. It looks like a bunch of Care Bears puked all over her house."

Marcella Greger lies on the floor in front of her couch next to an overturned coffee table. She's flat on her back, staring at the ceiling, her arms at her sides. She could be meditating except for the pool of blood soaked into the carpet, spreading out behind her head like a black halo.

During all my years of working with violent criminals, I've never actually seen any of their handiwork in person. I've looked at countless crime scene photos, none more gruesome than the ones taken of Carson's victims: four little boys between six and eight years old—around the same age he was when his mother was first arrested for prostitution—their throats neatly, deeply slit from ear to ear, the wounds gaping open like grins beneath their real mouths, which were set in grim lines of pale blue rigor. Their severed genitals lay in tidy little bloody piles where their Adam's apples would have eventually bulged if they had lived long enough.

I never asked him why he did what he did. Serial killers rarely offer explanations. By delving into their backgrounds and asking about everything else in their lives aside from the murders they commit, a good psychologist can usually find the answers that they didn't even know themselves.

Carson developed a habit of asking me questions about my own life that I came to discover was his way of answering mine.

On the day I spread out the photos of his victims in front of him and asked him to explain what he saw, he studied them without emotion then looked up at me and asked, "Why didn't you ever have kids?"

I understood immediately that he saw his slaughter and castration of boys of a certain age to be no different than my failure to procreate. We were both sending messages to our mothers.

I will never forget those photos, yet their grisliness didn't move me the way Marcella's body does.

Death can't be fathomed through sight, I realize. It can't be seen but must be felt, since it is the absence of something, not the presence.

Rafe starts to unwrap a Jolly Rancher, stops, and puts it back into his pocket. It's blue.

He takes out another one.

"The niece found her," he starts explaining. "She comes by once a week to check on her. Doesn't have a family of her own. Nothing valuable in the house. Smalls and Razzano went through it. Doesn't look like anything's missing."

"How could you tell?"

"Her purse is here. Wallet. Credit cards. Some cash. Car's in the garage. Door was unlocked but the niece says that's normal. I'd say she's been dead since yesterday," he finishes.

"Did you find a murder weapon?"

"A rainbow."

He says this in deadpan. I decide not to question him further. Considering the house she lived in, his answer seems appropriate.

"I'd say it was a single blow considering the lack of blood spatter. No rage. Nothing personal. Cold and calculated. I found this lying next to her and this under the couch."

He shows me a recently used coffee mug and a glass smudged with lipstick. A few drops of what smells like bourbon cling inside it.

"Do you think this means she knew her killer?" I ask. "It looks like she was having a drink with someone. The lipstick doesn't belong to the victim."

"Yeah. She's not wearing any."

"And it's too expensive."

Rafe stops clacking his candy against his teeth and gives me an amused stare.

"You can tell the difference between cheap and expensive lipstick? I worry about you, Danno."

"I've dated some women who wore expensive makeup and liked to talk about it."

"And you paid attention?"

"Maybe you can get some DNA from this?"

"DNA," he grunts. "This isn't the city. We don't have your resources. We'd have to send this to the state crime lab. It would take months to hear back."

Even if he had access to the latest technology, I know Rafe wouldn't use it. Forensic science is an unnecessary distraction in his eyes. He believes anything can be found out by asking enough people enough questions. His crime-solving philosophy is based on one simple belief: no one can keep his mouth shut forever.

He crooks a finger at me. I follow him into a bathroom where an image of a gallows with a stick figure dangling from it has been drawn on the medicine cabinet mirror.

I can't help thinking about Simon Husk's claim that the ghost of Prosperity McNab wrote the word "Fi" on his bedroom mirror in blood that turned out to be lipstick. This time there's no question.

"Is that blood?" I ask.

"Yep."

I examine the ghoulish artwork.

"I suppose I don't need to point out the similarity between this and what happened to Simon Husk when he was a boy."

"Nope. It's one strange coincidence."

The picture is carefully and neatly rendered. The artist was calm and unrushed. I can make out brushstrokes. I think back to the high-end lipstick on the glass and the makeup brush the owner would use to apply it. A woman did this.

"Who would have heard Simon's ghost story?"

"Hell, who hasn't heard it?"

"She's playing on the town's fears and superstitions. Whoever she is, she thrives on controlling and manipulating people."

"Who's she? You mean the woman with the expensive lipstick? You think the killer is female?"

"I do. Did the niece see this?" I ask, gesturing toward the drawing.

Rafe nods.

"I told her not to tell anyone, but I can't make her keep her mouth shut. Something this good, by now the whole county knows."

"But what is there to know exactly? You're not referring to the curse? Bloody cartoon aside, Simon Husk had a very strong link to the gallows, but Marcella Greger doesn't."

"Not true. She was the cousin of Anna Greger, the Dawes family nanny."

"The one who doused herself in gasoline and lit herself on fire?"

"The same."

I was a teenager when that happened. It was all anyone talked about for months, along with the inevitable gossip: Anna Greger was crazy, she abused the Dawes children, she professed her unrequited love for

Walker in her suicide note. Mrs. Dawes did it. Mr. Dawes did it. The butler did it. The entire town was spooked. Even my dad did all his drinking at home for weeks after it happened, refusing to go to the Rabbit or anywhere else. I remember thinking he was afraid to leave the house.

"And if you go back a few generations," Rafe goes on, "they're related to Peter Tully."

Peter was one of the first to be hung along with Prosperity. He was the only child of a widow who doted on him. He was nineteen and didn't leave behind a wife or children. His mother fainted at the execution and followed her son into the grave a month later. The lace handkerchief she gave him that he tucked into his coat pocket as the noose was put around his neck is on display in Nora Daley's attic.

Rafe shows me a rental contract for a safety deposit box.

"Found it in her desk. She also has the same number written on a piece of paper hanging on her refrigerator door."

"It must be important to her."

"I'm heading over there now to check it out. You want to tag along?"

"Sure."

"Explain to me again why you're wearing a suit?"

"I didn't really explain the first time. I have somewhere to go."

I don't know why I haven't told him about my impending meeting with Walker Dawes. I also didn't tell him about the note in Tommy's mailbox.

"Somewhere around here that requires a suit?"

"It's not really required," I reply.

It's more like I need it, I finish to myself.

Superman has his cape, I have my Armani herringbone.

THE UPS STORE IS located in a strip mall on the north side of Hellersburg along with the State Store, a Laundromat, a Rite Aid pharmacy, the Big Eats buffet restaurant, a Dollar General store, and a Christian thrift shop with a dusty front window displaying Bibles, crosses, angels, pictures of Jesus, and strangely enough, a life-size cardboard cutout of Elvis.

It's staffed by two heavily tattooed boys barely out of high school with identical mullets who I'm guessing spend a lot of time popping bubble wrap.

They each have a name tag pinned to their yellow polo shirts: Shane and Matt.

Rafe shows them his identification.

"I didn't know we had a detective," Matt says, squinting at Rafe's badge. "What kind of money you make?"

Rafe lays out Marcella's contract on the counter.

"Open this box."

"Don't you need a warrant?" Shane asks.

Rafe leans into the kid's face.

"The owner is dead. Her key is missing. Open the box."

Shane holds his hands up in a dramatic display of surrender and leaves to get the key.

Rafe takes it from him and heads to the wall of post office boxes and safety deposit boxes on the other side of an aisle of copy machines.

"Empty," he says upon his return.

He pulls out a photo of Marcella Greger he took from her house and shows it to the boys.

"Do you recognize her?"

"No."

"You haven't seen her in here lately? Think hard."

"Nah. Never seen her."

"Did anyone come in here yesterday or this morning and take something out of one of those boxes? Anyone at all."

"We got a couple regulars who come in every day to check their PO boxes," Shane replies.

"What about that woman?" Matt interjects excitedly.

"Oh, yeah." Shane gives us a lewd smile. "She was hot. Supermodel hot."

"Supermodel?" Rafe asks skeptically.

"Yeah, she was tall and had amazing legs."

"And her hair was tousled," Matt volunteers.

Rafe rolls his eyes.

"What color was this tousled hair?"

"Brown," insists Shane.

"Red," insists Matt.

"It wasn't red. It was brown."

"It was red."

"What was she wearing?" Rafe interrupts them.

"She was classy. She looked rich."

"Did she talk to you?"

"We tried to get her to talk to us. We asked her if she needed any help. We tried to talk to her about the weather."

"We said it was cold," Matt contributes, nodding.

"She ignored us."

"Hard to believe," Rafe comments. "What did she do while she was in here?"

"She opened up one of the boxes."

"Did she take anything out?"

"I think so. I'm not sure. Then she left."

"Anything else you can tell me about her? Anything at all?"

They fall silent and think.

"Hey, remember after she left what you said to me?" Shane says to Matt.

"Let's go to Sheetz and get an MTO?"

"No, you said she looked like a fembot."

"A fembot?" Rafe repeats.

Shane nods.

"More like a clone."

"Not a clone," Matt argues. "A cyborg."

"Definitely something with consciousness. It wasn't like you thought she was a machine. She just didn't seem completely human."

"It was her eyes, mostly. The way they stared at you."

"What color were her eyes?" Rafe asks.

"Brown."

"Green."

"Brownish green."

"They weren't blue."

Rafe sighs.

"So a supermodel or possibly a fembot came in here yesterday who may or may not have had red or brown hair and may or may not have taken something out of one of the lockboxes, then stared at you in a way that may or may not have been entirely human, then refused to make any kind of small talk with you and left. Is that correct?"

They look at each other and nod.

Back outside the snow has turned to freezing rain. I pull up the collar of my coat. Rafe yanks up the hood on his camouflage jacket.

"I shouldn't even be working right now," he says. "I've maxed out my overtime the past few days. I'm going to start this paperwork then grab a beer at the Rabbit and go home to bed."

"I need to get going, too," I tell him.

Rafe doesn't seem to hear me. He stares across the parking lot, blinking against the icy droplets blowing in his face.

"What is it?" I ask him. "What are you thinking?"

He slips another piece of candy into his mouth.

"I'm trying to figure out if they were the worst or the best witnesses I've ever interviewed."

fifteen

MY PHONE VIBRATES IN my coat pocket as I get into my Jag. I've been dodging Max's texts and calls. I'm going to have to touch base with him eventually, but I've been putting it off because I haven't decided yet how long I'm staying and I haven't accomplished any work. He's going to chastise me even though he has no business doing it. The problem with having a highly competent, efficient personal assistant is he sometimes makes you feel like you work for him.

I reach into my glove compartment for a bottle of Tylenol and some chewable antacids. I've been here for three nights and two were plagued with bad dreams, one a standard from my childhood with a new twist at the end, the other entirely new.

They both featured fathers and I can't ignore the subconscious message I'm sending myself. I need to visit my dad. I just can't do it quite yet.

I don't know what kind of relationship Walker Dawes had with his father or what kind of father he has been to his two children.

It's been said he bears a much closer resemblance to the first Walker Dawes physically and in temperament than to his own father, Walker III, nicknamed Trigger, who was a quick-tempered, jowly, unpolished cigar chomper who purposely mangled his grammar and never went anywhere without his black and tan coonhound.

Trigger's father, Deuce, had been a well-known disappointment to his pretentious dandy of a father. A sloppy, portly boy who didn't care at all about his heritage or personal appearance, he preferred the company of the Irish servants to children of his own class and listening to their folk tales over his father's dinnertime lectures on stock markets and labor disputes.

When the first Walker was struck down by the scarlet fever that would kill him, Deuce prayed harder than anyone that he would survive. He feared and disliked his father, but he feared and disliked the idea of running Lost Creek Coal & Oil even more. He only did it for a decade, handing over the reins to his son, Trigger, as soon as he was out of college.

Deuce's most notable public act as a Dawes was to sell the gallows and jail, but long before he did this, the miners liked to joke that his most courageous private act was to impregnate his wife. He was saddled with the explicit directive of providing a grandson to carry on his father's name, so it was assumed he'd have some difficulties in the bedroom. Rumors abounded about the various methods his wife employed to get him to make love to her, one of the favorites being that she rubbed powdered sugar into her skin to make herself smell like a cake.

He paced outside the bedroom door for an entire day while she was in labor. When the nurse finally brought the swaddled bundle out into the hallway for him to see, sweat droplets exploded from his forehead and he went deathly pale. She pulled back the blanket and a faint smile flickered across his lips before he passed out cold at the sight of the tiny pecker.

Like his great-grandfather before him, the man I'm about to meet doesn't tolerate nicknames. Apparently, he also doesn't want to share his full name with anyone else and broke family tradition by naming his own son Wesley instead of Walker.

As I drive onto the estate, passing through the stone pillars topped with a gold *W* and *D* entwined in black marble antlers, and head up the long, curving road lined by massive maples that must blaze with incredible color in the fall, I think about the Dawes men and the stories surrounding them and wonder at the fact that no one has ever seemed to know anything about their wives.

The first Walker was unique among the coal barons of his day in that he chose to build his home where his mines were located. Most of his peers lived far away on Fifth Avenue, Rittenhouse Square, or in Back Bay.

People speculated as to why he stuck around. Some said it was out of love for the area. Others said it was out of a pathological need for control. He was obsessed with knowing every detail of what went on inside his mines and his town. It was one of the many reasons the Nellies were doomed from the start. He had spies everywhere.

The house appears all at once looming pinkly on a low mountain ridge. The property abounds with the ostentation of formal rose gardens, fountains, and manicured topiaries, but they do nothing to alleviate the sullen presence of the dark woods and hills surrounding it.

Aside from the unusual color, the most striking features are the five gables stretching across the length of the roof like a child's depiction of a mountain range and the amount of diamond-shaped windows. When the sun shines, the mansion must glitter like a diamond, but on a day like today, this amount of glass only serves to make it seem filled with murky water.

A housekeeper answers the door and deposits me in an enormous great room dominated by a priceless gilded chandelier hung with crystal droplets the size of chicken eggs and filled with an eccentric mishmash of past grandeur. Persian carpets are scattered over the ebony hardwood floors. The windows are hung with heavy brocaded drapes. The furniture is an odd collection of pink and gold velvet sofas, highbacked dark oak chairs, and an excessive amount of end tables each displaying a Tiffany lamp and a figurine of either a circus performer or a waterfowl.

A pair of bronze stags prance across the mantel set above a fireplace of cerulean blue and sea green marble tiles and above them are hung oversize oil portraits of Walker the First, Deuce, Trig, and Walker IV. I stand in front of each one in turn trying to decipher what kind of man he was based on his stance, attire, and the expression in his eyes.

I decide to give them names worthy of the Seven Dwarves, another group of legendary miners: Cocky, Droopy, Feisty, and Bored.

There's not a single picture of any of the wives or of the only daughter, but Roscoe, the coonhound, has been memorialized. He lies fast asleep at his master's feet.

The housekeeper returns and leads me to Walker Dawes' study, a room I'm fairly certain hasn't been altered at all since the original one put his mark on it, his heirs not having the nerve or the inclination to touch anything. The walls are lined with books, most of them leather bound and appearing to be volumes in collections. The desk is a massive, immovable table of mahogany with roses carved into its legs. Stacks of papers cover its surface, and a chair of hunter green leather studded in burnished gold sits behind it turned toward a set of floor-to-ceiling windows that look out over the Dawes land extending to the mountains beyond. An intricately patterned rug of rich, dark colors and swirls of copper thread covers most of the hardwood floor. I don't know much about the prized rugs of the Middle East and North Africa, but I know enough to realize this one is very old and very valuable.

A set of matching ceramic urns, standing at least four feet tall, covered in scenes of Oriental men and women dancing with a red, snake-like dragon breathing black flames are positioned on either side of the doorway. I look closer and realize the people aren't laughing, they're screaming. They're not dancing, they're running for their lives.

The current Walker Dawes walks across the priceless rug without giving it a second thought and extends his hand to me.

He's dressed casually in brown corduroys, a bulky cream-colored cardigan over a blue chambray shirt, and perfectly aged buttery leather loafers that would barely leave a bruise if he decided to kick his son.

His hair is the color of lead. He wears it slicked back and still has plenty of it. He's in good shape. Time and the lush life haven't softened or widened him. I'd say he looks younger than his seventy-something years but not young by any means, despite the traces of a pretty boy lingering beneath the lined face.

He has a strong grip.

"The great-great grandson of Prosperity McNab shaking hands with the great-grandson of Walker Dawes," he says, smiling.

"I guess one of us should be nervous," I say, returning the smile.

He laughs and releases my hand.

"Come have a seat."

I start to follow him toward the desk when I'm suddenly immobilized by the sight of another large portrait of Walker the First, but this time posing in front of the gallows.

The picture is done in dramatic slashes of black and white, as if strikes of lightning had created it. Everything is sharp and jagged, including the planes of his face. The artist managed to capture both cruelty and delight in his expression.

The only color is a dot of red in the middle of his pleated shirtfront where a man might aim a bullet or stab an accusatory finger: the famed Dawes ruby.

I couldn't be more shocked if he had Prosperity's head mounted on the wall.

He notices me looking at the painting.

"Oh, that."

He shrugs away my discomfort.

"Walker the First. A show-off. Come. Sit."

I remain rooted to the floor. Next to the painting is a framed black-and-white photo of the "pluck me," circa late 1800s, one of the few buildings still standing in town originating from the time of the Nellies. Now it's Kelly's Kwik Shop.

The "pluck me" was the miners' name for the company-owned stores where they were forced to shop by the owners. Prices were much higher there and buying was done on "tick," meaning the purchases were recorded in a book and never revealed to the purchaser. Not that it would have mattered, since he was probably illiterate. If a miner and his family refused to deal with the pluck me, the manager would report him to his foreman and he'd not only be fired but be blacklisted and would find it impossible to get another job in the region.

Any thought of a miner ever seeing any actual cash money quickly became a fantasy. Most of the time what a man received at the end of the month was a "bobtail" check good for absolutely nothing except to show his current debt, and those debts never disappeared. They were handed down from fathers to sons. There were families in Lost Creek who were so deep in the tick that the men went their entire lives without ever receiving a dollar in cash from their labor.

Walker pulls a small, thin cigar from a tin sitting on his desk and lights it with a wooden match he takes from a drawer. He closes his eyes and blows a stream of blue smoke toward the windows.

"Sheridan Doyle. Crazy mother killed his sister and went to jail. Alcoholic father worked in the mines until he hit the disability jackpot. Young Danny somehow rises above his less-than-sterling parentage and earns both academic and athletic scholarships to the Ivy League. Bravo. That is no easy feat. Undergrad degree from Penn. Graduate degrees from Yale. PhD and JD. A shrink and a shyster. Never married. No children. Successful forensic psychologist. Three best-selling books. TV appearances."

I turn around slowly.

"Did I leave anything out?" he asks pleasantly.

"My shoe size."

"Twelve. Anything else?"

"Don't call me Danny."

"Sorry."

"You know a lot about me."

"I know a lot about everyone. Your grandfather, too. He's still alive at a very advanced age and just recently survived a bout of pneumonia. The first of the McNab men not to be killed by the mines. Do you smoke, Doctor, or should I call you Counselor?"

"I don't practice law. And no, I don't smoke."

"Please, sit."

I lower myself into a chair on the other side of the desk from him.

He gives me a patronizing yet affable smile. I'm amazed at his ability to seem appealing and repugnant at the same time, but I'm no stranger to his type. He's a textbook narcissist; a sophisticated playground bully who throws barbs instead of punches.

"A psychologist but not a psychiatrist. Interesting. Do you mind if I ask why?"

"I thought a law degree made more sense than a medical degree, since I knew I wanted to specialize in forensic psychology."

"But then you're not really all you can be, are you? You can't pre-scribe medication."

"I don't need to prescribe medication. I study and explain human behavior."

"In other words, you're not interested in trying to make anyone better."

"It's not my area of expertise."

"I saw you on some show a few years back," he goes on. "You were discussing the Wishbone murders. Jane Fonda was a guest, too, on an unrelated topic of course. Did you meet her? What was she like?"

"Aside from some radical cognitive bonding issues and bad taste in shoes, she seemed very nice."

He smiles again. A meaningless expression. A mask.

"All right, then. Enough small talk."

He pushes his chair away from the desk and opens a drawer. He glances in it then up at me.

"I want you to understand that I've had my life threatened many times."

"Someone has threatened your life?"

"I just said that."

"Recently?"

"I'm not sure. That's why I called you."

"Why would you call me? Why not the police?"

"Because I wanted to talk to someone with a brain. This might not mean anything," he says, standing up from his chair and putting his cigar in an ashtray. "I might be making a mountain out of a molehill or a vulture out of a canary, as it were."

He takes a small yellow bird out of the drawer and lays it delicately on the desktop.

"I suppose it's always disturbing to have someone give you a dead bird, but since I own coal mines this particular one takes on a menacing aspect. You understand the significance?"

"The canary dying meant the mines were filled with lethal gas," I answer. "Where did you find it?"

"That's the other thing that was disturbing. Right here. I just got back from New York last night and it was waiting for me."

"Who has access to this room?"

"Just the staff and my wife, and I can promise you nothing in the world could make my wife touch a dead bird."

I pick up the canary. Its neck hasn't been broken, which is the easiest way to kill a small bird like this one. I wonder if its killer suffocated it to mimic what would have happened to it in a carbon-monoxide-filled mine. I picture a pair of hands sealing it into a Ziploc bag and a pair of eyes watching it madly flap its wings then slowly weaken and die.

"How long were you in New York?"

"Just for a day."

"Did you hear about Simon Husk's death?"

"Of course. I knew him. His family and mine have had business dealings from time to time. Small ones."

"Some people are saying his death is related to his decision to sell the gallows back to you and your intention to tear them down."

"Yes, yes," he says. "I know. The big curse. Revenge of the Nellies. But if that were true, I suppose I'd be their number-one target. What do you think? Do you think a Nellie put the canary in my desk?"

"No, but maybe someone wants you to think a Nellie did it," I say. "Do you know a woman named Marcella Greger?"

"We had a nanny named Anna Greger."

"This would be her cousin."

"Anna Greger. I haven't thought about her in years. She killed herself in our house. Horrible ordeal. No, I didn't know her cousin or any of her family. Why do you ask?"

"I still don't understand why you called me," I say instead of answering him.

He puts the bird back into the drawer and takes up his cigar again.

"I wanted someone to know about this. Just in case something else might happen. But I didn't want to tell my family and I certainly didn't want to involve the police. Now you have your first clue if I end up dead."

"That makes no sense. You're lying."

My accusation elicits another unctuous smile from him.

"Would you believe that I simply wanted to meet you?"

"No."

I don't know what kind of stupid game he's playing with me, but I know that's exactly what this is for him. An amusement. A diversion. His type of wealth isolates a man. The very rich get very bored. They also get very jaded. It takes extremes to excite them, and what could be more invigorating than controlling a real live person as easily as a child moves a gingerbread marker across a Candyland board?

"But I did want to meet you," he insists. "I find you intriguing. Our culture loves to celebrate those who rise to great heights from very humble beginnings, but the truth is it rarely happens, and when it does it almost always involves a guitar or a football. You did it with brains and sheer determination to get away from here."

"You don't know anything about me and you certainly don't know what motivates me."

"Then what was it? Was it money that motivated you? That's an expensive suit. I'm sure you enjoy the fruits of your labor, but you could have made far more money in private practice. Or was it fame you were after? You make far too many appearances as an expert commentator on those lurid crime docudramas. Is it because you like to see yourself on TV?"

"You can't get a rise out of me," I inform him as I stand to go. "And if there's a reason for you calling me other than you had nothing to do on a sleeting January afternoon, I will figure it out."

He ignores my comments.

"It can't be because you wanted to make your hometown proud," he continues. "You're not like them. Surely you must feel much more comfortable here with me than you would drinking with the locals at the Red Rabbit. Have I hit a nerve?"

"No," I answer him.

I turn to leave and once again I'm stopped in my tracks by some artwork on his walls. It's been behind me hanging next to the door.

This painting I've seen many times before. I was practically obsessed with the image as a child after seeing it pictured in an anthology Tommy owned titled *Irish Tales of the Macabre and Supernatural*. I was mesmerized by the ravished sleeper's soft outflung arms wrapped in gauzy bed-clothes and her exposed alabaster throat and the foul incubus squatting on her chest staring out of the scene with a gargoyle's warning glower.

"Are you familiar with Henry Fuseli's *The Nightmare*?" he asks me. "It's one of the most reproduced images in European art. Unfortunately that's what this is, too. A reproduction. The original is in a museum in Detroit. Seems a pity to have it buried there, but I suppose it's an apt place to showcase a nightmare.

"Interesting theory those Victorians had, attributing bad dreams to malevolent spirits raping us in our sleep. They understood there's no such thing as safety. Anywhere. For anyone. Not even for a baby in her mother's arms."

His words make the skin crawl on the back of my neck, but I won't give him the satisfaction of letting him know he's getting to me.

I turn back around and offer my hand.

"Good-bye, Mr. Dawes."

He rises from his desk and takes it.

"Good luck solving your mystery, and if you see any dead coal miners, I'd advise you to run."

Run. That's what I want to do, but I manage to maintain my composure all the way back through the house until I arrive outside again, where I take big gulps of the cold air.

I most ardently don't believe in ghosts or spirits of any kind or that anyone has the ability to communicate with the dead, predict the future, or know which card I picked through telepathic means. But I do believe humans possess a sensory level that reaches beyond our accepted faculties. I've met people who for lack of a more accurate descriptive phrase give me the creeps. This isn't merely a mental sensation but a physical one, as well. Refined, polished, attractive, well-spoken, wealthy Walker Dawes is one of those people. I'd rather spend an afternoon with Carson Shupe.

The freezing rain has stopped, but it's still an unpleasant day and I'm surprised to see someone out walking. A woman comes toward me from the end of the driveway in a leisurely stroll, smoking a cigarette.

She's a leggy beauty in jeans, high-heeled boots that hit her midthigh, and a long black mink coat draped over her shoulders. Her hair has a chestnut sheen to it and is expensively unkempt. It might even be considered tousled.

She approaches without showing any sign that she's seen me, but heads right toward me, stops, and blows smoke in wreaths above her head the same way Walker did.

"Who are you?" she asks bluntly.

"Danny Doyle. I mean, Sheridan. Sheridan Doyle."

She stares openly at me. I try to read some kind of emotion in her steady gaze but get nothing but flat appraisal. Her eyes are an oxidized copper. Greenish brown. Brownish green. They're not blue.

"Which is it, Danny or Sheridan?"

"Both, I guess."

"I think I prefer Danny."

She reaches her free hand toward me, pulls open my overcoat, and appraisingly strokes my suit jacket.

"Gucci?" she asks.

"Armani."

"Really?"

She bites her lower lip.

"Double-breasted," she says appreciatively. "They're back in style."

"But with a modernized cut," I tell her. "Shorter length, and a peak lapel rather than a notch."

She takes her hand away and starts to stroke the lushness of her coat instead.

"You can't be from around here."

"I grew up in Lost Creek but I've lived in Philadelphia for many years."

"Why are you here now?"

"I'm visiting family."

I watch the rise and fall of the cigarette to her lips. I wonder with morbid fascination if the ring she's wearing is made from the same ruby that was pinned to Walker Dawes' chest the day of the execution. If it is, the stone was present the day Tommy's father stood clutching his mother's hand and watched his own father hang. It was an inanimate witness to the beginning of what my family would become.

"I'm visiting, too," she says. "I haven't lived here since I was a child. Scarlet," she introduces herself. "Scarlet Dawes."

"Anna Greger was your nanny."

I realize it's a strange thing for me to have said, but it was the first thing to pop into my head. I wait to see if she's put off by the question but she doesn't appear to be.

"Yes. She was."

"Did you know any of her family? Her cousin Marcella?"

"I didn't even know she had a family."

"You were here the night she killed herself?"

"I was ten."

"I'd imagine something like that would leave a lasting impression on a young child."

"I'll never forget the smell."

She takes another drag off her cigarette.

"You talk like a shrink," she says while finally offering up a smile.

The expression is pretty but not inviting.

"Do you have a lot of experience with shrinks?" I ask.

"Some."

She keeps staring at me with the bored yet wholly alert gaze of a cat.

"I should be going," I tell her.

"Do you have a card, Danny?"

I give her one.

She reads it and smiles.

"Ah, I was right. You are a shrink."

She continues to look at the card and I notice the crimson sparkle of the ring again and suddenly see myself, a pale, skinny kid wearing my school's red track uniform, crashing through the dense, dark woods surrounding our town. It's not a race. I'm fleeing from someone, something.

My pulse races, my breath quickens as if I'm actually running. I feel faint. I used to have panic attacks as a child but none were ever severe enough to make me pass out.

I see less and less of me as I get deeper into the trees, just a flash of bone white and blood red, until I disappear completely into the lawless shadows.

When I come to, she's gone and I'm facedown in the whitewashed gravel staring at the glowing orange embers of her discarded butt.

ON MY WAY BACK to Tommy's house I drive through town past the Red Rabbit and see Rafe's car parked on the street.

I slow down as I recall Walker's comment that I'd be more comfortable with him in his mansion than here with someone like Rafe at this very bar.

I park my car and go in.

It's barely noon on a weekday but there are about a dozen men sitting at the bar and the few scarred wooden tables. There's no music playing. No TV blasting. No women. No pool tables. No food. Barely any light. These patrons don't come here to unwind or socialize. They come here to drink. The reason they drink is to get drunk. Sex, noise, and conversation only get in the way.

I take a seat next to Rafe. He doesn't look surprised to see me.

He takes in the dirt on my coat, the tear in the knee of one of my pant legs, and the scrape on my nose and forehead, but doesn't ask what happened. He knows I'll tell him when I'm ready.

I used to come to the Rabbit as a child searching for my father before I learned that it was better to be scared alone in my house than to be scared by him at home with me. The Rabbit was never much to look at from the outside: a simple two-story square of whitewashed brick. Over time the paint had flaked revealing patches of pink underneath. At night the other buildings blended into the dark hills behind them, while the Rabbit glowed like a skull still mottled with flesh. I'd keep my head down the last fifty feet or so as I walked toward it and pushed open the heavy front door.

If my dad was in a good mood he'd sit me up on a stool next to him and order me a ginger ale. I'd look around me through the haze of cigarette smoke at the methodically drinking miners, many of them silent, others communicating with each other in low rumbles. All of them had showered after their shift but their necks, the palms of their hands, and the insides of their ears were still lined with grime, and the smell of sour sweat still clung to them. Their hooded eyes would occasionally flick in my direction, and I'd see the guarded curiosity and hostility of an animal that's been beaten but also fed by the same man.

I knew they had all just returned to the surface of the earth after spending eight hours working a mile beneath it. During the short days of winter, they became entirely nocturnal creatures, leaving their homes in darkness to go work in darkness only to return in darkness.

I could never figure out if they were more or less than human: gods or beasts? Should I respect or pity them? All I knew for sure was I didn't want to be one of them.

I stare at the old black-and-white framed photos of mines and miners hanging behind the bar in the midst of shelved liquor bottles and automatically fall into the silent reverie required by the atmosphere.

The building itself is on the National Register of Historic Places. A plaque outside explains its sinister role in the Nellies' crimes. This is where they met to plot and conspire against the mine bosses and plan their murders, or maybe it's where they met to drink and do nothing more.

No one will ever know the whole truth about what happened. I doubt anyone even knew at the time. Written statements were never taken. No journals or letters existed. The miners and their families were illiterate. The subject was taboo. People wouldn't talk; some because they were trying to protect the Nellies, but many because they were afraid of them. The Nellies could be just as deadly to their own kind as they were to their enemies if they thought someone was against them.

The bartender sets a beer down in front of Rafe as he swipes away an empty.

"I'll have the same," I say. "And a shot of whiskey. Make it two."

Rafe looks at me out of the corner of his eye. He knows I don't drink much.

"One of those for me?"

"Make it four," I call out.

The drinks arrive.

"What's the occasion?" he asks.

I raise the beer to my lips, take a few gulps, and throw back both shots.

Rafe watches me carefully.

"I just met a fembot," I tell him.

sixteen

WAKING THE NEXT MORNING from a dreamless sound sleep startles me almost as much as coming out of one of my nightmares. I marvel at the sight of my calm prone body extending down the length of the couch neatly covered with a blanket. The pillows are beneath my head where they belong. I'm not sweating, twitching, palpitating, or hyperventilating.

The sun is shining and the light reflects off the icicles hanging outside the windows, scattering Tommy's drab carpet with shards of rainbow. I can almost believe my talk with Walker Dawes and the note Tommy found in his mailbox were part of a bad dream I didn't have.

I told Rafe about both while drinking at the Rabbit and also about meeting Scarlet. He listened and didn't mock my suspicions about Scarlet, but he also didn't take them seriously.

He said we'd talk about it more today. He invited me to work at the police station. Tommy doesn't have an Internet connection and the nearest Wi-Fi is at the McDonald's in Hellersburg. When I tried to work there two days ago after bringing Mom home, I was informed by a large, pimply female employee half my age who called me "hon" that if I was going to sit there all day I had to buy more than a coffee. I ordered a salad. When I went there again yesterday evening, she told me her manager said I was going to have to order "something with meat in it."

I haven't even made it off the couch before I hear the tap of Tommy's cane. He comes into the room from upstairs, fully dressed and looking like he's on a mission.

We didn't say another word to each other yesterday about the note. We also haven't had a talk about Mom's situation.

"Is Mom still asleep?" I ask him.

"Fast asleep. She had a bad night so I got her to take a sleeping pill," he says guiltily. He could never have convinced her to take one willingly. "She should be out for a while still."

He heads for his coat and cap.

"Where are you off to at this hour?"

"Emergency breakfast meeting of the NONS."

I can't help smiling. He sees me.

"I know what you're thinking, but what happened to Marcella Greger is serious business."

"I agree, but it doesn't involve the Nellies."

"Everything here involves the Nellies."

He slowly lowers himself into his chair to sit while he puts on his boots.

"I was just thinking the other night about Prosperity back when he was just little Jimmy McNab staring at those pictures he loved so much daydreaming about coming to America. If he'd never seen those pictures he might not have ended up here. You and I would've never existed and Marcella Greger might still be alive."

I follow the reasoning behind the first part of his last statement, but the second is a little convoluted.

"I thought little Jimmy McNab ended up here because he got arrested when he was fourteen and his aunt put him on a boat to America rather than live with the embarrassment of the nephew she'd raised being put in jail. What did that have to do with the pictures?"

"He loved those pictures," Tommy begins.

I knew he'd take the bait. I've heard this tale countless times, just like all the other stories about Prosperity, but I never tire of any of them.

"He'd take any opportunity to go to the shop in town where they hung behind a counter. They were black-and-white ink etchings titled

Scenes of American Life. The first one showed cowboys and Indians racing toward each other across a prairie on crazy-eyed horses, guns blazing, tomahawks raised, all of them smiling with the maniacal glee of men who enjoy massacre. It was called *Land of Danger.*

"The second was a picture of a black locomotive, again racing across a prairie, with men leaning out the windows shooting at huge, bulky, hairy beasts who seemed to be all head (he'd find out someday they were called buffalos) and beautiful women with curls peeking out from beneath high hats cheering on the carnage. This one was called *Land of Progress.*

"The last one was his favorite and it depicted a serenely content farm family of four—a father, mother, son, and daughter—standing in front of bountiful fields stretching into the distance where they melted into a sparkling sea perfectly suited for swimming and boating. It was called *Land of Prosperity.*"

When I was a child, this was always the moment in the story where I'd butt in and point out excitedly, "Just like his name!"

To which Tommy would nod and say, "That's how he came to have that name. When he got to America he only spoke three words of English. Do you know what they were?"

"Danger, progress, and prosperity," I'd provide.

"Exactly," he'd reply. "Now, the men he worked with in the pits in Lost Creek were very familiar with the word 'danger,' and the word 'progress' held little interest for them, but 'prosperity' was an impressive-sounding bit of language. Before you knew it, that's what they were calling him."

Tommy catches himself as he realizes he's started to tell me a story I know well enough to recite word for word. He grabs hold of his cane and starts to get up. I make a move to help him and he waves me away.

"I was going over to the police station. Rafe said I could use their Wi-Fi," I tell him. "Will Mom be okay alone?"

"I should be back before she wakes up."

I wait until he and his truck rattle off down the street, then I get dressed in a pair of J. Crew broken-in chinos, a Tom Ford mulberry cable-knit crewneck, Zegna leather-and-waxed-canvas laceless wingtips, and a John Varvatos navy blue peacoat with a subtle metallic sheen. I'm anticipating a casual day.

During the drive to the station house, I notice a fair amount of vehicles parked along the main street and people milling around the gallows taking pictures with cameras and their phones again.

Parker hasn't taken another hostage. Rafe warned me about this. He told me since news of Marcella Greger's murder and the hanging stick figure painted in blood has spread, the town has lost its collective mind. For the first time since the living Nellies roamed these hills, doors are being locked, guns are being propped in the corners of bedrooms, spilled salt is being tossed over shoulders, and prayers are being frantically whispered upon hearing the usual bumps in the night.

Residents have been calling with reports of strange happenings that they insist can't be explained, funny noises, and sightings of lights bobbing in the woods.

A woman laid out a pink nightgown on her bed before she went to take a shower; when she came back the nightgown had been replaced with her green one. A man parked his snowmobile in his garage front end first, but when he went to take it out again, someone had turned it around. A microwave oven started without anyone pressing any buttons. Several dollars in loose change and a six-pack of beer disappeared from an unlocked car parked in the owner's driveway. The stools at the Red Rabbit were stacked on the bar right side up instead of the usual upside down. A garden gnome went missing.

Rafe has been unable to display the slightest bit of concern over any of these reports and has sent Billy and Troy and the two other officers employed by Creekside Township to respond to the calls, while he spends most of his working hours looking into the Marcella Greger murder even though the investigation has been officially taken over by the state police.

I find Billy Smalls standing inside the door of the station house staring in a kind of weary amazement at a rapidly talking, wildly gesticulating woman. Troy is supporting a swaying drunk by the forearm.

I greet them both then take a seat behind Rafe's desk, possibly the most impersonal workstation I've ever encountered. No family photos or sports memorabilia clutter the area. No notes or comics are posted on the filing cabinet with amusing magnets. Even the cup holding his pens is devoid of a logo.

I Skype Max. He appears on my computer screen, his elliptical bulk filling it like a satellite photo of a verdant planet. He's dressed like a forest in an evergreen mock turtleneck beneath a moss green suede jacket with a grass green silk pocket square.

"I haven't scheduled anything for you for the rest of the week and through the weekend," he begins before I can say a word. "When do you think you'll be back?"

"I'll be back in three days for Carson's execution."

Max says nothing. He reaches for his coffee mug offscreen.

"I thought you had decided not to go."

"He asked me to be there. Plus I had a nightmare about it," I explain. "It was my subconscious telling me I should go."

"Are you sure about that? Maybe you should talk to a shrink?"

"I know your feelings on this subject, but I feel differently."

He clams up and drinks his coffee, his way of showing his disapproval, but he's never able to keep quiet for long. Disapproval is one of his favorite topics.

"He sodomized, castrated, and murdered little boys," he erupts. "And please don't let the next words out of your mouth be that he's not all that bad."

"I would never say that. He is all that bad."

"How's your grandfather?"

"He's fine. It turns out there was no reason for me to come here after all."

"There was a reason," he says. "There are lots of reasons, I'm sure."

We finish our call. I settle in to do some actual work, but within a few minutes I'm distracted by the temptation to Google Scarlet Dawes. Once I do this, the floodgates of my curiosity are thrown open and before I know it I've moved well past the typical socialite photos of her at gala events and parties on the arms of tycoons and celebrities and go to a site of archived newspaper stories I often use when researching clients and their families.

Scarlet's life appears to be relatively uneventful except for two very eventful events both notable for the level of horror and tragedy surrounding them along with the fact that Scarlet was nearby for both though not implicated in any way. The first is the suicide of her nanny. The second is the accidental death of a classmate at the private school she attended as a teen.

I travel all the way back to the day of her birth and find a front-page newspaper clipping of Gwen and Walker Dawes taking their newborn daughter, Scarlet, home from the hospital. Gwen's wearing a chic, polka-dot dress and high heels just forty-eight hours after giving birth. She's holding the infant in one arm and waving with the other, her smile looking strained. Walker's smiling, too, but without showing any teeth. He has one hand on her shoulder and holds out the other in front of him like he's stopping traffic or heading for the end zone.

Only our local paper would consider this event important enough to make the front page and would use the headline "It's Not a Boy!"

I hear clicking and clacking coming from behind me. I crane my neck around and find Rafe looking over my shoulder at my computer screen.

He walks around and takes a seat on the corner of his desk.

"I've been doing a little poking around about Scarlet," I tell him, glancing back at my screen.

"Me too. Did you stumble on the story about the death of one of her classmates at her boarding school?"

"Just the bare facts."

"I made some calls. The girl died of an allergic reaction to penicillin. She knew she had the allergy and so did everyone else. No one could imagine how she'd end up taking it accidentally. She had tried to commit suicide before so they chalked it up to that. This was one of the reasons why she was there. It was a loony bin as far as I'm concerned, but the nice way of putting it would be to say it was a special school for very rich troubled girls."

"Why was Scarlet there?"

"We'd have to ask her parents."

We fall silent, each of us mulling around our own thoughts.

"Getting back to Marcella Greger and your theory," Rafe says, "have you come up with a motive?"

"Could it have something to do with Anna's death? Maybe Marcella knew something incriminating and Scarlet killed her to keep her quiet?"

"I don't know, but we're going to try and figure it out," Rafe replies. "We're going to start by talking to someone who was there. Let's go for a ride."

We're walking toward the door when a roar of engines comes from outside the station. Everyone inside stops what they're doing and heads for the windows.

"The *Ghost Sniffers!*" Billy Smalls cries out.

Two large vans have pulled up in the parking lot, one solid black and the other custom painted in an elaborate swirling montage of ghosts and ghouls surrounded by neon green. "The Mayhem Machine" is written out in bones dripping with blood.

"It looks like a diabolical version of the Mystery Machine from the *Scooby Doo* cartoons," I say.

"That's what it is," Billy explains, barely able to contain his excitement. "They're kind of based on *Scooby-Doo,* but they're not funny and they use real people."

The passenger-side door of the Mayhem Machine opens and a young woman gets out. She's dressed completely in skintight black leather. The only areas of exposed flesh are her hands, throat, and considerable cleavage, and all of it is covered in tattoos. Flames leap up her neck licking at her jawline, giving the impression that she's peering out of a burning building.

Her face might be considered pretty but I can't tell because I'm too distracted by the various metal rings protruding from her nose, upper lip, and eyebrows. Her long, straight, jet-black hair has an iridescent gleam to it and oozes down her back like an oil spill.

"Define 'real people,'" Rafe comments.

"That's Bambi," Billy tells us.

I think of the clean, perky, fiery-haired cartoon Daphne with her lilting voice and pink tights from my youth. I almost want to cry.

"And that's Brick."

A hulking brute comes around from the driver's side. Despite the cold, he's not wearing a coat. I'm not sure he could find a coat to fit over his massive upper arms and shoulders, one of which is tattooed with a blood-soaked woman being devoured by the undead. His head is shaved except for a spiky black Mohawk down the center. He sports a thick utility belt hung with a walkie-talkie, a flashlight, a hatchet, a water bottle, a crucifix, and a canister of hair gel. He has a skull ring on every finger and his nails are painted black.

A tall, gangly, goateed African American in a purple tracksuit, untied red high-tops, a gold ball cap with the bill worn to the side, dark reflective shades, and a long fur-lined purple trench coat disembarks from the other van.

Troy steps up beside us.

"Z Mac," he says. "Short for Zombie Master."

I look over at Rafe, who stares at the ceiling.

I'm afraid to ask but I must.

"Where's Velma?"

Z Mac joins Bambi, who's begun combing the air with a device that looks like a cross between a waffle iron and a calculator, while Brick trudges back to the other van and pulls open the side door.

A small, trim man with a perfectly round pink-cheeked face wearing glasses set in perfectly round tortoiseshell frames jumps out. He, like Bambi, is dressed entirely in black. They may in fact be wearing the same leather jeans and combat boots in the same size, but his upper body is differently attired in a turtleneck and a long black suede coat with its hem flapping at his heels.

"There's Velma," Troy says.

"Velma is a man?"

"Kind of," Billy replies.

A crowd of onlookers has already started to gather around the Ghost Sniffers. I don't know where they came from so quickly, but I imagine the sight of these newcomers to have the same hypnotic pull as an alien spaceship setting down in the town square.

Velma disregards the traffic slowing as it passes by and the gawkers trickling toward them. He says something to his companions, then turns and marches toward the station and pushes open the doors double-handed like a tiny gay gunslinger.

"Excuse me," he addresses no one in particular. "Who's in charge here?"

We all look at Rafe, who doesn't say anything.

Troy and Billy step forward together and introduce themselves.

Velma gives them an appraising look before pulling off one black leather glove one finger at a time and extending his hand in midair waiting for one of them to shake it. Troy goes first.

"We always make our presence known with local law enforcement before we begin an investigation as a courtesy so there won't be any misunderstandings," Velma says briskly.

"We appreciate that," Billy replies.

"Of course we're expecting to experience the most activity at the gallows and the jail, but we'd also like to get inside the house where Marcella Greger was killed."

"That won't be possible," Rafe speaks up. "It's still a crime scene."

Velma gives him a once-over, too. A slight wince crosses his features as his eyes land on Rafe's corduroy blazer and skinny knit tie worn with a plaid flannel shirt.

"And you are?"

"The guy in charge."

"Well, Guy in Charge, can we see crime scene photos?"

"No."

"You're no fun at all. Can I bribe you? Can I buy you some doughnuts or a sports jacket from this century?"

Rafe narrows his eyes until they are nothing more than two bright blue slits set among the rest of the lines in his face. His candy chewing has slowed to a contemplative rhythmic clicking.

"The investigation has been taken over by the state police," he explains, "and I'd pay good money to watch you try and bribe one of them."

"Where's Wade?" Troy asks, hoping to change the subject.

"Oh, Wade," Velma sniffs. "He's in the van having a drink. The

temperamental genius. He's still pouting over losing that fan-favorite reality show award to that blond tranny Real Housewife. When he found
out he threw up. I kid you not. Blech! All over the couch."

"He seems way too classy to do something like that," Billy says.

"Oh, he is. He was mortified. But don't let his public façade fool
you. He has his moments. Once at a party at Woody Harrelson's house
that got completely out of hand he pissed all over Woody's patio!
Scout's honor. Fortunately he and Woody are good friends and Woody
thought it was hysterical. I can assure you he'll never let Wade forget
that one."

Velma finally notices me.

"Oh my God," he gasps. "Is that the John Varvatos shimmer peacoat? In navy? I didn't know he did it in navy. He does everything in
black and gray, although he does have a prewrinkled black-and-white-
checked shirt with a fine line of aubergine shot through it that I'm completely jonesing for."

"I almost didn't buy this coat," I confide in him. "His clothes are a
little too rock and roll for me."

"Nonsense. You look amazing. I should've gone with my first instinct and bought one in black instead of this old thing. I'm too short to
pull off a duster."

His gaze finally makes its way down to my feet. He lets out a clipped
shriek.

"Laceless wingtips?"

I nod.

"Who *are* you?" he asks breathlessly.

Before I can answer he holds up his hand requesting silence as he
receives a communiqué through his Bluetooth ear bud.

"His Highness has finally deigned to grace us with his presence."

He steps back and holds the door open. Everyone in the station, including the impossible-to-impress Rafe, moves closer and peers outside
at the open van waiting for the renowned psychic's appearance.

A teeny brown and white dog in a green argyle sweater comes flying
out of the van and proceeds to high-step jauntily across the icy parking
lot until he enters the building, where he rushes crazily from person to

person sniffing at ankles and occasionally pausing to gaze soulfully into someone's eyes.

"Wade Van Landingham is a rat in a coat?" Rafe asks.

"He's a fox terrier," Velma replies with a languid haughtiness, "and that's a cashmere cardigan."

The dog comes to a skidding halt in front of Rafe, who towers over him. Their eyes lock. Wade sits up in a begging position, throws his head back, and flails at the air with his little paws like he's paddling to stay afloat.

"He senses something special about your aura," Velma explains.

All movement ceases and Wade closes his eyes. The dog holds the position sitting back on his hind legs with his paws crossed in front of him for at least a full minute. No one moves or speaks or even seems to breathe. He finally breaks his trance and addresses Velma with a few high-pitched staccato barks.

"He says you feel guilty about the lives you took during the war," Velma translates. "He says there's a Vietnamese soldier who wants to speak to you from the other side."

Rafe doesn't respond in any way. He knows how easy it is to re-search the backgrounds of the local police officers and how anyone knowing he'd been in Vietnam could take a wild guess that he might have killed an enemy soldier. I know all of this as well, but I also know his story of killing a soldier in hand-to-hand combat who was "just like" him, and I'm taken aback for a moment, but the feeling quickly passes. As for everyone else in the room, their awe is palpable.

"Let's see how good he really is," Rafe says, breaking the silence. "Let's see if he can read my mind."

He places his middle and index fingers at his temple and glowers down at Wade, who holds Rafe's stare for a few seconds until his entire body begins to shiver. He lets out a loud yelp, turns, and runs away with his tail tucked between his legs.

Rafe grins broadly.

"He's not bad," he says.

Velma shoots him a scathing look and chases after his canine charge.

On our way to Rafe's car we pass Velma surrounded by the rest of the paranormals. Wade is lying on his back cradled in his arms performing a very convincing dead faint, but turns his head and opens his eyes as Rafe walks by. I swear the dog winks.

"I ALMOST QUIT AFTER that," Dave Rosko says, throwing a shovelful of snow off his driveway into his yard. "I walked out of that house and said to myself, that's it. I can't ever look at something like that again."

He's a short, stocky man with a grizzled crew cut, a lightning bolt scar on his forehead from a quad accident, and a bumper sticker on his truck that reads: I Support PETA: People Eating Tasty Animals. When his mother wasn't able to do it, he identified his father's remains after the explosion in Lost Creek Mine No. 6. He's been Barclay's fire chief for twenty years. Rafe tells me it takes a lot to disturb his sensibilities.

"You think you can handle it because you've seen it in movies," he continues, "although I gotta tell you I never saw anything like that even in the movies. She was . . ." he begins with a grimace, then pauses.

He lets the shovel fall to the ground and crosses his arms over his chest while pulling one knee up into a partial fetal position.

"She was kind of like this, protecting herself from the pain. Her skin was completely charred but she was still recognizable. Her face—"

He stops altogether and stares hard at the sky.

"People don't burn fast. You could see the expression on her face. It was still there. The agony. Her mouth was open, screaming. Most fire victims die of smoke inhalation. It's not a good way to go either, but at least they don't know the pain of being burned alive."

He shakes his head like he's trying to get rid of the image.

"Wasn't there a police investigation?" I ask Rafe.

"Not much of one. We found a suicide note and a gas can and part of a lighter in her room."

"What did the note say?"

"'I want to die. I hate it here.'"

"'I hate it here'?" I repeat the words. "That sounds like something a child would say. Where did you find it?"

"In the kitchen. It was in her handwriting. There were notes from her posted on a bulletin board in the pantry. We compared them. It looked authentic."

"Still," I say skeptically, "suicide? The only instances of self-immolation I know of have been related to extreme political or religious protests. Women traditionally commit suicide by taking an overdose or cutting their wrists, but almost always in a bathtub. They're concerned with not leaving a mess behind for others to clean up."

"Well, Anna Greger sure as hell wasn't worried about a mess," Dave says. "Accelerant fires burn hot and fast. The entire room was a loss. We found her near the windows. She'd pulled down the curtains."

"She had second thoughts?" I ask.

"Looked that way. Would be hard not to. But she'd poured a whole can of gasoline all over herself. There was no way she could've put it out on her own once she lit up."

"Suicide?" I ask again.

"I admit I never felt right about that explanation," Dave says, "but there was the note and—"

"There were no suspects," Rafe joins in. "No motives. She was a single woman with no immediate family who took care of Walker Dawes' kids and lived with them full time. She didn't have a husband or boyfriend. Who would want to kill her? And kill her like that?"

"How did the Dawes family react?" I ask Dave.

"The wife was hysterical. Walker was pretty shaken up, too, but he did a good job of concealing it. We never even saw the little boy, Wesley. He was only five, I think. Then there was the daughter, Scarlet."

He shakes his head again.

"She saw it."

"What did she see?"

"Her nanny burning."

"She said that?"

"I'll never forget it. She said, 'I saw Nanny burning.' Cool as a cucumber."

"She was in the room with her?"

"Mrs. Dawes told us Scarlet had bad dreams and sometimes she got up in the middle of the night and went looking for Anna. Problem was she also said Anna always slept with her door closed and if the fire had been started when the door was closed and someone came along and opened that door, the back draft would've created an explosion. The whole hallway would've went up with her in it. The burn pattern was all wrong. The fire started while the door was open."

"So the night she decides to kill herself Anna leaves the door open? And Scarlet just happens by? No one thought this sounded suspicious?" I say.

Rafe and Dave look at each other.

"What were we supposed to be suspicious of? To think this cute little girl had something to do with it? She was ten years old. We figured she was in shock. Something like that happens, you can't blame her for getting her facts confused, except . . ."

"Except what?"

"She didn't act like someone in shock. She wasn't upset at all. She gave us the facts like she was reading them off a script."

"How did her parents react to her statement?"

"I got the feeling Walker didn't want us talking to her at all, which I guess is understandable considering what had just happened. But her mom insisted she talk to us. She was a nervous wreck. Pacing the whole time. Wringing her hands. After Scarlet said something, she'd look at us, not at her, like she wanted to be sure we heard what she said. I have to say she was a creepy kid."

"You just said she was a cute little girl."

"Not creepy-looking, mind you. She was beautiful, all dressed up in a long nightgown with lace around the neck. She had these big green eyes and long shiny hair. Looked like a doll. But there was something off about her. I raised five kids and none of them ever looked that good when they just got out of bed."

"She was too calm," I state.

"Not just calm. It was like she was bored. When she finished talking to us, she looked right at her mom and asked if she could have some ice cream."

None of us have anything to say after that. We stand in the cold and

snow without speaking at all for a length of time that would be impossible among any of the people I know back in the city.

Dave reaches down and picks up his shovel.

"One more thing that's always kind of bugged me about that night. It's probably nothing, but I was one of the last guys out, since I was the youngest and I got all the crap work. I was lugging out some equipment when Mrs. Dawes caught hold of my arm and said, almost begging, 'Can you help me?' I thought she was talking about cleaning up the fire damage, and I told her we didn't do that. They'd have to call a private contractor."

"Sometimes I wonder though," he says while his eyes travel along the chimneys across the street, pausing for a moment at each plume of smoke. "I wonder if that's what she was talking about."

seventeen

M Y MOTHER HAD TO have killed her baby because there was no one else who could have done it. Anna Greger had to have killed herself because there was no other way it could have happened. Neither of these scenarios were ever actually proven beyond a reasonable doubt. The explanation given for each event came from the necessity for an explanation and the inability of anyone to come up with a better one.

Now the case of Marcella Greger's murder looks as if it's heading down a similar path. Two theories are currently circulating: a random psycho broke into her house and killed her even though there was no sign of a break-in or a struggle and nothing was stolen and it would be highly unusual for a psycho to have the proclivity or take the time to carefully draw a picture of a stick figure hanging from a gallows on the bathroom wall in blood. Or the ghost of Prosperity McNab did it. In my opinion, the chance of either proving to be true is about the same.

My suggestion to Rafe that Scarlet Dawes could be involved is too outlandish. It's as inconceivable as the thought that someone other than Anna Greger lit herself on fire or that someone other than my mentally ill mother would have had a reason or opportunity to kill her infant and bury her in our backyard.

But what if the explanation for all three of these tragedies happening in this tiny town is an unthinkable one? Does that mean it must be otherworldly?

My mind drifts back to my case files sitting in Tommy's living room and the crime scene photos of Baby Trusty.

Or could the answer be a monster did it?

MY FATHER'S HOUSE SQUATS on a muddy slope at the very edge of the street at the end of its row as if unwanted and gradually shunned there over time, almost hidden now by vines and rogue shrubberies and a sprawling rhododendron on one side that's grown as high as the roof. Although practically opaque with dirt, the windows aren't broken and suggest someone is living here, however it's obvious no one ever looks out of or into these bleary panes of glass. They're the eyes of a beast staring slyly and stupidly at the outside world, concealing secrets and plotting destruction.

I'm convinced this structure has a memory, and when my father dies, I'm going to have it torn down. It's the only merciful thing to do.

I get out of my car and start up the front walk toward the porch. My tsunami guilt rises up before me, a gigantic shimmering wall poised to crush me. It's grown bigger in the last several hours.

"Where's Molly? Where's my baby? I can't find my baby!" my mom shrieked at the top of her lungs while being hauled off in handcuffs.

Those were her words. Even after my dad found the body and called the police. Even after they explained to her that her baby was dead.

"Where's Molly?" she kept screaming.

She's crazy, everyone said. Only a crazy woman could look at her own dead baby and ask where she is. I agreed. My mom was crazy. I abandoned her. I didn't stand up for her.

But Tommy did. Tommy never wavered in his insistence that Mom was incapable of killing anyone, least of all her own child. And who would know better? Mom was his child. He'd been dealing with her problems for twenty-five years. I'd only been in her life for five, and she'd been taking care of me.

The guilt crashes down all around me. I stand perfectly still on the bottom porch step and wait for it to do its damage then ebb before confronting my father.

I continue making my way up the steps. No matter how many years I stay away, I can never approach the front door of this house without my heart racing and muscles tensing. In my head, I'm already running.

I'm about to knock when the door opens and my dad is standing in the shadows, his silver beer can and the white globe of his belly in an undershirt the only parts of him fully visible.

The surprise makes me take a step back and I'm certain he's been watching me from inside along with the house, the two of them muttering to each other about what a useless, chickenshit of a boy I am.

"You finally decided to come see me," he says. "I heard you was in town taking care of Tommy. What a wasted trip. Someone that old you just let 'em die."

He takes another step toward me and comes farther into the daylight.

My eyes drop instinctively to his feet. He's wearing slippers with tears in them where the padding shows through. He can't do much damage with those.

"You know there are tribes in Africa who take their old people and stick 'em up in a tree with a basket of fruit when they get a certain age and just leave 'em there 'cause they can't keep up anymore. Someone should've stuck Tommy up a tree a long time ago," he goes on.

He's become an old man himself, his drinking having aged him well beyond his actual years. The skin on his face is sallow, spotted with broken capillaries like someone has dipped a finger into a pool of blood and flicked it at him. Deputy Dawg bags hang beneath his foggy eyes. I wonder how much of his stomach's girth is the result of his diet and how much is caused by the bloat that accompanies the beginnings of liver failure.

I feel him studying me.

"Takes a lot to get you out of that ivory tower of yours."

"I don't live in an ivory tower." I'm able to find my voice. "'Ivory tower' is a reference to academia."

"Jesus. Still can't say a goddamn word around you without you correcting it. So what color is your tower? Green 'cause it's covered in money?"

I swallow back the burning in my throat.

"I don't have a tower."

He takes a gulp from his beer and lowers his gaze to my feet. He stares at my shoes. To him they represent Management.

"How much you pay for those?"

"Not much."

My dad openly, almost happily, resents my success. When I was younger, he took my aspirations as personal insults. He thought the only reason I got good grades was to try and make him feel stupid, the only reason I wanted to go to college was because I thought I was better than him.

If he believed in evolution I'm sure he'd probably be convinced the only motivation Man had for learning to walk upright was so he could rub the monkeys' faces in it. But he's a creationist. He believes he was made in God's image.

"You here for a reason?"

"I wanted to talk to you about something. How are you doing?"

"I'm doing great as you can see."

Despite the outward appearance of his home and his person, I'm sure he is doing great because he's doing exactly what he wants to do: nothing with a beer chaser.

He hasn't worked in almost forty years but has somehow still been able to constantly upgrade his TVs, trucks, and power tools, the only things he cares about, and he was doing this even before I started sending him money.

"I'm glad to hear it."

I wait for him to ask about me, knowing he won't.

"I'm kind of busy right now," he says.

Crazy or not, I tell myself, a mother knows her own child.

"I really need to ask you something."

"How many years it been since I seen you and you suddenly need to ask me something? In person? Face to face?"

"Yes."

"Well?" he says.

"Was the dead baby Molly?" I'm able to push out.

"What? What'd you just say to me?"

I think he's going to hit me and I have to fight the urge to bolt. I clench my trembling fists and stick them into my coat pockets so he can't see them.

"Mom said it wasn't Molly but no one believed her. I have to know the truth. I don't care if you didn't stick up for her at the time."

"You listen here, boy. Your mother's fucking loony tunes. She killed her own baby and of course she's gonna lie about it."

"Dad . . ." I choke out the painful syllable.

I've always wanted to be able to say that word and have it mean something other than "Stop!"

"If that baby wasn't Molly, who the hell was it? Huh?"

"I don't know."

"And if that baby wasn't Molly, where's Molly? Huh?"

These were the same questions Rafe and I were asking earlier, but we were seriously trying to come up with answers. Why would Dad ask them? How would they even occur to him unless he's already asked them of himself?

"You should go," he says.

He takes a final gulp of beer and holds out the empty can to me.

"Pitch that for me."

I walk back to the street, holding the can in one hand, waiting to hear his door slam before laying my cheek against the roof of my car the way the teachers used to make me put my head down on my desk in shame when I finished my tests before everyone else.

eighteen

SCARLET

MY FRIEND COURTNEY HAD a pair of red shoes, too, but they were hideous, nothing like the ones that belonged to the yellow-haired girl I watched clip-clop across the Lost Creek elementary school gym. Technically, Courtney's weren't even shoes. They were ankle boots, flat and scrunched, the same color as a clown's nose. She tucked her jeans into them and wore them with one of her many drab oversize sweaters. Their boldness was completely out of character for her, and I often wondered what possessed her to buy them.

Courtney had her share of problems. She was an asthmatic bulimic who was addicted to pain medication, plagued with phobias, and had been discarded by her parents because they found her multiple suicide attempts to be inconvenient, especially the one that occurred during her father's bid for a senate seat.

I went to school with other girls who had even lengthier résumés of woe and ill-treatment, castoffs from wealthy families who didn't want to deal with them and their so-called problems: addicts, anorexics, suicides, manic-depressives, sluts, and kleptos. Bonsai Girls I called them after the mutant miniaturized trees everyone admires and wants to have but no one can keep alive except a trained expert. These girls were freaks of nature, too, their psyches stunted and deformed just like those tiny tree limbs.

Of all the Bonsai Girls, Courtney was the most rarified, the most delicate, the one requiring the most attention and skill to keep alive, the one whose loveliness and fragility and ability to exist in a world dominated by the large and loud impressed even the most callous soul.

I liked her well enough. She was no threat to me. My family had more money. I was prettier, smarter, and had a far superior wardrobe. I was better than her in every way I wanted to be. The only area where she excelled and I didn't was in getting people to love her. This didn't bother me because I've never had any desire to be loved. I prefer being feared. It gets the same results but without any hugging.

I never gave Courtney much thought until the arrival of Jacqueline, a newly transplanted fabulously discontented French Bonsai who had a penchant for stealing both things and people. Her parents chose to discard her after one too many expensive objets d'art disappeared from their home and she slept with both her mother's lover and her father's mistress.

We hit it off immediately, spending countless hours together blowing smoke rings and discussing how pointless everyone's existence was compared to ours. Despite her brooding Gallic ennui, she had a surprising sentimental streak. The first time I told her this, she blushed as adorably as Heather the Holiday Inn waitress.

Jacqueline had only one flaw I could discover: she was hopelessly smitten with the tragic, sweet, and wheezy Courtney. This didn't concern me at first, but eventually she started spending too much time with her, and when they weren't together, she talked about her endlessly.

The solution to this annoying state of affairs came to me during English class. Along with assigning us the usual literary crap penned by frigid nineteenth-century British females deemed appropriate for American girls of a certain age, we had a teacher who also tried to engage us in what she called "thought exercises." She presented us with moral dilemmas we might encounter in the real world and we had to write a short essay explaining what we would do and why.

One day the question was what happens if you fall in love with your best friend's boyfriend?

It wasn't much of a thought exercise in my opinion. There were only two answers: forget about the boy and stay true to your friend, or screw over your friend and go after the boy. In one scenario you're a drip, in the other you're a skank. I'm not either.

I wrote I would kill my friend, and when her boyfriend came to her funeral I would win his love by consoling him. This would be a win-win situation. I'd get the guy without betraying my gal pal.

The teacher refused to even grade my essay and I was sent to the school shrink, which was no big deal since we all saw him once a week anyway. More important, it gave me an idea for a way to get Jacqueline back.

Courtney had mentioned to me that she was allergic to penicillin when she saw me taking it when I had strep. She told me how it made her break out in these disgusting hives and how it made her trachea swell shut. I was skeptical. My brother, Wes, was allergic to cats, but all that happened to him was a runny nose and itchy eyes.

The infirmary always kept a small supply of the drug. It was easy enough to steal and easy enough to dissolve into a can of Dr Pepper that I brought to her one afternoon when she was studying alone in her room while her roommate was somewhere else.

I stayed and watched just to make sure everything went well. It turned out she was right: she really was allergic. From the way her eyes bulged and she clawed at her throat I could tell she was suffocating, and the hives were beyond disgusting; they covered her entire body like a film of scalded milk.

"I'm doing you a favor," I explained to her, and I think she understood what I meant.

She had tried to kill herself many times and failed; I took care of it for her. One more thing I was better at than she was.

However, my plan didn't work. Jacqueline was so devastated by what happened to Courtney that she had a nervous breakdown and dropped out of school. It was for the best. She was starting to bother me.

I've been thinking about Courtney because I've been thinking about the yellow-haired girl. I'd like to track her down and find out what happened to her, maybe drop in and pay her a visit and see if she still has those shoes.

I told Gwen I'm not leaving until I find out the truth behind Anna's letter and that involves finding a person, too, but I know I don't have the patience to mount a search on my own. I don't want to hire someone. I don't know what I'll find and I might not want to share the information with anyone, including a private investigator.

I did conduct a little Internet search on Danny Doyle, though. I should have known from the suit but I was still surprised to discover the extent of his success and fame. For a psychologist, that is.

Walker wouldn't tell me why Danny was here the other day, but I assume from the questions he asked me that the visit might have had something to do with Marcella Greger, although I don't know why he'd have any interest in that. I'm intrigued by him. I like go-getters. I can't stand the whiners who comprise most of the human race. "Boo hoo! My life sucks. Life isn't fair. Wah wah!"

That's why I've always secretly approved of the Nellies. They failed miserably, but at least they tried to get what they wanted. Anna used to fill my head with tales of their bravery and sacrifice. I knew her stories were biased and I couldn't believe everything she told me, but most of it sounded plausible.

She was related to one of the executed Nellies, a boy named Peter Tully. He was the only child of a widow who adored him, and she was so devastated by his untimely death that she died of a broken heart a month later. That's the nice version. Anna said she took some kind of poison and it was an agonizing death. Probably a lot like Courtney's.

Anna loved to tell me this particular story and I always suspected the reason behind it was because she liked rubbing in the fact that my own mother didn't love me at all. She could barely stand to be in the same room with me. If I were to die, she'd go on living just fine.

I thought I had resolved all my feelings of abandonment and betrayal by Anna a long time ago, but this note her cousin discovered has reopened all those scabbed-over wounds. I don't understand why she didn't tell me herself.

The only explanation I can come up with is that she was waiting until I got older. Maybe if she hadn't had her accident, she would've told me.

Everyone else called it a suicide. I called it an accident because I knew she didn't have any idea how upset I was going to be when she told me she was getting back together with her old boyfriend, the scum who got another woman pregnant and married her instead of Anna. They were running off together into the sunset and she was going to leave me behind with Gwen. Even this wasn't the part that bothered me the most. I couldn't get past the idea that she never stopped loving this jerk and was willing to forgive him. It really bothered me.

I guess it was a suicide and an accident. She accidentally caused her own death by disappointing me.

Walker and Gwen are having breakfast in the east-wing sunroom. Untouched silvery snow reaches over the grounds before blending into the lavender-shadowed hills. The sun is shining and the icy glare makes it almost impossible to look outside for too long.

I could live here someday. Not full time, obviously, but this place does have its charms. I know Wes won't fight me for the house. He hates it. He thinks it's haunted. And Gwen has no power anymore. I'd just have to get Walker out of the picture.

I walk over to the table and give Walker a kiss on the cheek. He's reading a newspaper and an iPad and doesn't look up at me but smiles and squeezes my hand I've laid on his shoulder.

I don't kiss Gwen. Instead, I toss a day-old newspaper onto the table in front of her. I know she must have already seen it but I can't help my-self.

"Look at that," I say. "Someone killed her."

Gwen's already poor color pales even further as she glances down at the front-page story about Marcella Greger. She reaches for her Bloody Mary.

"Isn't this cozy? One big happy family. Except for Wes, of course," I comment as I take a seat. "By the way, I think I'm going to visit him and the wifey and the girls in New York."

"That's a good idea, Button," Walker says.

"When?" Gwen asks, a note of panic in her voice.

"Not for a few days. I have some business to take care of first."

Clarence brings me a cup of coffee. I point to Gwen's drink and tell him I'll have one of those, too.

"So, Daddy," I say brightly and give Gwen a wink, "what do you think about what's going on around here? Did you hear about Marcella Greger's murder? She was Anna's cousin."

"I did hear. Terrible. The local consensus seems to be there's a random crazed killer roaming the countryside, since the woman didn't seem to have any enemies."

"So you don't think the Nellies have risen from the dead?"

He puts down his paper and smiles at me.

"Wouldn't this be the first place they'd come?"

We both laugh. Gwen downs half her drink.

"But how do you explain the gallows painted on her bathroom wall in blood? That doesn't sound like a random psycho. And what about Simon Husk?"

"Please, Scarlet. You sound like one of those NON people," Walker says.

Clarence brings me my Bloody Mary along with a bottle of Tabasco. He remembered I like things spicy.

"I guess it all depends on how you look at it," I respond. "Some people want them to remain standing forever as a reminder. Others want them torn down because they are a reminder. They consider them to be a black eye not only for the state but for the entire country."

"Let me tell you something about our country," Walker begins to pontificate, leaning back in his chair. "Not so very long ago my great-grandfather had ten men executed with hardly any evidence against them. The whole region, the whole state, the whole country rallied behind him and applauded his efforts to get rid of the riffraff that wanted to undermine capitalism with their unions. No one stood up for them. No one supported them and their struggle to try and provide safer working conditions and a fair wage for the common man or if they did, they kept it to themselves out of selfishness and fear.

"An individual's power put up those gallows and collective shame has kept them up. Nothing is more American than that."

He rises from his chair and I wonder if he's expecting us to applaud.

"Now, if you'll excuse me, ladies. I have some work to do."

Gwen stands, too, and watches her husband leave the room. She looks uncertainly back and forth from me to the door like she's trying to decide if she should make a break for it.

"Are you going to kill me, too?" she asks, trying to keep her voice from quavering.

I take the cap off the hot sauce and start shaking it into my drink.

"Kill you, too? Are you accusing me of being a killer, Gwen? What a drama queen you've become lately. Would you like me to kill you?"

She begins to speak and a sob catches in her throat. She swallows it and composes herself.

"Please stay away from my son."

I finish stirring my drink with a piece of celery then take a loud, crunching bite out of it.

"I have no interest in your son, lady. He's nobody to me."

I TRY TO HANG out at the house but everything reminds me of Anna. Not long after she died I was sent away to a boarding school. Prior to that I went to a private school, but it was close enough that I could still come home on weekends. I've never spent any substantial time in this house when she wasn't here.

Anna and I didn't have the smoothest relationship. We fought a lot, but only because we were both strong-willed and wanted our own way. When we agreed on something, all was well. When we didn't, things could get a little tense, but I respected the fact that she was the only person who ever stood up to me. She said it was for my own good. She was trying to provide the guidance and discipline a child needed from her mother that I didn't get from mine. I wasn't always receptive to the idea, but I knew she always had my back. She was the one person I could depend on.

I'll never forget the day she told me she was leaving.

One of the groundskeepers had shot and killed a rabid raccoon on our property. Anna, Wes, and I were out taking a walk when we came upon him pouring gasoline on the animal about to light him on fire.

Anna explained the disease to us, how it affected the brain and could turn even the most docile of creatures into killers that had to be destroyed. Even in death, their corpses were still dangerous. Only the cleansing power of fire could successfully defeat them.

Wes started to cry when the raccoon began to burn and Anna had to take him back to the house. I stayed and watched.

Later that same day she sat me down and explained about her boy-friend and how they were moving out west. She said she loved me and Wes, but she wanted to have her own children. It had never been her plan to spend her life taking care of Walker Dawes' children. She had taken the job on a temporary basis one summer to make money for col-lege and the only reason she was going to college was because her boy-friend had dumped her. Her intention had been to marry him right out of high school and stay in Lost Creek, but he got this other girl preg-nant.

As I listened to the familiar story, I seethed inside. I couldn't under-stand how she could be so stupid and selfish.

Unlike the raccoon, she wasn't dead when I lit her up. She was asleep under her blankets. The wet splash of the gasoline on her face woke her but she was disoriented and I was fast and once her hair began to burn, the pain and panic drove her from the bed and I was able to fin-ish dousing her everywhere else.

I said the same thing to her that I said to Courtney: "I'm doing you a favor." And I was.

She was about to completely screw up her life. This guy would never be true to her. He was going to hurt her again. And it was obvious she was never going to get over him. I won't deny that I was very upset over how she was behaving, but I also wanted to help.

I DECIDE TO SPEND some more time in Lost Creek. I find the busi-ness card Nora Daley gave me and easily find her street.

Her house is a well-kept, tasteful white house trimmed in green that stands out from its sagging neighbors freckled with peeling paint. Clean, white lace curtains hang in every window pulled back to reveal a single white candle on every sill.

I knock and the door is quickly answered by Birdie, the activities

secretary for the NONS, holding a pot of coffee in one hand. She's wearing another one of her hand-knit sweaters. This one is neon pink patterned in yellow, orange, and red lightning bolts.

"Oh," she says upon seeing me.

She glances at the pot as if it might tell her what she should do next.

"The museum isn't open today. It says so on the sign."

"I'd like to see the museum, but that's not the main reason I'm here," I tell her. "Can I come in?"

She looks at the pot again, frowning slightly. It's still not helping her.

"Is Nora here? She invited me."

Nora steps up beside her. I get the feeling she was standing just out of my line of vision listening the entire time.

She makes a frank appraisal of my Valentino studded miniskirt and tights, Balmain camouflage cotton top, Fendi motorcycle boots, and ankle-length fawn suede duster. I don't know what her problem is. This is very hayseed for me.

"We're not open today," she echoes her friend.

"Yes, I know."

"Then why are you here?"

"Now that the gallows are coming down, people might forget about the Nellies and I think that would be a shame. I seem to remember hearing somewhere that you've always wanted to put up a statue. I might want to make a donation."

Nora is nattily dressed in a pair of dark green polyester slacks, a high-necked white blouse, and a sweater vest covered in cardinals and accessorized with a pine-tree-shaped brooch made of green and gold crystals.

"Come in," she says.

The interior of the house is as tidy as the exterior and as carefully put together as its owner.

"I'm sorry I didn't properly introduce myself the other day when we met at Kelly's Kwik Shop. I'm Scarlet Dawes."

Nora puts on her glasses hanging from a beaded chain around her neck and examines me.

"Scarlet Dawes?" Nora asks me. "The daughter of Walker Dawes?"

"Would you like some coffee?" Birdie eagerly offers.

"No, but I'd like to see the museum. Do you think you could make an exception for me?"

"Sure, sure," Nora says briskly and starts ushering me toward a staircase.

"Normally we'd be open but we had to take a day off. Things have been bonkers around here. The amount of people," Birdie informs me. "It's the first time since Nora started the museum almost forty years ago we've ever had lines."

"So Marcella Greger's death was good for you?"

"We'd never say that," Nora replies, shocked.

"Poor Marcella," Birdie laments. "She was such a kind, good soul. No one can figure out why anybody'd want to kill her."

"I thought the Nellies did it."

"That's not funny," Nora says.

"Rafe says it's some lunatic," Birdie offers.

"Who's Rafe?"

"Rafe Malloy. He's a police officer in town. Our only detective," Nora explains.

"Does he have a granddaughter named Heather?"

"Yes. He has quite a few grandchildren."

"Rafe says it's a lunatic," Birdie repeats.

"I heard you the first time. A lunatic? Really?"

"Here we go," Nora announces as we reach the top of the third flight of stairs. "Watch your head."

She opens a door with a key. We have a few more stairs to go before reaching a spacious attic that takes up the entire top of the house. Birdie flicks a switch and the peaked ceiling is lit up with white Christmas lights that act as stars in the sky over an impressively detailed model of Lost Creek set up on an old Ping-Pong table covered in green felt.

"This side is the town as it looked during the time of the Nellies and this side is how it looks now," Nora explains proudly. "Rick Kelly made it. It took him two years to complete it. He's Moira's brother."

"It's impressive," I say.

"We had a group of paranormal investigators spend the night here last night," Birdie rattles on. "They have their own TV show. They found evidence that this room is haunted."

"What evidence?"

"They wouldn't tell us. We have to wait and watch the show."

"There are no ghosts in this house," Nora insists. "I think I would have seen one by now."

"What about Wade Van Landingham going into that trance and starting to growl and shiver and scratch at that corner over there?"

"It was all nonsense."

"Who's Wade Van Landingham?" I ask.

"Their psychic," Birdie answers. "Nora didn't like him."

"He chewed up one of my mother's handmade doilies," she says hotly.

"He sounds interesting."

The ladies lead me to the exhibits. I was expecting something amateur, but each item is enclosed in a wood and glass case accompanied by a detailed description typed on an index card.

I walk slowly past one of the tickets the Original Walker issued for the executions bearing his signature with its gold seal still intact, the bloodstained collar from the priest who lost his tongue after he blabbed information to O. W. that a Nellie told him in confession, the dented tin flask smuggled in to Footloose McAnulty his last night in prison by the very wife who had always tried to get him to quit drinking, a newspaper clipping detailing the construction of Walker's Wonder complete with a sketch of the amazing gallows able to accommodate four men at a time, the petrified ear of the informant Mickey Duff that was sliced from his head by Prosperity McNab and nailed to the door of the Red Rabbit, a brass door knocker with LEWELLYN engraved on it, one of the two men the Nellies were accused of killing, Fiona McNab's hairbrush and the small wool cap her son, Jack, wore while watching his father hang, the white hood worn by Kenny Kelly, and the noose that choked the life out of him.

On the walls behind the exhibits is a framed series of an artist's renderings of each of the executed Nellies sketched during the trial.

I take a closer look.

"Is something wrong?" Birdie asks

"I met someone here in town recently who looks a lot like Prosperity McNab. Danny Doyle."

Nora nods her head excitedly as if making this connection has just won me a prize.

"Prosperity was his great-great-grandfather. His mother was a McNab and married a Doyle."

"We're all very proud of Danny," Birdie chimes in. "He's a famous psychologist in Philadelphia who puts murderers in jail. He's in town now visiting his grandfather Tommy."

Hanging beside the sketches is a haunting painting done in shades of green and gray of a woman on her knees in the dirt with tiny fearful faces peering out from the folds of her tattered skirts. She's pleading with a well-dressed man in shiny riding boots on a blood bay horse. His hand is raised and holds a coiled whip.

It's titled *Nellie O'Neill Pleads for Her Children*.

Beneath it in another glass case is the lace handkerchief Peter Tully's mother gave him that had to be pried from his dead hands. I wonder how much it would cost.

I reach into my purse and take out my checkbook.

"So, Nora," I begin, "how much do you need for this statue of yours?"

nineteen

I SPENT LAST NIGHT AT the house but I kept my room at the Holiday Inn. I go back there, watch a movie, and fall asleep.

When I wake up, I'm starving and I want a drink.

I'm glad to see Heather is working again tonight. I wave at her and she gives me a brilliant smile.

A few tables are occupied and two women sit at the bar. I wonder if Anna and her cousin, Marcella, ever got together for a drink. I never thought about her having any kind of life outside of our house.

From the way Marcella talked, it sounded like she and Anna confided in each other a lot. Part of me regrets acting so hastily. It might have been worth my while to have had a lengthier conversation with her, but she really got on my nerves.

"Hi," Heather greets me happily. "I was hoping you'd be back. Jack and Coke?"

"Good memory," I reply.

"Extra strong," she adds.

"And do you have a bar menu?"

She hurries off and returns with a drink, a laminated menu, and a bowl of complimentary stale party mix.

"So how did your dad like Tweety?" she asks me.

"Oh, he loved him," I tell her, smiling. "Thanks again for giving me directions to that pet shop."

"No problem. I go there sometimes to play with the puppies and the hamsters. I'd love to get a pet, but the place where I live doesn't allow animals."

"Do you live alone?" I ask while perusing my food options.

I can't find a single item that isn't deep-fried or covered in an artificial cheese sauce.

"I have two roommates."

"Boys?"

She blushes and shakes her head. A cloud of girlish perfume wafts toward me. She smells like a sugar cookie.

"My grandpa would go ballistic if I lived with guys," she adds.

"Is this the grandfather who's a cop?"

"He's not a bad guy or anything like that," she explains. "He's just extra protective of me. My mom was his first kid with his first wife, and I'm his first grandkid."

"That's a lot of firsts. Why don't you sit down and talk to me for a minute? You're not that busy right now," I urge her.

She glances around at the mostly empty tables and the bartender sitting on a stool with his eyes closed and his iPod plugs in his ears appearing to be fast asleep except for the slight nodding of his head in time to his music.

I push a chair out from under the table with the tip of my boot. She smiles at me in wonderment as if I've just performed some amazing feat of magic.

"Has your grandfather told you anything about that poor woman who had her head bashed in?"

"No. He never talks about work."

"It would go against his ethics?"

"I don't know about that. I think it's more about going against the rules of his job. He loves rules. I heard him tell my mom once he likes being a cop because he likes never having to ask if something is right or wrong. All he has to do is enforce laws. He said after Vietnam, he never wants to have to pass judgment or make a moral decision again."

"What happened to him in Vietnam?"

She shrugs.

"He was a soldier."

I notice her eyeing my bowl. I push it toward her. She takes a small handful after checking for management spies. She's adorably moral.

"Tell me, Heather," I say. "Does your grandfather know Danny Doyle? He's some famous shrink who lives in Philadelphia but he grew up here."

"Sure, Grandpa knows him. He's known Dr. Doyle since he was a little kid. When he went away to college he was so proud of him, you would've thought he was his own son. That's what my mom tells me."

"Do you know him?"

"He hardly ever comes back here. I've never met him."

"You must have a boyfriend," I goad her. "A pretty girl like you. Come on. Tell me."

Her telltale blush heats her cheeks again. She bows her head and starts picking through the bowl for the yellow cereal squares and the cheese sticks, pushing aside anything brown.

"I do kind of have a crush on someone."

"What's his name?"

"I can't tell you."

"Of course you can."

I sip my drink and watch her. I know she can't keep her secret for more than a few seconds.

"Troy," she reveals breathlessly.

"Is he cute?"

"Very."

"So? What's your status?"

"What do you mean?"

"How involved are you?"

"Oh, we're not involved."

"Why not?"

"For one reason, he works with my grandpa."

"He's a cop?"

She nods.

"What's the other reason?"

"I don't know."

She gives up her previously finicky manner of eating and starts tossing handfuls of the snack mix into her mouth.

"We've gone out drinking a couple times. Him and his friend Billy; he's a cop, too. Me and one of my girlfriends. And we meet up with other people. We've never gone out on anything like a date."

"Why not?"

"He's never asked me."

I place my hand over the bowl. She looks at me, surprised. I hold her gaze.

"Heather," I say quietly but firmly. "You can't wait for him to ask you. Men are completely content to play video games and wank off to Internet porn. If you want a man, you have to go after him. Call him."

"What?"

"Call him right now and tell him to meet you for a drink when you get off work."

"I can't."

"Heather, remember our talk the other day? Life is short. You have no idea how short it might be."

I take my hand off the bowl and place it over her hand instead.

"Think about that poor Marcella Greger woman. Do you think when she woke up that morning she had any idea that someone was going to come to her home and kill her?"

Heather slowly shakes her head.

I squeeze her hand.

"Don't waste another second. Call him. Do it now," I command her. "And tell him to bring his cop buddy for me."

I CAN SEE WHY Heather has a crush on Officer Troy Razzano. He's darkly good-looking with big brown eyes and a flashy smile; one of those pretty Italian boys who will be twice the size he is now in another ten years and resemble every small-time actor playing a background *paisan* on the most recent mob show du jour.

His friend, Officer Billy Smalls, looks and talks like a twelve-year-old Marine. He has ears that stick out and enormous hazel eyes set in a little boy's angelic freckled face that makes his tough talk and attitude hard to take seriously.

They aren't as conversationally challenged as I thought they might be; however, the topics are severely limited and I'm unequipped to speak to any of them. It's obvious the three of them know all the same people and are going to spend the night talking about them along with the hopes of a local speedway reopening in the spring and the latest highlights from a few of their favorite TV shows.

I watch them and think about how much their contentment with their pathetic lots in life would bother Walker and his abhorrence of mediocrity and belief that abject failure is better than bland survival. He once told me he'd rather have me be a crack whore than a soccer mom.

I didn't tell Heather my last name when we first met only because when people around here find out who I am they stop being who they are. I knew sweet little Heather would be intimidated by me if she knew I was the daughter of Walker Dawes and would be impossible to pump for information.

I toyed with the idea of not giving the boys a last name either but decided to be honest.

I was right about Heather. She can barely look me in the eyes anymore. Troy seems cowed, too, but the information thrills Billy.

"I can't believe I'm sitting here with Scarlet Dawes. Seriously, how much freakin' money do you have?" he asks, grinning at me over a shot glass of Jägermeister.

"A lot," I say, grinning back.

"Drinks are on you!" he proclaims joyfully, and signals for the whole bottle.

The evening progresses and as I knew would happen, I get bored.

Troy has managed to stay relatively sober while Billy is almost too drunk to walk. He barely makes it to the men's room for the fourth time. Troy and Heather have become fairly cozy and I can tell by the way Troy winces at the sight of Billy stumbling across the room that he's concerned for his friend's welfare but would also like to ditch him. I volunteer to drive Billy home. His car can stay in the hotel parking lot overnight.

Troy and Heather pledge me their undying gratitude.

Billy has a surprisingly tidy little bachelor pad complete with state-of-the-art electronics, a Coors Light dartboard, and a framed poster of a mostly naked starlet whose name I've never been able to remember. Within moments of our arrival, he's pouring more shots.

I sit down next to him on the couch and he starts talking about his job, trying to impress me with his selfless pursuit of protecting and serving. The next thing I know he gets up and disappears into his bedroom. He comes back with his gun.

"Look at this," he slurs, waving it in front of me. "You wanna hold it?"

"It's not that heavy," I say, acting surprised. "What kind of gun is it?"

"A Glock .40," he replies, taking it from me and moving in for a kiss. "It's heavier when it's loaded."

I give him his kiss and even let him do a little groping before breaking our clinch and asking, "How do you load it?"

"You really want to know?"

I smile and stroke the inside of his thigh stopping just short of the bulge straining against his jeans.

He grins.

"It's okay. Lots of women are turned on by guns."

He gets up, returns with a magazine, and shows me the bullets inside.

"There's fifteen here and the gun holds one in the barrel."

He takes one out and demonstrates how to depress the spring-loaded mechanism in order to put it back in.

"It's hard to do. The tension in the springs is really tight. Female officers usually don't have the hand strength to do it. They have to use this gizmo called a sissy loader."

"A sissy loader? Do you think I'd need a sissy loader?"

He sets the gun on the coffee table and reaches for me.

"No. I'm sure you can do anything you set your mind to."

We start making out. He's not repulsive. There was a time when his pawing, panting, and sucking might have aroused me a little if I knew he was also going to be useful to me in some other nonmasturbatory capacity, but my desire for sexual manipulation has dwindled over the years.

The Bonsai Girls were crazy for sex. They called it love, but Jacqueline and I knew there was no such thing. The tingling they felt in their private parts had nothing to do with the ache in their souls. Finding someone to take care of the first didn't mean the second would be cured. We had our own term for their romantic obsession with boys and sticky nocturnal fumblings with each other: friction fictions.

I was fully prepared to complete the deed with Officer Smalls, knowing the alcohol and bliss would knock him out immediately afterward, but my plan proves unnecessary. He passes out with me straddling him, the condom still in the wrapper, his fly only partially undone, holding one of my breasts in each of his hands. I watch his head roll over to one side and wait for him to lose his grip.

I pick up the gun, slap the magazine into it, and point it at his head. I won't use it. I don't like guns. They're for the unimaginative. Anyone can pull a trigger. But I take it with me anyway, just to be on the safe side. There's a killer roaming the countryside.

The bar food didn't do it for me. I'm still hungry. I know everything will be closed at this hour. I'll have to go back to the house if I want to eat before tomorrow.

I dig Danny Doyle's business card out of my purse and call the number on it. I get voice mail. Of course it's his office.

I use the Internet white pages on my phone to look up Tommy McNab's home number.

On the fifth ring, a man's voice thick with sleep and concern, answers.

"Hello?"

"Is this Danny?"

"Do you know what time it is? Who is this?"

"Scarlet Dawes."

He doesn't say anything. The silence lengthens.

"Danny? Is that you? Are you still there?"

"Yes."

"Let's have lunch tomorrow. It must be something in the air, but since I've been back here I've had a craving for a bacon cheeseburger."

twenty

DANNY CALLED CHAPPY'S A restaurant, but it's nothing more than a wood-paneled dining room furnished with tables and chairs straight out of a church bingo night. Hanging directly inside the front door is a portrait of a balding man with thick glasses and a lopsided smile revealing bad teeth wearing a white T-shirt and a paper fry cook's hat. HERM is written on his hat in an elaborate script, the way children's names are embroidered on Mickey Mouse ears. I assume he's the proprietor.

The sole waitress in a yellow polo shirt and mom jeans looks me over. She's a sour-faced woman of an indeterminate age and familial relation to Herm.

Beneath my mink, I'm wearing Balenciaga brocaded skinny jeans, a taupe Alexander Wang long-sleeved silk Henley, and a rope of diamonds and hand-carved jade beads.

She doesn't seem to know what to do with me. I spot Danny on my own. He's already here, drinking coffee, sitting at a table set with paper place mats advertising local businesses and a milky white glass vase filled with plastic flowers. I push past her.

He stands up as I approach. He has manners. How cute.

"I've never had a burger here," he tells me while I take off my coat and sit down, "but I hear they're good."

"What have you eaten here?"

"The gravy. A lot of gravy. Over just about anything you can think of."

He pushes a menu toward me. All the entrees are comfort food: stuffed pork chops, roast beef and mashed potatoes, chicken and waffles, liver and onions, ham pot pie. "Bowl of gravy" is listed among the traditional side dishes of french fries, coleslaw, and onion rings.

"You don't strike me as a gravy kind of guy."

"I'm not anymore but I used to be. I was hungry all the time."

"That's right. You were poor."

The waitress appears instantly. I can tell I'm going to have a problem with her.

"Can I get a drink here?"

"Coffee, tea, and pop," the waitress shoots back.

"That's not what I meant. I'll have tea."

"You know what you want?"

"I just got here," I reply, making no effort to keep the irritation out of my voice.

"Most people who eat here know what they want before they get here."

"I'll have a bacon cheeseburger, rare."

"You want it medium," the waitress says.

"I want it rare," I repeat slowly. "It better be rare."

The waitress shrugs and turns to Danny.

"You?"

"The stuffed pork chop with mashed potatoes and extra gravy."

"Good choice," she says and walks away.

"You weren't kidding about the gravy."

He smiles at me. I believe it's a genuine smile. I have a thing about fake smiles. Fake orgasms, too. Faking in general.

"I never eat it except when I come back here."

"You said you live in Philadelphia?"

"Yes. What about you? Where do you live now?"

"Paris. I also have a place in New York but it takes a lot to get me to come to the States."

"What brought you this time?"

"Identity theft."

"Someone stole your identity?"

"Yes. I'm here to get it back."

The waitress returns.

"Here you go, hon."

She sets down a cup of tea in front of me and refreshes Danny's coffee.

"Thank you, hon," I reply.

She gives me a dirty look.

"I don't like her," I tell Danny. "She has a bad attitude."

"Can I ask why you called me at three in the morning?"

He's trying to divert my attention away from the waitress. It won't work.

"What can I say? I'm disoriented. Jet lag. I didn't know what time it was."

"Can I ask why you called me at all?"

"I'm going to be here for a little while and I need someone to entertain me."

"You want me to entertain you?" he asks.

"Did I offend you? You sound offended."

He smiles again. I'm not so sure this one is sincere.

"No. It's just . . . I'm not going to be here much longer. I'm going back to Philly."

"That's too bad. We could've had some fun."

I shake a few packets of sugar into my tea.

"Why did you want to see Walker? Don't tell me he's a serial killer?"

"Nothing like that."

"Did it have anything to do with Marcella Greger? You asked me about her."

"No, but we could talk about her if you want."

"Why would I want to talk about someone I don't know?"

"She was your nanny's cousin. It's rare for one family to experience two such bizarre and violent deaths. Statistically, it almost never happens."

"You sound like you're preparing expert-witness testimony."

He laughs.

"I'm sorry. Force of habit."

He takes a sip of his coffee and watches me while trying to seem like he's not watching me. Shrinks: they're so predictable. Always looking for a psychosis here and a syndrome there.

I've dealt with a few. The first I can barely remember it was so long ago. I can still recall his office, though, filled with toys and dolls and art supplies.

I was six. Gwen and Anna were up in arms because I had killed a cat, although technically speaking, I never admitted to doing it. When Anna accused me, I said, "I didn't kill it. It was still alive when I left it hanging in the tree."

That one still makes me chuckle.

I didn't know what Anna expected. She was always telling me stories about the Nellies being hung. How it was the worst way to kill someone. How it took so long for them to die. How they were forced to hang there with the ropes cutting into their necks, having the life choked out of them, suffocating in front of their loved ones, their bowels emptying and the blood vessels in their eyeballs popping while they bit off their tongues.

Her tales were riveting. Of course I was going to be curious and want to experiment. Kids will be kids.

Anna told Gwen what I had done, a small betrayal but still a betrayal. Neither Gwen nor Walker would have ever dreamed of punishing me or, worse yet, having a heartfelt conversation with me. They're both consummate avoiders. Walker talks around things and Gwen retreats inside her icy loveliness, where it seems rude to intrude. However, they also both loved their property and taking strolls around it, and I'm sure the thought of dead critters found dangling in the oaks and maples when they least expected it was very unappealing to them. I'm pretty sure this is why they decided to seek professional help for me. Nothing came of it. I told the shrink what he wanted to hear and I learned how to bury.

After Anna died, I was sent to another shrink, Dr. Brown Ball. (She had a large brown ceramic ball sitting on the top shelf of her bookcase and I could never figure out what it was for. I suppose it was meant to be decorative even though it was the antithesis of the word. She also had a gray cube but it didn't excite me the way the ball did.)

Gwen and Walker were concerned that I might suffer some kind of trauma after watching Anna burn. I pretended I did. I gave Brown Ball some of the best performances of my life. Boo hoo! I miss my nanny. I have nightmares about my mommy and daddy catching on fire, too. I'm afraid to have birthday candles on my cake. Then I miraculously got better.

But my all-time favorite shrink was the psychiatrist at my boarding school, Dr. Slow Puller, so named because a girl once heard some teachers talking about going out with him and his reluctance to bring out his wallet and pay at the end of the evening. We took it one step further and assumed it also described his sex drive.

I had the best time with him. To this day I miss our sessions. I let him think I was a complete psycho. He thought I killed Courtney. It was so obvious, although I never let on that I knew what he was thinking, just like I won't let Danny know I'm on to him, too.

"From what I've heard Marcella's death wasn't that bizarre or violent," I tell him. "Someone hit her on the head. Big deal. And Anna's was a suicide."

"A suicide doesn't count?"

"Not really."

"You seem detached from your nanny's death."

Oh, boy, here we go. Shrink-speak!

I take a drink of my tea.

"It was a long time ago. Believe me, I was devastated when it happened. My parents sent me to a very good psychiatrist. She helped me a lot."

"I'm glad to hear that. Did you have anything to do with your nanny's death?"

I'm impressed. Even Slow Puller never came right out and asked me.

"I was ten."

"That's not an answer."

"What would you do if I told you I did it?"

"Nothing. What could I do?"

I sit back in my chair and play with my beads. I'm not afraid of him.

"How about an exchange of information? You tell me something, I'll tell you something. I'd like to know how you feel about your mother."

"My mother?"

"Yes, your mother. Your mentally ill, baby-killing, ex-con mother."

"I love her."

I'm stunned. I expected so much better from him, yet at the same time, I realize this means he fully understands the rules of the game.

"That's awesome!" I cry. "You love her. What a perfectly meaningless thing to say."

"Do you love your mother?"

"Oh, no," I scold. "It's still my turn. How can you love someone who betrayed you like that?"

"My mother is mentally ill. She can't be held responsible for her actions."

"That's a nice, neat rationalization, but you've never really believed it deep down inside, have you? When you were a kid you blamed her. Why couldn't she be normal like the other moms? And you must have hated her for getting sent to jail and leaving you."

I watch him carefully. He's good at hiding his feelings.

He toys with the handle of his coffee mug and stares for a moment into the black liquid before raising his equally dark eyes to me and saying blandly, "Hate's a strong word."

"She killed your sister," I remind him.

"I have no memory of my sister. I was only five years old when she died, and she only lived for a week. It's not as if I lost a person I knew and loved."

"That's cold," I say and mean it.

"I'm not saying her death hasn't made an impact on me. I think about her all the time, but not in the form of a person. She's become a sort of symbol to me."

"A symbol of what?"

"My life that didn't happen."

I have one of those, too, I think, but don't reveal to him: a life that didn't happen.

"Now it's my turn," he says. "Why did you kill Marcella Greger?"

I didn't see this coming, yet at the same time, I saw this coming. He's going for the brutally direct approach. He's hoping his outrageous accusations will shock me into confessing.

I'm losing interest in this game.

Our waitress appears with our meals. She sets a burger and fries down in front of me and a plate of something unidentifiable covered in rubbery brown goo in front of Danny.

"Enjoy," she says and saunters off.

Danny reaches for his knife and fork.

"The others I can understand," he says while sawing away at his gravy. "Anna was your nanny. You had an intimate relationship with her. There would've been endless opportunities for her to wound you. And that girl at your boarding school, what was her name? Courtney. At that age in that setting, the reasons for you wanting her dead would also be endless. Maybe she started a nasty rumor about you or stole a boyfriend. Or maybe she stole a girlfriend?"

He pauses to stick a bite into his mouth and chew contemplatively.

"But Marcella Greger I can't figure out," he goes on after he's swallowed. "How could that little old lady get in the way of the fabulous Scarlet Dawes?"

I blink at him.

He cuts off another bite of pork chop and holds it aloft.

"A toast," he says. "Not so very long ago one of your ancestors stood by and watched one of my ancestors die a grisly death, and now here we sit having lunch together. *Salud!*"

His phone rings.

"Do you mind if I take this call? It could be important."

"I don't mind."

I dig into my burger. Herm got it right. It's barely cooked and the beef is surprisingly good.

Danny holds his phone away from his ear.

"I mentioned to a friend of mine that I was having lunch with you.

He's a police officer here in town. He says he'd like to talk to you. Something to do with an encounter you had last night with Officer Smalls."

"No problem," I tell him. "I'll be there as soon as I'm done eating."

I take another bite. Blood dribbles down my chin.

I reach into my bag for my new handkerchief.

THE POLICE DEPARTMENT IS housed in a small, serious, brown brick affair. The interior is low ceilinged, poorly lit, badly heated, and furnished with cut-rate office-supply-store metal desks and chairs constructed with the sole intention of making people want to stand up. It smells of overheated coffee and pine-scented disinfectant with an underlying odor of vomit near the front doors.

Officer Billy Smalls sits in front of a desk wearing the expression of a child told to sit in the corner. The man on the other side of the desk is much older, with a head of short, spiky gray hair like the bristles of a steel-wool brush and some of the bluest eyes I've ever seen. Traces of his former good looks are still evident in his face, but the clothes are pitiable even for someone in a profession not known for its fashion sense: a blue tie with orange stars on it, a flannel shirt, a pair of hopelessly wrinkled and outdated khakis, and some kind of hiking boots with yellow laces.

Billy notices me first and he blushes all the way to the tips of his big ears. He gets even pinker than Heather.

"Hi, sweetheart," I gush from across the room.

I walk over and plant a big kiss on his lips.

"I missed you."

His blush darkens to the color of a plum and I swear I can feel heat coming from his skin. I hope he doesn't burst into flames.

"You must be Heather's grandfather," I say to the other man at the desk.

"Yep."

I extend my hand.

"I'm Scarlet Dawes."

He takes it but he doesn't stand up. He doesn't have Danny's manners.

"Rafe Malloy," he says.

"What can I do for you boys?"

He gestures to another metal chair sitting next to the one where Billy sits. He really doesn't have any manners.

"Have a seat," he says.

I debate leaving. I only came because I thought it might be fun to mess with the local po-po, but I expected to be treated well.

I shed my coat and hang it over the back of my chair, letting it drag on the dirty floor. Nothing says *I'm better than you* than mistreating an object that's worth a year of your pay, Rafe Malloy.

He reaches into a bowl filled with hard candy and extracts a pink piece.

"Care for one?" he asks.

"No, thank you."

"Why did you come back here?"

The abruptness and irrelevance of his question catches me off guard but I recover quickly. It takes much more than a bumpkin cop to rattle me.

"To visit my family."

He unwraps the candy and puts it into his mouth, where he clicks it noisily against his teeth.

"I thought you didn't get along with your family."

"How would you know anything about that?"

He leans back in his chair, puts his hands behind his head, and studies me. I'm sure he expects me to get nervous and agitated. He has an effective gaze, the kind that would break most people's resolve and get them to say just about anything in order to get him out of their heads. It won't work with me, though. No one's ever been able to stare me down.

"You missed your daddy? Is that what you're saying?"

"I have a good relationship with my father."

"Walker Dawes doesn't care about anyone but Walker Dawes."

"I suppose you know him well enough to make that determination?"

He shrugs.

"Rich people."

"You don't like rich people, do you?"

"Not particularly."

"Do you know a lot of them?"

"Don't have to."

"But you'd like to be one."

"Not particularly. How about you? Do you like rich people?"

I reach for a piece of candy. I take a green one then put it back and take a pink one, too. I slowly unwrap it. I get the feeling this is pissing him off.

"So I hear you and Officer Smalls had quite a night last night."

"We did."

"Ending at his apartment?"

I put the candy in my mouth and suck.

"Yes."

"Where you decided to steal his gun?"

"Steal his gun? Why would I do that?"

"His gun is missing and you're the last person seen holding it."

"I was holding a lot of things last night."

I glance at Billy, who grows even redder. I notice Troy not far away at another desk trying to look busy while straining to hear every word we're saying. The same can be said for everyone else in the station.

"I'll tell you what," I say. "I didn't take it, but I'll buy him a new one."

"Guy in Charge!" a high-pitched voice calls out.

Everyone turns their attention away from me and toward an emaciated Goth cherub wearing bedazzled granny glasses and an Hermès foulard scarf rushing toward Rafe. I can't imagine where he's come from.

"Guy in Charge! I'm so glad we found you. Wade has been frantic with worry over you."

A terrier in a bluish-green fur jacket and matching boots and tam comes rushing out of nowhere. He slides to a stop directly in front of Rafe and begins hopping straight up and down on three-inch-high legs that appear to be spring-loaded.

"He says you're in grave danger," the cherub adds.

"For Chrissakes," Rafe growls.

The dog sits back on his tiny haunches and lets loose with an ear-splitting howl.

"Get that animal out of here!" Rafe shouts.

"Don't call him an animal. You'll hurt his feelings. He's only trying to help."

The little dog leaps onto Rafe's lap then up onto his desk, where he sits frozen in a begging position with his eyes closed.

"What's he doing?" I ask.

"He's in a trance," the cherub answers.

"Is this the great psychic?"

The dog returns to all fours and begins barking at Rafe in a strange staccato that almost sounds like a form of speech.

"Do you speak dog?" I ask him.

"Shut up," Rafe tells Wade.

The dog keeps barking.

"I said, shut up!" he yells and slams his open palm down on the desktop.

Wade does what he's told. He walks around in a circle then lies down facing me with his muzzle between his front paws and stares.

I get up from the chair. I've had enough. This isn't fun or even mildly amusing.

I take a big handful of candy and dump it in my purse.

"I'm going. Feel free to search my purse or my father's house or my rental car. You're not going to find Officer Smalls' gun."

Rafe gets up from his chair, too. I expect him to try and stop me or maybe offer an apology, but he says, "Hold on. I'll walk you to your car."

Our journey is a silent one except for his clacking and crunching. I think it's over but he pulls another piece of candy out of his coat pocket, a horrible camouflage thing with a hood.

"Your granddaughter's sweet," I say. "I've really enjoyed spending time with her. I've been considering hiring a personal assistant. Maybe I should offer her the job. She could come live with me in Paris. What do you think?"

"The farthest she's ever been is Monroeville Mall to do some Christmas shopping. She won't even go to Pittsburgh. But if she wants to go, why not?"

He's bluffing. My suggestion has to terrify him. He's underestimating me. He doesn't think I can convince her.

We end at my car. He shoves his hands into his pockets and starts rocking back and forth on his heels while squinting into the spitting snow like he can see the future.

"Seems like you made a big impression on Danny," he says without looking at me.

"I did?"

"He told me he met you at your father's place. Then he called me after your lunch today while you were on your way over here and we talked about you some more."

"What did he say about me?"

"He said you're fascinating."

"Fascinating?"

"Yeah, well. You know how it is. He's a shrink. He loves it when he meets a crazy person."

I step up beside him and lean in very close until my lips are almost touching his ear.

"Can I give you some advice? You're out of your league."

"Can I give you some advice?" he says, still staring at the sky. "You're wrong about that."

We hear a skittering sound behind us and both turn.

Wade comes tearing across the parking lot and stops beside Rafe.

I reach down to pet him and he snaps at me, his needlelike teeth barely missing my fingers.

I'm not upset. I understand his jealousy.

"Really, Wade?" I say as I pull the collar of my mink up around my neck. "Teal faux fur? So last season."

twenty-one

DANNY

THE WISHBONE KILLER WAS a psychopath. He wasn't a rich, beautiful one like Scarlet Dawes. He worked odd jobs and had long, greasy hair and an unkempt beard that led to the prison guards describing him as Jesus on a bender.

He didn't have Scarlet's sophistication either, or her intellect, but he was much more personable. It was impossible to have a conversation with him and not be entertained by his self-deprecating stories and attracted to his affability. Each time I interviewed him, I could easily understand how he was able to convince a certain kind of woman that he was someone she wanted to keep around, who would make her laugh and who would care for her emotionally and spiritually while she paid the bills until that fateful surprise turkey dinner he inevitably made for her that ended with their pinkies tugging at the wishbone to see who would come away with the bigger piece.

Twelve of them lost.

Friendliness was his affect, his particular con to manipulate and use others to get what he wanted. Scarlet's is simply her presence. She doesn't have to do anything. She knows only too well the appeal of wealth and physical beauty. Most people are as helpless in the face of it as the proverbial deer in the headlights, a constant source of crushed fenders and smashed windshields in these parts.

Rafe is convinced Scarlet killed Marcella Greger, and so am I. He's also begun to seriously wonder if she murdered her nanny and a high school classmate, too. I have no doubts about this either. He has no evidence placing Scarlet at Marcella's house or a motive or even a case at this point since the state police have taken over, but I know he won't be dissuaded.

I agreed to have lunch with her as part of my own investigation. I wanted to see if my suspicions were correct. I knew they were based on very little. I wasn't able to get a confession out of her and I didn't think I would, but after a meal at Chappy's combined with the information I've been able to gather, I know what she is.

Rafe wouldn't give me any details about what went on between Scarlet and Billy Smalls, but he did tell me his granddaughter Heather was involved, too, along with Troy Razzano.

I've decided after my earlier date with Scarlet that I deserve a drink. I've chosen the Barclay Holiday Inn's atrium poolside bar and grill. If I happen to run into Heather, who just happens to be a waitress here, maybe I'll ask her a few questions.

I'm leaving in two days to attend Carson's execution. I told Tommy I can come back again soon to help with Mom, but he insists he wants me to return to my job and get on with my life. He also pointed out that he won't be around that much longer and soon enough Mom will become my sole responsibility. It was one of our more depressing conversations.

I take a seat at the bar and find out that Heather called in sick tonight. I have a feeling Rafe is behind her sudden illness. If she's crossed Scarlet's path, it's probably a good idea to keep her under lock and key.

I think about going back to Tommy's house, but the sensory overload of the blaring music, six competing TV screens, and the overpowering scent of chlorine mixed with burnt nacho cheese has already lulled me into a dollar-draft-night stupor. I order a beer from the kid behind the bar. He looks to be about Troy's and Billy's age. Unshaven with a thick crop of messy hair and a pierced lower lip, he's listening to his iPod and nods.

I gesture at him to take out his ear buds.

"How can you hear anything?"

"Can't. I read lips."

"You must be good at it."

"People only order like five different things here."

"Junior," he thinks to add, pointing at himself.

"Me Danny," I say.

He smiles suddenly and waves at someone behind me.

"Anything happen at the gallows last night?" he calls out.

I turn my head and see Bambi and Z Mac walking to a table. Z Mac's dressed like a normal human being tonight and I wouldn't have noticed him at all in Philly, but since he's the only African American within a hundred miles of here, he sticks out.

Bambi's in the same leather catsuit she was wearing the other day at the police station and I can't help wondering if it's actually her skin.

"You gotta wait and watch the show, man," Z Mac calls back.

"I wonder if Wade's coming," I comment.

"I doubt it," the bartender says. "He was in here last night and kind of embarrassed himself. That guy was crazy. I had to cut him off."

"You served alcohol to a fox terrier?"

He shakes his head.

"Virgin piña coladas. Don't get me wrong. I wouldn't mind if he came back. He's a big tipper."

A woman sitting a few bar stools away gives me a smile. I nod back. She takes it to be an erotic invitation and pushes a tangle of limp, margarine-colored hair out of her eyes, licks her lips, and turns toward me, strategically positioning her cleavage for fullest exposure. One of her breasts is marked by a dull red blotch that could easily be a scar where an ex-husband stubbed out a cigarette during a heated argument, but I have a feeling twenty years ago it was a rose tattoo.

The next step in the courtship is her attempt at conversation.

I'm drinking my beer as quickly as possible, but it's not fast enough. She gets up from her stool and heads toward me.

"Hey, baby."

I smell lilac and cinnamon behind me.

Brenna slides her arm around my shoulders and glares at the woman at the other end of the bar.

"Back off, sistah. He's mine."

"Thank you," I tell her as she takes a seat beside me and the other woman picks up her drink and heads for greener pastures.

"No pro-blay-mo."

"What are you doing here?"

"Frackers," she says.

"Frackers?"

"Didn't you see all the trucks outside? They're staying here while there's work in the area. I had a date with one. He turned out to be a total jag-off."

She reaches for a bowl of pretzels. Junior brings her a beer. I signal for a refill.

"So you're pro-fracking?" I ask her. "At the very least it's providing you with a new pool of potential sex partners."

She ignores my gibe.

"Oh, yeah, I'm thrilled. Can't wait to get fire out of my kitchen tap."

She takes a few gulps from her beer.

"First they rip up the land for coal. Now they're going to poison everything sucking up the gas."

"We have to get energy from somewhere," I say, goading her on.

"The wind and the sun can provide energy, but nobody takes that seriously. You know why? No one can make money off them. No one can own the sky."

"You're sounding rather subversive tonight." I try joking some more. "Where's that capitalist spirit? What happened to a job's a job?"

"Sometimes I just want to grab my guns and my pots and pans and my books and throw them in the back of my truck and drive the hell away from here and live in the middle of nowhere and never have to see anyone ever again. People are fucked."

"Why don't you?"

"Do you know how big my family is? I have nine brothers and sisters. All of them married multiple times with tons of kids who have kids, too. When I haven't been living in the midst of them, I've been living with a bunch of soldiers. I know I could never stand a life of isolation for long, but it's fun to think about."

"What's that like?" I ask her. "Having a big family?"

"They can drive you crazy, that's for sure. But I can't imagine what it would be like without all of them."

She looks like she's going to say more, then she catches herself.

"I'm sorry. I forgot about your sister and your mom . . ."

"It's okay."

"You don't have much of a family."

"No."

"But you have Tommy," she points out, encouragingly. "And your dad."

"My dad and I never got along very well."

"I'm sorry," she says again.

"Me too."

We fall into a comfortable silence while we drink our beers until I notice Scarlet walking into the bar. At first I don't believe it. My shock must show on my face because Brenna asks, "What's wrong?"

Before I can begin to formulate an answer to that question regarding this particular person, Scarlet spots me and slinks over.

She smiles, but just like the ones she gave me earlier today, there's no warmth or joy in it. She's forced her lips into an expression the situation requires and nothing more. Happiness is the most difficult emotion to playact I've learned from my years of studying human performances under the most desperate circumstances. Everyone has experienced negative feelings such as grief, anger, jealousy, and fear, and therefore has a well of knowledge from which to draw if they find it necessary to put on a show; however, the same can't always be said for the positive. The type of person who has to fake happiness is usually the type who can't feel it.

"Danny," she says. "I thought you would've been done in by all that gravy, but here you are out whooping it up with some of the local talent. Who's your friend?"

I feel Brenna stiffen beside me and her face becomes the impregnable mask of soldiering.

"This is Brenna Kelly. Brenna, this is Scarlet Dawes."

"We met once a long time ago," Brenna says. "You wouldn't remember."

"Try me."

"The elementary school after the explosion in number six. You were there with your nanny. I was there with my sister. She lost her husband. They'd only been married for two months."

"Are you the little girl Anna tried to get me to talk to near the swings?"

"You did talk to me. You told me I had ugly hair," Brenna answers without a trace of emotion in her voice.

"I remember. You did have ugly hair. It's not much better now."

I'm not sure exactly what's taking place between the two of them, but I sense it's much more serious than a hair critique, or maybe hair critiques are much more serious than anything I previously imagined.

Scarlet's eyes widen, and if I didn't know better I'd think she was going to give Brenna a hug.

"Your sister was the girl with the red shoes," she says almost gleefully.

"Moira."

"Why does that name sound familiar? Don't tell me that cow behind the convenience store counter used to be that skinny little blond disco queen?"

Brenna doesn't flinch, demonstrating the exquisite self-control required by her former profession, but I feel the anger coming off her in waves.

Scarlet is obviously getting some personal satisfaction from all this. She leans forward as if about to take Brenna into her confidence.

"Does she still have those shoes?"

Brenna doesn't respond.

"Please tell me she still has those shoes."

Brenna gets up quickly, almost knocking over her stool, and pulls some crumpled bills from her purse, tossing them onto the bar.

"I gotta go."

"Wait, Brenna."

Scarlet smiles at me again.

"Did I just ruin your evening? She's not going to believe you if you tell her we're just friends. No one ever does."

"I don't know what just went on here between the two of you, but you obviously upset her and I think it was intentional."

"I'm innocent as a lamb," she says. "Have a drink with me?"

"No."

I hurry outside to see if I can catch Brenna in the parking lot.

A freezing wind has kicked up since I went inside. The snow clouds above are the same shade of white as the snow on the ground. It's not exactly dark and not exactly light and difficult to tell where earth and sky and day and night begin and end.

I find her about to get into her truck.

"How can you have anything to do with that . . . that . . . that thing?" she stutters at me in her rage. "Are you sleeping with her?"

"What? I barely know her."

"She seemed to know you pretty well."

"I just met her the other day."

She begins pacing back and forth rather than get in her truck and leave.

"What was she talking about?" I ask her.

She continues pacing. I don't think she's going to answer me and I know better than to ask again. I think she might belt me.

"Moira's husband," she blurts out. "They were only married two months. He died in the explosion. She, she . . ." Her voice begins to quaver. "She went there to identify him. She wore this dress and shoes he bought her on their honeymoon."

She stops and draws in a sharp breath. She begins pacing again. Tears glisten on her cheeks among the melting snowflakes.

"It was out of respect. I suppose she looked ridiculous. Who cares?"

She's openly crying now.

"She loved him so much. She was so happy. She wanted to have a bunch of babies. Instead . . . instead . . ."

She doesn't have to say more. I think of the Moira I know, unmarried, childless, and not exactly the happiest person I've ever come across.

Brenna regains her composure with a swipe of her coat sleeve across her face.

"She never got over it," she finishes.

THE SNOW IS COMING down hard by the time I get back to Tommy's house. His truck is gone. He could easily end up stranded somewhere tonight or be in an accident. I curse again the fact that he refuses to get a cell phone. He's impossible to track down.

I close the door behind me, hang up my coat, and brush the snow-flakes from my hair.

My concern is situational, I tell myself. This man has managed to survive for ninety-six years without any help from me. I never worry about him when I'm back in Philly. It's only because I'm here in his house that his welfare weighs on my mind.

I know I can't expect him to babysit Mom all the time, but after my dealings with Scarlet today, I'd feel much better if someone were here with her.

I don't think Scarlet Dawes is going to attack my mother, but Marcella Greger probably never dreamed the gorgeous heiress would show up at her house one day and crush in her skull with a rainbow. Or did she? Marcella Greger knew something Scarlet didn't want her to know. I'm convinced of that. But what?

Scarlet is a very specific kind of murderer. She wouldn't have thought she was doing anything wrong in killing her nanny and her classmate. In her mind, they needed to be eliminated. Each had done something unforgiveable in her eyes and their further existence would have gnawed at her.

I highly doubt she runs around randomly killing for the sake of kill-ing. Someone has to get under her skin or get in her way, but how far under her skin or how much in her way?

I told Brenna before she drove off that she and Moira should be careful. I let her think my concern stemmed from Marcella's anony-mous killer still remaining at large. I couldn't tell her the real reason, that all these years later Scarlet remembered a young Moira and even the shoes she wore, and it excited her. I'm fairly sure it's not a good idea to rouse strong feelings in Scarlet, even positive ones. Especially positive ones.

It's barely ten o'clock, too early for my mom to be asleep if she's well. I need to check on her.

I go into the kitchen and put on a pot of coffee. I'm going to try and get some work done tonight.

On my return to the front room, I give the deer head a caress on his nose then take one of the dish towels from his antlers and cover Fi's portrait with it.

I start making my way up the stairs, almost welcoming the cold lump of dread in my stomach. The sooner it begins, the sooner it will be over.

I don't know how many times I've made this trip, my stomach bunched in a knot of wariness, my pulse thudding heavily in my throat, never knowing what I might find when I finally enter my mom's room.

The door is slightly open. I peek inside. The curtains are drawn. The lights are on. She's lying on the bed in her bathrobe staring at the ceiling.

A cup of cold hot chocolate sits on the nightstand. A piece of lint floats in the skin on top.

When I was a child, this was always the worst way to find her. If her eyes were closed, I could tell myself she was sleeping and run away, but if they were open and she wasn't moving, I knew she could be dead. I was never able to see her chest rise or hear her breathing, so I got in the habit of putting a mirror under her nose to see if it fogged up.

I'm wondering if I should do that now when she turns to look at me and gives me such a start, I jerk backward against the nightstand and slosh cocoa onto the carpet.

I go to the bathroom for a towel to clean it up.

"I'm sorry, Mom. Would you like me to make you a new cup of cocoa?"

"I'm not feeling good tonight, Danny," she says dully.

"Then this is the best place for you to be. You should get some sleep. Let me help you get under the covers."

She sits up and I move to her side.

"I heard someone killed Marcella Greger," she tells me. "I didn't do it."

"Of course you didn't do it."

"She hated me, but I didn't hate her. If someone killed me it might've been her. That would make more sense."

I pause in tugging the comforter out from under her.

"What are you talking about? I didn't even know you knew Marcella Greger. Why did she hate you?"

"Because her cousin Anna hated me. I stole her boyfriend."

"What are you talking about?" I say again.

"It was an accident."

My mother accidentally stole someone's boyfriend. I'm not sure how someone does this, but it sounds like something she'd believe.

"He said I trapped him," she goes on. "I didn't mean to. I didn't even want him. You don't trap something you don't want. It was more like the time that possum fell in the window well. It was his own fault. Then he couldn't get out. When I tried to help, he got mad at me. Hissing and baring his teeth. I kept telling him, 'I'm trying to help you.' But he didn't care. He blamed me for not being able to free him."

"I don't think possums can feel blame. He was probably afraid of you."

"His eyes were shiny and black with hate," she insists.

I push her feet beneath the blanket and pull it up over her legs.

"I told him we didn't have to get married."

"The possum?" I ask, smiling at her.

Mom's delusions don't usually involve talking animals, but anything is possible.

"He wanted me to kill you. I wouldn't do it. I already loved you."

The content of her story has taken a serious turn.

I sit down on the edge of the bed.

"You've lost me, Mom. Who are you talking about?"

"Your dad."

"What are you saying? Dad wanted you to have an abortion when you were pregnant with me?"

"I wouldn't do it, then he said if I was going to have his baby, I had to marry him. He said he wasn't going to let me find some other guy to raise his kid."

This sounds like something my father would say.

"Tommy wanted to shoot him," she adds.

"Dad?"

"The possum. I wouldn't let him. I put a board down for him and he crawled out in the middle of the night."

She sighs and sinks into her pillows.

I trace her jumbled thoughts back to her original statement the same way I used to help her separate the colorful tangle of her embroidery threads.

"Dad was Anna Greger's boyfriend?"

She nods and rolls over onto her side, pulling her knees to her chest, her signal that she's done talking.

"I'm too tired to make you breakfast," she mumbles.

There's no point in explaining what time it is.

"It's okay, Mom. I can make my own."

Back downstairs, I pour a cup of coffee and sit alone at Tommy's kitchen table thinking about my father and how much I don't know about him.

Dad and Anna Greger? But why not? They were the same age living in the same small town. There's no reason why they couldn't have been involved before he met my mother.

The foreboding feeling I had when I asked him if the dead baby in our yard was Molly returns, and I finally realize why his response troubled me so much at the time.

He wasn't shocked by my question, and for someone who found his child murdered and watched his wife go to prison for it, this particular question should have been inconceivable. He didn't even seem to wonder or care how I had come up with such a wild idea. He exhibited his usual reflexive anger and defensiveness, but strip away his bluster and he was a man almost willing to have a rational conversation on the subject. Then who was that baby in our yard, huh? Then where's your sister, huh?

I meant what I told Scarlet about my feelings for my sister. I was too young to understand death. I didn't even understand babies. Molly was a week old when we lost her. All I knew about her was that she was soft, smelled like talcum powder, and my mother loved her.

Mom kept telling me about all the fun we were going to have together, how we were going to be a family, repeating this word "family" over and over again as if I didn't know its meaning or had never taken part in one.

Maybe Mom, Dad, and I didn't make a family after all, I remember thinking. Maybe we needed Molly to complete it. I thought she was going to solve all our problems. I loved the idea of her for that reason, but I can't say that I loved her. I was never given the chance.

This didn't keep me from thinking about her, though. I imagined her to be the complete opposite of the heavy, bristly, black goblin that had clung to Rafe's back as he fought his way through the jungles of hell.

Molly was feather light and translucent, her presence marked only by a pale rosy shimmer dancing before my eyes as if she were dusted in the pink sugar our mom favored for her heart cookies.

I never knew when she'd appear. I could never conjure her to help me deal with the worst of my melancholy, my loneliness, or my fear. She would appear at the oddest moments, times when I didn't think I needed her, but it would always turn out later that I did; moments like now, when her tiny spirit hovers near me and seems to whisper that I may yet find a way to save us all.

twenty-two

PROSPERITY'S STANDING IN LINE at the company store waiting for his pay and watching the waning light outside. Another summer has passed. Before long, the days will grow short and he'll leave for the mines in darkness, work in darkness, and get home in darkness, his life no better than an earthworm's.

Each day since he's arrived in Lost Creek he's watched the coal dust stream from the doors and windows of the colliery settling on everything, even the petals of wildflowers and the wings of birds. The interior of the building is always filled with a foggy blackness, and the silent shadows of men appearing and disappearing in the sooty haze makes him think of damned spirits floating in the storm clouds of hell, which was probably where they were all going to end up no matter how many rosaries they said. He knew God was male and therefore his biggest concern was making sure he was obeyed, but the Virgin Mary was a woman and a mother and she would have been appalled at the mess.

Bill Fahey had been in prison back in Ireland and he said a far more cheerful lot of men could be found there than in these mines. Prosperity had discussed the possible reasons why with him: was it the filth they lived and worked in, their constant exposure to danger, the strain of the physical labor?

There was something more. He knew what it was but he would

never say it out loud because to hear the words spoken would make his fate all too real.

His turn comes and he steps up to the counter.

The superintendent, Llewellyn, looks down at a sheet of paper in front of him and begins to read, "Coal mined . . . twelve cars at sixty-six cents a car. Total—seven dollars and ninety-two cents."

He knows better than to put his hand out yet. He waits.

"Less . . . two kegs of powder at two dollars and fifty cents a keg—five dollars. Two gallons of oil at ninety cents a gallon—one dollar and eighty cents. Repairs to one drill and one lantern—thirty cents. Replacing one pickax—sixty cents. Total—seven dollars and seventy cents."

Llewellyn looks over at the company store manager keeping track of the books who nods his head.

"Wages for the week—twenty-two cents."

A few coins are extracted from a steel box and dropped into Prosperity's hand. The nod meant he was in the tick on his household account. This was nothing new. The debt would be more than his meager earnings and it would reappear again next week even if he could pay it off.

Fi wasn't going to be happy, but she never was. She had proven to be a difficult woman to manage. Sometimes he had to strike her, yet despite the problems between them, nothing could diminish the awe he felt for her as a mother. Her endless patience with Jack, her protectiveness, the sweet smile she bestowed on him for the most undeserving reasons made him think of his own valiant mother, and he'd fiercely miss the care from her he never knew and the green woebegone hillside where she had lain all these many years among a multitude of tiny deaths.

He jingles the coins in his hand while watching a pair of emaciated canines doing the deed in the middle of the rutted dirt road not far from the steps of the store's porch. Eyes glazed with hunger, ribs protruding from beneath patchy, flea-bitten fur, their tongues lolling, panting for all their worth; they're probably enjoying the act more than he ever did on the rare occasions when Fi was willing and he had enough energy to get it up.

He gazes longingly at the Rabbit where a pint and the camaraderie of the Nellies were waiting to help dull his pain.

He knew a man could endure the worst kind of poverty and abuse if he had even the slightest expectation of something better, but that was what was missing in the company town: hope. There was no hope here, and its lack created a vacuum that had the power to suck the very souls out of men. Only shells were left behind.

He looks around him as he crosses the road. There seem to be more men than usual wandering about, but on closer inspection he realizes they're not men at all. They're hard, blackened carcasses of men.

A giant hand reaches down from the sky. A woman's slim, milky white hand wearing a flashing ruby ring. It touches them one by one and they shatter into piles of smoldering onyx bones.

I sit bolt upright on the couch gulping for air and instinctively look toward Fiona. Her portrait's still wearing the dish towel I covered her with last night.

Tommy's sitting at the kitchen table having breakfast.

He glances my way, not at all concerned. I must not have screamed.

"Still having those nightmares?"

"No. Not exactly. They're different nightmares now. Sort of."

I look around at the open folders and papers scattered about. I fell asleep in my clothes again.

"Come have some breakfast," Tommy suggests.

He raises his bowl to his lips and slurps up the sugary cream left after the cereal is gone.

I join him, pour a cup of coffee, and put my face over the steam, hoping the caffeine will seep directly into my pores.

"I had a strange talk with Mom last night," I tell him.

"That would be a first," he says with a wink.

"Is it true that Dad was dating Anna Greger before he met Mom?"

He puts the bowl down with a clunk and makes a noise that's a cross between a snort and a gag.

"Not dating. He and Anna were engaged," he replies. "And he had met your mother long before he started sniffing after her. They went to school together. They always knew each other."

"What happened?"

"As hard as it is for a father to speculate about the amorous dealings of his daughter, I think it was what you youngsters call hooking up. I don't think it was serious for either one of them, but then your mother got pregnant and it became very serious."

Tommy reaches across the table and pats my arm when he sees my face fall. No kid who comes from a failed marriage wants to know that he was the reason his parents married in the first place.

"Did you know Fiona was pregnant with Jack when she and Prosperity got married?" Tommy asks, trying to distract me from my gloominess.

"No."

"Did I ever tell you about the day they met?"

I look up at him and know he must see the curiosity in my eyes. Could there be a story about Prosperity that I haven't heard?

"I don't think so,"

Tommy grins, claps his hands together, and leans back in his chair, settling into storytelling mode.

"Each day on the way to and from the pit, Prosperity and his best mate, Kenny Kelly, and all the rest of the miners were forced to walk by the superintendent's house," he begins. "It was a lovely three-story affair with a fresh coat of white paint, a picket fence, and a tree-lined path leading to a front door with a real brass knocker. As they passed, their steps would slow and they'd all stare sullenly at the Welsh name on the mailbox, Llewellyn. How they hated this man. But that's another story.

"One particular day, he and Kenny were late heading home and were all alone on the road as they approached the super's house. A girl was leaving it carrying a sewing basket. She had a sweet face and a fine shape to her.

"Prosperity asked Kenny who she was. Kenny told him her name was Fiona and she was a maid for a family in Barclay but did sewing for other folks, too. He also thought to add that she was an orphan like Prosperity. He knew his friend would find this fact interesting.

"Prosperity ran after her and tried to talk to her but she wouldn't have anything to do with him.

"'Don't waste your time. I have my sights set higher than a boy in the pits. Look at me. What do you see?' she said to him.

"'A beautiful girl with a foul disposition,' he replied.

"'Foul disposition? Just because I don't want nothing to do with the likes of you? That makes me foul?'

"'In my book, yes.'

"'You've never opened a book in your life.'

"'That's only because I can't read them. Otherwise, I'd be opening them all the time.'

"This made Fiona smile.

"'What's your name?' she asked him.

"'Prosperity.'

"'What's the name your mother gave you?' she persisted.

"'My mother died before I was born.'

"'Before?'

"'Before.'

"'Mine died after. What about your da?'

"'Never knew him. But I'm named after him. James Michael McNab.'

"'I never knew mine either. And I got nothing from him. Not even a name.'

"'We've got a lot in common then.'

"'We got nothing in common except our Irish blood.'

"'I'd say that's enough.'

"She slowed almost to a stop and gave him a look that made his heart beat faster when he realized the meaning behind it. She was paying attention to him.

"'You're a patriot, then?' she asked.

"Jimmy was his own country and owed allegiance to no one else, but at that moment he would have marched off to war against any foe she chose.

"'I am,' he proclaimed.

"'I suppose you're too young to run with the Nellies?'

"Her question surprised him, not only because he was obviously too young but because people rarely spoke the name of the Nellies out loud and definitely not in front of someone they didn't know well and could trust completely.

"'I am too young,' he said gravely, 'but I plan on getting older.'"

"'Would you think of joining then?'"

Tommy stops. He takes a drink of his coffee and closes his eyes. I wait for him to continue the story. He doesn't.

"That's it?" I ask him.

"There was more, of course, but it starts to drag after that."

"So what is the point of the story?"

"Does there have to be a point?"

He gets up from the table and stretches.

"Are you trying to tell me Prosperity joined the Nellies so he could hook up with Fiona?" I press him.

"Who knows? Although it's true Fiona was an avid supporter of the Nellies. She thought they were heroes."

The phone rings. Tommy grabs up his cane and hobbles into the other room.

"It's for you," he calls out a moment later. "Brenna Kelly. She sounds upset."

My mind flashes to last night and our encounter with Scarlet and her fascination with Moira's shoes.

"Hi, Brenna. What can I do for you?"

"Remember you told me you owed me a favor after I gave you a ride the other day?" she says in a rush. "Well, I have a big one to ask."

"I can barely hear you. Is that a siren?"

"Please, please," her voice breaks off into a clipped sob. "Can you come to the mine?"

TOMMY COMES WITH ME. We take his truck. I can tell his concern is greater than he's willing to admit because he lets me drive.

An alarm is never a good thing, but at least we both agreed what I heard in the background was the chirp of a police car and not the enormous scream of the town's siren announcing an accident at a mine.

Tommy's heard it several times; I've only heard it once. I was sitting in my sophomore English class. It began as a low, moaning wail that rose to a shriek, eerily human yet inhumanly immense, as if the earth itself were crying out in pain.

We all stood, the terrible sound pulling us to our feet, not knowing if we should run or hide or fight. We instinctively knew it meant death, and we were right.

Twenty-eight men died that day from an explosion in Lost Creek Mine No. 6, including Moira Kelly's husband, Dave Rosko's father, and Nora Daley's son.

Tommy doesn't say a word until we arrive at the mine. Nothing out of the ordinary seems to be happening. One police car and Rafe's car are here, but there are no fire trucks or ambulances or any other emergency vehicles present.

Rafe's talking calmly to a few of the miners I recognize from my run here a few days ago. Billy and Troy are drinking coffee.

Tommy smiles in relief.

"It's nothing. Probably someone broke into the office and stole a few paper clips," he jokes.

Then he notices Alphonse Kelly. He and Tommy are good friends even though Alphonse is in his early eighties. He's one of the "kids" as Tommy calls them who hang out at the union hall, except his health has been failing lately. It takes a lot to get him out of his home these days. Tommy knows this, and the sight of the sickly old man in an ancient military-green Carhartt and flap-eared cap standing off to one side of the others, alone and stoop-shouldered, staring worriedly at the gaping black hole in the side of the snowy hill brings his dread crashing back.

"What's Al doing here?" he says.

He barely lets me park the truck before he opens the door to get out.

I join Rafe and the other men. Brenna is with them, too.

The air around them buzzes with the energy required to control their combined panic.

Brenna seems to relax a little at the sight of me.

"So what's this favor I can do for you?" I ask lightly, trying to improve the atmosphere as best I can.

The four other miners I met before are here, but I notice both of her brothers are absent.

"We have a situation," Rafe answers for her.

"Rick's gonna blow up the mine," the one named Todd says.

"Don't say it like that," J. C. counters. "He's not gonna do it."

Dressed in identical coal-stained blue coveralls, steel-toed rubber boots, and battered miners' helmets with American flag stickers on the sides, the only way to tell the men apart is by their faces and their height.

Todd's the shortest of the four, and the youngest, chubby-cheeked with a mustache and a wad of tobacco under his lip. J.C. is taller, looks to be the oldest, and has shrewd gray eyes and a scar that starts beneath his nose and travels down the middle of his chin like someone began to cut his face in half but thought better of it.

"Rick's sitting down there with a bunch of dynamite. He says he's gonna kill himself by blowing up the mine," Jamie joins in.

He's the tallest, wiry, with a goatee.

"That way his wife and kids will get his life insurance, plus they can sue Walker Dawes."

"How is the financial gain part of the plan supposed to succeed since you all know the truth?" I ask them.

Shawn, dark-eyed, broad-shouldered with an angular face, speaks for the whole group by folding his arms across his chest and shrugging.

I instantly understand that none of them would ever rat out their buddy, and their buddy knows this.

"Rick didn't want any of us to get hurt so he made us all come back up topside," J. C. further explains. "We wanted to stay. We figured if we did we could find a way out of it. There's no way he'd blow up all five of us, but Carl said it has nothing to do with numbers. If Rick turns crazy enough to blow up his brother, he'd have no problem blowing up four more guys, so we might as well go."

"It made sense to us," Todd confirms guiltily.

"So Carl stayed?"

"Yeah."

"Why didn't you try to overpower Rick? It would have been five against one."

"He had a gun. He brought this old revolver of his with him in his lunch pail," J. C. goes on.

"You don't want to shoot a gun in a coal mine," he adds for my edification.

I don't know the exact chemistry and physics principles supporting this fact, but I'm willing to take his word for it.

"So the situation right now is a suicidal man is sitting in a coal mine with his brother armed with a handgun and a bunch of dynamite?" I summarize. "This is awful, but I don't understand why I'm here."

"You're a shrink." Shawn speaks for the first time.

Brenna places her hand on my arm.

"I thought maybe you could talk some sense into him," she says pleadingly.

I glance around at all their faces except for Rafe, who turns away from me and begins unwrapping candy. Tommy—who should be fine with what they're asking, even happy at the thought that his grandson might be able to save the day—looks dumbstruck.

The idea is so far beyond possible, I can't even begin to consider it, then I suddenly realize what they must actually be asking of me.

"You mean through a phone or a radio?"

"Nah," Todd replies. "He won't talk to anyone willingly. You'll have to go to him and make him talk to you."

"We know it's asking a lot," J. C. concedes.

"Yeah. It takes a half hour in the mantrip to get to the room where we was cutting. Who knows what could happen in the meantime?"

"Don't say that, Todd," Brenna scolds.

I don't know what I'm showing on the outside, but on the inside I've dissolved into a puddle. I must not look too good, though, because Tommy takes me by the arm and leads me away.

"Listen," he says. "I know how afraid you are of the mines. I know about your nightmares."

"How? I never told you."

"You told me plenty, but you were always hysterical at the time and probably don't remember."

"All these years you've known?"

"It doesn't matter."

"It's embarrassing."

"No, it's not. Those men over there would never be able to put on a suit and testify before a jury or sit down and have a chat with a serial killer. They'd be as afraid of doing your job as you're afraid of doing theirs.

"You don't have to do this, Danny. No one will think less of you."

I know he's right. They wouldn't think less of me because it's not possible. Right now they think nothing of me.

We walk back over.

"I'll do it," I say.

I expect saying the words out loud will give me some sort of confidence boost, but I'm wrong.

My heart is already pounding much too fast. My mouth has gone dry and my legs feel weak. I take some comfort in the fact that I'm probably not going to make it into the mine; I'm sure I'll pass out first.

"Come on over to the trailer and we'll get you fixed up with some boots and coveralls," Brenna says.

"It's okay. I'll go like this."

She and all the men look me up and down. Beneath my knee-length slate gray Tom Ford overcoat are dark-wash jeans, an Yves Saint Laurent Henley, a Boss Orange shawl-collar cardigan, and a pair of vintage Prada boots.

"Your clothes are gonna get ruined," Todd points out.

"It's okay. I want to keep them on."

I take off my coat and give it to Tommy.

J. C. hands me his helmet and also his heavy leather tool belt.

"I highly doubt I'll need any tools. Or were you planning to put me to work?" I attempt some levity.

"It's for the dog tag."

He shows me the brass plate on the belt inscribed with his name and social security number. I know what it's for. Sometimes it's the only way to identify a body.

"You're Joseph Cameron Hewitt now."

"It's up to you, Danno," Rafe says, finally weighing in on my decision.

"Almost forgot," J. C. says. "Here's your self-rescuer."

He hands me a canteenlike piece of equipment.

"If something goes wrong you got enough air for an hour."

A MANTRIP IS THE flat, battery-powered cart that takes the miners to the face where they're cutting coal. It rides on rails, and as Silent Shawn and I begin our downward-sloping journey into the inky darkness, I try to think of it as the world's most horrific amusement park ride: it might end in a stroll down the fairway eating cotton candy and cheesy fries, or it might end in men digging for days only to find bits and pieces of you and a brass tag with someone else's name on it.

Top that, Pirates of the Caribbean.

I try not to look at the walls of black rock speeding past or, more important, at the ceiling. This part of the tunnel is only a little over four feet tall. If I were to panic and stand up, I'd be knocked unconscious. It's a tempting thought.

I've managed to stay composed so far except for the sweat pouring down my back, dripping onto my face, and oiling the palms of my hands. This reaction isn't caused by heat. After the miners explained to me that they all wear long johns under their coveralls, they convinced me to take Al Kelly's coat. I'm glad I did. Along with being dark, cramped, and damp, it's also cold down here.

The tunnel suddenly opens into a broader area with a slightly higher ceiling called the mains, short for the main section. I've spent enough time listening to my dad and Tommy and other miners talk about their work to recognize that this mine has been dug by a method known as room-and-pillar, in which the coal is removed in a series of rooms or entries with blocks of coal left in to keep the roof from collapsing. I count six numbered entries. Running between each one at about fifty-foot intervals are the crosscuts that allow access from one corridor to the next. I don't know how the men keep track of all of them.

Though a little less claustrophobic, the mains aren't much of an improvement over the setting in my dreams. Now instead of being trapped in a tunnel, I'm lost in a huge black maze.

"I appreciate you taking me down, Shawn."

"No problem. Can do it in my sleep. Truth be told, most of the time I'm on this thing, I am sleeping."

I glance back at him calmly rolling a wad of tobacco around beneath his lower lip and carving at his thumbnail with a pocketknife.

The boys of my youth jumped off anything, attacked anyone, ventured anywhere no matter how dark or perilous without giving any thought to what harm might befall them. I could never decide if they were brave or stupid until I finally came to realize they were neither; they acted that way simply because no one ever taught them to value their lives. I was convinced it was the same mentality that led them into the mines.

Watching Shawn, I reassess my findings. All people value their lives and everyone is afraid of dying. It's a particular manner of death that leads to phobic behavior. Even now as I'm experiencing my worst nightmare in real life, I'm not afraid of dying; I'm afraid of the mine killing me.

"How far are we going to go underground?"

"'Bout a mile and a half."

"I probably shouldn't have asked that."

"Probably not."

I close my eyes and in my mind I start running a mile and a half. I see the road stretching out before me, a pitted gray empty country road with no end in sight.

I have no idea what I'm going to say to Rick Kelly. Walker Dawes was right when he suggested that I haven't hung up a shingle and gone into private practice because I don't care about making people better. I don't. I have enough trouble dealing with my own problems and those surrounding my family.

I do what I do because I'm fascinated by the workings of the human mind, especially the minds that have failed society. I want to understand the criminals, crazies, outcasts, and dropouts and their unorthodox, sometimes destructive and violent, almost always unacceptable means of survival.

Rick, who was described to me before I began my descent as the most normal of normal guys, a nice, easygoing family man who hardly ever raises his voice and whose only vice is an inexplicable love of rap music, is exactly the kind of man who should value his life but has decided he doesn't want to survive, while Carson Shupe would have done anything to survive including murdering young boys; it was the only thing in his mind that gave him a reason to keep getting up in the morning.

We finally come to a stop. Alongside the fact that every inch we've traveled looks exactly the same to me, the ins and outs of the mains have me completely confused. If I were to be left alone, I could never find my way out of here.

I try to push this thought out of my mind and fill it with bright, airy, generous images. Everything I come up with centers around my mother: the beautiful summer day we painted our garage Pepto-Bismol pink; the colorful cookies we used to make to share with our neighbors; her sitting in Tommy's rocking chair near the sunny front windows knitting another addition to her rainbow coalition of hats.

Shawn gets off the mantrip and motions for me to follow him. The ceiling has become low again. He moves quickly, even gracefully, hunched over like a gorilla, using his miner's hammer as a walking stick.

I try my best to keep up with him and to keep my panic at bay. Everywhere I look I see nothing but black nothingness, yet I know I'm surrounded by something impenetrable.

In the light cast by our two helmet lamps I think I see movement. I've been placing my hands on the moist rock walls to help keep my balance. I drop them to my sides.

"Are there rats down here?" I ask Shawn.

"Haven't seen any, but we got spiders big as Labrador retrievers."

I hear him chuckling to himself.

A face suddenly appears out of the gloom, reminding me so much of the faces seared to the seam wall in my nightmare that I almost faint.

I jerk back and bump into the wall that I'm convinced moved and I jump forward to get away from it.

The two men pay no attention to me.

"How's he doing?" I hear Shawn ask Carl Kelly.

"Not good. He's not himself."

"Brenna got Danny Doyle to come talk to him. He's a shrink, you know."

A moment of silence passes while Carl considers this new development.

"I don't know if that's a good idea, but I'm willing to try anything. What are you gonna say?" he asks me.

"I don't know."

"You know he's got a gun."

"Yes."

"He's right over there."

They point into the midnight abyss of solid black rock. I see nothing.

I maneuver my lamp until I can make out a miner sitting against a wall. He has his own lamp turned off.

I tap my helmet.

"What if all the lights go out?"

Shawn spits a stream of tobacco.

"Then you'll be in the dark."

I join Rick Kelly, concentrating on the task at hand and trying to ignore once again where I am. It's not easy.

"I'm Danny Doyle," I say to him, taking a seat next to him. "Tommy's grandson. We met here at the mine a couple days ago."

"Oh, man," he unexpectedly wails. "They sent me a shrink. I'm not crazy."

"No one thinks you're crazy."

"Then why'd they send me a shrink?"

"Your family and friends thought maybe I'd have better luck talking to you. Since that's my job, getting people to talk just like"—I pause and look around me at our dungeon surroundings—"this is your job."

"Not for too much longer. Tim's bankrupt. He's going to close down."

His face and clothes are covered in soot. He'd blend in completely with the coal behind him if it weren't for the white rings around his eyes and the emotion shining in them.

He suddenly looks as frantic as I feel.

"Who knows about this?" he says. "Who's out there? Does my wife know?"

"Just the guys on your crew, Brenna, and your dad's here, too."

"My dad? He's sick."

"Your dad loves you."

"I know my dad loves me. I don't need a shrink to tell me that. I'm not fucked up."

I glance at the handgun sitting in his lap and the pile of dynamite lying next to him.

"No one thinks you're fucked up," I assure him.

"You made a long trip for nothing. I don't feel like talking."

"Don't you think you owe them an explanation?"

"They can figure it out."

"That's the thing about suicide. The person doing it thinks the people they leave behind will understand, but they almost never do."

"I got no way to make a living. My wife's got no way to make a living. We got kids and bills," he says, ticking off the reasons.

"There are resources. Programs, people who can help you."

"Don't give me any of that liberal helping-hands bullshit," he says loudly.

I expect an echo but the chamber we're in is too compact and the walls too dense for sound to travel.

"I want to work. You understand me? I want to work. My wife wants to work. We're not freeloaders. We don't want the government paying for us."

"I'm not talking about welfare."

"We don't want anyone paying for us."

My mind races trying to come up with anything I can say that can help this man solve his problems.

"When I was a kid I didn't want to go to Heaven," he tells me. "You know why? Because it sounded so frickin' boring. No one had a frickin' job. What do angels do all day?"

"You'd rather toil in hell than lounge in Heaven. Interesting."

"Don't call me interesting. I'm not a chapter in one of your books."

"You've read my books?"

"I can read."

"I didn't ask if you could read. I asked if you've read my books."

His eyes flash angrily.

"Turn your lamp off," he says.

"Excuse me?"

"Turn your goddamned lamp off," he repeats through gritted teeth.

Even though Rick is armed with a gun and explosives, there's still a part of me that would rather risk more of his wrath than do what he's asking of me, but I know I won't be able to reason with him if he stays mad.

I turn off my light and my sight is gone. I close my eyes; I open them. There's no difference in what I'm seeing. I hold my hand up two inches in front of my face. Nothing.

Next to me I feel the tension flow out of Rick's body. I realize that he likes the dark. More than that, he likes this mine.

I think of all the times I've heard Tommy talk about the mines he's worked in as if he were talking about women. Some were unpredictable, some complained more than others, some were silent and serene, some were generous, some were tough and hard to please, but the miners entrusted their lives to all of them without question. Each lady enfolded them in her depths and looked after them while they took the riches from inside her.

Rick's overwhelmed by his obligations and responsibilities. He can't keep his head above water. He's a drowning man.

"You want to kill yourself in the mine because you're not afraid of dying here. You like it here. But you're afraid of something. You're afraid of drowning."

"How'd you know that?" his disembodied voice asks.

"Everyone has a particular means of death that terrifies them more than any other and they fall into the four categories of the elements. There's sky, fear of dying in a plane crash or falling from a great height;

water, fear of drowning; fire, fear of burning in a fire or explosion; and earth, fear of being buried alive."

"What are you afraid of?"

"Being buried alive."

"Then you're in the wrong place. I could tell you're petrified. Your voice is shaking."

I have nothing to add on this subject. I clench and unclench the hands I can't see.

"If you're so afraid, why are you doing this? Don't say to help me. You don't know me."

I try to recall all the reasons I gave myself before I made the decision to come down here, but only one seems to make any sense to me now.

"I wanted to be useful."

He says nothing to this and I have nothing to say to him. This isn't a good sign in a psychotherapy session.

"You're trying to solve a problem for your family but I don't think you want to die," I try. "People who succeed at killing themselves do so because they want to die."

"What are you saying?"

"I'm saying you're not going to do it."

"Is that a dare?"

Bad idea. I search for another avenue of self-discovery.

I know how much he cares about Lost Creek. I've seen the scale model he made of the town on display at the NONS museum in Nora Daley's attic. The details are painstaking. It required not only time and craftsmanship but love.

"You know, maybe you're right. Maybe you don't have a reason to live. I mean, look at this shithole you live in."

"Reverse psychology? That's the best you got? You suck at this."

Third time's a charm.

"What about your children?"

"Now you're gonna try and convince me I should keep living for my kids? Man, you really suck at this."

"Your kids need you."

"Don't talk about my kids. You got kids?"

"No."

"Why not?"

I begin to list the reasons: "Selfishness, fear, a dislike of clutter."

"Your problem is you think too much," he tells me.

"We're not talking about my problems."

"I'd rather talk about your problems."

"My biggest problem is I'm sitting in a coal mine."

"Don't you have a messed-up mom? The one who went to prison for killing her baby?"

I nod, then remember he can't see me.

"Yes."

"Is that why you became a shrink?"

"It might have had something to do with it."

"She's one strong lady from what I've heard."

I don't think I've ever heard my mother described this way.

"I mean, her illness," he explains. "She had spells, right? But she always came back to you and kept being your mom. That must've been hard for her."

I envision my mother clawing her way through the crushing terrain of her illness to get back to me, her blue sky.

She wanted me to be an astronaut. She made me a tablecloth covered with celestial bodies and all of them were happy.

"Rick, I'd like to hire you. I'll pay you five thousand dollars if you get me the hell out of here."

The silence is maddening. It's louder than the streets of Philly at rush hour.

"You expect me to take your money?"

"It's not charity. It's not even a loan. I can't leave without you. I'm paying you to do a job."

More silence, then I hear a sigh and the lamp on his helmet snaps back on, spraying a glorious shower of white light across his filthy features.

"I can't take your five grand," he says, "but I'll do it for two."

twenty-three

I LEFT THE SCENE AT the mine in the capable hands of Rafe and left Rick Kelly in the capable hands of Dr. Versey, who agreed he should be put under a seventy-two-hour psychological hold.

Rafe didn't know how things were going to shake out in regards to criminal charges. No one was ultimately hurt, but threatening to blow up a coal mine, even an empty one, is no small matter. Just to be on the safe side I put Brenna in touch with a friend of mine who's one of the best defense attorneys in the state and adept at vindicating people who have committed their offenses under extreme emotional duress.

Back at Tommy's I immediately stripped and took a long, hot shower with the rock-hard lye soap he used to scrub with after every shift. I held out my hand to him and he placed the grainy cake, the color of old snuff, in my palm with all the sober majesty of an aged king ceding his scepter.

In return I gave him the garbage bag containing my clothes.

Sporadic bursts of Kellys showed up throughout the rest of the day, all of them bearing some type of casserole or baked good as if the ordeal of helping their emotionally embattled kinsman return to his senses must have given me an insatiable appetite. Tommy and I made small talk with them about everything under the sun except for the topic of Rick; no one came close to asking me to disclose anything he might have said to me.

Mom was feeling better and played the charming hostess. She chatted and made coffee and never showed a sign of her illness, yet everyone present knew her history and could probably sense my nervousness at having her on display. A condition they once feared or pitied or maybe discounted or even ridiculed had shown up in their own lives and become suddenly real to them. They looked upon Tommy and me with a new awareness and regard. Rick's alarming actions were brought on by desperation and will hopefully never be repeated; his situation is a far cry from my mother's, yet once a family witnesses a loved one's disintegration they can never escape the constant dread that it might happen again and that the next time it will be worse.

I did my best to appear fine on the outside, but it took most of the day before I stopped shaking inside.

Rafe told me to stop by his house when he got off work so we could talk. As I stand outside his front door, the exhaustion of the day finally catches up to me. I'd like nothing more than to stretch out on his couch and fall asleep while he sits in a big easy chair drinking a beer watching an action movie or a favorite sitcom. I assume this is how an evening at home with Rafe would sound and look. After all these years of knowing him, I've never been across his threshold.

As a child, I imagined Rafe's home to be similar to Superman's fortress of solitude. High on a hilltop he would retire after a day of writing speeding tickets and mopping up the countryside to contemplate the woes of humanity and the peril of driving seventy down a one-lane country road.

As an adult, I was surprised to discover he lived in a small unremarkable house badly in need of a fresh coat of paint and a new roof. Tommy and I were driving by once while he was in the front yard, shirtless, on a tractor mower. We stopped to talk to him. He asked us if we wanted beers then hustled off to put on a shirt, but not before I saw the four puckered gunshot wounds in his chest he had picked up in Vietnam.

At the time he was between wives. He's had two more since then, but the house is the same. Either he moves wives in and out or he always keeps this house on the side just in case.

He greets me at the front door in jeans and a Penguins sweatshirt. It strikes me that my entire life I've only seen him in a police uniform or most recently the visual cacophony I've come to refer to in my mind as his detective clothes.

It's strange to see him look like a regular guy.

"I'm making dinner. Come on in."

It's also strange to think of him cooking.

We're about to step inside when the Mayhem Machine comes roaring down the road and into Rafe's driveway.

Velma hops out of the van. He's swapped his duster for a billowing black cape and is also wearing a fur hat that looks like a large gray cat curled on top of his bald head.

He drags out a small toboggan and places it firmly in the snow. Wade leaps out and onto the middle of it where he remains sitting imperially in a shiny lavender ski jacket, matching earmuffs, and four tiny blond UGGs while Velma pulls him toward the house.

As soon as he sees Rafe, Wade goes crazy. He starts barking uncontrollably and chasing his tail while somehow managing to stay on the very limited surface of the little sled. The need for the contraption becomes apparent when his agitation gets the better of him and he tries to propel himself into Rafe's arms but falls short and soundlessly disappears into the deep snow like a toy dropped into a child's bubble bath.

Much to my amazement, Rafe bends down and pulls him out of the drift then slips the shivering dog into the pocket of his sweatshirt.

"What are you doing here?" he asks Velma. "I thought you were leaving today."

"Tomorrow. We want to go back to the gallows one more time. We experienced some very promising activity last night."

"What are you doing here at my house?" Rafe says.

"Oh, well, Wade insisted on seeing you again."

"Am I still in danger?"

"No. Now Wade's insisting there's a tortured soul from the other side who needs your help crossing over."

I'm surprised to see Rafe's highly skeptical look soften into one of possible consideration.

"You actually believe in this stuff?"

"What I believe isn't important. All that matters is what Wade believes."

Rafe reaches into his pocket and pulls out the little dog. He holds him up in the air by the back of his jacket. Wade hangs limply in the air.

"Is he yours?" I ask Velma.

"Wade doesn't like the O word," Velma replies, then silently mouths the word "owner" to us.

"He also doesn't like the T word. 'Trainer,'" he mouths again. "But yes, I'm both."

"And you really think he can see ghosts and predict the future?"

Wade begins to whine. Rafe sets him back on the sled.

"Wade was a rescue dog," Velma begins, "and one of his little quirks was he'd suddenly for no reason start barking and running in circles then run into a corner and sit up in a begging position and shake all over looking positively terrified. I said to my partner at the time that he looked like he was seeing a ghost, but we had no idea what was really causing it.

"This same partner of mine loved candles. We had hundreds of them. I finally figured out that Wade went into his little freak-out whenever Justin struck a match. I talked to someone at the shelter and she told me that Wade's previous owner used to throw lit matches at him. When they found him he had burn marks all over him."

"That's terrible," I say.

Velma nods vehemently.

"I know. Well, the idea had been planted in my head. All I have to do is strike a match to get him to perform. Other trainers use whistles and hand gestures. Don't get me wrong. Wade is a brilliant dog. He responds to those, too."

"You use his fear to make money?" I ask incredulously.

"Wade has a wonderful life. Now if you don't mind, we were hoping to get this on film."

Rafe reaches down while Velma rattles on and picks up Wade again and returns him to his pocket.

"I'm confiscating your dog," he says, and goes back inside his house.

"Wait! Wait!" Velma calls out.

"He can't do that," he says to me.

"He just did."

He starts pounding on Rafe's door.

"Don't bother," I tell him. "He'll give him back when he's ready to give him back."

"We have a show to do!"

"Come back in an hour or so. He won't keep him longer than that."

"I'm calling our lawyer," Velma huffs.

"Call away."

He starts to stalk off then stops and reaches inside his voluminous cape and brings out a Fiji bottled water.

"Here," he says handing it to me. "It's the only water Wade drinks."

I watch until the van is completely out of sight before going inside.

It's instantly apparent to me that Rafe is a man who never puts anything away, but since he doesn't have that many belongings, the habit doesn't overwhelm his surroundings.

Clothing and dishes are piled everywhere, but the clothing is clean and folded and the dishes look clean, too, stacked in various spots around the room. A flashlight, pocket knife, screwdriver, roll of masking tape, and a can opener are neatly lined up on a windowsill. The top of a desk set in a corner of the room is functioning as a pantry and liquor cabinet. Bottles, canned goods, a loaf of bread, and a box of Wheaties sit there along with a scattering of Jolly Ranchers of every color but pink.

I'm not sure if he has a fear of drawers and cupboards or can't be bothered to take the time to use them. Whatever the reason, he does all his living out in the open.

An entire bookcase is filled with framed photos of his five grown daughters at every stage of their lives along with those of his numerous grandchildren.

Mixed among them I'm surprised to also find photos of him with each of his ex-wives: him as a blue-eyed boy in a suit wearing a tie he probably had to borrow clutching a brown-eyed girl in a simple white dress, both smiling breezily, their confidence stemming from the fact they were too young to imagine life beyond twenty-two; in front of a

flower-festooned church altar, the big Irish Catholic wedding to Glynnis Kelly, her in a sparkling ivory ball gown, Rafe in a tux this time, grinning broadly, drunk already, a man with a good job, good bennies, the
first mistake of a marriage behind him, settling down now to the real
thing; at the VFW, in a suit again, not a tux, middle-aged, with a safe
schoolteacher in an eggshell suit trimmed in lace holding a bouquet of
gardenias, not smiling this time, serious about this one, serious about
life; a picnic table outside the Lick 'n' Putt, the remnants of chili dogs
and slushies in front of them along with their miniature-golf scorecards,
with a woman to warm his bed and his leftovers, which he thought
would be reason enough to make it work.

I follow the smell of sautéing green peppers, garlic, and onions into
the kitchen. Rafe is busy at the stove. Wade stands behind him intently
watching.

A plateful of shredded blackened chicken topped with a handful of
fresh herbs sits on the table along with a stack of flour tortillas.

"Is this cilantro?" I ask Rafe.

"Yeah, how 'bout that? We ignorant yokels stumble across exotic
stuff now and then."

I take his ribbing in stride. Normally I'd feel a sting, but after what
I've been through today, nothing can bother me as long as it's happening
aboveground.

Wade rises up on his hind legs and paws at the air.

"What's he want?" I ask.

"I think he wants you to take his coat off."

I lean down and unzip the little parka. Underneath he's wearing a
black T-shirt with "Doggie Style" written across it in miniscule silver
studs.

"Velma says this is the only water Wade drinks."

I set the Fiji bottle on the counter.

Rafe ignores it and fills a bowl with tap water he sets on the floor.

"Pour us a drink, too," he says.

I follow his gaze to a bottle of vodka. He's been mixing it with
Mountain Dew.

I refresh his drink and get myself a glass.

"You know if you two start seriously seeing each other you're bound to wind up in the tabloids," I warn him, glancing at the happily lapping terrier.

I look in his refrigerator for an alternative mixer. Beer, beer, milk, and more beer. I end up settling for straight vodka after discovering one lone lime.

"Come on," he says.

I begin to follow him then realize he's talking to Wade.

The little dog trots after him back into his living room.

Rafe turns on his TV and searches through the channels.

"Here's that show about meerkats," I hear him say. "You should like that."

Wade jumps onto the couch, circles the cushion a few times, and lays down.

Rafe returns to the kitchen and tends to his vegetables on the stovetop.

"You never told me the whole story about Scarlet and Billy's gun," I say to him.

"Not much to tell. She took it."

"How did she manage that?"

"She got him to take her back to his place. He was shitfaced. He said she talked him into showing her his gun, had sex with him, and when he passed out afterward, she took it and left."

"You believe all this?"

"Not the part where she had sex with him, but everything else."

"She admitted to it?"

"Not to taking the gun, but she took it. There's no other explanation."

"It doesn't make sense for her to take a gun."

"It makes perfect sense. I think this woman has already killed three people that we know of."

"A gun is too pedestrian for her. Shooting someone is murder. There's no other way to classify the act. If she was responsible for those other three deaths, I highly doubt she thinks of them as murders."

"Then what the hell are they?"

"She's a psychopath. They don't conduct their lives according to the same moral codes and standards of behavior that the rest of us do," I explain. "Their social interactions are nothing more than plans to outmaneuver others in order to get what they want. They have no guilt. No remorse. No conscience. What seems a crime to us is an act of expediency or entitlement to them."

"A problem solved."

"In a sense, yes."

Rafe turns off the stove and makes himself another drink.

"Do you think she was planning to kill Marcella Greger, though, or it just happened?" I ask him. "The sculpture she hit her with was a weapon of opportunity."

"A can of gasoline and a dose of penicillin aren't exactly things you carry around with you," he replies. "Those murders were premeditated."

"But I'm sure they had special meaning to her. There was a reason she decided to set her nanny on fire and poisoned a friend. I just can't see her shooting someone. It may sound strange, but I think she'd consider it to be tacky."

He grabs two plates from a stack on the counter and sets them on the table, then leaves the kitchen. He returns carrying two envelopes and a folder.

He hands me one of the envelopes.

"What's this?"

"Marcella Greger's niece brought this to me at the police station. Marcella didn't have much, but she did have a will, and the lawyer who drew it up for her had this letter and instructions to give it to her niece when she died."

I take out a four-page handwritten letter.

"Don't bother reading any of that," Rafe tells me. "Get to the last paragraph."

"'I'm enclosing a copy of a letter from my cousin, Anna, I found in her belongings,'" I read out loud. "'The original is in my lockbox at the UPS store. I'm not as young as I used to be, plus accidents happen. If you're reading this it means I'm dead and I didn't have time to tell anyone about this.'"

He hands me the other envelope. Inside is a single piece of paper.

On May 24, 1974, Gwendolyn Dawes caused the death of her one-week-old infant, Scarlet Dawes. I knew of a man who had a daughter of the same age he wasn't able to care for and agreed to switch the babies.

It's signed by Anna Greger.

"Gwendolyn Dawes killed her baby? That can't be true. What about Scarlet?"

"Look at the date," Rafe says.

It's the day before Mom killed Molly.

"Sit down, Danno."

My head is whirling. I have all the pieces; I just can't fit them together.

"I really struggled with this. I thought about burying all of it and not telling you anything. No good can come of it. Nothing from the past can be changed. There's no way to get any justice in the future—"

"What are you talking about?" I interrupt him. "What's going on?"

"Listen to me carefully. When I came back from Vietnam, I found myself in some truly fucked-up way missing it."

"You said Vietnam was like being in hell."

"It was. That's what I didn't understand. I was back home. I was a civilian again. That's what I wanted, but I felt like a stranger. I didn't belong anymore. It wasn't anybody's fault. It was just a fact.

"I couldn't hate the war the way protestors did, and I was the one who should've hated it because I was the one who was there, but that's exactly why I couldn't hate it as much as they did. They didn't know what they were talking about. They were free to imagine whatever they wanted, but it wasn't abstract to me. It was personal. The deepest emotions I would ever feel in my entire life I felt in Nam; not between some woman's legs, not winning a championship football game, not teaching my child how to ride a bike, not getting a promotion at work, but in a jungle on the other side of the world killing people who had never done a damn thing to me."

People who were just like you, I think silently to myself, remembering our talk from long ago.

He sits down across the table from me and fixes me with his piercing stare.

"It may have been the worst thing that would ever happen to me, but it was also the most significant."

He hands me a folder with a state police seal on the front.

"We were able to lift some DNA from the lipstick smudge on the glass," he explains. "I called in a big favor and was able to get a rush job through the state crime lab."

"Is it hers?"

"I don't know that for sure since I didn't have a sample from her to compare it to so I compared it to someone else's."

"What good does that do? Especially when you don't know it's hers to begin with?"

"We both know it's hers," he says with a dark finality.

I open it and study the results of the lab test.

"You've seen enough of these reports. You know what this means?" he asks me.

"It's not enough for a match but the two subjects are related. A child? A sibling? We know she has a brother."

"Yeah, she does have a brother, but I didn't run this against Wesley Dawes' DNA," he says. "I ran it against yours."

twenty-four

DON'T TELL HER, RAFE insisted, but I convinced him that she probably already knows. This could be why she's shown an interest in me and why she put that note in Tommy's mailbox. It seems like something she would do. She loves to mess with people's minds. It's the same reason she drew the hanging man in Marcella Greger's bathroom.

He still didn't want me to talk to her, to let her know I know, but I told him I have to confront her. She's my sister, I explained, but quickly added that I have no delusions about a future with her. I'm not going into this meeting with sentimental hopes of a tearful reunion, that we'll throw our arms around each other and erase the past.

I know who and what she is and the impossibility of changing either. She has no moral boundaries and there's no pill to cure this. No method of rehabilitation. No school of psychotherapy that can explain or fix her. Not even a fairy tale could provide a happy ending to our story. Unlike Wendy tending to Peter Pan's shadow, no one can sew a conscience back on.

He agreed to let me talk to her but only if we met in a public place.

I suggested a drink at the Red Rabbit to her almost as a joke. She agreed.

I'm waiting at a scarred wooden table in a dark corner nursing a beer trying to silence my mind but having no luck. Rage has pushed aside all other emotions including the grieving I will need to do over what my mother and Tommy and I have endured.

My rage is a brilliant red and sits perched on my shoulder, not square in the middle of my back the way Rafe's hate once did. It burns hot against my cheek and casts a golden ruby glow over everything I see. It's not a burden like hate; on the contrary, its righteous urgency makes me feel weightless.

In my work I've encountered every level of depravity, viciousness, and selfishness, but I've never come across anything as heinous as what my father has done.

My father conspired with an old girlfriend to take a child from her mother and a sister from her brother and sent his mentally ill wife to jail for a horrendous crime she didn't commit. I recite the words calmly in my head. I feel like standing up in these booze-flavored shadows and saying them out loud, just as calmly, to the half-dozen raggedy men tossing back shots and sucking down beer chasers.

They wouldn't be shocked. They'd take it all in stride. One more day in a company town.

Why did he do it? For what? Money? He certainly doesn't live like a man who took a payoff for selling a baby and keeping his mouth shut for Walker Dawes.

I realize now when Walker shook my hand the other day he wasn't seeing just the great-great-grandson of Prosperity McNab, but the brother of the girl he raised as his own daughter.

Scarlet just found out. Rafe and I are fairly certain of this. Marcella knew. It's why Scarlet came back. To talk to her, to confront her, to silence her: it all finally makes sense.

Walker knows the beast he has lived with all his life, the monster he unwittingly brought into his home thinking she was an innocent stolen babe, is finally going to turn her reptilian gaze on him.

No wonder he was curious about me. He was evaluating our genes.

The door opens and Scarlet stands in silhouette under the outside light against a backdrop of black sky swirling with snowflakes.

Her entrance causes no stir. The men glance then go back to their methodical drinking. Boss's daughter. One more player in a company town.

She takes her time crossing the room, pausing to look at the old photos of miners and local landmarks on the walls and propped behind the bar. She orders a drink and brings it with her.

I study her face: the heart shape of it, the slightly upturned nose, the wide-set eyes; it's my mother's face slightly modified. I never noticed the resemblance before, but I wasn't looking for it. Now I can't see anything else.

She pulls out a chair for her mink then one for herself.

"How did it go the other night?" she asks me. "Did you get some?"

"How much do you know?"

"About your sex life? Nothing. But it can't be too good if you were going after that."

"Do you know who you are or do you only know who you aren't?"

This question gives her pause.

She drinks while staring at me but doesn't answer.

"The identity theft you were talking about at Chappy's," I go on. "Marcella Greger knew about it, too. It's why you killed her."

She continues staring at me. There's nothing in her eyes. They're as flat as the glass ones stuffed into Tommy's deer head.

"What do you know?" she finally asks.

"I know you're my sister."

Her gaze doesn't waver, but I can tell she's been mentally slapped.

I don't hurry her. I sit across the table and wait for her to decide what her next move should be. Rage burns hotly and contentedly beside me. I'm sure at this point my skin has melted from my bones and nothing is left but one of the charred skeletons from my dream.

If she reaches out and touches me, I will collapse into a pile of ash.

"I like it," she finally announces. "I love it, actually. Because of me the entire Dawes fortune is going to end up in the hands of Prosperity McNab's great-great-granddaughter. Talk about revenge. Talk about poetic justice."

She smiles and takes a sip of her drink.

"That's it? That's your reaction? That's all you've got to say? All you can think about is money?"

My outburst surprises her. It surprises me, too. I had planned to conduct this conversation without passing judgment or displaying emotion like I would any clinical interview with a psychopath.

I try to get my composure back.

"What about Wesley?" I ask. "And his children? Won't they inherit, too?"

Would she be capable of killing an entire family? I wonder. How would she do it? It would have to involve explosives.

"I guess we can share," she says, not sounding pleased with the idea. "I'm not unreasonable."

"Then you have no intention of going public? Of letting the world know what happened?"

"Is that why you got upset? Is that why you're all mad and mopey?"

She smiles at me again.

"I'm sorry, but we can't let anyone else know. Don't take it the wrong way. I'm not embarrassed or appalled. I don't care that my real family is white trash. I'm thrilled to find out that you're my big brother."

I watch and listen in amazement, knowing there's nothing I can do or say that can make her understand that there's something terribly wrong with her. She can't feel empathy or compassion. Half the time she doesn't realize she's hurting people and the other half she doesn't care.

"And there isn't anyone else who knows," she continues. "Believe me, Gwen isn't going to say anything, and Walker doesn't know—"

"He doesn't know?" I interrupt her. "How is that possible?"

The man I met knows everything that goes on in his home and business. There's no way anyone, even his wife, could keep something this big hidden from him. Scarlet should realize this, but her narcissism would make her prone to missing details about others.

"Trust me, he doesn't know. That just leaves you and me. You didn't tell Candy Cop, did you?"

"No."

I think about Wade's insistence that Rafe is in danger. Could the little dog be onto something?

"What about Mom?" she says.

Hearing her call my mom "Mom" makes my stomach lurch. There's no affection or even regard attached to the word. She makes it sound indecent.

"What about her?"

"I'm kind of disappointed in her. How does a woman let someone steal her baby? And then when the other baby was found, how could she have believed it was hers? Don't good mothers have some kind of intuition, some kind of maternal tracking device? Where was her due diligence?"

"Mom always knew the dead baby wasn't her baby," I say in Mom's defense, "but no one believed her. Except for her father. Even I didn't believe her. I thought she did it."

When I look at Scarlet again, I still see pieces of my mom, but trapped in something cold and hard like her reflection seen in shards of broken glass.

"I suppose you think we should tell Mom. She's spent all this time wondering what happened to me and wondering who that dead baby was in her backyard."

"No," I say forcefully. "No, she shouldn't know. Her mental health is too fragile. It could cause her to have a psychotic break or it might not register at all. Nothing good could come of it."

I don't want Scarlet anywhere near my mother, but thinking about my love for Mom reminds me of something.

"You've forgotten someone. There's someone else who knows."

Scarlet gives me her full attention.

In my head I picture the first Walker Dawes standing near the gallows nodding his head to the executioner.

So this is how it feels.

"Our dad knows," I tell her.

"Anna's boyfriend," she says slowly in the same tone of eerie giddiness she used when talking about Moira's red shoes.

She finishes her drink, gives me one more stunning, empty smile, and stands to go.

"I'm sorry, Danny, but this is a lot to take in. I'm going, but I have one more question for you. What were you hoping to get out of all of this?"

"What do you mean?"

"Why did you tell me?"

"If you had found out first would you have told me?"

"Good question. Assuming I hadn't run into you the way I did and I didn't know you at all? Would I have sought you out or any member of our family? Probably not. I'm only being kind. I'm only thinking of all of you. I think we can both agree you'd probably be much better off not knowing."

She slips into the glossy heavy black fur.

"One more thing," she says. "What's my name?"

I conquered my worst fear today only to come face to face with a brand-new one.

"Molly," I tell her. "You're Molly Doyle."

I FIND TOMMY DOZING in his favorite chair with a book in his lap when I arrive back at his house. I go into the kitchen and pour milk into the battered saucepan that never leaves his stovetop.

"There he is. Our hero," he says to me upon waking.

"Don't call me that. I didn't do anything heroic. I went into a coal mine, something you did almost every day for forty years."

"But you were afraid of the mines," he says. "You put aside that fear to help someone else. That's bravery. That makes you a hero."

One of his coughing spells wracks his body. He reaches for his empty coffee can and spits.

"But I want you to know there's no shame in being afraid of the mines," he says once he settles back into his chair. "I never knew a man worked in them who wasn't. Every shift you think, 'This might be my last glimpse of the sky, my last breath of fresh air,' but you put those thoughts aside and concentrate on your job.

"I had a fellow work with me, a bolter. The most dangerous job in the mines. He went in and secured the roof for the rest of us. Young, strong, fearless as they come. One bright sunny Sunday afternoon he slipped and fell down his basement stairs. Broke his neck and died.

"Everyone took his death very hard. It seemed like a slap in the face, some kind of joke. He survived all the danger around him only to die in an almost silly way."

He clasps his big, scarred, knotty hands together over the spine of his book.

"The randomness of life. Hard workers end up in the poorhouse while the lazy make fortunes. Health nuts drop dead of heart attacks in their forties while someone like me lives into his nineties. Terrible people have good things happen to them and decent people have awful things happen to them. There are no guarantees. No foolproof ways to protect ourselves from anything. If you stop to think about it too much, you'll go mad."

I wait for him to say more.

"And?"

"And what?"

"Don't you have some words of wisdom to add?"

"No. I just wanted to tell you not to think about it too much."

I shake my head at him.

"Come into the kitchen with me."

"I'm not going to be around that much longer," he says while raising himself out of his chair with his cane.

"Don't say that."

"It's a fact you're going to have to face. Don't feel bad about it. I've lived much longer than I had a right to."

He follows me and takes a seat at the table.

"My only regret is that I never made it to Ireland."

"Put it on your bucket list."

He laughs.

"I'm too old for a bucket list. The only list I have is the list of instructions for my funeral."

"What does it say?"

"Blue suit."

I set a cup of hot chocolate in front of my chair and a half cup of hot milk in front of him. I pour in a little maple syrup and give him his bottle of Jameson.

"What's wrong, Danny? You look like you've seen a ghost."

I sit down and try to steady my voice.

"Grandpa," I begin, "tonight I've got a story to tell you."

twenty-five

SCARLET

GWEN IS A STRIKING woman even in her seventies. She doesn't need to wear makeup and rarely does, but today she's dusted her face in perfumed powder, rouged her cheeks in pink, smudged the lids above her worried blue eyes in copper, and painted her lips in harsh ruby. She's trying to hide her disease. Alcoholism doesn't disfigure, but it discolors and ages.

She thinks I might kill her and she wants to look good when her body is found.

"I love the countryside," she says from her vigil at one of the floor-to-ceiling windows in the great room.

I don't know what she's looking for. A knight in shining armor? A guardian angel? The pizza delivery guy?

I just ordered one: pepperoni and double cheese.

"I guess it's ironic that you're part of two families who've made vast fortunes raping it," I comment.

I take the wrapper off a piece of Rafe's candy. I have a little pile of it sitting here on a marble-topped end table set in an elaborately carved base covered in gold leaf.

I know most of the stuff in this room is priceless, but the reason for having it isn't any different from what motivated Marcella Greger to accumulate her treasures. It's all crap to me.

Gwen turns and looks at me, holding her chin a little high, at an angle, to pull the flesh tight beneath it.

"When I was dating your father, he brought me here and I fell in love with his family's estate, the house, and the land."

"Did you fall in love with *him*?"

"I thought I did, but I didn't know him. He put on a good show while he was courting me, but once we were married he became a different man. Cold, controlling, self-obsessed. All the Dawes men were that way. I worried Wesley might turn out the same but he didn't."

She stops speaking at the mention of her son.

Her hair is long and loose today. It falls below her shoulders in a satiny cascade of white that blends in with the ivory silk of her blouse. She's wearing pants of the same color and some of her family's diamonds in her ears and on her fingers.

I'm fire; this woman is ice. There's no resemblance between the two of us. I never thought about it before.

"Go on," I encourage her.

"You think you know everything," she says, her voice trembling, the calm she's been struggling to maintain dissolving away.

"I'm pretty sure I do. My *real* brother filled in all the blanks."

"You don't know everything. Even I don't know everything. There are only two people left alive who know everything."

"Owen Doyle . . . ?"

"And Walker."

I stop clacking the candy against my teeth. This can't be true. Walker would have never brought someone not of his own blood into his house. He would have never raised a miner's child as his own, and especially not a McNab.

He has always believed I'm his daughter. His love for me is genuine. I'm his Button. And not because I'm cute as a button. Walker despises cute things. He explained the nickname to me once. It was in reference to the alleged red button the president would press to launch a nuclear attack. I was the most powerful object in his world. I was his little doomsday missile.

"Anna's confession or whatever you want to call it is only partially true. It's true that my Scarlet died and was switched with the Doyle baby, but I never knew about it."

"I don't get it."

"I always suspected there was something terribly wrong with you but . . ."

Her voice catches in her throat.

"I used to blame myself. I thought I must be a monster. What kind of woman doesn't love her own child?"

She stops herself once again. The look she shoots me is pure terror. I don't know what she thinks I'm going to do to her. I don't know if I should be insulted or flattered.

"It's okay, Gwen. I always knew you didn't love me. You were a lousy mother. It wouldn't have bothered me except you were a good mother to Wes."

"Please leave him alone."

"Stop bringing him up and maybe I will."

She turns away from me. I watch her take a tissue out her sleeve and dab at her eyes.

"Until Marcella Greger came to me several months ago and showed me that note, I didn't know that you weren't my real daughter or that I had killed her."

"I still don't get it."

"I went to Walker and showed him the note. I knew he was the only one who might know what Anna had been talking about."

She's openly crying now. Tears roll down her cheeks and leave damp spots on her silk.

"I killed her. I killed my own child. It was an accident. You have to believe me."

Her words come rushing out in a string of violent hitches.

"It was a difficult pregnancy and a difficult birth. I didn't want anything to do with my baby at first. I didn't care. I was sick and in pain. I was doped up half the time on medication; when I was lucid people were always forcing her on me, telling me how much she needed me.

"I took her into bed with me one night. I wanted to love her. I wanted her to love me. But I had taken a lot of pills and I was drinking. I passed out on top of her," she finishes in a whisper. "I suffocated her."

She raises the tissue to her face again. This time it comes away smeared in shades of beige and rose and streaked in black.

"Anna found us. I never knew. I was unconscious through the whole ordeal. She went to Walker. He was the one who decided to cover it up. His plan was to dispose of the body in a way that no one would ever find it and make it look like a kidnapping, but then Anna came up with her idea, one that would serve her own ends."

"What were those?" I ask, her tale finally beginning to interest me.

"She wanted to run away with Owen Doyle, but he had a wife and a child and now a new baby. She had never been able to convince him to get a divorce and leave with her. This plan solved her problems. The wife and baby would be out of the picture."

"What about Danny?"

"I don't know what they planned to do with him."

"This still doesn't make sense. Anna died when I was ten. Why did they wait that long? Why didn't they leave right away?"

"They couldn't. Owen had to stay through his wife's trial and play the wronged husband and grieving father."

"But why wait ten more years?"

Gwen stops her sniffing. She comes paddling up through the murk of her misery and briefly resurfaces into her usual crystalline perfection.

"Anna grew attached to you. She didn't want to leave you."

She gives me time for the full meaning of her revelation to sink in.

"That's right," she says, a note of triumph in her voice. "You killed the one person who loved you."

I think back to the day Anna told me she was leaving. She seemed sad when she should have been happy, but I thought she was faking to make me feel better.

"No," I say. "I don't believe any of this."

Gwen's brief recapture of poise melts away.

She wipes again at her face vigorously this time, almost rubbing it.

She's trying to remove all the makeup. Now she wants to be a clean corpse.

"You understand he did it to protect me," she says.

"You've got to be kidding me," I scoff at her. "Walker Dawes never gave a thought to protecting you. If anything he was protecting himself. You think he wanted to live with the stigma of a boozehound wife who killed her own baby?"

The idea appeared in my mind uninvited and the words poured out before I could stop them, but after hearing them I realize they could be true.

Protecting his reputation was more important than holding firm to his principles. I was never his beloved child. I was a random convenient nobody brought in to solve a problem. I was a replacement part.

If it's true, then Gwen was another victim. If she had been held accountable for what she did, she would have been forced to get help. She might have had a healthy life instead of drinking it away trying to drown the voices in her head that were constantly telling her there was something wrong with her daughter and herself.

"Do you understand what he did to you?"

"He was protecting me," she repeats.

"Do you understand what he did to Arlene Doyle?"

She breaks into more sobs.

"Yes. Oh God. That poor woman. Her family . . ."

"Why would Anna claim you switched the babies in her note? She was pretty devoted to you. I think she could have forgiven you for the accident, but why would she want to make you sound guilty when it was really Walker who covered it up and destroyed an innocent family?"

She continues crying. I wonder if this is the first time she's allowed it, or did she go to her room after Marcella Greger and then her husband presented her with this incomprehensible truth, possibly the same room where she unknowingly killed her child, and wept? Has she done it every day since then?

I think this is only the beginning of her tears. She has aged centuries in the past few minutes, no longer even looking human to me, more like a part of this ravaged countryside she claims to love so much that's also been ripped open and robbed.

"Excuse me, miss."

I turn and see Clarence in the doorway.

"Your pizza's here."

"Great."

He notices Gwen's condition.

"Is everything all right, ma'am?"

"Mrs. Dawes is under the weather today," I answer for her. "She's going to go to bed.

"I'll check on you later," I tell her.

I'm done with her for now. She doesn't need to say anything more. She doesn't have to explain to me why a descendant of Peter Tully decided to place the blame entirely on her and let her husband off the hook. Anna told me the story many times of Peter's mother fainting at the execution of her only son and how she poisoned herself and followed him into the grave a month later. In my purse I have the lace handkerchief his mother had painstakingly sewn in the hopes Peter would wear it in the pocket of his wedding suit someday, but had clutched it in his cold dead hand at the age of nineteen instead.

In Anna's mind Walker's cruelty was to be expected; he could be excused, but not a mother who didn't know her own child.

I INTRODUCE MYSELF BUT feel it's unnecessary. He knows who I am, and he's known I'd eventually show up on his doorstep someday. He's been expecting me for thirty-eight years.

Fear flickers through his eyes, but then I almost sense some relief on his part. Looking around at the dank, dark, dirty house, I can tell this is a man who stopped living a long time ago. He did an unforgivable thing with the intention of freeing himself, but ended up trapping himself in a tomb of his own filth instead.

"Dad," I say with a smile. "We need to talk."

I walk past him while handing him the copy of Anna's letter that I took from Marcella's house. I took the original from her lockbox, too.

He doesn't say anything at first. He's absorbed in the piece of paper. His lips move as he reads its contents.

I can't believe Danny and I are descended from him. We must get our brains from Mom, but hers are mush.

I catch sight of my reflection in a mirror hanging on a wall the color of tobacco-stained teeth.

I don't look like a Molly. It's a sweet name. A cute name. I'm definitely a Scarlet. But Molly should have been my name and this might have been my house. My life would have been vastly different from the one of wealth and privilege I had with the Daweses, but if I never knew that life, I couldn't miss it.

Lost Creek isn't so bad. Chappy's makes a good burger. The Kelly girl found great red shoes somewhere. Danny survived and made a success of himself.

Who am I kidding? Being poor sucks. Anna understood that. Anna saved me. Anna put me in the castle.

"It's a lie," Owen announces.

This man is going to be one big disappointment after another.

"Come on, Dad. Let's not go there. I know it's the truth. I've had a nice long talk with Gwen. Danny confirmed it, too."

"How would Danny know?"

"I forgot to ask at the time, but Danny is much too levelheaded to make up something like this or to believe it if he didn't have irrefutable evidence. I suppose that's why I didn't doubt him."

"Does Tommy know?"

"Tommy who?"

His house is disgusting. He never washes a dish or does a load of laundry or even throws out a beer can, but he has a state-of-the-art, five-foot-long plasma TV mounted on his wall.

He notices the bottle of Jack Daniel's and the six-pack of Coke I brought with me. The bourbon has been heavily laced with Gwen's sleeping pills.

I glance upstairs.

"Are the rooms up there a little less disgusting?"

"Danny's old room hasn't been touched in years."

"Grab a couple glasses and let's go."

He and his beer gut roll into the kitchen and come back out with the glasses followed by the rest of him.

I follow him up the stairs and regret putting myself downwind of him. He reeks of sweat and liquor. I give Gwen credit. She keeps her boozing as hidden as possible. She always smells good, but there's no perfume and mouthwash that can cover up slurred speech and hand tremors.

Danny's room turns out to be truly depressing. I can only hope it used to be better when he was using it. There's a twin bed and a rocking chair and a dresser with a lamp on top of it. That's it. Not one sign of his childhood or teen years remains. No toys. No posters. No sports memorabilia. The walls are painted an institutional gray and the comforter on the bed is plain navy blue. No cowboys or superheroes or dinosaurs romp across it.

It's pathetic, but it has a window and will serve my purpose just fine.

"Take a seat, Dad."

I gesture at the rocking chair.

"I'll make us a drink."

"I'll have mine straight."

"You'll have it with Coke. Live a little."

He's still holding Anna's note.

"I'm not sure why she wrote this," he says to me. "Maybe putting it down on paper was a type of security for her if anything went wrong."

I realize he's moved past any discomfort or trepidation he initially felt over my coming here. He's confiding in me like I'm an old friend. This must have been a difficult secret to keep all these years. It probably feels good to finally get it off his chest.

"What could have gone wrong?" I ask, handing him his glass.

"Hell," he replies, almost laughing. "Everything."

"You must have really loved Anna to take such a risk."

He downs half his drink. I wait to see if the cola successfully masks the taste of the pills. Apparently, it does.

"She was more into me than I was into her. She was kind of obsessed with me."

I take in the red, veined nose, the bruised pouches of skin beneath his bleary eyes, the jowly chin, the lank gray hair like motor oil smeared across the top of his flaking scalp.

He's overweight but not obese, his bulk not the honest, hard-won pounds of someone who can't stop eating but the bloat of sloth and ill use.

"Why not just get a divorce?" I ask rather than question his irresistibility.

"Divorcing Arly would've been a huge mess, plus I had my kid to think about. And Anna wanted to leave. I didn't want to leave here."

"Of course not. Who would?"

He's finished his drink already. I make him another one.

"You cared about Danny? You didn't think taking his mother away from him and having him live with the stigma of her crime was taking good care of him?"

"Arly's nuts. I really thought at the time he'd be better off without her. I realized after she was gone that she was actually a good mother."

"If you didn't care that much about Anna, why did you do it?"

"The money, I guess. Walker didn't pay me outright. Anna said he wouldn't want there to be any kind of traceable evidence. I worked in his mines, you know. So we set it up that I pretended to hurt my back and the disability checks started rolling in. Big ones."

I've known some self-absorbed people in my time, but this guy blows them all out of the water.

"You don't think you did anything wrong, do you?"

"The Dawes baby was already dead," he answers. "We didn't have anything to do with that. And as for you, you got to be the daughter of a millionaire. If you think about it, I did you a favor."

"What did you say?"

He takes a healthy swig.

"I did you a favor."

I watch while he finishes off his latest drink and I make him one more.

"It must've been a big shock for you when Anna killed herself."

"It didn't make sense. That's for sure. We were all ready to leave. I knew she was sad about leaving you. She liked you. But not sad enough to kill herself.

"Anyway, I know she didn't kill herself. I figured it out. She was murdered," he says as I hand him one more full glass. "And I know who did it."

"Who?"

He yawns.

"Walker Dawes. He found out she was leaving and he wanted to make sure she kept her mouth shut. Permanently."

I have to smile at the thought of Walker in his designer dressing gown lighting the nanny on fire.

"Wouldn't he have killed you, too?"

"I guess he figured seeing what he did to Anna would be enough of a warning to me."

It doesn't take much longer before he begins to doze off.

I go out to my car and get the rope.

Back in the room, I walk over to him and yank his head up by his hair and slap his face a couple times. He comes awake but only barely.

"Can you hear me?"

"Yeah."

"I want you to write something for me."

I put a piece of paper in front of him and a red marker in his hand.

He gives me a bewildered look when I tell him what to write, but the drugs have already made him too groggy to argue or ask questions.

"I don't believe in revenge. Vengeance is a petty emotion for small-minded people," I explain to him. "But Anna believed in it. She used to love to talk about the Nellies and how someday they'd get back at the Dawes family. And all that time there I was a direct descendant of Prosperity McNab living in their midst. Enjoying their wealth. Holding them hostage without even knowing I was. And Anna knew eventually I'd get their fortune."

I dangle the noose in front of his eyes. The fog in them clears momentarily and he tries to get up but his arms and legs are like lead.

I wait for him to pass out then put the noose around his neck and tie the other end of the rope to the bed frame. I push the chair to the window and throw it open.

Dumping him is harder than I thought it would be. Eventually he goes tumbling out. The bed slides across the room and slams against the wall. The rope is pulled taut and I hear a snap and thud.

I peer outside. He's not dead yet. His body jerks and twitches.

"This is for Anna," I call down to him.

twenty-six

DANNY

MAX IS OVERJOYED TO see me. He's not a hugger or even much of a smiler; he's a blinker.

His lids flutter rapidly behind the lenses of his glasses while he takes my coat and my briefcase and leads me to my chair behind my desk where he makes a motion for me to take a seat. I do and he stands back surveying me with a mix of fatherly or motherly pride and shocked concern like I've just taken my first steps but they're into a busy road.

"Is my charcoal Calvin Klein back from the cleaners?" I ask.

"Yes," he says eagerly and rushes to the closet where I keep a few suits for court.

"I have to be at the prison in twenty minutes if I want to be able to talk to him before they move him to the execution chamber."

"Are you sure you want to do this?"

Max appears dressed for mourning in a black shirt, black tie, and a black blazer with a crow feather sheen to it, but he's not wearing this out of any respect for Carson; I know he's glad he's about to be removed from the living.

"Not really, but I promised him."

"Will you come back here afterward or do you want to go home and get some rest?"

"I'll come back here. I need to work."

I get up from the desk and begin to undress. He hands me a shirt and drapes a suit and tie over my chair before returning to the closet to retrieve a pair of shoes.

He sits on the couch with a brush and begins buffing them.

"We have a grand jury date for Mindy Renee Trusty."

"Good."

"It's hard to believe this isn't going straight to court. Do you think there's a possibility we won't get an indictment?"

"She suffocated her newborn son with loose change she found at the bottom of her purse because he was going to be an inconvenience. It sounds like a slam dunk," I reply. "But she's a pretty, blond, nineteen-year-old girl who can appear as harmless as a baby seal when she wants to."

I wonder what Scarlet would think of Mindy Renee, another attractive female psychopath from a respectable family.

I open the bottom right-hand drawer of my desk where I keep a mirror and check the knot in my tie while listening to the shushing of Max's brush.

All the legitimate research on the subject concurs that psychopaths are born not made. The environment they're raised in can influence what paths their behavior takes, but nothing can keep them from their lifelong course of callous manipulation and inflicting pain on others in order to get what they want.

Walker and Gwendolyn Dawes didn't create Scarlet. She would have been the same monster if she had been left with us. Only her victims would have changed.

"Your trip back home this past week got me thinking about some of my own demons from my past," Max says. "I was a coward. I tried to run away from myself. I wanted to completely erase who I was, and most people knowing me now and knowing my past would think that's exactly what I did, but I learned something very important during my journey. You can't make a new you by denying the old you. You have to find a way for them to happily coexist."

He brings me my shoes.

"There's more Stacy in me now than there was when I was in Stacy. I was constantly trying to destroy her. I didn't like her. But I realize now

I did like her. It was other people telling me there were things wrong with her that made me not like her."

"Thank you, Max," I tell him. "I appreciate what you're saying and why you're saying it. I'm fine. Everything went very well."

"Are you sure?"

Could Mindy and Scarlet pick out each other in a crowd of normal people? I wonder. Do they give off a scent or a telepathic signal that only their kind can detect?

Humans are as much a mystery to psychopaths as we would be to a visitor from another planet. They're trapped in a sense, alien life forms that can adapt their behavior to seem like us when needed but who can never fully comprehend us. I imagine some of their insatiable need to control others stems from a warped attempt to ease their own loneliness.

"You look haggard," he says, doing little to conceal the concern in his voice. "Don't get me wrong. It's a good kind of haggard," he says, backpedaling. "A sexy selfless kind of haggard, the kind that says, 'I've been up all night doing calculations that will cure world hunger and re-pair the ozone layer.'"

I smile wearily.

"What exactly would I be calculating?"

"You know what I mean."

"I admit I didn't sleep well this past week, but I promise you I'm fine. Really."

I stand to go.

"I'll call you when it's over."

He holds up his fist to me. On the back he has written: DON'T GO BACK.

THE GATES OUTSIDE THE prison are lined with protestors. Placard-carrying, fist-pumping opponents of the death penalty jostle with angry, bullhorn-wielding victims' rights advocates and others who believe kill-ing Carson Shupe is our duty.

The people who were personally touched by his crimes will be in-side already, sitting silently in hard metal chairs staring at the floor or the curtained glass panel where he will soon appear strapped to a gurney; or they're at home somewhere waiting for a phone call and the relief that will come in knowing that it's all over, only to be quickly permanently replaced by the realization that it can never be over.

Official lines of communication have already been closed, but I've been allowed three minutes with him. The warden is doing me a favor. I can't say he's a friend of mine, but he's a personable man and we've had many dealings together. He's also set to retire soon and has plans to write his memoirs. He's already asked me how to find an agent.

There isn't enough time left to move Carson to an interrogation room. I'm taken to the death-watch cell, where he's been for the last thirty-six hours along with a round-the-clock guard.

The chaplain is waiting outside the cell, too.

"He's not religious," I tell him.

"I'm here for the people who are," he replies.

Carson is sitting on his bed dressed in what looks like white surgical scrubs and slippers. A Milky Way wrapper lies next to him.

He notices me looking at it.

"Do you know your last meal can't cost more than twenty dollars?" he asks me.

"What did you have?"

"What could I have for twenty dollars? Definitely not anything worthy of a last meal. I told them to bring me a candy bar and take the rest of the money and make a donation to the prison library in my name. Maybe they'll buy a copy of one of your books."

He looks even smaller than usual. His fingertips are bloody and raw. He's been chewing on them again. Under the circumstances, no one has thought it necessary to take him to the infirmary.

"How was your trip?"

"Good."

"Is your grandfather okay?"

"He's fine."

"Your mother?"

"She's fine, too."

"I didn't think you were going to come."

His lips twitch and purse into something resembling a smile.

"I thought you were going to chicken out."

"I try to keep my promises, but in all honesty, I don't want to be here."

"Because you feel bad for me or because you feel bad for yourself because you feel bad for me?"

"Both."

"Time's just about up," the warden says from outside the door.

Two corrections officers I don't know come in and begin shackling Carson's wrists and ankles.

"Do you think I deserve this?" he asks me.

My rehearsed response leaps to my lips, the one I've been called upon to offer in almost every venue imaginable, from post-trial interviews, panel discussions, and cocktail parties to blogs, book-signing Q&As, and even pillow talk, but I've never been asked by a man who is about to experience it firsthand.

It suddenly sounds as dry and irrelevant as it probably always has. Inside my head I hear myself droning on about how capital punishment in its most elemental form is imposed as a means of retribution, but far greater philosophical issues are involved when it comes to a society agreeing to put people to death, how we must consider the reason behind the crime and not the crime itself when making this decision.

I can't stop my thoughts from turning to my father. I don't support the death penalty. It's ineffective as a deterrent and I've never understood the rationale behind a punishment where the recipient isn't alive to endure it, but thinking about what my father's done, my animal instincts are stirred and I suddenly appreciate the need: it's a way to cleanse our species.

"Yes," I tell him. "You deserve this."

"You're wrong," he says, lowering his voice into the rasping, almost sensuous whisper that he used while torturing his victims, "but I forgive you."

I step outside the cell. Carson follows in a shuffle.

"I guess this is it. Is she here?"

I already checked for him.

"No."

"You don't have to stay then. I won't see you. I'm going to close my eyes. I was only going to keep them open if she was here."

"You're not going to let go of any of it? Not even at the very end?"

His lips make a few involuntary flutters and I wonder for the first time if maybe this tic of his is an unconscious expression of the kisses he was never given a chance to bestow.

"You're confused, Doctor. My mother never gave me anything to hold onto. Not even her hand."

His pain is real. It's how I know he's not a monster, just a man, which makes this final act all the more tragic and all the more necessary.

I'M SITTING IN MY idling car at the gate of the parking lot when I get a call from Max.

He's surprised when I answer.

"I was ready to leave a message. Shouldn't you be watching the big send-off?"

"He told me I didn't have to stay."

"Imagine that. Carson Shupe has an unselfish moment."

"Unselfishness had nothing to do with it. What's going on?"

"We just received the strangest fax here at the office. It was sent from a UPS store with a 724 area code. Isn't that the one from your hometown?"

"Yes," I say, immediately awash in a bad feeling.

"It must be from your mother or father. I'm sending you a scan of it right now."

Neither my mother nor father has sent a fax in their lives.

It appears on the screen of my phone written in red.

I recognize my dad's terrible handwriting immediately from all the notes he used to pen to the school lying about the so-called accidents that led to my absences.

I stare at the words, knowing in my heart that he would never express this sentiment unless he truly had a gun to his head. The use of the past tense confirms this. As he was writing, he knew he was going to die.

The letters swim in front of my eyes before they dissolve into a crimson haze:

You were a good son.

twenty-seven

I CALLED RAFE RIGHT AWAY. I knew in my heart that it was too late. Scarlet wouldn't have bothered to send confirmation if the deed hadn't been done. I knew she sent a fax because she wanted to think of me in my office watching a machine slowly spit out the physical piece of paper with its ominous past-tense message penned in faux blood signifying the end of any chance for me to confront my father. She wanted me to hold it in my hand, to be enslaved by its permanence, unable to perform the aggressive act of crumpling and throwing it away; deleting blips from a screen requires no emotional investment.

Rafe was already at Dad's house. He wouldn't give me any details other than to say my father was dead. He wouldn't tell me what had been done to him except to assure me Scarlet was involved.

I made him promise to keep my mother and Tommy safe. He said they were.

His greatest fear now was no longer protecting his citizenry but keeping Scarlet from escaping. He had no legal reason to detain her. He didn't even have a reason to talk to her. There was still no concrete evidence against her. All we had were outlandish theories and a handful of coincidences and what Scarlet had was an enormously wealthy set of parents who would do everything in their power to make certain none of her story was ever revealed.

Even the DNA at Marcella Greger's house couldn't help us. We had no proof that it belonged to Scarlet Dawes, only that it belonged to a relative of mine, and those were results that could never come to light since Rafe didn't have legal cause at the time to have the test performed. He needed a court order to compel Scarlet to give a DNA sample in order to prove she was there and he couldn't get one.

He called the Dawes estate looking for her. Walker talked to him and informed him that he heard about Rafe harassing Scarlet with questions about a police officer misplacing his gun and that if he ever wanted to talk to her again about anything he would have to go through their lawyer.

I suggested to Rafe that I might have better luck. He told me to stay the hell away from her. He said I'd done a brave thing going down in that coal mine to help Rick Kelly, but I shouldn't let it go to my head. I wasn't invincible.

Bravery is playing no role in my pursuit of her. I'm also not doing it because I'm inflamed by a desire to bring her to justice, even though this is something I want. My actions are beyond my control; I need to ask her what Dad's message meant.

Once Rafe realizes he's not going to talk me out of it, he asks me if I'd be willing to wear a wire. I tell him I have a small tape recorder in my briefcase. I use it to record interviews. I'll put it into my coat pocket.

I've called her over and over and she doesn't answer. I'm within ten miles of Lost Creek when she finally does.

"What do you want? You're really starting to bother me."

"I want to see you. I'm back in town."

"I thought you were in Philadelphia. I thought you had so much work to do."

"I got your fax."

"I didn't send you a fax."

"Okay. I mean, I got a fax from my father."

"How sweet."

"I just found out someone killed him."

She falls silent. I don't press her.

"I had an opportunity to meet him," she says. "Briefly. You can't tell me you had any feelings for that man."

I have feelings for him. Plenty of feelings, and I know his death isn't going to make any of them go away; it will only amplify them.

Like most children of abusive parents, I always secretly hoped for our miraculous day of reconciliation. Carson Shupe hoped for his until the moment an IV dripping poison was stabbed into his vein.

I longed for that propitious occasion when my father would tearfully express his love for me, tell me he'd always been proud of me, and ask for my forgiveness.

I'd accept his apology and listen compassionately as he explained that he was just one of those guys who couldn't express his feelings well and then we'd share a beer and talk about guns and carburetors and football and all the other rites of rural manhood I was never initiated into.

I'd make excuses for him. He was only human, after all, and his own life hadn't been an easy one. He was allowed some anger and bitterness. I'd rationalize away his behavior refusing to accept the sad, simple reality that some people are mean, selfish, and incapable of love, and these people often reproduce.

I knew this day would never come, but as long as he was alive, I could pretend it might. Scarlet had not only taken my father from me, she'd taken the last of my hope.

"I want to see you," I say again, appealing to her vanity and need to control.

"I have a plane to catch."

"Please, give me ten minutes. I'd consider it an expression of sisterly love," I add when she doesn't respond.

"Fine. Come to the house."

I'VE SPENT THE DAYLIGHT hours driving back and forth from one side of the state to the other and it's almost dark by the time I drive down the winding lane to the Dawes mansion.

In town and along the salted roads, the snow is already mixed with mud and melting into slush, but here it's remained as pristine as when it first fell. The treetops and hillsides are unmarred. Their pure white iciness glitters softly beneath a bright moon of the same color.

The house looks like a snow queen's castle out of a children's wintry fairy tale. Every window is lit from within, throwing rays of crystal onto the vast front lawn and bathing the brick in a frosty pink.

Scarlet is alone, standing in the circular drive beside the trunk of a dark sedan.

She's covered from neck to knee in her black mink and from knee to toes in a pair of chocolate brown alligator-skin boots. The glossy fur of her coat shimmers with undertones of peacock blue each time she moves, and her hair gives off glints of red-gold that almost seem like sparks. Everything about her screams wealth and privilege. I wonder what the same woman, the same genes, would have looked like if she had been left with us, if she had grown up living in Lost Creek instead of owning it.

Her mind would have remained the same; this is all that matters.

I don't know exactly what I'm going to say to her, but I've decided to use the blunt approach. I think she responds better to what she believes is my do-gooder earnestness.

She's smoking. She takes the cigarette from between her lips and blows.

"The police aren't going to let you on a plane," I tell her.

"The police can't stop me from doing anything."

"You got sloppy. There's no way out of this."

"Me? Sloppy? What are you talking about?"

"You left DNA at Marcella Greger's house. That's how we found out you were my sister."

She smiles.

"So Candy Cop does know."

"And the fax. The boys working at the UPS store will identify you."

"Those boys at the UPS store? That's the best you can do? I sent a fax. It doesn't prove anything. I visited the cousin of my dear departed nanny. That also doesn't prove anything."

"It's over. It's all going to come out now."

"You underestimate my resources. Gwen and Walker will do everything in their power to keep this as quiet as possible."

"Money can only go so far."

"It's not just money, Danny, or even a lot of money, but one of the biggest fortunes that's ever been dug, pumped, and blasted out of the planet earth. Don't be naïve."

"The same fortune that got the Nellies executed," I remind her.

She doesn't seem interested in this fact.

I decide to try another tack.

"You said you met our father. How did that go?"

"He didn't have an ounce of remorse over what he did to your mom or you. Or even me. He said something about how he gave me a better life by giving me to Walker. He said he did me a favor. Can you believe that?"

I gesture at the house and the beautiful surroundings.

"I'd say he did do you a favor."

She finishes her cigarette and tosses it into the snow.

"I'm going now."

"Wait," I almost shout the word.

She's amused by my desperation but also obviously irritated.

"I'm worried about you. You've suffered a huge emotional trauma, and I don't think you're dealing with it."

"I really don't care."

"How can you say that? You've just found out that your entire life has been a lie.

"You're not one of them," I say, pointing at the sparkling mansion.

I place my hands on my chest.

"You're one of us."

She studies me with her blank eyes that also somehow manage to be full of knowledge, but of things I don't want to know.

I sense I've gone too far.

She can't be part of anything. I've encountered the isolation of her kind before. She's a lone entity whose only requirement of others is that no one gets too close.

"You're going to try and psychoanalyze me? Try and find out what I'm feeling?" she says. "I finally get it. I'd be the biggest catch of all for you, wouldn't I? The best freak head you could mount on your wall of forensic psychology fame?"

I take a step back from her. I don't know why. She can't hurt me. She's a woman; I'm a man. I'm fairly certain I could take her in a fight and I know for sure I can outrun her.

Nothing in her voice, gaze, or posture gives signs that she's upset with me, but I know this doesn't mean anything. She doesn't feel rage the way other humans do. She encounters an obstacle and makes a calculated decision whether she can walk around it, over it, or if it needs to be permanently removed from her path. I fear I've just become a big boulder on the road to her contentment.

She brings her hand out of a fold in her coat holding Billy Small's gun. I don't have any time to react before she pulls the trigger.

I don't feel any pain at first, just a pressure in my chest that knocks me off my feet. I slam into the snow with the quiet thud of a child falling into a drift about to make the imprint of an angel. I didn't hear a gunshot but my ears won't stop ringing.

I must be in shock because all I can think is I didn't get to ask her about Dad's note. I didn't get to tell my mom I'm sorry I didn't believe in her. I didn't get to tell Tommy he's the best man I've ever known.

"What are you doing?" I'm able to ask her.

I drop my gaze from her face to her feet. I see the stitching, the exquisite quality of the leather.

"You're the biggest disappointment of all," Scarlet says.

"Don't hurt Mom," I say before my throat fills with blood.

"Shut up. You should be thinking about me right now. Not her."

She's practically standing on top of me. I feel her foot pressing into my stomach the way Dad used to do.

I try to look up at her. I begin to shake uncontrollably.

She makes a disgusted sound.

"Blood on my Blahniks. I should've never come back to this shitty little town."

Another shot rings out. This one I hear. I wait for death. It comes in the form of a dark suffocating weight on my chest.

I see the thick glossy pelt. It's a bear, I think. Tommy killed a bear and it fell on me.

In my delirium, I smile at the idea.

I know I'm dead because an angel appears above me. A snow angel dressed in white fur with a halo of opalescent hair blowing behind a kind, alabaster face as old as the heavens themselves. She says nothing, but a single tear like a diamond clings to her pale cheek.

twenty-eight

THE GRANDSON OF PROSPERITY McNab stands on a dais in the middle of Lost Creek especially erected for the occasion. He's surrounded by hundreds of townspeople and onlookers. His doomed ancestor looked out on a similar scene, except today it's green and sunny and the atmosphere is lighthearted. Conversation and laughter waft through the soft spring air, and everyone is dressed in bright, festive colors. The only black present is paired with Steelers gold.

Nora Daley is introducing him after talking at length about the history of the Nellie O'Neills, the good works of the NONS, and the surprising end to their struggle to raise enough money to put up a memorial statue.

There's been no attempt to hide the identity of the generous donor who paid for the statue. The fact that the money came from a descendant of the man who was responsible for executing the Nellies who then turned out to be a descendant of one of the Nellies instead has been taken almost in stride here after the initial shock passed.

The entire story was too incredible to keep quiet. Scarlet was wrong about the Dawes' fortune being able to do so. It spread rapidly and soon became the biggest scandal the county has ever seen aside from the rise and fall of the Nellies. The legitimate media has had to treat the allegations delicately since there's no verifiable proof and since Walker Dawes has remained completely silent, but there are plenty of pseudo-news outlets nowadays that thrive on unconfirmed gossip, speculation, and innuendo and have no compunction about putting it out in the world for others to judge.

Nothing can be done to bring Walker Dawes to justice. In a court of law it would be his word against hearsay and a piece of paper written by a dead woman that incriminates his wife, not him, and part of which is a lie.

There's no forensic evidence. The infant Scarlet has been dead too long to be able to retrieve DNA from her body, and we weren't able to get any from Molly because Walker had her cremated before Rafe could get a court order to stop him.

His crime is too old and he's too rich for anything to be done. A child was taken from her mother and a mother was taken from her other child. Another child was lost and never mourned. Another mother permanently damaged without understanding why.

He won't be punished by our judicial system but he is being tried in the court of public opinion and not faring well.

To everyone's surprise, he didn't run away. He has other homes but he's stayed here in the estate the Original Walker built. The rumors are he never leaves the house even to take a walk around his property, and he's plagued with paranoia, which has led to him firing most of his house staff. He's also handed over the reins of Lost Creek Coal & Oil to his son, Wesley. No one thought that would happen until he was lying on his deathbed. Maybe in a sense he's already there.

I've managed to stay out of the limelight as much as possible. For once I don't want to be an expert witness or any kind of witness at all. My recovery has been slow and has given me a good excuse to avoid interviews.

Tommy has become an undisputed media darling. He's even assisting a young filmmaker in the making of the definitive Nellie O'Neills documentary in which Tommy is set to star as the narrator.

I see the director on the fringes of the colorful crowd with one of his cameramen. Another roams through the spectators. Billy Smalls, carrying a newly issued Glock, and Troy Razzano in dress uniform patrol the perimeter. News vans line the streets.

From my seat on the dais along with Rafe, Wesley Dawes, and the other eight founding members of the NONS besides Nora and Tommy, I have a good view of everyone in attendance and it does seem to be everyone. I start picking out the people who played a role, no matter how small, in the strange and wonderful week of my homecoming three months ago that almost ended in my death.

According to the EMTs who accompanied me in a Life Flight helicopter, I was briefly dead. A four-day coma would follow. When I finally opened my eyes, I was greeted by the sight of Tommy asleep in a chair and Brenna and Moira Kelly watching Jerry Springer on a TV mounted in the corner of my hospital room.

Moira's face loomed over me for a moment. I thought I detected the beginnings of a smile but it was quickly replaced with a frown.

"Some people will do anything to get attention," she said.

Moira is here along with Brenna and easily sixty members of their clan including Rick, his wife, and their children. Alphonse sits on the dais next to Birdie, smiling and waving and occasionally shushing all the cries of "Hi, Grandpa!"

The widow Husk and her family occupy a prominent place up front. Marcella Greger's niece and the rest of the Greger and Tully families stand next to them.

All four of Rafe's ex-wives are here, his five daughters and their spouses, and his nine grandchildren ranging from eighteen-year-old Heather to newborn Henry, who's already been christened Wee Hen in a family dominated by women, a nickname I fear he's never going to shake.

I see Tommy's doctor, who made the call that brought me home in the first place; the girl from McDonald's who wouldn't let me use their Wi-Fi unless I ordered meat; Matt and Shane from the UPS store, who were finally able to put a name to their fembot; Dave Rosko and an entire crew of firemen complete with truck; Herm Chappy, the undisputed king of gravy; my mining buddies Todd, Jamie, J. C., and Shawn; Parker Hopkins, looking unusually alert and dapper befitting the fact that he is no longer a volunteer but is now a paid groundskeeper; and even the manager from Carelli's Furniture has put aside her earlier trepidation and decided to embrace the bloodthirsty Nellies.

The only noticeable absence is my mother. She didn't want to come and Tommy and I didn't encourage her. She doesn't like crowds.

There's really no reason for her to be here. It seems like the entire town has stopped by these last few months to offer their sympathies and apologies one and two and three at a time. She barely makes it through the conversations but is always happy to have company.

I can't tell what she's feeling inside. It's impossible to know how all of this will ultimately affect her, but in her own way, I think she's better equipped to deal with the inconceivable than the rest of us.

I've consulted with other psychologists and psychiatrists while trying to decide what my course of action should be, but I think the best advice has come from Rafe, who told me to "leave her alone."

He's sitting beside me now in an actual suit where the pants and jacket match, a solid-colored dress shirt, and a Bottega Veneta tie I gave to him as a gift for solving the crime of the century and vindicating my mother.

He keeps tugging at the knot, trying to loosen it, as if he's afraid silk is a live thing that might try to strangle him.

Thundering applause welcomes Tommy to the microphone.

He tries to appear unmoved but I see tears glimmering in his eyes.

"If we can get this many of you to come out for a statue, you better believe I'm counting on all of you being at my funeral."

Laughter erupts from the crowd.

"As you all know, I'm a shy, retiring man who tends to keep his opinions to himself."

More laughter, clapping, hooting, and hollering.

"My grandson, Danny, is the public speaker in the family."

I receive my own round of applause.

"I was going to let him say a few words, but I knew we wouldn't be able to understand half of them."

More laughter. For once I don't take offense. I glance at Brenna, who smiles back at me. I take it for what it is: good-natured ribbing.

"I'm not going to bore you with a speech. Everyone knows my feelings on the Nellies and my grandfather, Prosperity McNab, and if they don't by now, I've done so many interviews lately, it's easy enough to find out. I'm even on . . . what's it called, Danny?"

"YouTube."

"That's right. I'm on the YouTube."

The crowd bursts into laughter again and cheers riotously.

"During one of those interviews I was asked, What do you consider yourself to be first: Irish or American? I said I consider myself to be a retired coal miner."

More applause.

"When you get to be a relic like myself, people are always asking you for words of wisdom," he continues once everyone calms down. "It gets annoying."

More laughter.

"The reason why is because you can't grasp at thirty or fifty or even seventy what becomes blindingly obvious to you in your nineties. I can try and explain things to you. I can advise you. You can listen politely and nod your head, but you can't truly understand.

"But I will tell you this much: no matter what age you are, the amount of satisfaction you're going to take from life all depends on your perspective.

"It can be a terrible day when you reach your ninety-sixth year and realize this is all there is, or it can be a wonderful day when you realize that yes"—he pauses and gestures at the people gathered around him, the town, and the hills beyond—"this is all there is."

Nora gives Tommy a pat on the back and waits behind the microphone for the applause to die down before introducing Wesley Dawes.

I was able to meet with him alone before the ceremony. He was nothing like his father. Relaxed, unpretentious, empathetic: the kind of man who would probably prefer having a beer at the Red Rabbit over having cocktails at the Dawes' mansion.

We talked briefly about our shared sister. He said he couldn't remember a time when he wasn't afraid of her, yet he was never absolutely sure why he felt this way. She never abused him. She didn't even torment or tease him the way children were expected to behave in a normal sibling relationship.

Without comment, he then showed me a photograph of his wife and two daughters, aged five and three. I'm glad Scarlet didn't live long enough to dispose of them.

We don't talk at all about his mother. I've met with her several times since she shot and killed her daughter and saved my life.

Only one person knew Gwen Dawes owned a gun and it wasn't her husband. Not long after the gruesome death of her children's nanny she decided she wanted some protection. She knew it didn't make sense. It was a suicide after all. The young policeman she consulted agreed with her but said he didn't blame her for wanting to feel safe after something like that happened in her own home. So Officer Rafferty Malloy found her a gun and filled out the paperwork for her permit.

"This was an unfortunate moment in our shared history," Wesley proclaims. "I say 'our history' because the Dawes family and the residents of Lost Creek are irrevocably intertwined. My ancestors could not have existed without yours and your ancestors could not have existed without them.

"I'd like to think we've finally come to a moment in time where we no longer have to draw lines, where we no longer have to think of each other as the employer and the employed, the user and the used, but as people who share a love for this place, who have made a commitment to stay here through thick or thin, and who will work together to find a way to have more thick than thin."

This suggestion is met with shouting and clapping. I hear Rafe unwrap a Jolly Rancher and the clacking begins.

"It's my pleasure on behalf of the Dawes family to officially donate the land on which the gallows and jail stand to the town of Lost Creek in all perpetuity complete with a yearly income to maintain the property.

"And now, Mr. McNab, I'm supposed to give you this bottle of champagne to use to christen the memorial statue."

Tommy takes the bottle and walks down the dais stairs to where the cloaked statue and the artist who created it stand in the middle of the town square.

Everyone is dying to know what the NONS finally decided on. They managed to maintain an uncharacteristic level of secrecy about the project, but Tommy was only too anxious to share the submitted designs with me.

It's true the purpose of the statue was to immortalize a great tragedy, possibly a horrific miscarriage of justice, but even so, the proposals all seemed too dark and grim for me.

One was a Nellie waiting to be executed, wearing his hood, his wrists and ankles shackled, the noose already around his neck. Another showed several miners toiling at their jobs, expressions of agony on their faces with flames licking at their feet. Yet another was done in the style of the Vietnam Memorial in Washington, D.C., only instead of names set against a coal black background, the Nellies' faces were carved into the wall like the faces in the recurring nightmare from my youth.

The veil is dropped to an appreciative round of gasps then cheers.

A solitary miner walks to the pits with his young son on his shoulders. The boy smiles down at his dad who appears to be whistling.

I'm sure it's not supposed to be anyone in particular, but to me it's Prosperity and his son, Jack, at the same age I was when I first began to understand how I was related to them. It was also the same age when I began to question if my own father's treatment of me wasn't okay.

I haven't been back to my father's house since he was murdered there. I stayed true to my earlier decision to have it torn down. Beforehand, I had no interest in wandering through the rooms where I grew up, and where he sat for decades with his terrible knowledge, and going through his personal effects searching for answers or shreds of sentimentality. Some of the Kelly sisters volunteered to dispose of his belongings and furniture for me, and in return they kept whatever they wanted or any profits from selling it.

He left no instructions regarding a funeral other than the location of his burial plot. He had no family or friends who cared about his eternal rest. Tommy found a priest who came to say a few words as his body was lowered into the ground. He and Rafe were the only ones there. I was still in the hospital and unable to attend.

Some people have been worried for me that I wasn't able to properly say good-bye to him. I can't make them understand that I did, but in a way that only my father and I could appreciate.

Against his own wishes, Rafe gave me the crime scene photos. I pored over them one night sitting in my apartment listening to the city sounds outside my window and knowing no matter how late the hour, it would never be completely dark here.

I was able to distance myself from them at first, regarding them as clinically as I would similar evidence from my work. It wasn't until I came to the full-length shot of my father hanging out of my childhood bedroom window at the end of a noose that I finally felt grief.

All I could see were his feet. They were bare. He wasn't wearing shoes or slippers. They dangled pale and harmless, reminding me of some kind of vulnerable newborn creature. I realized I'd never seen his actual feet before, just what covered them. They were flesh and blood underneath.

I knew at that moment that I would never be able to make peace with his actions, but that didn't mean I couldn't make peace with him. In order to do it, I've had to keep my emotional distance and regard him as a man and not my father, but I'm okay with this. I don't need him to be my father.

I have a father. He's sitting next to me, offering me a piece of candy.

BACK AT TOMMY'S HOUSE, Mom is busy in the front room fluffing pillows on the couch and adjusting Fiona's portrait. The coffee table is set for a tea party.

She's changed her clothes four times but has finally settled on a white eyelet dress that wouldn't look appropriate on anyone over the age of eight except for her.

Max is assisting her. He's wearing the neon pink hat she began knitting for him when she first met him in my hospital room. The sequins spell out MOXIE.

He refuses to take it off. He's even color-coordinated the rest of his outfit. His shirt and shorts are the same alarming color, although the Birkenstocks at the ends of his surprisingly skinny legs are black. The comparison to a flamingo is almost too easy to make.

He's taking us to the airport. Brenna and Moira Kelly are going to take turns staying with Mom while Tommy and I are gone.

Max didn't have to do this, but since the shooting, he's become clingy. I wasn't able to return to work for a month and then only in a limited capacity. Now that I'm back to operating at full capacity, he's started accompanying me everywhere I go. I was self-conscious at first, but I've begun to enjoy the bewilderment on people's faces as they try to figure out who the quietly possessive, uniquely attired, iPad-tapping individual is: An avant-garde personal assistant? A gay bodyguard? My genie?

Rafe is at the kitchen table using the new laptop I bought for Tommy. I've also upgraded his Internet capabilities.

Since the airing of the *Ghost Sniffers'* wildly popular Lost Creek episode and Tommy's ascendancy into pop culture social media superstardom, the NONS website has devoted an entire page just to Tommy, and he's considering starting a blog. Of all the incredible happenings around here recently, this might be the most unbelievable.

"When you get to be my age, you end up seeing a lot of things you wished you hadn't lived to see," he says to me when I join him where he's hovering behind Rafe.

I follow his gaze to the computer screen, where Rafe is Skyping with Wade Van Landingham, who's sitting poolside in a Hawaiian shirt and tiny bedazzled Ray-Bans.

Velma sticks his head into the picture, too.

"Wade misses Guy in Charge. He's insisting on coming to spend a few weeks with him this summer even if it means pushing back his usual month on Johnny Depp's yacht."

Rafe flashes us one of his inscrutable grins. I know he has big plans for the little dog's visit. I'm having a vision: I see camo waders and a fluorescent orange ball cap in Wade's future.

"All the attention Wade's received from the Lost Creek episode has been fabulous for his career. He's been offered a part in a Tom Cruise movie. He's going to play a dog."

"Pshaw," Tommy snorts.

Outside the front window I see a silver sports car pull up and park across the street. I tell Tommy, Rafe, and Max we need to get going.

They say their good-byes to Mom while I leave them and go to greet Gwen Dawes.

Like my mother, she has dressed for this occasion in a lilac sheath, matching pumps, and a rope of pearls. She carries two boxes: one is plain cardboard, the other has an elaborate fleur-de-lis pattern and is topped with a red foil bow.

She gives the plain one to me.

"Thank you for agreeing to this," she says.

"My mom wanted to do it."

"I'm leaving tomorrow to begin serving my sentence," she tells me. "I'll also finally receive help for my drinking problem."

A legion of Dawes' lawyers worked out a plea agreement where Gwen Dawes will serve two years in a minimum-security prison for the shooting death of her daughter, Scarlet.

Considering her age, wealth, the mountain of extenuating circumstances, and the fact that she did save my life, she could have fought the charge and might have been able to avoid incarceration altogether, but it was obvious from the few times I talked to her that she wants to go to jail; she feels she deserves it.

"Once I'm released, I'm going to live near Wesley and his family."

"I think that's a good idea. I met him earlier today. He seems like a good man."

"I wonder what she would've been like? My Scarlet?"

I know the question isn't directed at me. It's meant for the cosmos. I assume she's coping as best she can. The truths she's had to face have been every bit as awful as the ones my own mother has had to endure.

I don't know this woman at all. Certainly not well enough to judge her. I do know she has a conscience. She had begun her own campaign to expose her husband. She put the note in Tommy's mailbox.

"And Walker?" I ask her.

She leaves her reverie of the daughter she never knew.

"He has to live with himself."

I take her inside where my mother is waiting and introduce them to each other, a wild rose and a hothouse orchid who have both managed to survive in the same scorched earth.

"This is Gwendolyn Dawes," I tell Mom. "And this is my mother, Arlene Doyle."

Gwen's eyes are damp with tears as she hands Mom the box.

Mom takes it from her and eagerly opens it. Inside is a collection of tiny pastel-colored cakes adorned with candy petals.

"Your son told me how much you like sweets."

"Thank you," Mom says. "And, here, I have something for you. I made it."

She gives Gwen one of her purple TOLERANCE hats.

Gwen begins to cry.

"It's okay," Mom tells her.

She rushes off and returns with a box of Kleenex. Gwen takes one and dabs at her eyes.

As I turn to go I hear Gwen tell my mother she has one more gift for her.

She reaches into her purse then asks for my mother's hand.

"This belonged to your daughter," she says.

I watch as she slips the Dawes ruby onto my mother's finger.

Mom holds up her hand, delightedly tilting it this way and that, watching the sparks of fiery light in the stone's depths.

She has no idea of the value men have placed upon it and that makes it all the more precious.

ALL SYSTEMS ARE GO with Max's Toyota. The trunk is packed. Max is behind the wheel. Rafe is in the backseat. Tommy's riding shotgun.

"Is that it?" he asks me, staring at the box.

"Yes."

He reaches out his hands to me through the open window.

"We can put that in the trunk," I tell him.

"No."

He opens it and takes out a carved rosewood urn sealed with a golden lid and places it on his knees.

This is how he will make the entire drive, with the ashes of his granddaughter sitting in his lap.

twenty-nine

ON A WINDBLOWN IRISH hillside surrounded by humped graz-ing land crisscrossed with stone walls like a sloppily stitched blan-ket, we finally find her grave.

The name was worn away by the elements long ago, but the three of us agree this one belonged to Jimmy McNab's mother. We can easily picture her young son sitting here beside the bleached headstone, bat-tered now by the winds until it's as smooth as glass, discussing his future with her. He was going to America, the land of danger, progress, and prosperity.

Tommy stares hypnotically out at the wild gray sea. We can smell the salt from here and hear the thunder of the waves.

The sight of the three of us in our dark suits and impractical Sunday shoes tromping through the fields and up the hill to the little cemetery has brought out a small knot of onlookers gathered at the bottom of the road. All of them are men. I can make out various caps and walking sticks and one bicycle. A border collie keeps running up to join us. Each time he circles us, sniffing, and returns to the men where he reports back with several sharp barks.

Without saying a word, Tommy moves on, gripping his own stick, away from the little graves, toward the nearest cliff face. Rafe and I fol-low, him holding a bottle of whiskey and me carrying Molly's ashes.

He stops only a few feet away from the edge. The wind is fierce here. It fills up his suit jacket and whips it around his skinny frame. His tie flaps behind him like the tail of a kite.

I fear he might be blown off the island but if it happens, I know he'll spread his arms and smile and whoop and fly off happily to his own death.

"This is the place," he says.

I give him the wooden urn. He takes off the golden lid and without saying a word, shakes her ashes over the ocean.

The wind catches them and blows them back onto land. We turn and watch the cloud of her remains dissolve over the snail-gleam of the road behind us and the green of the hills.

Each of us takes a shot glass out of our pants pockets. Rafe pours.

A few of her ashes still float in the air. I watch them drift and fall and land on the back of my hand and in my drink. I think of Prosperity, not so many years after the conversations he had here with his mother, as dawn broke on his last day on earth. He would have been lying on a wooden bed a world away in Lost Creek jail watching the ever-present flakes of black soot twirl in the gray light of dawn looking the same, like snowflakes dressed in mourning.

Tommy raises his glass.

"The one who has suffered the most isn't here. I feel this is the way it should be. We, as the men in her life, should be able to take care of at least this one crushing task for her.

"To Arlene," he says.

We drink. Tommy drops his head and I can tell by the shaking of his shoulders that he's crying. Rafe goes to him. I've never seen Rafe hug anyone, not a wife, not a grandchild, not the teammate who hit the double that scored the winning run when the police department played First National Bank.

Watching the two of them I suddenly understand that a man's life story is written before it even begins, all of his choices made for him by a history he's helpless against yet he believes is of his own making.

I know now what Tommy has always known and why he has always felt such affection for his ill-fated ancestor. Prosperity McNab's decision to band with the organization that would bring about his infamy and his death had nothing to do with the various reasons history likes to claim. He joined their ranks not because he had an interest in bettering conditions in the mines, or a desire to wreak vengeance on the rich and the racist, or even a wish to impress the woman he loved with his patriotic zeal for the *ould sod,* but because he couldn't help feeling drawn to a group of men who fought in the name of a mother who had committed an extraordinary act for her son.

acknowledgments

I'M FAIRLY CERTAIN THAT I'd still be working on *One of Us* and might be doing so for the next twenty years if it weren't for my agent, Liza Dawson, who once again saw me through the doubt, panic, and bouts of self-loathing that always accompany the writing of one of my novels. Thank you, Liza, for your unflappable encouragement and magical ability to get me to do what needs to be done without actually telling me what it is that I need to do.

The greatest gift a writer can receive is a smart, passionate, intuitive editor who seems to have an immediate understanding of her work. I received such a gift earlier this year in the form of Karen Kosztolnyik at Gallery Books who turned out to be a lovely incarnation of the nagging voice inside my head that tells me I'm not done yet. Thank you, Karen, for your insight and care. Every suggestion you made was dead-on except for your original thoughts on Wade but don't worry; we both forgive you.

Thank you, Mom, for always being there for me; Roy, for your unwavering support and elbow grease; and Molly Meghan, for your rock 'em sock 'em spirit and steadfast devotion to me. And to Tirzah and Connor, my sweet babies who are now amazing adults, without you my life would be a dull, plodding thing with no shine or sizzle to it: thank you, Fate, for giving them to me.

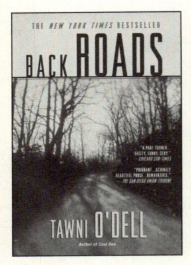
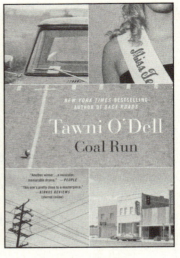